NEPHIL'S DESTINY
BOOK 7 OF THE CHOSEN CHRONICLES

Sirena Robinson

Supposed Crimes LLC • Matthews, North Carolina

Published in the United States.

ISBN: 978-1-944591-40-3

www.supposedcrimes.com

This book is typeset in Goudy Old Style.

PROLOGUE

"REACH WITHIN yourself, Amaya. Feel the power there. Let it rise up within you." Michael paced back and forth, watching the teenager concentrate. "Do you feel it?"

Amaya struggled to listen to the Angel, reaching for the power that lurked just below the surface of her mind. It was always there, always just out of reach. She could feel it, could brush it with her fingertips, but couldn't wrap her hands around it and pull it to the surface.

"It's normal for this to be hard. A Nephil's power is designed not to manifest until puberty. You're in the midst of that right now, so training you at this stage is very important. It's imperative you be able to control your powers as they arise. Without proper training, you will be very dangerous."

Her eyes snapped open, and she glared at Michael. "You sound like Gabriel."

Michael smiled softly. "Your father doesn't want me to teach you anything, Amaya. If it was up to him, you'd be in Heaven, safely ensconced within the Gates where he could guard you at all times."

Gabriel appeared in a flash of light. "Michael. What is it you think you're doing?"

Michael regarded his brother mildly. "We're training."

"I've made my opinions on this matter quite clear."

"We were just discussing that, actually." He picked up a bottle of water and drank deeply. "Alaria and Braxton have asked me to help her. She's having bursts of power she cannot control. It's time for them to learn, Gabriel."

Gabriel turned to Amaya, his expression belying concern. "You should have called for me."

Anger and hurt rose within her, and she jumped back when he reached out to touch her. "Why? So you can lie to me some more? So you can trick me again?" She pressed herself against the wall. "You lied to me! You made me trust you and love you, and you betrayed me!"

Both Angels jumped when the lightbulbs on the ceiling flickered and exploded. Michael looked at Gabriel. "Perhaps you should return at another time. Her abilities are manifesting, but her control is shaky."

"Don't talk about me like I'm not here!" Amaya's voice echoed through the warehouse they were using to train and the walls shook as a wave of power rolled off her.

Michael grabbed Amaya by her shoulders, pulling her into his chest and pressing her face into his shirt. "Calm yourself, child. Breathe deeply."

Gabriel stood several feet away, his arms crossed. "Michael, it's apparent she needs to come with me. She needs appropriate instruction in her abilities. She's more powerful than we thought she would be. Without learning how to control what lives within her, she could be a danger to everyone. Let me take her to Heaven."

"No!" Amaya yanked herself free from Michael and threw out her hands, screaming when the whole building rocked on its foundation.

Flames leapt from the ground and climbed the walls, engulfing the building within moments. As Amaya panicked from what she'd done, she sent out more and more power, knocking back both Angels as they tried to get to her. Tears streamed down her face and she stared at her hands, not quite believing that she had caused the fire.

"Amaya, no!" Michael's yell went unacknowledged as Amaya turned and ran, flashing as soon as she was clear of the protections the Angel had placed on the building.

She landed on a rocky beach, falling forward when she hit the ground and catching herself on her palms. Her throat burned, and hot tears fell from her eyes. Cold earth and rocks bit into her jean-clad knees as she knelt, pressing her hands to her face as she sobbed.

It had been three years since she'd found out about her paternity. In those three years, she'd been sent to live with Michael and train, had met the other Nephilim supposed to help her take down Lucifer, and had been separated from her siblings since her abilities had begun to manifest.

Easing back to lean against a log, she drew her legs up to her chest and stared at her hands. Unlike Lux, who had magic and wielded it like a surgeon with a scalpel, Nephilim powers came in bursts, manifesting as the host grew and matured. The more powerful the parents, the more powerful the Nephil and the more unpredictable the powers.

Amaya looked up when she heard a pop and relaxed when she saw Deacon, Michael's son, appear.

"Dad said there was a little—event—in training today." He lowered himself to the ground next to her. "Want to talk about it?"

"Gabriel showed up. He wanted to take me to Heaven to train me. He doesn't think I can control myself."

Deacon lifted one eyebrow and stared at her. At seventeen, he was a year older and seemed eons wiser. "So you blew up the building you were in and took off? Yup. That'll show him."

Amaya sank her teeth into her lower lip and stared out at the lake. "I really screwed up, didn't I?"

"Nah. You just had a bit of an accident. Dad'll smooth things over with Gabriel, and it'll all be fine. They were screaming at each other in the office when I left to come find you." He draped his arm around her shoulders. "It's cold out here. Much warmer back home."

"I don't want to go back yet."

Always the amiable sort, Deacon jerked one shoulder. "Okay. We'll freeze then. No biggie." He toyed with the ends of her hair. "What did you think running away would accomplish?"

Amaya leaned her head on his shoulder. "I wasn't thinking. I can feel so much stuff inside me, and I don't know how to control it. I don't know when it's going to come out, and I don't know what to do with it. Everyone keeps telling me how special I am and how I have this particular thing I was born to do, and all I want to do is go home to be with my parents and my brother and sisters. I miss them! I don't want to have to do this, Deacon!" She wrapped her arms around his neck and cried. "I don't want any of it! I wish they'd never let me be born!"

Uncomfortable with tears, Deacon patted Amaya's shoulder awkwardly. "It could be worse."

Sniffling, she sat back and stared at him. "How? How could it be worse?"

Wryly, he smiled. "Do you know who my mother is?"

Amaya shook her head. "No. I didn't think you did, either."

"I didn't until a few days ago. My dad finally told me. It's Lilith. The Devil."

Amaya sat back and stared at the lake again, unsure what to say. After several moments of silence, she looked at him, studying the side of his face for a long time before speaking.

"You win."

Deacon laughed and shook his head, grabbing her hand in his own. "Yeah. I win." He squeezed her fingers. "They're going to come looking for you."

"I know."

"Do you want to be here when they come?"

She shook her head. "I don't want to see him, Deacon. Not now, maybe not ever. What he did, I just can't."

Deacon stood, pulling her to his feet. "Let's go then."

"Go where?"

"Anywhere. Let's be stupid and reckless and have some fun. Where do you want to go?"

The beach lit up as Gabriel and Michael appeared. Gabriel strode purposefully toward the two young Nephilim. "Amaya Samantha Winslow, you will return with us right this instant."

Deacon looked down at her, a grin on his face. "Well, what's the verdict?"

Amaya looked between Deacon and Gabriel, her heart pounding in her chest and her stomach twisted in knots of excitement. Leaping into Deacon's arms, she wrapped her arms around his neck and hugged him tightly.

"Let's go!"

Deacon flashed an instant before Gabriel reached them.

CHAPTER ONE

DECEMBER 25TH, 2052

"MERRY CHRISTMAS." Amaya Winslow hopped onto the couch and handed a wrapped package to the man sitting next to her. "It's not much, but, well, it's the Apocalypse, so what can you do?"

Deacon laughed and reached down to snag a bag from the space between the end table and the couch. "Not much. Here's yours. Are Zeke and Lux coming?"

She shook her head. "They're with their parents. Where's everyone else?"

Deacon rolled his eyes. "Carys convinced them to have a party down on Earth. Denise is thrilled about it. Dev went to keep an eye on her, and Zane went to keep Dev company. The normal. Dad's supervising to make sure they don't get out of hand. I'm surprised to see you back. I thought you were with your mom and dad for the holidays?"

"I was." She stared down at the bag in her hands. "It's hard to be with them knowing that I still don't have a good handle on things. I worry that they're in danger when I'm around. Eden and Donovan are still so young, and Finley is scared of me. She doesn't want to share a room anymore. I had to sleep on the couch."

Deacon scowled. "Your sister is a pansy."

"No, she's right. I'm dangerous right now. Mom and Dad want me there. I miss them, so I want to be there, too, but until I figure out how to control everything, it's dangerous. I get mad and blow things up, remember?"

He chuckled. "How could I forget? I don't think Gabriel's ever forgiven us for that little jaunt."

"Three years. You'd think he'd stop holding a grudge." She giggled at the memory and bounced in her seat. "Enough about that. Open the present!"

Humoring her, Deacon tore into the package, scattering bits of paper on the floor. He ripped open the box, revealing a soft, steel blue, cable knit sweater. Running his hands over the fabric, he lifted it from the box, holding it up and toying with the loops for the two buttons at the top.

"It's gorgeous."

"Aradia's been teaching me to knit. She's got that loom and has been making wool with the sheep she and Gage have, so I got her to give me some and I made it."

He looked up. "You made this? Amaya, that's amazing."

Amaya blushed. "It's actually pretty fun. Knitting. Try it on."

Deacon jumped up, stripping off his hoodie and pulling the sweater over his head. The cuffs hung a little past his fingers, but it fit reasonably well. "I love it." He dropped back to the couch. "Now open yours."

Amaya opened the bag and pulled out several sheets of shredded newspaper before getting to a wooden box. She lifted it out, her fingertips moving over the smooth wood.

"Open the box. The real present is inside."

She lifted the lid, her face splitting in a wide smile as she saw the small carved chess pieces inside. The board was folded in quarters laying in the bottom.

"Did you make this?"

"I found the board, but most of the pieces were missing so Zane helped me carve some of them, but I did most of the work. I thought maybe we could play. I know you used to play with your dad all the time when you were little."

"He played with all of us. So did Mom." Amaya picked up one of the pieces and turned it over in her hands. "I love it, thank you." Setting aside the box, she folded her legs beneath herself and stared at him, the light from the fireplace playing over her face. "I've been thinking."

Deacon snorted into his beer bottle. "Uh oh. That's never good."

Laughing, she grabbed his hands. "No, it's nothing bad."

"Spit it out already, Winslow."

"I think that I'm ready to leave. I feel good about my powers and controlling them, and I think I'm ready to go out on my own a little. I want you to come with me."

Deacon stared at her as he processed what she had said. "Maya."

"What? I'm the only one that can kill Lucifer, other than maybe you, and I see no reason for us to continue to sit here on our asses and wait while people are out there fighting and dying every day. Let's go do it! Let's go do what we were born to do! Come with me, Deacon."

"We don't know how to kill Lucifer." Deacon tightened his grip when she started to pull away. "No, don't get mad at me. I'm not saying I don't want to go with you." He cast a look around. "Truth be told, I'd love to get out of here. I agree it seems wrong for us to be living up here like this while the rest of the Nephilim are fighting a war. But our fathers would never allow it, and you know that. Even if they would, we don't know how to kill him. God isn't telling them how it's done, and Gage hasn't been able to figure it out."

"I don't care what our fathers would allow." Amaya dropped his hands and stood to pace. "I'm tired of being some weapon and not knowing how to do anything. We train and train and train, but we don't get anywhere. All I've heard since I found out about all of this is that I'm special, and I have to stay safe because I have this bigger purpose. I'm tired of hearing it. I'm sick of hearing that I have this bigger purpose. It's time for me to go out there and prove it." She threw her hands out to emphasize her point. "I want to do something, Deacon! I don't want to sit here anymore!"

"What do you think would happen if we just packed a bag and ran away? How long do you think it would take before they found us?"

"There are cloaking spells and wards. We know how to protect ourselves."

"Okay, just for a second, let's pretend that we could keep both Gabriel and Michael from finding us. Do you really think we could avoid Braxton and Alaria? Or Aradia and Gage? Damon and Greer? Zeke? Zane? Lux? Dev? Denise? Carys? Elisa? Or any of the other ten thousand Nephilim and Warriors they'd have looking for us?" He smiled gently. "I know how you feel. I feel the same way because we're in the same boat, but there's nothing we can do about it right now other than wait and see how it turns out."

"I don't want to wait and see how it turns out. I want to get out there and do something about it!" She flopped back down onto the couch. "This is ridiculous! It's like I'm a prisoner! I can't leave and go do anything without being dragged back here where they've decided I'm safe. I'm not a person. I don't have rights. I'm a weapon they intend to detonate whenever they figure out how to use me." Tears flooded her eyes. "You don't know how that feels. No one does."

Deacon reached out and smoothed a lock of her hair back from her face. "No, no one knows how you feel. I'm sorry." He laid his hand on her shoulder. "I wish there was something I could do."

Amaya looked away. "It was a stupid idea. You were right. It's trouble when I have an idea."

Unsure how to help, Deacon wrapped his arms around her, hugging her close. "It's a good idea. It's the circumstances that are trouble." He kissed her temple. "Let's play a game of chess. There's no use in dwelling over this. It's Christmas, and we should be celebrating. Another holiday we managed to survive."

Amaya turned quickly, wrapping her arms around his neck and clamping her mouth on his. Surprised by the onslaught, Deacon sucked in a breath and grabbed her by the shoulders. His body tensed as her taste flooded his senses, and it was all he could do to move her back from him.

"Whoa, Maya, what was that?"

Amaya stared up at him. "If you have to ask, I was doing it wrong."

"You were doing it just fine, but why were you doing it?"

Hurt flashed across her face. "If you don't want to, just say so. There's no reason to be mean about it." When she leaped to her feet, Deacon reached out and pulled her back down, holding one of her wrists firmly in his hand. "Let go of me!"

"No." His voice calm, Deacon leaned back against the couch. "Last I checked, you and I are pretty good friends and haven't seemed to be on the path to anything else. If that's changed, or if it's in the process of changing, then we both need to be on the same page with it because it's a pretty serious shift."

Amaya blinked several times in rapid succession. "What kind of twenty-one year old man are you?"

He laughed warmly. "The kind who doesn't want to ruin a friendship on a whim. I'm not interested in being the way you get your mad out, so if that's what this was, rethink it." He touched her face gently. "If it wasn't, then we can try it again."

"My, my, how touching."

Both jumped at the sound of an unfamiliar voice and whirled, facing a blonde woman who stood at the bottom of the stairs, flanked on either side by a man, one of whom was shirtless and clad only in leather pants and the other who wore a full three-piece pinstriped suit.

Deacon shoved Amaya behind him as they stood, clenching his hand and conjuring a sword. "Who are you and what are you doing here?"

The woman giggled. "Is that anyway to greet your mother? Come here, Deacon darling, and give Mommy a hug and kiss."

Deacon's stomach clenched and knotted. "What do you want, Lilith?"

"That's 'Mother' to you, you ungrateful whelp." Lilith's voice turned sharp, and she gripped the railing tightly, her knuckles turning white. "Who's behind you?" She turned her head to the side. "Come out here, little girl, and let me get a look at you."

"She's a human. She's nothing."

The man in the suit lifted one eyebrow. "Son, I can sense a Nephil a mile away. Don't lie to us."

Lilith stepped off the last stair and crossed the room on needle-thin heels. "You're protecting her. Is she special?" When Deacon didn't answer, Lilith made a considering noise in the back of her throat. "Where is your father, darling? I have business with him."

"Does Lucifer know you're here?"

"I'll be the one asking the questions." She glanced at the two men. "Azazel, check the main floor for other Nephilim down here. If you find any, kill them. Beelzebub, take the upstairs. I want to find Michael." She turned back to her son. "Step aside and let me see the girl. I want to see the type of woman my son was going to fuck."

Temper flared in Deacon, and he lifted the sword slightly. "Don't talk about her like." He grabbed Amaya's wrist and jerked her back when she started to step out from behind him. "I won't let you hurt her."

"I never said I was going to hurt her, but I can promise you I won't stand by and allow my own flesh and blood to sully himself with a Nephil." Lilith tapped one blood-red fingernail against her lips.

"Why are you here, Lilith?"

She lifted one eyebrow. "I warned you once about who is asking the questions here. And I already told you I have business to discuss with your father."

The room filled with light as Michael appeared, his sword drawn. On one side of him was Gabriel, and behind them were a dozen Nephilim. Michael looked at Lilith with mild disregard.

"We have no business. Leave my home or die here. Your choice."

"Oh, but we do." Lilith sauntered across the room and ran her hand up Michael's lapel. "I've been searching for this place for two decades, Michael. How lucky did I get that when I arrive, here is our son." She smiled brightly at Deacon. "You've had him long enough. It's my turn."

Michael exchanged a look of disbelief with Gabriel. "You can't be serious. He's a grown man who has chosen his path. He fights with the Nephilim. Deacon is free to go or to stay, but you cannot force him to leave with you."

"I want him. He's mine. I carried him and birthed him. You stole him from me, and I want him back. It's not fair what you did, Michael, and it's my turn." Lilith stomped her foot and turned to Deacon. "I'm your mother! You're supposed to be with me!"

Beelzebub appeared back at Lilith's arm, his face twisted with fury. "You lying bitch. You told us Lucifer was sending us to wipe out the Nephilim here, not for you to have some sort of custody dispute with Michael over that fucking whelp!"

Lilith's eyes flashed, and she whirled on Beelzebub. "You answer to me! Not Lucifer! I'm more powerful than he is, and you will answer to me!"

"Not today."

Michael smirked when Beelzebub disappeared. He sensed a second flash as Azazel followed suit. "I suggest you cut your losses and get out of here. You can't take us all on."

Lilith looked at Deacon, her gaze imploring. "Come with me, son. It's time for you to know your mother."

"I don't think so."

Eyes flashing with fury, she stomped her foot again. "Fine! I can see you've been corrupted by your father. I won't ask again, Deacon. This was your last chance. The next time I see you, I'll kill you." She looked past him at Amaya. "As for you. If I ever see you put your filthy Nephil paws on my child again, I'll make sure Abalam gets ahold of you and has as much fun as he wants."

Michael didn't move until Lilith was gone. Once she was, he turned to the Nephilim behind him. "Pack what you need. We leave in thirty minutes. The position of this nonplace is compromised. Gabriel, can you begin forming another?"

Gabriel nodded. "I will. Amaya, are you injured?"

Amaya stepped out from behind Deacon. "I don't think she knew who I am."

"If she had, she would not have gone. We got very lucky." Michael looked at them both. "Come into my office. I think we need to have a quick talk before you pack." He glanced to Gabriel. "I'll handle this."

Gabriel nodded reluctantly. "Handle it well. I do not wish to repeat this lesson at a later time."

Confused, Amaya followed Deacon and Michael into the office that he used and sat down. "What lesson is he talking about?"

Michael waited until Deacon sat down before perching on the desk. Reluctantly, he spoke. "Deacon, are you and Amaya involved with one another? Romantically?"

"No. Why?"

"Why does Lilith think you are?"

Amaya blushed. "I kissed him. I was kinda mad about something and reacting, and I think she saw part of it, but it's not like we're sleeping together or anything."

Deacon glared at his father. "And it wouldn't be your business if we were. What does this have to do with any damn thing?"

Michael held up his hands. "Your mother is a very jealous and vengeful Devil. She is also very powerful. I have known her for more years than you can even comprehend, and I have seen her soul twisted beyond recognition. The thing she is now is so possessive and jealous that she would not hesitate to target and hunt down anyone she thought was encroaching on her territory. I'm afraid since you are her son, she views you as that territory."

"I'm not her son. She's a fucking egg donor. Nothing more."

Michael silenced Deacon with one look. "I don't disagree with you. I've raised you since you were an infant. As far as I know, today was the first time she had lain eyes upon you since the moment you were born. She is no kind of mother, but Lilith is delusional. In her mind you are more hers than you are mine since she was the one to carry and birth you. An act, I might remind you, we will forever be indebted to her for." He glanced sharply at Amaya when she started to speak. "I don't want either of you to misunderstand what I'm saying here. I don't care one way or the other whether the two of you are involved or not. If you were, it ends today."

Deacon crossed one leg over the other and stared at his father. When he spoke, his voice was even and calm. Too calm. "You don't get to make that decision."

"In this particular case, I do. Not because of anything to do with the two of you or any desire to be patriarchal toward either of you. I cannot overstate how lucky we were today that those three Devils did not realize who Amaya was. If she had used even the tiniest bit of her power, they would have, and she would no longer be safe. If Lilith knows you two are together, it is a very short matter of time before they know who you are, and then you are not safe. She is crazy, and anyone she thinks is important to you is going to be her target. We cannot let her know who Amaya is or they will come for you, and they will not stop because they'll know what you look like, where you were, and they'll have your scent. Your anonymity is the one singular thing keeping you safe right now, and we cannot risk losing that, Amaya." Michael looked at them both, his expression pained. "I don't say any of this to hurt you or because I want to say it. I say it because I love you both and I want to protect you. If the time comes that we have defeated Lilith and we know how to kill Lucifer, I'll step back and you two can figure things out for yourselves and do whatever it is that you want with no interference from me. I cannot promise you'll get none from Gabriel, but I'll keep my nose out of it."

Amaya leaned forward in the chair. "But she knows there was someone. Won't she be trying to figure out who that is?"

"Yes." Michael met her gaze steadily. "Which is why it is of utmost importance that we leave here immediately. You are going to come with us, and I am going to send Deacon to Damon and Greer for a few weeks. We'll rotate some of the Nephilim staying with me to other assignments, I'll move to several other nonplaces, and we will take precautions to ensure that Lilith cannot find her way back to us. The two of you will not be in the same place for a while. It's not something I want to do since you need to train together in order to defeat Lucifer, but we can't take the risk at this time. I can't force you to do as I say, but if you don't, I fear for what Gabriel will do, Amaya. He may force you to go to Heaven with him."

Deacon looked at Amaya. "Dad's right, as much as I hate to admit it." He reached out and took her hand, squeezing it tightly. "Friends?"

The word constricted her heart in her chest, but Amaya nodded. "Friends."

CHAPTER TWO

DECEMBER 10TH, 2060

AMAYA SAT in the library, her hair pulled back into a messy ponytail at the back of her head. She was on the floor instead of the couch or one of the chairs, surrounded by piles of books. Many were open, others were bookmarked or turned over to mark a page, and still others were stacked in piles with sticky notes stuck to the covers, handwritten notes scribbled on them denoting what she hoped to find therein.

In front of her were the scrolls, held open with empty tumblers, bottles of liquor—whatever she could find to keep them flat. Several notebooks were stacked next to one of her legs, and she held yet another in her lap, tapping a pen against the page as she studied one of the volumes, trying to make sense of the Aramaic by translating it into Latin, then into English.

She glanced up when the door opened and smiled tightly when Zeke came through the door. "Hey. Couldn't sleep?"

Zeke shook her head and rubbed her belly. "No. My back is killing me." She lifted an eyebrow at the piles of books and scrolls. "What are you doing?"

"Working. There has to be a way to kill Lucifer and Lilith's children, and Lucifer, and I'm going to find it. Some prophecy, some abstract mention somewhere." Amaya looked around, slightly surprised when she realized how many books were on the floor. "I've made quite a mess, haven't I?"

Zeke laughed. "Yes, you have. Is there someplace I can sit without disturbing whatever system you have going on, or should I just continue to stand where I am?"

Amaya carefully climbed to her feet and stepped over the fortress of books she'd somehow walled herself into. "Give me just a second. I'll clear a spot off." She looked at Zeke suspiciously when the other woman winced. "Are you sure you're okay?"

Zeke waved her hand dismissively. "I'm fine. I'm just seventeen fucking months pregnant and uncomfortable. That's all."

"When are you due, anyway? It has to be soon."

"A few days. I only got to see a real doctor once, and she figured it was around Christmas. Aradia thought a little before, so sometime between now and Christmas." She hissed when her stomach tightened and a pain shot through her back. "I hate this backache. I'm on the verge of waking Dev up to come down here and give me a massage."

Amaya finished clearing off the couch and grabbed Zeke's elbow, leading her to it and helping her sit down. "Where's Lux?"

"She went with Gage to the Warrior compound that your mom and dad are staying at. Why?"

"Sweetie, I think you're in labor. I remember when my brother was born, and this is what it looked like."

Zeke glared at Amaya and shoved a pillow behind her back, trying to get comfortable. "I am not in labor. I would know it if I was. There would be contractions, and my water would break, and bloody stuff would come out. All sorts of nasty things happen to a woman's body when she has a baby. I just have a backache."

"You're just stubborn." Amaya looked at her watch, paying attention to the time. "How does your back feel right now?"

"A little better. I got the pillow where it's supposed to be."

"I'll get you some water. Hang on a second." She rifled through the pages on the floor until she came up with an unopened bottle. Twisting off the cap, she handed it to her friend. "Here, drink this."

"Thanks." Zeke drank the lukewarm water and set the bottle aside, resting her hands on her stomach. "I haven't wanted to bring it up, but I do need to know who's going to deliver the baby when it does come. I assumed it would be Aradia, but she's gone now, and Lux hasn't ever done it. She doesn't even know how. Hell, of those of us left, you're the most qualified to deliver me."

Amaya blanched. "I was, like, seven when my brother was born. That hardly makes me an expert."

"Neither Lux or I had any siblings, so it makes you more an expert than us. Obstetricians are pretty hard to come by lately in case you hadn't noticed."

Zeke shifted again as another pain tore through her back. She rubbed her side absently and surveyed the room, taking in the fire in the fireplace and the piles of books and papers. Turning back to Amaya, she noticed her friend staring at her wristwatch intently.

"What are you doing?"

"Timing your contractions."

"I'm not in labor."

"Your back is hurting periodically. The pains are coming every—" she looked at her watch, "—nine minutes. How long have they been coming?"

"A few hours. It's just a backache."

"Are you stubborn or stupid?" Amaya looked at Zeke drolly. "You're due in a maximum of ten days, you're having pains every few minutes that look suspiciously like contractions, and I can see your stomach tightening up when you do."

"I can't be in labor. I have no place to deliver the baby and no one here to do it."

"We live with an Angel. Michael will figure out something." She stood and extended a hand. "The first thing to do is to get you away from my work before your water breaks and you get amniotic fluid all over several thousand years of priceless prophecies. We'll get you settled into bed upstairs and I'll wake up Dev."

"My water hasn't broken." Zeke pointed out reasonably, sighing as Amaya heaved her to her feet. "I can't have a baby until that happens. It's just not possible."

"I understand that, but your water doesn't have to break for labor to start." Amaya guided Zeke toward the stairs. Halfway up, Deacon stumbled out of his room, his hair standing on end and a towel slung over his shoulder. He blinked at them rapidly.

"You're either up really early or really late."

"She's up early, I'm up late." Amaya supported Zeke's weight up the rest of the stairs. "Heading out for a run?"

"I was planning on it. I can wait a few minutes if you want to join me."

"Not going to be able to do that, unfortunately. Zeke's in

labor."

Growling when Deacon's eyes lit with surprise, Zeke bit off her next words with an angry huff. "I am not in labor. Amaya thinks I'm in labor." She grunted as a wave of pain worked its way through her and doubled over, wrapping her free arm around her stomach. "Jesus Christ, I need a hot bath and a pain pill. This backache is killing me!"

Deacon lifted his eyebrows. "I'll go tell Dad."

"I'm not fucking in Goddammed mother-fucking labor you son of a bitch!"

The door swung open and Dev came out into the hallway, rubbing his eyes. "What's going on?"

Her tone mild, Amaya was the one to answer. "Zeke is in labor. She's in denial about such, but her contractions are about nine minutes apart. I've been timing them. She is under the impression that because her water has not broken, that she cannot possibly be in labor."

They all stared when a splash of clear fluid hit the floor and wetness spread across the front of Zeke's pants. She looked between the other three people, redness coloring her cheeks. Amaya put her hands on her hips and stared at Zeke drolly before speaking.

"And I suppose you just pissed yourself in the middle of the stairs? Or are you finally going to admit what I've spent the last half an hour telling you?"

"I guess I am in labor." She reached for Dev, squeezing his hand. "Oh, God, the baby's coming and we don't have anyone to deliver him! What if something goes wrong? What if I can't push him out? What if I need a C-section? Aradia was supposed to do this! So many things could go wrong!"

Amaya gripped Zeke's shoulders and ushered her up the stairs and down the hall toward the bedrooms. "Calm down, sweetheart. It's all going to be fine. Dev, find a tarp or some plastic to put down on the mattress. Birth is bloody business. Deacon, we're going to need towels. A lot of them. Let's get you changed into a clean shirt. Might as well leave the bottom bare since that's where all the action is going to be. How long have you been having the back pain?"

Looking embarrassed, Zeke closed her eyes. "Since about four yesterday afternoon. It was just little pangs at first. I could ignore it for the most part. I only got a couple an hour and then they started coming more and more often through the night. By four this morning it was every fifteen minutes, and now it's every, what did you say, nine?"

Dev gaped at her from where he was stripping the sheets off their bed. "You've been in labor for thirteen hours and never said a word?"

"I didn't realize it was labor until five minutes ago. I thought it was just a really bad backache. I thought labor would be pains in my stomach, not my back."

Amaya grabbed one of Dev's shirts from the door and handed it to Zeke. "Put that on."

"Don't you dare let her put that on!" Dev snatched the shirt and clutched it to his chest. "I don't want my clothes ruined with blood and goo. She has a whole drawer of my shirts that she's pilfered. Use one of those."

Amaya cocked one eyebrow. "She's getting ready to push your progeny out of her lady parts, and you're pitching a fit over whether she's wearing a shirt you like while she does it? Really, Dev, that's kinda crazy."

Zeke bent to open another drawer. "He's really funny about his clothes. I should have warned you." She pulled out a shirt and yanked it over her head. "Is the bed ready for me to get into?"

Deacon appeared with a stack of towels. "Here are all the towels I could find. I gathered up the rest and put them in the wash."

Michael entered the room behind Deacon, his gaze going to Zeke. "Ezekiel, how are you?"

She looked at him, fear and excitement shining in her eyes. "I'm not sure. I wasn't expecting this tonight. I'm not entirely sure what to do."

He crossed the room and laid his hand on her stomach. "Your child is well and anxious to be born. Would you like for me to fetch Lux?"

Zeke laughed. "Does Lux actually know how to birth a child?"

"I don't know if she's ever done it, but I'd think Aradia had taught her something about it."

She shook her head. "If we need her you can go get her, but she's dealing with a lot with Gage right now. I don't want to pull her away from him unless we need to. We'll manage here. Women have been doing this forever, right? And you'll be here, won't you? I mean, you're not leaving, are you?"

Michael took her hands and led her to the bed, helping her onto the mattress and tucking a blanket around her legs. "No, I'm not leaving. I won't interfere unless something goes wrong, but I'm not going to let anything happen to you or the child." He stroked her hair gently. "For today, think of me as your own Guardian Angel." He looked at Deacon and Amaya. "Deacon, I'd suggest occupying yourself elsewhere. Ezekiel won't want more company than necessary during this. Amaya, do you need anything else for the delivery?"

Amaya looked around the room. "We need baby things." She looked at Zeke. "Do you have anything for the baby?"

"A few things. Some clothes we scrounged and diapers."

Deacon leaned against the door. "Get me a list and I'll go on a run. I'll take Carys and Elisa with me. It'll keep them out of here and out of your hair while you're doing this."

Amaya slipped from the room and down the stairs so that she was out of earshot, Deacon trailing behind her. She grabbed a pad of paper from Michael's desk in the office and one of the pens from his top drawer.

"I'm going to give you the list from most important to least important, but if all Zeke and Dev have is clothes and diapers, then they are sadly lacking in things. I should have been paying more attention. With Damon and Greer gone, Zeke didn't have anyone to tell her what to get, and Dev's mom died when he was little. I'm the only one who has any siblings. God, since when does having a younger sister and brother make you a fucking expert on babies?"

Deacon laughed. "Since the world ended apparently. What're my top goals?"

"A bassinet or crib for the baby to sleep in, bottles, breast pump, diapers, clothes, swing, so on and so forth." She looked up from her list. "Be careful going out. You'll want to find some baby stores or something. Going house to house would take forever to find stuff. That's going to mean towns or cities."

Deacon took the list from her. "I'll be careful. Take care of that baby."

"I need to do something. I feel pressure!" Zeke grabbed Dev's hand and bore down, sweat dripping off her forehead as she pushed.

Amaya looked up from where she sat at the foot of the bed. "Pressure means push, sweetie. Push on each contraction." She touched Zeke's knee and pushed it slightly to the side. "I see hair!"

Zeke blushed. "I've been too big to do much grooming lately. Oh, God, here comes another contraction!"

Amaya laughed, turning her face into her shoulder. "The baby's hair, goofy! I see the head. What kind of friend do you think I am that I would criticize you when you're in labor?" She laid a towel on the bed to soak up the bloody fluid that gushed out when Zeke pushed. "Then again, I didn't think we were the kind of friends that stared at each others' vaginas for hours on end."

Zeke huffed as the contraction ended and she relaxed. "Not my fault I've been pushing for two hours." She looked at Dev. "It's your fault."

He leaned down and kissed her gently, his eyes shining with love. "I take full responsibility. You're doing so great, Zeke. So great. I'm absolutely in awe of you, baby. Isn't she great, Amaya?"

Amaya glanced up. "Hmm?" She shook her head. "She's wonderful. Hey Dev, could you get me some Vaseline or lube or something?"

Zeke sat up, bracing herself on her palms. "What's wrong?"

"Nothing's wrong, but the baby is getting ready to come out, and I think something to help make him more slippery might help you not tear." Amaya patted Zeke's knee. "You're doing fine. Just relax."

Dev reappeared with a tube of lubricant in his hand. "Here." He passed it to Amaya. "Is there anything else you need?"

She looked around. "Scissors would be good and run some water in the tub. Warm but not hot. He's going to be here soon."

Zeke gritted her teeth and dug her fingers into the sheets as a contraction ripped through her. "God this hurts! Now I know why human women love those epidurals they all got!"

"You're doing fine." Amaya squirted lube on her hands and slipped one finger between Zeke's body and the baby's head, rubbing the lubricant into her skin to ease the child's exit. "I'm going to try and rotate the baby to get the shoulders out, okay?"

Zeke nodded. "Okay."

Concentrating, Amaya placed one hand slightly below Zeke to support the baby's head as it slipped out as she pushed and gently pushed one of the baby's shoulders up to angle them.

"One more push, Zeke. A little one, please." She held up a finger when Zeke bore down. "Not that hard. Gently. Good. Okay, the shoulders are out."

"This feels weird."

Dev ran back into the room. "Did I miss it?"

"Just in time, Daddy." Amaya glanced up. "Come here with

those scissors." She looked to Zeke. "This is the last push. Slow and gentle."

Zeke closed her eyes and pushed, the baby slipping from her body and into Amaya's waiting hands. Amaya grabbed a towel, turning the baby over and rubbing his back vigorously. Within seconds, cries filled the room, lusty and loud. Zeke burst into tears.

"I want to see him! Give him here!"

Amaya nodded to Dev. "I need something to tie the cord off with. A string or cord. Something."

Dev raced into the bathroom and returned with dental floss, thrusting it into Amaya's hand. She tied the cord and handed him the scissors, gesturing to a spot right above the green floss.

"Cut right there." Waiting while Dev sliced through the cord, Amaya wrapped the baby in a towel and laid him on Zeke's chest, watching with tears in her eyes as her friend met her son for the first time.

"Oh!" Zeke pushed back the towel to see his face. "Oh, Dev. He's beautiful. Look at him. Just look at him!"

After encouraging Zeke through several more contractions and delivering the placenta, Amaya gathered up the remnants of birth in a towel and tucked both into a garbage bag. She snagged the laundry basket and picked up all the other bloody towels before balancing the basket on her hip and heading for the door.

"Amaya."

She turned at the sound of Zeke's voice. "What is it?"

"Where are you going?"

"I thought you'd want to settle in and bond."

Dev took the basket from her and sat it on the floor, gathering her into a hug. "Don't be silly. You stay as long as you want to stay."

Zeke held out her hand, pulling Amaya down onto the bed with her. "I don't have a single fucking clue what to do with him." She laid her head on Amaya's shoulder. "But I love him anyway."

Amaya ran one finger down the baby's cheek. "Well, I think we should likely wash you both off and get some clean sheets for this bed. The plastic underneath should have protected the mattress from all the goo." She pressed her cheek to Zeke's hair. "What are you naming him?"

"We'd decided on a name when we found out we were having a boy. Naming him after my mom if a girl, and after my dad if a boy." Zeke looked at Dev, who nodded slightly. "But we had to change things a little when everything happened recently." She reached over and took Amaya's hand in hers, gripping it tightly. "You're my best friend. Well, you and Lux. I don't know what I would do without you, Amaya. I love you. I wasn't a fan of your father. For a while I hated him, but at the end, he was trying. He tried to make things right with me, with Zane, and with you. He died saving you. For everything he was, I think he'd have died for any of us."

Dev cleared his throat. "She's rambling, so I'll get to the point. We decided to honor both your fathers, Amaya. Yours and Zeke's. So, we decided to name him Caleb Gabriel Damon Deveraux. It's a hell of a name, but we think he can rise to the occasion."

Amaya bit the inside of her cheek to keep from crying. "It's beautiful. He's beautiful." She kissed Zeke's head. "Let's get you guys cleaned up, hmm?"

An hour later, once Zeke and the baby were tucked into a clean bed, Amaya finally managed to slip out of the room and down into the kitchen. She went to the cabinet, pulling out a bottle of scotch and plunked it down on the counter while she fished a snifter from another cabinet. Filling the glass, she drained it in one gulp, reveling in the burn of alcohol in the back of her throat.

She refilled the glass, drained it, and filled it again. Tears burned her eyes and throat, threatening to spill over. Angry at herself for wanting to cry, with Zeke and Dev for making her want to cry, and with Gabriel for being the reason she wanted to cry, she grabbed the edge of the counter and rocked back and forth, forcing herself to breathe in an effort to quell the tears. When that didn't work and several slipped down her cheeks, she heaved the glass at the wall, shattering it and splashing alcohol onto the tile floor.

Grabbing the bottle, she turned it up and gulped straight from the opening, not even bothering to get a second glass. Tears ran freely down her face, and the alcohol burned her throat. Grief and anger bubbled up within her, gripping her heart and squeezing until she felt she couldn't breathe.

"You son of a bitch!" The shout surprised her as it burst from her lips. "Why did you do this to me? You made me hate you! Why couldn't you just have kept letting me hate you?"

Michael appeared at the door. "Amaya, what's wrong?" He took in the nearly empty bottle and the glass on the floor, then the tear tracks on her face. "Come here."

Without questioning, she ran into his arms, burying her face in his chest and let the tears take her.

CHAPTER THREE

IT WAS insistent drumming that woke Amaya. Or hammering. Some sort of constant pounding. Opening her eyes, she immediately realized it was her head. Gripping it between her hands, she rolled to her side and groaned, gagging at the taste of her mouth.

Struggling not to vomit, she dashed to the bathroom and shoved her face under the faucet, gulping water greedily. As soon as it hit her stomach, a wave of nausea rolled through her and she hit the floor on her knees, wresting open the lid of the toilet and puking up still cold water and splashes of stomach acid.

Collapsing to the floor in a heap, Amaya wondered briefly how it was possible to sweat so much and be so cold at the same time. She was still lying there, wishing for death, when Deacon opened the door to her bedroom and poked his head in.

"Maya? You up?"

"Shh. Don't yell."

Deacon grinned and walked into the bathroom. "Hangover?"

"Hangover from hell." She peered up at him. "What do you want?"

"Griffin is downstairs. She says she has some information for us. Lux and Zane are here, too. She's pissed no one came to get her when Zeke went into labor."

Amaya stuck out one of her hands and waited until Deacon pulled her to her feet. "They're all going to have to wait until I get a shower and brush my teeth."

"I'll relay the message. Do you want some breakfast?"

"What time is it?"

"Noon."

"How long was I asleep?"

"About fourteen hours. Dad said he poured you into bed about ten last night. You needed it, though. You'd been up more than thirty-six." He reached out and tugged on one of her curls, watching it spring back when he let it go. "I'll make you some oatmeal. It'll be nice to your belly."

Twenty minutes later, wearing sweatpants and a hooded sweatshirt with her hair in a messy bun, Amaya slipped down the stairs and into the kitchen. Zeke was sitting at the breakfast nook holding Caleb, who was sleeping. Lux was next to her, cooing over the baby. Dev and Zane perched on barstools, Michael was leaning against the stove, Deacon sat at the kitchen table, and Griffin was standing at the end of the island looking supremely uncomfortable.

Deacon nudged a bowl toward Amaya as she sat down, and she picked up a spoon, tasting the warm oatmeal hesitantly before deciding it was going to sit on her stomach just fine. Groaning with delight when Michael handed her a mug filled with coffee, the spoon clattered into the bowl and she grabbed the cup with both hands, drinking deeply, not even caring that she burned her tongue.

"I would be really annoyed when Gabriel would come see me in the middle of the night or early in the morning, so I tried to wait until you'd all be awake. I'm sorry I woke you, Amaya."

Amaya jerked her shoulder when Griffin spoke. "Not your fault I got drunk and passed out. What's going on?" She glanced up from her bowl. "What wisdom have you come to impart on us?"

Griffin held up a hand when Michael started to scold Amaya. "Don't. She's okay. I remember how bitter I was when I did this. I'm sure I was rude on more than one occasion." She flicked her wings, still not used to the feel of them, and thought about sitting down. Just the concept of trying to figure out how to position the wings to settle into the chair was enough to change her mind and she remained standing. "It's been decided that I'll pick up where Gabriel left off since it is his abilities I have. I know this is awkward for all of us, and I want to assure all of you that I'm not here to rock the boat.

I don't want to take over for Michael, and I don't want to boss anyone around. I want to help." She locked her gaze onto Amaya's. "I'm not here to get in your way."

Amaya inclined her head slightly. "Then we won't have a problem." She spooned another bite into her mouth, chewed, and swallowed. "What do you know?"

Griffin looked longingly at the coffee pot. "Michael, can Angels drink? I don't remember if they can or not."

"We can eat or drink. Would you like a cup of coffee?" Michael reached for a cup and poured coffee into it.

Griffin took the cup and sipped, sighing contentedly before speaking. "The one thing I hated the most about Angels was when they would come and give me some information but not enough to do anything with. I hate that I'm about to do the same thing to you. I've been sent with information on what you must do and how you can accomplish it, though I'm afraid the details that I've been given are sorely lacking." She scowled. "This brings back not so good memories of my time doing God's bidding."

Deacon folded his arms on the table and leaned forward slightly. "What do we need to do?"

"I think you already know most of what I'm going to tell you. You have to kill Lucifer and his two progeny. Unfortunately, because one of them is still gestating, if you wish to kill him before birth, that will necessitate killing Lilith as well."

Amaya looked up from her bowl. "I thought Lilith is more powerful than Lucifer? How are we supposed to kill them both?"

Michael crossed his arms. "Lilith was more powerful than Lucifer when the Fall occurred. However, Lucifer has grown more and more powerful in his position as the ruler of Hell while Lilith has remained stagnant. Simply by nature of God recognizing Lucifer as a ruler was he given certain abilities and power. It's a complex situation, and she certainly had more power than him at one point in time, but I do not believe she still does. I do believe she is fully convinced she is the most powerful. I also am convinced Lucifer would like her to continue to believe the lie."

Griffin cleared her throat. "That having been said, you may or may not have to kill Lilith, depending on whether the child is still gestating when you go after it." She looked at Amaya. "In order to kill Lucifer, you need a weapon. One that only you will be able to use and one that may only be used once, not dissimilar to the knife I was given to do the Choosing. Unlike that, you won't be able to pick up any old blade and do the job. It must be done with this particular weapon. It is the one singular thing with the power to do it. Do you understand?"

Amaya nodded. "I understand. What weapon is it?"

Griffin sipped her coffee before answering. "How familiar are you with Biblical history?"

"Not much at all. I know a little, but it's not like we had Sunday School growing up. Why?"

"Surely you've heard of Moses and Aaron and the rod Aaron had that turned into a serpent. He was gifted with it by God in order to demonstrate His power to Pharaoh. Do you remember that much?"

Annoyed, Amaya dropped her spoon into the last few bites of the oatmeal and shoved the bowl away from herself. "Yes, I remember that much. Get to the fucking point. What does a stick have to do with anything?"

"It wasn't a stick. Rod is a general term. In Aaron's case, it was a sword with a blade made from sapphire and a handle forged in the fires of Hell." Griffin looked at Michael. "You can see where I'm going with this by now, I'm sure."

Michael inclined his head. "God created Aaron's rod on the sixth day of Creation at twilight. It was the final thing He made before resting. It's incredibly powerful. It was given to Adam as he left the Garden of Eden, and it's been used several times throughout human history by those chosen by God for higher purposes. After Aaron had it, it was buried in the ground and is said to remain there until someone pure of heart and intent withdraws it."

Zeke looked up from staring at her son. "It's the Sword in the Stone. King Arthur, Sir Lancelot. That old story. You're talking about the Sword in the Stone. That's real?"

"I can assure you that neither of those men were nearly worthy enough to wield this weapon, though Aaron's rod is where those myths began, yes." Griffin ran her hand over her arm absent-mindedly. "Amaya, you need to find this sword and use it on Lucifer. It is the one thing that can kill him. There's no need to take him to Purgatory to do it. Stab him through the heart, and he will die as long as both of his children are also dead. As long as his bloodline lives, so will he."

Deacon ran his hands through his hair. "Where is the sword?"

Griffin scowled. "I don't know. God won't tell me."

"Figures." He sighed deeply. "Okay, what about the other ones. How do we kill them? Just as important, what are they? We know Serafina and this new baby aren't normal Cambion. Are they Devils? By that logic, if two Angels had children would they have baby Angels?"

Dev laughed. "Cherubs."

Michael glared at both men. "Don't make light, boys."

Griffin shifted from foot to foot, obviously uneasy. "In all seriousness, the reason they are not normal Cambion is because they are the children of Lucifer. Lucifer rules Hell the same way that God rules Heaven. In the same way God has His son in Jesus who was born to Mary, Lucifer is reproducing through Lilith. They will be just as powerful as Lucifer if they are allowed to survive. We don't believe he is aware of that yet or he likely would not have sired them." She took a deep breath and expelled it slowly. "There is another weapon that will destroy them, or other Devils, if used upon them. Like the Choosing knife, this weapon has been cleansed in the blood of Jesus Christ and made pure. Also like the Choosing knife, it is good for one shot and one shot only."

"But there are three of them." Amaya sat up straighter. "One weapon, two kids and Lilith. The math doesn't work. Even best case scenario and we take out Lilith and the baby in one fell swoop, we still need two."

"This particular weapon can be severed and made into several." Griffin finished the coffee and crossed to the sink, placing the cup in the soapy water. "I am referring, of course, to the Spear of Destiny. The spear wielded by the human who pierced the side of Christ while he hung on the cross."

"Of course." Deacon laid his head in his hands. "I don't suppose you know where this one is?"

"It is contained within the Ark of the Covenant. A container ordered made by God to contain certain artifacts such as the tablets on which the Ten Commandments were written and a jar containing manna which has fallen from Heaven. It was gathered by the Israelites on their journey to the Promised Land and has been stored there ever since."

Michael straightened slightly. "Are you saying that Amaya is going to eat the manna?"

Amaya wrinkled her nose. "I'm not eating anything that's been in a box for several thousand years. There's probably nothing left."

Michael shook his head. "In the time of Moses when he led the twelve tribes of Israel to the Promised Land, each day God sent manna from Heaven to feed them. For forty years they lived on nothing but this substance. Manna is whatever God needs it to be. For the Israelites it was food. For you it could be the strength or knowledge to kill Lucifer and Lilith." He looked at Griffin. "Is she to eat it?"

Griffin nodded. "They both are. This is their fight, not hers alone. To review, they must find the Ark of the Covenant. Within it will be manna, the tablets, and the Spear. The Spear can be separated into several blades, sharpened, whatever they need to do to it. They must not cut flesh or they are useless. Any instrument used on it must be cleansed in Holy Water. The manna must be eaten after the Spear is separated and they have found Aaron's rod. Only then will they have everything they need, and the rest will be made clear."

Amaya drew her legs up into the chair and rested her chin on her knees. "You don't know where the Ark is?"

Griffin shook her head. "I wish I did, but no, He didn't tell me. Michael, do you know where either of those things are?"

"No. I didn't keep track of them. Unlike the Holy Grail, they weren't taken to Heaven because they were specifically left on Earth to be used by humans during the End of Days." He refilled the coffee pot and pushed the button to start it perking. "We'll need to find them as soon as possible, though."

Lux stood. "My dad can help. This will give him something else to focus on. Can someone take me back to him?"

Griffin stepped forward. "I'll take you. I'm leaving anyway." She offered a smile. "If you need me for anything, please don't hesitate to call for me. I'll answer."

Amaya didn't speak until Lux, Zane and Griffin had disappeared. She looked at Deacon, her green eyes reflecting worry. "Well, fuck."

Deacon nodded. "My sentiments exactly."

CHAPTER FOUR

DECEMBER 12TH, 2060

AMAYA WAS back in her fortress of books when Deacon found her. She was sitting on the floor with her back against the couch and a book in her lap with several others spread out around her and a bottle of scotch at her feet. A glass dangled from her fingers with an inch of liquid in the bottom.

"Are you just having a drink, or are you getting drunk again?"

"I haven't decided yet." She glanced up and offered a sad smile. "Grab a glass and join me."

Deacon lowered himself to the floor next to her. "I don't need to get drunk every night to deal with things, Amaya. I wish you didn't, either."

Annoyed, she sat the glass down on the floor and shifted away, turning to stare at him. "It's hardly every night, and in case you haven't noticed, I've been dealing with a lot lately!"

"And instead of dealing with it, you're drowning it." He snagged the glass from the floor and drained it, reaching up to place it on the end-table. "You could talk to me, ya know."

"There's nothing to talk about. Gabriel and Aradia are dead, Griffin's back, my parents are in a tailspin, and nothing is going right. Now, instead of coming with the answers, the baby Angel comes with even more questions, and we're supposed to go off gallivanting like Indiana Jones and the Caped Crusader!"

"You're mixing up your pop culture references." He bit the inside of his cheek to stop from laughing. "It's Indiana Jones and the Last Crusade or Raiders of the Lost Ark, whichever you prefer. The Caped Crusader was Batman, I believe."

She goggled at him through just slightly watery eyes. "What the fuck does it matter? It's yet another hoop to jump through when God could just snap his fingers and that damned trunk could be sitting right there in front of us with everything we need in it. I'm sick of everything being so hard. I'm damned tired of all the death." She rose to her knees and grabbed the bottle, reaching around Deacon to get the glass back. Filling it up, she drank deeply, savoring the burn of alcohol sliding down her throat. "We have to slaughter a baby. An infant."

"Not a baby. Satan's child. Who will be just as powerful as he is and could pick up right where Lucifer leaves off. It's a threat to the whole world."

"And none of that changes the fact that yesterday I helped Zeke bring a life into this world and tomorrow I might end another one before it starts. Do we just assume that it's going to be evil? Do we not even give them a chance to decide to follow God or Satan? Is that the kind of legacy we want to leave Earth with? One of blood and mercilessness? Are we really the type of monsters that are going to kill children simply for the sin of being born?" She finished the drink and poured another. "You have the same mother they do. How easily could this have been you?"

"I've thought about that, but my Dad is an Angel. That gives me some balance. They might not even have souls. They're not human. It's not like walking up into the nursery and slitting Caleb's throat. It is different."

"How is it different?"

Deacon plowed his hands through his hair in frustration. "It just is. Do you think they would hesitate to kill that baby up there? Or a hundred thousand others? Do you think they would hesitate to slaughter every Nephilim before birth if they could?"

Amaya stared sullenly into the fireplace, the flames reflected in her eyes. "I think we're not Cambion and that just because they would do it should not be taken as permission for us to stoop as low."

"Maya." Deacon's voice softened. "We knew it wouldn't be easy."

"It was never supposed to involve killing babies!" She tightened her grip on the glass, the alcohol in her system making her vision fuzzy and her words slightly slurred. "I didn't sign on for this."

"We don't get a choice in it."

"We always have a choice."

"They aren't human! They're Devils! We are not talking about a Cambion or a human or even a vampire. We aren't discussing something that has the capacity to choose good or evil. We are talking about a Devil. One with the potential to be even worse than Lucifer."

"My mother was a Devil! She chose good instead of evil!" Amaya swore when tears splashed down her cheeks and dripped into the denim stretched across her knees. "Just being a Devil doesn't automatically make something evil!"

Realization dawned and Deacon sighed deeply. "Dammit." He reached out and touched her knee, wincing when she jerked away from him. "I'm sorry. I didn't think."

"That's pretty obvious." She took a deep, shuddering breath. "How many people need to die? How many times do we need to prove to God that we're fighting? The Choosing is the one thing. One sacrifice, one choice. Then it's not. Three more things. Stop the flow, seal the gate, fix Lucifer's chains. They fail at the last one not because they couldn't do it but because God lost faith in them. Why did God lose faith? Not because of them, but because of other people making bad choices! Women hosting Cambion, Devils mating with women, demons mating with women, people worshiping Satan. So he requires the Nephilim. Thousands of women volunteer. They're honored to stand for God. The Warriors and Hunters view it as their duty. It's their birthright to have Nephil babies. Now, here we are, two armies of half-human things fighting each other for Earth and now God says it's still not good enough, here are these three more things to do. Get Lucifer's sword and destroy it. Check. Kill Beelzebub and all of his kids. Check. But wait, there's more! Can't let them get too close, we have to add in a couple more hoops to jump through to keep them from getting to the finish line. Except this time, the hoops are children. Children that have to die. So we get to choose. Do we save Earth by killing Lucifer, or do we save our own souls?"

Deacon picked up the bottle and refilled the glass, taking it from her fingers and sipping. "For what it's worth, I don't think anyone ever thought it would turn out this way."

"That's not worth much."

"What are you going to do?"

Amaya took the cup back and guzzled it, tipping her head back to stare at the ceiling. "I don't have a fucking clue. No one thinks about how it actually feels to be the one who has to push the red button."

"You don't have to do this alone. I can be the one to take care of them. I don't like seeing you like this."

"Being asked to do what we're being asked to do should have this effect. It shouldn't be easy."

"I never said it's going to be easy. I think it's easier for me than it is for you because everything is very gray for you with Alaria, but it's less that way for me. It's a big picture issue. I don't want to have to do any of this, but I will because the alternative is way worse. If we keep going the way we're going, or if we fail at this, Earth will die. All of us. That baby that was just born up there will die. And not an old man. A young man, or a child, or still a baby. Sooner rather than later, they will win if we don't stop them now. That's how I can know I'll do what needs to be done no matter how repulsive I find the idea." Deacon laid his hand on her cheek. "I'll probably never forgive myself for it, but I will do it because I believe that it's necessary. It's okay if you can't."

Amaya finished her drink and stared at the wall. "I'm not upset because I can't do it, Deacon. I'm upset because I can."

Braxton sat at a weathered kitchen table, an oil lamp his only light and a kerosene heater in the middle of the room. In front of him was a map, and he was studying it intently, making notations on a pad of paper at his elbow. When the room lit up with a flash of light and he heard the fluttering of wings, he glanced over and felt his heart constrict in his chest when he saw Griffin.

Looking as uncomfortable as he felt, she walked to the table and gripped the top of one of the chairs. "I need to talk to you about Amaya."

Braxton dropped the pencil onto the table and looked up at her. "Alaria's already asleep. Can it wait until morning? Is she okay?"

"She's not hurt. She's at Michael's. Ezekiel delivered a healthy baby boy."

"We heard." He pushed back from the table and stood, putting some distance between them. "What's going on, Griffin?"

Alaria appeared at the door, her hair mussed from sleeping and rubbing her hand over her eyes to wake up. "What's going on? Why is Griffin here?"

Griffin turned to face Alaria. "I came to speak to you about Amaya."

"Is she okay? Is she hurt? What's wrong?" Alaria grabbed Braxton's arm, panic rising in her throat.

"She's fine. She is having a very hard time dealing with the task which has befallen her. I thought maybe one of you could talk to her about it."

Alaria released her grip on Braxton's arm. "What's she having a hard time with?"

"You know Lilith is pregnant. I informed them recently that in order to kill Lucifer, they must finish severing his ties to other beings, which includes his children."

Alaria wrinkled her nose and sat down at the table, crossing her legs. "I think we all kind of assumed that would be the case. Did she not realize that?"

"She doesn't believe the children are inherently evil. She thinks they should be able to have a choice and that killing them is proving we are just as bad as they are."

Braxton leaned against the counter. "I think we proved that a long time ago, personally."

Alaria glared at him. "Letting Serafina and the other one live would be letting two new versions of Lucifer continue to exist. It would only be a matter of time before we ended up right back here. This is a war, Brax. Sometimes we all have to do things we don't want to do to make sure that we end it once and for all. Think about human history and the atom bombs. Yes, you killed a lot of people with them who weren't soldiers, but you saved a lot more by doing it and ending the war. By them doing this, they are saving a hell of a lot more people. And they're Devils! Devils are evil."

Griffin locked her gaze onto Alaria's. "Amaya feels you were a Devil and still chose to fight for God. If that was possible, then perhaps these children would make the same choice given the chance. She believes Deacon had the potential to be evil and chose to follow his Angelic nature."

"Deacon is half-Angel, and I used to be an Angel. It's totally different than creatures born to Lucifer and Lilith. Totally different. I always wanted to be human. It had nothing to do with picking the right side and everything to do with getting what I wanted. It wasn't until later I started fighting for God and good and whatever. At first it was totally selfish. I thought it would be over with the Choosing and we'd all go our own ways and I'd have a nice life on Earth doing whatever I wanted. I wasn't choosing good. I was choosing me." She looked at Braxton and Griffin. "Don't look at me like this is news. You've both known that for thirty years. We all met when I was still evil."

Griffin fisted her hands at her hips. "Perhaps you should tell her. She's having a problem separating Lilith's children and you."

Braxton pushed off the counter and twisted the top off a thermos, pouring himself a capful of coffee. "If you think it would help, of course we'll do whatever we need to."

"I also think she's having some difficulty grieving for Gabriel. She struggles with seeing me here. She views me as a threat to your union and doesn't trust me."

Alaria snorted. "I can't imagine why she would think such a thing. I'd be pretty upset too if my father's dead wife suddenly reappeared. She knows the only reason I'm human is because of the Choosing. Gabriel told her. She knows everything about what happened before. I can see her being scared you coming back is going to wreck everything that's happened since."

"I can assure you my intentions are purely platonic." Griffin pulled out a chair and sat across from Alaria, keeping to the edge so her wings didn't get pinned in behind her. "Each time they dragged me out of Heaven, I felt different. I don't want to say less human, but that's the best way I can think of to describe it. I felt less human. My emotions were dulled, and I didn't feel things like I used to. Now that I'm an Angel, it's magnified. I don't feel things at all like I once did." She started to lean back, then jerked when her wings got in the way. "Honestly, I understand Gabriel so much better now than before. I don't know how Michael is like he is. He seems so much more human than Angelic. I find myself even starting to talk like Gabe, and every once in a while I have a memory I know isn't mine."

Alaria tied her hair back into a bun. "They're Gabe's. Sharing Grace is one thing, but he gave you all of his when he died. You got everything. His power, his emotions, his memories, all of it. I'm surprised you haven't been remembering more of what he had." She looked at Braxton. "Amaya needs to know you're not going to run away with Griffin and leave me here some woman scorned or whatever it is she's cooked up in that pretty little head of hers. I knew she was having a hard time dealing with Gabe, but I didn't realize it was this bad."

Braxton sipped his coffee. "I think I should be the one to go. It's me she's doubting, so she needs to hear it from me."

Griffin cleared her throat. "I suspect she has some doubts about Alaria as well."

Alaria lifted her eyebrows. "I'm certainly not going to run away with you. Why is she worried about me?"

"Because of Gabriel's death. It is her fear that you still retained some feelings for Gabriel and his death will bring them back to the surface."

"For someone who started this talk with how Amaya doesn't trust you and won't talk to you, you know an awful lot about how she's feeling." Alaria stared steadily at Griffin. "How do you know all this?"

"I keep an eye on her." Griffin looked embarrassed. "She has developed a penchant for drinking at night and often vents her feelings once she's had a few. She's struggling, Alaria."

Alaria reached out and took Braxton's coffee, finishing the small cup and setting it down on the table. "We'll go talk to her, but the time has come for her to handle things without us. We raised her to be strong and capable. She can do this. I know she can." She smiled softly. "She's allowed to struggle. We all do. I'd be more worried about her if she didn't have feelings about everything going on. It's because you took on so much of Gabe that you can't see that." She looked at the blonde pointedly. "I seem to remember you struggling to get through things and managing to do it just fine. Amaya has a strong spine and a sharp mind. She'll get through it and be fine."

Griffin lifted her shoulders slightly. "Perhaps you're right, but I'd prefer that you both speak to her. I'll wait here while you ready your things."

CHAPTER FIVE

DECEMBER 13TH, 2060

THE MANOR

AMAYA DRAGGED two black backpacks from one of the closets on the main floor and laid them on the couch in the living room. She had already brought in boxes of supplies and lowered herself to the floor to sort through it, tucking what she decided was useful into the bags and laying everything else aside.

Each bag got some of the same things. A thin solar blanket, water purification tablets, protein bars, compass, paracord, lock-pick kit, fire-starting kit, filet knife, sleeping bag, and various other odds and ends. In one pack she placed a small two-man tent, and in the other she tucked a small cooking set with pans and dishes.

Weapons and ammo came next. Holy Water went in each, both in bottles and in aerosol cans. Each bag also got a rosary so they could make more. Two stakes went in the front pockets, and extra clips, shotgun shells, and the corresponding firearms were added. She gathered bags of salt and gunpowder for wards and the herbs she would need for protection spells and the bundles that went in pillows. Leaving enough room for a change of clothes for each, she zipped up the packs and moved on to the utility belts.

A pistol fit in the holster on one side, with a place for a buck-knife and a machete or small axe on the other. Each belt also contained several grenades and two extra clips of ammunition so that it was within easy reach. She added a multi-tool to a small pocket on each belt and tucked several cans of spray paint into the loops.

When she heard noise in the kitchen, she glanced up and did a double take when she saw her parents. Rising, she went to Alaria and Braxton, wrapping one arm around each.

"What are you guys doing here?"

Alaria kissed Amaya's forehead. "I'm happy to see you, too." She looked past her daughter to the packs. "Getting ready to leave?"

"We're waiting for word on where the Ark of the Covenant and the Sword in the Stone are, so I wanted to be ready."

Braxton laughed. "Another generation of Indiana Jones, I see." He hugged Amaya tightly. "Let's sit down for a few minutes." He waited until they were all settled in chairs in the living room before taking Alaria's hand in his own and speaking again. "Where is everyone?"

"Zeke and the baby are asleep upstairs. Dev and Deacon went to Gage's to work on finding this stuff, and I stayed here to pack our stuff in case they find it. I think Michael is in his office. Do you want me to get him?"

Alaria shook her head. "No. Griffin came to us last night and told us that we needed to talk to you about a few things. She brought us."

Amaya lifted her legs and folded them beneath her. "What do you need to talk to me about?"

Braxton cleared his throat. "Amaya, you're about to do something very dangerous, and you need to be on top of your game when you go out there. The last thing we want is for you to do something stupid because of stuff going on with us." He closed his eyes tightly and swallowed. "Griffin thinks you're afraid I'm leaving your mother and that your mother is in love with Gabriel."

Amaya stiffened, her muscles freezing and her eyes hardening. "I'll kill her. I haven't talked to that woman, so if she knows those things, it's because she's been eavesdropping."

Alaria's eyes darkened. "You really think that?"

"Not really! Or at least I don't want to." Amaya stood and plowed her hands through her hair, pacing. "I don't know what I think. I hated Gabriel, and then he died the way he did. Saving my life. He died to save my life! And it makes me not hate him so much, and now I don't know what to feel about it. Part of me is worried with Griffin back you're going to remember how you felt about her and leave Mom." She gestured wildly at her father before turning to her mother. "And an equally stupid part of me is worried since Gabriel is dead you're going to only remember the good things about him instead of all the really bad things and start remembering how much you loved him and decide you don't want Dad after all." She held out her hands. "I know it's crazy, but I'm all mixed up inside and I don't know how to stop from thinking it."

"Sit down, Amaya." Braxton's voice was soft and calm. He didn't speak again until she had dropped back into the chair. "You're assuming I ever forgot what I felt for Griffin or your mother ever forgot what was between her and Gabe." He leaned forward and took Amaya's hand in his. "Sweetheart, neither of us were ever disillusioned enough to think those feelings ever went away."

Alaria nodded. "There will always be part of me that loves Gabriel. I loved him for millions of years. That never goes away, but I made a choice to walk away from it and to be with Brax, and I haven't regretted a single moment of it. We chose to be together in spite of all the hardships and in spite of our pasts." She smiled at Braxton. "Even when we shouldn't have been together, we chose to be."

Braxton squeezed Alaria's fingers before addressing Amaya. "Grief is complicated, and there is no right way to do it. I grieve for Griffin because she was ripped from Heaven. I grieve for the life she lost and what she now has to do. I don't regret the last thirty years with your mom and I don't intend to ever walk away from that. As for Gabriel, you are allowed to love and hate him, to grieve for him and be angry with him, to feel whatever it is you feel, and all of that is okay. There is no right or wrong answer to this. Feel whatever you need to feel for as long as you need to feel it, but do not let worrying about us get in the way of what you have to do. There's nothing to worry about. I promise you that."

Amaya rubbed her hands over her face. "I feel like I'm acting like a brat, and it's not a feeling I like very much. I've been waiting for this my whole life, and now it's here and I'm getting pissed off over little things I should have seen coming, and I'm letting all this shit bother me when I know deep down it shouldn't."

Alaria patted her daughter's knee. "Then suck it up and deal with it. You've got to have your head on straight, and that means not worrying about all the other shit." She looked over at Braxton. "I'm going to go up and see Zeke and the baby."

"I'll join you. I think Amaya has enough to keep her busy for the moment." He stood, stooping to kiss Amaya's hair before following Alaria up the stairs.

"Did you find it?"

Deacon held up his hands as he appeared in the kitchen, a grin spreading across his face. "You could at least let me fully materialize before pelting me with questions."

Amaya wrinkled her nose and tapped her foot, waiting for five seconds. "There. You're all here. Did you find it?"

He nodded to a scroll under his arm. "Well, we have a starting point, so there's that, anyway." He cleared off the island and spread the parchment, securing the edges with coffee cups. "Gage found a reference to the Ark in some old Atlantean literature. It was apparently in the temple. Graciela had it there with her."

Amaya closed her eyes. "How the hell are we supposed to get something that was in Atlantis? Was it moved? Did it get brought through the portal?"

"We don't know. I'm going to talk to Dad about the options and see what we can do about it. If it was still there when the city sank, it's somewhere at the bottom of the ocean or was destroyed."

Michael entered the kitchen. "The Ark couldn't be destroyed. It was Heaven made. There's nothing on Earth strong enough to destroy it." He laid his hand on Deacon's shoulder as he studied the scroll. "Typically things of great importance, such as the Lucifer gate, that were in Atlantis were removed before the city was destroyed. However, I have no idea where else the Ark could be. Did Gage remember seeing it there?"

Deacon shook his head. "No, but they weren't looking for it, either. Is there a locating spell Lux could do to find it?"

"I don't know of one." Michael tapped his fingers on the scroll, considering the options. "I'm going to need some more time to decide on the best course for this one. Did you have any more luck on finding Aaron's rod?"

"That one we did have some luck on. According to legend, it was initially given to Adam when he left the Garden of Eden. There are many references to it throughout Biblical times and who it was handed down to until it was planted in the ground for whomever was worthy. What Gage thinks is that it was planted at the entrance to the Garden."

Amaya glanced up. "The Garden of Eden is a real place?"

Michael nodded absently. "Of course it is."

"And it still exists?"

He lifted his head to look at her. "Yes, of course. Why wouldn't it?"

"Because no one has lived there in several million years."

Michael rolled the scroll back up and tucked it under his arm. "The Garden is similar to Purgatory in that the only people who can access it are those who already know it's there. I can teach you how to get to it. I'm afraid if the sword is there, getting to it is not going to be as easy as just walking up to it and grabbing it. The Garden is self-contained. Once you're in, the only way out is through. The sword may be there when you enter, or you may not find it until you are exiting, if it's there at all."

Amaya scowled. "This doesn't sound fun."

Michael's expression was serious. "It's not going to be fun." He looked at Deacon. "You're sure this is where Aaron's rod is?"

"As sure as we can be about it. It's not on Earth. We know that much. We know it's not in Hell, Purgatory, or Heaven, so our options are very limited. We think the Ark is in Atlantis, so I can't imagine they would both be in the same place. It doesn't make good sense."

"I agree with you." He sighed deeply. "Okay. Check your packs, take today and get some rest. I'll prepare what you need, and you'll leave in the morning." Looking at them both, he shook his head solemnly. "I don't envy you the things you're going to have to do. If the Ark was in Atlantis, it is not able to be found in this time. Remnants of Atlantis were removed from Earth to make sure humans would not find evidence of the city having existed."

Deacon blinked rapidly. "How the hell are we supposed to find it then? And where did it go if it was removed from Earth?"

Michael pursed his lips. "I don't know where the artifacts went. I was not involved in that particular quest. However, unless I can convince God of another way, I suspect I'll have to take you back to Atlantis."

Amaya gaped at him. "What do you mean? Atlantis is gone. It's been gone for a very long time."

"And yet your parents were there thirty years ago. It is possible. I can bend time and take you back if necessary, and if that is the only way to get the Ark, then that is what I will do." He smiled. "Don't give yourselves headaches over it too much. As I've said before, time is very fluid to an Angel. It is possible for an item to exist in one time and not in another, but to be introduced to that time by being removed from another. Tampering with time must be taken seriously and done with utmost caution, so it is done very little by either side. The ramifications can be serious if care is not taken, but it can be done safely. If there is no other way to get the Ark, or if it does not exist in this time, I will ensure you can retrieve it from Atlantis without damaging the timeline."

Deacon let out a low whistle as his father left the room. "Time-traveling? That's just weird."

Amaya leaned on the island. "What isn't weird about this? He's right, though. My parents did it. So did Lux's and Zeke's." She bounced on her heels. "I got our bags packed all except for clothes and food."

"Well, let's finish packing and then just enjoy the rest of the day, I suppose."

"My parents are here. They're upstairs with Zeke and Caleb."

Deacon glanced over his shoulder as he rifled through the fridge. "Cool. Are they staying for dinner?"

"I don't know. Griffin has apparently been spying on me. She's been listening in to our conversations and then tattling to Mom and Dad she's worried about me."

He emerged from the refrigerator with a bottle of water and an apple. "We're all worried about you. You're drinking too much, sleeping too little, and you just don't look good." He studied her pale skin and the dark rings around her eyes. "That's not a secret, Maya. You know we're worried."

Flickers of annoyance rose within her. "I don't need you to be worried. I'll be fine."

Deacon sat the water on the island and caught her hand as she tried to brush by him. "I know you'll be fine, but it doesn't change the facts." He held tight when she tried to pull away. "I'm your friend. I care about you, and you just lost your dad. You're struggling with what we have to do, and I want to be here for you. I just wish instead of chugging half a bottle of scotch you'd talk to me about it."

Amaya laid her hand on his chest, clenched his shirt, released it, then laid her hand there again. She rested her forehead against him, the heat from his body seeping through his t-shirt and into her skin.

"It's hard to talk to you." She looked up at him, green eyes locking onto blue. "Do you remember the night Gabriel and I were talking in here and you came in after?" She toyed with the cotton of his shirt, rubbing it between her fingers. "We were standing right here."

Deacon's body tightened and tensed with the memory of her pressed against him. He turned her hand over in his, sliding palm against palm and twining their fingers. "I remember. It's one hell of a memory. We never talked about it. Everything happened so fast after that."

"I feel like we've been dancing around each other. We're friends, but we don't get too close because if we do we start to get onto sticky ground. It's been that way since we were teenagers. That makes it hard for me to lean on you because I'm afraid if I get too close, if I rely on you too much, then we'll step too far into it and have to jump back, and then I'll lose my friend, too."

Deacon's eyes bore into her. "You know better. We've known each other for way too long for you to even entertain the idea that I would ever let anything get in the way of our friendship." He grasped her chin in his hand and turned her face up to his. "I want to help you with whatever you need."

Heart pounding in her chest and her stomach twisting into knots, Amaya's fingers clenched his t-shirt. "What if what I need is you?"

"Then ask." He ran his thumb over her bottom lip. "We'll have plenty of time to figure things out once we leave here tomorrow."

"What about Lilith?"

Deacon grinned. "We're going after them. I don't think her finding out anything is a worry at this point. The time to be concerned about that is over." He leaned down slightly, his breath warm on her face.

Amaya's eyes drifted shut in anticipation of the kiss. Deacon released her hand and slid his down to her hip and around her waist, drawing her closer to himself. Her lips tingled as she waited anxiously for his to make contact and her heart pounded so loudly she was afraid he could hear it. Just before he made contact with her, someone clearing their throat from behind them made them both freeze.

"Sorry to interrupt." Dev stuffed his hands in his pockets and looked sheepish.

Deacon didn't release Amaya. He turned his head and looked

over his shoulder. "Then don't."

Dev chuckled. "Sorry, dude. Zeke sent me to get Amaya. You'll have time to do whatever you were going to do after you leave. I'm not going to be the one to piss off the lady who just gave birth."

Deacon glared at his friend. "I want to do it now, not later. Go away."

Amaya laughed and ducked under Deacon's arm. "Pack some canned food for us, would ya?"

Dev waited to speak until Amaya had disappeared up the stairs. "Want to talk about it?"

"It's none of your business."

"No, it's not. Want to talk about it anyway?"

Deacon opened the pantry and starting yanking out cans at random. "I was going to kiss her. You interrupted. End of story."

"We both know that's not what I meant. Dude, you and Amaya? When did it start?"

"Eight years ago."

Dev choked on a gulp of water. "Eight *years* ago and I'm just hearing about it now? Jesus fucking Christ, why in the hell haven't you said anything?"

"We aren't doing anything. We started, and that was when Lilith found the first nonplace. Dad made us promise to stop because it endangered Amaya if Lilith found out who she was. So we stopped. There hasn't been anything since until right before Aradia and Gabriel died and nothing since until your fucking miserable timing."

"Is it serious?"

"How the hell should I know? I've managed to kiss the girl a grand total of two times in eight years, and both of those times she was the one laying it on me." He scowled. "I'm sick of being celibate."

Dev sat down on one of the stools. "Deac, it's Amaya we're talking about. You'd have Zeke and Lux up in arms if you're just looking to get laid. Hell, me too for that matter. If you just need a piece, drop down to Earth and get it, but look outside here. We don't need that kind of drama."

"I didn't say I was just looking to get laid. I don't know what the hell I want, and there's no way to figure it out if every time I touch her someone walks into the room." Sighing, Deacon walked into the living room and returned with the two packs, cramming cans into them. "If anything, at least being away from here will mean some privacy to figure things out."

Dev laughed. "Don't count on it too much. If I learned anything from my turn at this, it's that there's very little time for the things you want to do and too much time spent fighting and scavenging." He helped his friend finish loading the packs. "I worry about the two of you going down there during the winter. It was winter when Zeke and I went out, but we were in a huge house in Los Angeles with all the luxuries the Cambion had to offer. I doubt the two of you will have that."

"We'll manage. We've got tents and sleeping bags and can make a fire. It'll be fine." Deacon zipped up the bags and sat them back on the couch. "The only thing left to put in there is some clothes, and I'm not doing that until Dad tells me where we're going."

Dev laughed and flopped on the couch. "Hopefully it's somewhere tropical. Jamaica would be nice."

CHAPTER SIX

"I HAVE determined that the entrance to the Garden of Eden is somewhere in the Sinai Peninsula. I believe it can be accessed by crossing the Gulf of Aqaba." Michael pointed to an area east of Egypt on the map. Before he spoke again, he shifted his finger up half an inch to point to an area inside the peninsula. "Here, in the center of the southern tip, is Saint Catherine's. It's the oldest monastery in the world, and one of the only ones still standing. In all of human history, this monastery has never been destroyed."

Deacon lifted his eyebrows. "Cambion specifically targeted the monasteries. How did this one escape their notice?"

"It didn't. They tried to siege against it and failed. Saint Catherine's is the place where Moses took his audience with God. It is also the location of Mount Sinai."

Amaya snapped her fingers. "The burning bush? That was true?"

Michael snickered. "All the things you have seen and yet you doubt the downright pedestrian. Child, most of the destories in the Bible are true in one way or another. Some happened, some didn't, others I have no idea whether or not they did. I've told you before that I have no inclination to read all the versions of that blasted book your kind insists on putting out, but certain things bear weight, even with the Angels, and the relationship between God and Moses is one of them. Moses was chosen to speak for God to the human race, and you, Amaya, have been chosen to save them. It's a very fitting parallel that you should find your answers in the same place that he did."

"Are you saying that I'm going to go to this place and have a chat with a flaming shrub?" She stared at him skeptically. "Come on, Michael, there are limits to what I'll believe and that's pushing it."

Michael looked amused. "Is it less likely than having a chat with a man who sprouts wings out of his back? Or talking to someone in their mind instead of with words? Perhaps you weren't there when we traveled to Purgatory. Did you miss the tale of when Greer and I battled in Hell or when the six traveled back in time to Atlantis? This world is full of unbelievable things. God appearing to a human in a way that he could understand is the least of them all."

Deacon laughed. "Point, set, and match." He looked at Michael. "Okay, so we go to this monastery. I'm assuming there are people there to talk to?"

The Angel inclined his head. "Yes. It is heavily guarded by Warriors, and there are still priests there. They stayed in their posts when the rest of the world fled, and they still stand. I believe they'll be able to help you get to Eden." He looked at his son. "You will need to be careful. Your eyes and hair identify you as Cambion, not as Nephil, so they may be very suspicious of your presence. If you need my assistance, call for me immediately and I will identify you as my son."

Deacon fiddled with a lock of his white-blond hair. "I suppose I had to get something from my mother." He sighed. "As long as they don't shoot before they ask questions, we'll be fine."

Amaya rubbed her hands on her knees. "Wear a hat."

"It's going to be, like, eighty degrees in Egypt."

"It'll keep the sun off your face." She grinned at him. "Can you transport us to Saint Catherine's?"

Michael shook his head. "No. While Saint Catherine's has never been breached, Lucifer knows of its history, and he knows of its importance to us. It is being watched. Any flashing near the monastery would draw attention. I would be able to get myself in undetected, but I cannot bring the two of you in. Deacon, you are known to your mother. She has a feel for your powers, and they know you are going to be with Amaya. It is imperative you do this without the use of your powers as much as possible."

"Does that include flying?"

"I believe you can fly. As long as it is done at night, and as long as you are sure no one is going to see you. I would use that as a last resort in the event you are unable to use a car." He turned back to the map. "There are several ways to get to Sinai, but I have determined what I believe to be the safest for you. It avoids the most populated areas and will keep you near the coast, so the towns you stumble onto will likely be resort areas. There will be places to sleep, shelter from bad weather, and likely ample food due to the nature of the areas."

Amaya leaned over to see where he was pointing. "We're getting dropped off in Spain?"

"At the southernmost point of Portugal. From there, Deacon will either fly you into Africa, or you can find a boat. Given the shark and crocodile populations in that area, I highly suggest flight." He glanced up when Amaya stiffened. "They can't get you from a hundred feet in the air." He sighed. "From there, you'll come into Morocco and head west along the coast into Algeria, then Libya, and finally into Egypt. You'll cross the Gulf of Suez just outside of Cairo and then head south to Sinai. It's three hundred and fifty miles through the mountains from the banks of the Suez. I fear most of that trip will be by air or on foot."

"Are there any villages once we cross into Sinai?" Deacon studied the map intently, memorizing the route.

"There may be some very simple structures, but I would not anticipate finding any villages or towns once you enter the mountains. They have all likely been destroyed. I would anticipate you will need to be sleeping in your tent once you're there. Deacon, I want to stress to you how important it is not to exhaust yourself. I know you're accustomed to flying for long periods of time, but the altitude is greater and breathing will take a larger toll on your lungs. You may find you are unable to fly as much as you are here. I also caution you against flying during the day much and only doing so at night when you are confident you cannot be seen."

"So basically not at all then."

"That would be best if it can be managed, but I understand if it cannot." Michael folded up the map and handed it to Deacon. "There are times when flying will be your only option. The reality is that if you walk, it will take at least a week to reach Saint Catherine's from the time you get to Sinai. Carrying food for that long is a hardship, and sleeping exposed for seven nights is a danger, even in such a sparsely populated place."

Amaya looked around the room nervously. "Okay, then." Her gaze settled on her parents, who had sat silently while Michael talked to her and Deacon. "I hate it when you two are quiet."

Braxton laughed. "It's a lot to remember and a lot to handle." He stood and crossed the room to place his hand on her shoulder. "I want you to be careful and to stay safe. Both of you." His other hand landed on Deacon's shoulder. "We've all spent your entire lives preparing you for this. There's no turning back now, so all we can do is worry about you while you're gone and know that we did our jobs and that you're as prepared as you can be."

Alaria shifted in her seat. "If I could, I'd yank the plug on the whole damn thing and go deal with this myself." She smiled ruefully. "Unfortunately enough, that's not an option."

Amaya staunchly ignored the tightening in her chest. "We'll be okay. We can take care of each other, and we'll get it done." She laid her hand over Braxton's. "I've been raised right."

Alaria joined Braxton, sliding her arm around his waist and resting her head against his arm. "I know you might disagree, Amaya, but I do wish Gabriel could be here to see you do this. I wanted him to see how strong and capable and amazing you are. I always thought maybe if he saw you the way we did that he could chill out and things would relax some."

Braxton squeezed Amaya's shoulder and took a step back. "He knew. He had to know, somewhere deep down, that she's capable of this. For everything he was and wasn't, he loved her more than anything else." He bent to kiss Amaya's head. "Try to remember the good and not the bad, and don't dwell on what's happened and who we've lost. Think about what we'll gain if~when~we defeat Lucifer."

Michael stood. "I agree with Braxton." He exchanged a look with Deacon before continuing to speak. "I'm very proud of you both. Are you ready to go?"

Deacon held out a hand to Amaya. "Ready?"

She nodded and laid her palm against his, sliding skin over skin until their fingers were twined. "Let's get this party started."

Michael transported Deacon and Amaya to Portugal with as little fanfare as possible. They were deposited on a beach surrounded by rocky outcroppings, with one path leading up to what appeared to be houses.

Deacon turned in a circle, taking in the blue and green water, the sunny weather and the sand beneath his feet. Expelling a whistle through his breath, he looked at Amaya, shielding his eyes from the sun with one hand.

"We have our route. We need to get to Gibraltar to cross over into Morocco and then straight along the coast until we hit Egypt from there." He sighed deeply. "I understand Dad's reasoning, but this is going to be a long fucking trip."

Amaya inclined her head slightly. "I know. Better safe than sorry, though." She placed her pack on the ground and shucked off her jacket, tying it around her waist. "At least it's warm."

"We need a car, fuel, and a map of the local area so we can get to Gibraltar. We're also going to want to stay as out of sight as possible. We don't know who might be around."

She started up the hill to the road. "Doesn't look like many people are here."

"This wasn't a very populous area to begin with. It's likely most of the people are gone or dead, but there will be some stragglers around." He slid a hat onto his head to hide his white-blond hair. "I need to invest in a bottle of hair dye."

They walked companionably for half an hour, keeping their weapons at the ready as they made their way into the village. Once the beach and cliffs gave way to pavement and buildings, they split up in search of fuel and a working vehicle, knowing both were necessary to make substantial progress during the day.

Deacon left Amaya rifling through the contents of a general store and wandered across the street. He shifted some rubble and felt his face split into a grin when he saw a garage door. Rounding the building, he jimmied open the side-door and peered into the building with his light.

"Amaya! I found a garage!"

Amaya exited the store with a box in her arms. "Like where someone parks their car?"

"Kinda. It's a place where people brought their cars to be fixed. Looks like there's a couple vehicles in here. Let's check it out."

Shrugging, she walked across the street and entered the building with him. Together, they checked every inch of the garage to make sure there was nothing in there that could be a threat. Satisfied, Amaya holstered her pistol and clicked on her flashlight, shining it over the three bays with cars sitting in them.

"Well, if any of them have a full tank of gas and an engine that works, we'll be on our way."

Deacon dropped his pack on the ground. "I'll work on the cars.

Check the office for any supplies or a map while I check on this."

Amaya left him checking engines and tinkering with cars. She found the office up a flight of stairs and rifled through the papers on the desk, looking for a map. Finding nothing, she sat in the chair and opened the drawers on the desk, thumbing through the contents until she pulled out a yellowed tourist book. Happy with her find, she tucked it into a pocket on her pack and slipped into the shop's small kitchen to scrounge for anything useful to take with them.

She found two empty gas cans under the sink, a can of ravioli in a cabinet, and half a box of crackers on top of the fridge. A second office yielded four bottles of water and a box of cookies, and she found two pounds of coffee grounds next to a broken coffee pot.

Gathering her find into a box, she hefted it and wound her way back into the garage where Deacon was wiping his hands on a rag. He glanced up when she entered the room and pointed to a blue SUV.

"I got that one running. The tank is almost full, and I was able to leech fuel from the other two to finish filling it up. I found a couple gas cans in the closet back there and filled them up, so I figure we've got about four hundred miles' worth of fuel. It's enough to get started."

Amaya slid the box into the backseat. "By the time we clear the debris away from the door to get this thing out of here, four hundred miles will be more than we can make before dark." She fished the map out of the box. "But I found a map and looking at it, I'm not even sure it's four hundred miles to Gibraltar, so we might make it there today after all. I guess we'll just have to wait and see."

Deacon took the map and spread it on the hood. "Dad dropped us in Portugal, so we're here." He pointed to an area. "Africa and Europe kinda-sorta almost meet at Gibraltar, which is technically, I think, in Spain. There's a thin channel of water between the Atlantic and the Mediterranean that's the Strait of Gibraltar, which is where we'll cross into Africa. From there we hug the coast heading East."

Annoyed, Amaya stared up at him. "Yes, I know that. How far is it from here to the nasty crocodile and shark infested water we need to get across?"

He studied the map for a long moment. "Looks like three hundred or so miles. It's about ten miles across the water. I can do that in just a few minutes. We'll aim for the other side tonight and find a place to sleep in Morocco, then find another car and move on in the morning."

Satisfied with their plan, Deacon and Amaya worked together to clear the rubble away from the garage doors in order to get their vehicle out. Within an hour they were in the car and maneuvering through the narrow streets toward the highway that would lead them south.

CHAPTER SEVEN

DECEMBER 15TH, 2060 – MOROCCO

AMAYA WOKE slowly, the sun warm on her face despite the chill in the air. She rolled onto her back, scraping her unruly hair from her eyes and securing it with the band around her wrist. Squinting against the bright sun, she sat up and rolled to her feet, casting a glance around the room.

It had been near dark by the time Deacon had flown them across the Strait of Gibraltar. They had found a beach house set far away from the others and warded it heavily against demons and Devils, sweeping a half-mile circumference before barricading the doors and crawling into bed.

She stepped through the balcony doors out onto the deck and shivered as the wind blew through her clothes. Seeing no sign of Deacon, she ducked back into the bedroom and entered the bathroom to brush her teeth, relieve her bladder and dig a sweatshirt from her pack before going in search of her companion.

A glance at her watch told her it wasn't quite seven a.m., which meant they had time to scarf down breakfast and comb through the house for anything usable before going out to search for a car.

Barefoot and with her hair tied back in a messy bun, she stepped back out onto the deck and followed it around the outside of the house to the side with the kitchen on it. As she rounded the corner, she stopped, her stomach clenching and her heart speeding up in her chest.

Deacon stood on the deck, wearing a pair of sweatpants with his chest bare. Beneath his bare feet was a thick blue mat, and he stood in the center of it, his eyes closed and an expression of concentration on his face.

Amaya stood and watched as he moved in deliberate, graceful movements, his body stretching and flexing. She recognized the motions as tai chi, a martial arts technique that focused on the relationship between body and mind.

A thin sheen of sweat shone on his chest and shoulders, and his hair was slightly long, just brushing over the nape of his neck and hanging down to tease his cheekbones. Amaya pressed her hand to her throat and devoured the sight of him, taking in every inch.

Deacon's wings were visible on his body at all times in the form of two tattoos that ran down either side of his spine from shoulder to hip, curling down over his sides and disappearing into the waistband of his pants. As he turned, she was given a perfect view of the muscles in his butt as he flexed and bent.

Feeling like a voyeur, Amaya considered announcing her presence but couldn't quite bring herself to do so. She raked her eyes over his broad shoulders, taking in the strong planes of his chest, the hard muscles of his stomach and the narrowing of his hips. She studied his hands, the wide palms, scarred knuckles and long fingers, and remembered how they had felt anchoring her body to his.

Lifting her gaze to his face, she drifted over the dramatic slash of his cheekbones, his full mouth, strong jaw and straight eyebrows. She knew the exact shade of his eyes, even though they were closed. A cold, icy blue that bored into her and made her feel like he could see into her soul.

"Are you planning to stand there and watch me all morning, or are you eventually going to say something?"

Embarrassment flooded Amaya when Deacon spoke. Her face flushed red, and her heart tripped in her chest, slamming against her chest hard enough that it hurt. She cleared her throat and desperately tried to think of something that made what she had been doing seem even slightly less creepy. Unable to think of anything, she took a deep breath.

"I'm sorry."

Deacon picked up a towel and wiped it over his face and chest to remove the sweat from his skin. He turned to face her, his gaze intense as he took in her windblown hair, baggy sweats, and panicked look.

"No problem. We'll just get this out of the way now instead of later then."

Amaya cocked her head to the side, preparing to question him. Before she could form the words, he strode across the deck and grabbed her, crushing her against him and lifting her off her feet. She had time to suck in one breath before his mouth clamped onto hers.

The kiss was demanding. He plundered and dominated from the very beginning, pressing her against the banister and stroking his hands over her body, gripping her hips and jerking them into his. Amaya's fingers bit into his arms as she struggled to keep up with the storm of emotion he had unleashed within her.

His mouth was insistent on hers, taking everything she offered and more. He parted her lips with his tongue, brushing against hers and groaning when her taste flooded his senses.

Deacon slid his hands beneath her sweatshirt, sighing when he felt bare skin against his palms. He stroked his hands up and down her back, kneading her muscles and relishing the feel of her flesh under his hands.

Amaya returned the kiss eagerly, her arms sliding around his neck as her mouth responded enthusiastically to him. She threaded her fingers through his hair, gripping the silky locks and tugging on them before releasing them to splay her fingers on the back of his skull.

A slow burn started in the middle of her gut and speared through her until every inch of her body was on fire. She arched toward Deacon, feverishly pressing her body against his and groaning deep in her throat when he slid his hands down from her back and over her ass, gripping her flesh to lift her onto the banister.

They came apart slowly, both out of breath. Amaya stared down at him, intense green eyes locking onto cold blue. His grip on her was gentle, and he loosened it even more until his fingers were laying on her skin instead of grasping it. After several beats, he cleared his throat and managed to put together a reasonably coherent sentence.

"I think that gives us both something to think about."

Amaya blinked rapidly, her heart still pounding and her stomach not quite in its normal position. "I don't know what to say."

Deacon leaned forward and nuzzled her neck with his nose, his breath warm and his laugh a rumble. "Speechless is good." He eased back and lifted her down from the bannister, placing her on her feet. "For the record, this isn't the way I intended to start the morning, but I'm not one to pass up an opportunity when it presents itself."

She looked up at him, still unsure. "Why did you do that?"

Amused, he tucked a wisp of hair behind her ear. "Because I wanted to and I thought you wanted me to. Things certainly seemed to be moving in that general direction." He studied her, growing serious. "If I did something wrong, tell me."

"No, no, that's not it." She ran her hands over her face. "My brain is a puddle of mush. I can't even think straight." She smacked his arm when he laughed. "Don't laugh at me!"

"I'm not laughing at you." He pulled her close and hugged her tightly. "I'm not used to seeing you like this. It's kinda cute."

Snorting, she breathed in deeply before stepping back and out of his arms. "Where do we go from here?"

"East toward Egypt." He grinned when she gaped up at him. "Bad joke, I know." He led her back into the house. "I figure we just take it as it comes. We've known each other for many years, and I think we can feel our way through things okay."

She trailed after him, arms crossed. "I don't know if I want to just play it by ear. Feelings get hurt when people aren't on the same page."

Serious, he looked at her over his shoulder. "What page are you on?"

Frustrated, she tossed up her hands. "I don't know! It's not like I can ask you out on a date!" She flopped onto the couch, coughing when a cloud of dust erupted from the cushion. "I've known you since I was born. This is both kind of weird and comfortable at the same time."

"I can count on one hand the number of times we saw each other before we were teenagers." He pulled on his shirt and stooped to dig through their supplies, pulling out granola bars and bottles of water. "We hardly have a familial relationship, Maya."

"That's not what I meant. I meant that we've been friends for so long that it's kind of weird to be talking about being more, but then again it's you, and there aren't many people I'm more comfortable with than you, so it kind of makes total sense."

Deacon lifted one eyebrow and sat down across from her. "That was the longest run-on sentence in the history of the English language." He bit off a chunk of granola and chewed. "But I get what you mean."

Amaya ripped into her own granola bar. "Are you sure this is something we should be doing? Lilith—"

"I don't give a flying fuck about Lilith." Deacon's voice was razor sharp. "We agreed to not do this eight years ago because of the danger to you. We're going for Lucifer. The time to worry about that bitch is done and over with." He crumpled the wrapper in his hand. "There's no one here to tell us what to do, so unless you've changed your mind since the other day in the kitchen, I see no reason why we can't see what happens."

"I haven't changed my mind." She reached out and laid her hand on his. "I just don't want to mess things up with you, Deac. I love you too much for that."

He squeezed her fingers. "I love you, too. Which is exactly why we won't mess it up." He finished the granola bar. "Let's get packed up and find a car. It's nearly eight. We need to get on the road."

Lucifer stood at the top of the cliff, the wind blowing through his hair and his hands on his hips. Behind him, bodies were scattered on the ground, and demons lit them on fire. The smell of roasting flesh filled the air, wafting to his nose on the brisk breeze. Inhaling it, he held the scent of death within his chest and savored it, his mouth watering.

Lilith approached him, her hands resting on the mound of her bulging stomach and Serafina next to her. He glanced back at them and swallowed a smile at the sight of his family. Each time he looked at the child it seemed she was taller. Every glance to Lilith and her stomach was more swollen with pregnancy, her skin glowing slightly brighter as she reveled in what was happening within her body.

"It was a good victory here today." Lilith surveyed the burning bodies. "Many Nephilim died."

"As did many Cambion. We lost a hundred demons on top of it. The victory came at a steep price." He smiled as his daughter hugged him. "There's Daddy's princess. Do you like what you see, my darkling?"

Serafina grinned up at him, her teeth bared. "I love it, Papa. Can I go play with the bodies?" She bounced up and down, rocking from side to side to swirl her skirt so it flared away from her legs. "I want to cut them open and play with the insides."

Lucifer smiled indulgently. "Don't get your dress dirty. You know Mommy hates it when you dirty your pretty dresses."

Lilith watched adoringly as their daughter scampered off to find a non-burning body. "Evil burns bright in our girl. Her powers are strong, Lucifer. She will be magnificent as she grows."

"I know. I can sense what is in her. Even greater than that is what I sense in the son you carry." He caressed the curve of her stomach. "He yearns to tear his way from your body and roar into life. He's going to devour this entire world, my love. When we're done here, we'll storm the gates of Heaven and rip God from His throne. I'll tear the Grace from every Angel in Heaven and take the Streets of Gold for myself. Every soul there will know my wrath."

Lilith purred and pressed her body against his. "We'll rule it together, won't we? We'll make everyone worship at our feet. Our son will siphon the powers of God and we will rule the universe with an iron fist." She shivered. "It makes me wet to think about it."

"The only thing that stands in our way is Gabriel's daughter." Lucifer gestured to Abalam, who left the group of demons he'd been instructing to approach. "Has there been any information on the witch?"

"We've gotten word that she is with the other Nephil residing with the ex-vampire somewhere on Earth. We don't know precisely where yet, but the intel is that she has left the protection of Michael for the moment to be with her father in the wake of Aradia's death. It would be an opportune time to move on capturing her if that's what you have in mind."

"It is." He looked at Lilith. "And Amaya. What do we know of her?"

"Nothing. We know from the battle in Purgatory what she looks like, but she hasn't used her powers anywhere that we can detect it. All efforts to find Michael's hiding place have been unsuccessful."

Lucifer sighed. "I haven't been able to draw either of them into the dreamplane either. This is a huge problem. I want that witch. We failed in Purgatory, and I won't accept failure again." He looked at Abalam. "Send out word to all Cambion, Devils, and demons. I want Lux Windsor. The one who brings her to you will get a great reward. Do not fail me on this." He turned back to Lilith. "And what of the whelp sired by Michael?"

"He is on Earth, though we do not know where. Azazel reported two days ago that he sensed Michael transporting two Nephilim to Earth. One felt like Deacon. I'm not sure who the other one was."

A flash of worry crossed Lucifer's eyes. "Was it in proximity to Saint Catherine's monastery?"

"No. Well outside the sentries' view on the monastery. It does not appear that they are going for Eden."

Abalam cleared his throat. "They may not know about Aaron's sword."

Lucifer turned back and stared off the cliff. "Oh, they know about it. God knows about it. He made the fucking thing, and He loves to give them just enough to go off of right when they need it the most. Fucking bastard won't keep His damn nose out of things and just let them play out. Always interfering. You can bet your ass He's told them about the Rod and the Spear." He turned around, his eyes gleaming. "If Deacon is on Earth, so is Amaya. Find them, Abalam. Send Azazel to Saint Catherine's. I want him to stand back and watch. He is not to engage. We can't get in to the Garden, so if they're going for it, we have to wait until they come out with the Rod to make a move on it."

Abalam nodded. "I'll relay the message to Azazel immediately. What of the Spear?"

Lilith hissed. "Yes, what of that damn thing that can kill the rest of us with one well-aimed poke?"

Lucifer tapped his fingers against his chin. "In retrospect, we should have prioritized finding the Spear well before now, but we were very sure we could find and kill Alaria and Gabriel's daughter before she reached the age where she was a threat. It was an unacceptable miscalculation on my part, and for that I apologize to you all. Typically I would have had Beelzebub find it for me. He always did excel at such things. Unfortunately, he's dead." He considered the quandary for several more moments. "Have the witches begin doing locating spells for it. They'll need to search Earth, Heaven, Purgatory, and Eden. If it's none of those places, they may need to look back in time. Get some of the Cambion to delve into the literature we have and find out where it's last known location was. If we can't find it in the present, we'll figure out where it was in the past one way or the other."

Abalam inclined his head. "I'll begin arrangements immediately." He prepared to disappear but stopped when Lucifer held up one hand. "Is there more?"

"One last thing." Lucifer laid his hand on Abalam's shoulder. "You have served me very well, and that should be rewarded. You will have Beelzebub's seat. From this point onward, you are no longer a minion but a trusted friend. You are my brother, Abalam. Succeed and you will rule with me. Fail and you will know unspeakable pain." He brought the man in close and kissed him squarely on the mouth. "Serve me well. I won't forget it when it comes time to choose a mate for Serafina if you do."

Abalam took the hand Satan offered. "Your will be done."

Lilith spun in a circle, her dress flaring away from her legs and her hair streaming behind her. She tipped her head back and stared at the sky tinged red and black from the battle and smoke and breathed in a lungful of the scent of charred flesh.

"Your will be done." She straightened and spread her arms to encompass all the burning bodies. "We're going to see Heaven burn."

CHAPTER EIGHT

DECEMBER 21ST, 2060

SINAI PENINSULA

DEACON WINCED as the hammer he was using struck his thumb instead of the yellow plastic spike anchoring the tent to the ground. He shook his hand to relieve the pain and slammed the hammer into the barb, driving it into the dirt.

Amaya glanced up from the fire she was building. "Don't break that. We only have four, and without them, the tent blows away."

"The tent won't blow away with us in it." He tucked the hammer back into his pack and sat back. "Keep the fire small. We're only going to be here a few hours. Long enough to eat and sleep. As soon as it gets dark, I'll take off again."

She lifted one eyebrow, torn between amusement and annoyance. "Someone needs a nap."

Deacon ran his hands through his dusty hair. "I need a shower and something other than canned tuna to eat and about twelve straight hours of sleep. My wings are very functional, but ten hours for the last three nights is taking its toll, especially with needing enough height to get over the mountains." He gratefully took the bottle of water she held out and drank deeply. "Carrying you isn't a big deal, but add in almost two hundred extra pounds in packs and I'm flying more than five hundred and fifty pounds through the air. We're making shitty time because I can't go very fast, and I'm tiring out quicker than I thought I would."

"You're not a pack mule. Give yourself a break. We've still made better time than if we'd been walking. We should get there tomorrow, right?"

"If the fucking map is right, yeah. I should be able to get us to within about ten miles of the cathedral by dawn. Then it's a two-or-three-hour walk down to it. We'll have to be careful from there to make sure we're not being seen. If Dad is right, Lucifer has this area under surveillance and we'll need to take extra care not to endanger the people at Saint Catherine's."

Amaya used her knife to open a can of soup and dumped it into the small pot she'd pulled from her pack. "I agree with you on that. I haven't sensed anything so far. This area of the world is very quiet."

"Not much infrastructure to begin with and a very tribal population. It reverted quickly. Not many Warriors over here, so it's been pretty much left alone aside from the major cities, which are all but destroyed." Deacon unlaced his boots and pulled one off, then the other, flexing his toes and peeling his socks off. "In some ways, Africa is one of the safest places on Earth right now."

"Are we in Africa or Asia?"

He shrugged. "I'm not sure it matters. Kinda in between right now. I think Egypt technically owns Sinai, so Africa still. Well, owned. Egypt doesn't exist anymore."

She stirred the soup slowly. "This is a fucking geography lesson from start to finish. I'm learning about an area of the world I knew absolutely nothing about." Pouring the noodles and broth into the two small metal bowls, she handed one to Deacon and kept one for herself. "Do you think governments will come back soon?"

"I don't know. It's been a long time. Over here they've been without governments since the very beginning. Even in the United States it's been almost twenty years without anything. No military, no elections, no nothing. It'll take a while for people to start forming governments again. I'd imagine the Warriors will have a lot to do with that. People listen to them." Deacon laughed. "Especially to your dad. Can't you just see Braxton as the new President?"

Amaya giggled. "God, my mom as the First Lady. That's a hilarious mental image." She spooned a bite of soup into her mouth and swallowed. "There's so much work to do, even if we get through all of this. Just reestablishing communication is a bear of a task."

"Not really. That's what the Nephilim can be used for at first. Quicker than an e-mail. NephilCom. It'll be a multi-million dollar company."

"Tell Gage now before things get going so he can start it." She smiled around the spoon. "It feels good to talk about it like we actually stand a chance."

Deacon reached out and tucked a strand of hair behind her ear. "We do. We always have." He finished the soup and poured a splash of water into the bowl to rinse it. "How much water do we have?"

Amaya counted the bottles. "Six bottles. It's enough to get us there. Not enough to wash off with, but enough to finish the trip."

"Are these priests at Saint Catherine's going to speak English or Egyptian?"

She shrugged. "Damned if I know. Even if they speak Egyptian, I'd say the Warriors will speak English."

Deacon cast a look around the rocky canyon. "What would you think about me flying low and doing a little scouting for a creek to wash off in? I'd feel better after a bath."

"I think the sun is shining and you flying around could draw unwanted attention."

"Attention from who?" He spread his arms. "We haven't seen a living creature since Libya, Maya. Even when there was civilization here there weren't many people, and the ones that were here didn't live in the fucking mountains."

"It's still a risk. We'll be at the monastery tomorrow, and I'm quite sure they'll have water there. According to the map, it's not too far to the Gulf of Aqaba, and there's an oasis, too. Feiran. The atlas says it's where Moses turned a rock into a river and made water for the Israelites, so if that's true, you can bet your ass it's still there. This whole area is just chock full of Biblical significance." She pulled off her shirt, leaving her clad in a thin tank. "I want to be clean as badly as you do. I have dust in places dust should never be, but I'd rather be dirty than dead."

"Have you read the whole atlas?"

She nodded. "I like to know things." Gathering up their dinner dishes, she tucked them all away and zipped up her pack. "If you want to hike and look for some water we can do that, but I don't think you should fly anywhere while it's light outside. The last thing we need is for some stray demon to see you and tell your mother. I don't want to have it out with her in the middle of nowhere."

"That assumes there are any self-respecting demons who are anywhere near Egypt."

"If they are watching the monastery, then they're not far from here, which makes it that much more important to be careful."

Knowing she was right but still not liking the fact, Deacon scrubbed at the dust on his arms with his hands and stared out at the desert. "Everything is brown here. There is literally no color but brown."

Amaya chortled. "We're in the desert. It's supposed to be brown." She poked at the fire with a stick she'd picked up the first night in the Peninsula and kept in her pack since. "Do you want to take the first watch or sleep?"

"I'll take watch. You grab a few hours."

She rose to her knees and then stood, peeling off her sand-crusted jeans and shaking them off. Clad in underwear and the tank, she paused next to Deacon and laid her hand on his shoulder.

"If you're still interested in being anything other than my friend by the time we get to Saint Catherine's, it will be a minor miracle in and of itself. The last thing I wanted you to see at this point in whatever the hell kind of relationship we're in is my stubbly legs, greasy hair, and filthy face."

Deacon chuckled and looked up at her. "If I was deterred by those things, I wouldn't be worth your time." He squeezed her fingers. "Get some sleep. I'll wake you in a few hours."

They broke down the tent as the sun was setting below the horizon and waited for dark at the foot of the mountains. The tendrils of smoke from the extinguished fire rose into the air, and Amaya shivered as a cool breeze whipped through the hills and valleys of the Peninsula. Once the sky had darkened and the last fingers of orange and red were gone from the sky, Deacon stripped off his shirt and reached within himself, the tattoos that ran along his back moving and flowing over his skin.

The lines of black and grey turned to feathers that glowed and moved along his back. Slowly, they rose up off the skin, black feathers that shined in the moonlight. The ends looked as if they had been dipped in blood, so deep was the red color. Amaya watched in awe--as she always did--as he flexed his wings, stretching them completely out.

"I'll never get over that as long as I live." She smiled when he brushed one of the wings against her face. "It's amazing."

Deacon flicked his wings. "Not really." He helped her strap the second pack to herself. "Ready?"

She hooked her arm around his shoulders and smiled when one of his snaked around her waist. "Let's get there. Tomorrow we get clean water and a bed to sleep in."

He flapped his wings and lifted them both off the ground, soaring through the air. Amaya couldn't help but grin as her stomach lurched when her feet left the dirt. Even after flying with him a hundred times, those first few seconds were always exhilarating.

If she was honest, it wasn't just flying that was exhilarating. In order for Deacon to support her weight and the weight of their packs, she had to be carefully balanced and pressed against him. Feeling the solid places of his body so tightly against hers was nearly as thrilling as the moment he propelled them from Earth.

He flew for several hours uneventfully. When the sky began lightening from black to gray, Deacon scanned the ground for a place to land that would give them the easiest path to walk the rest of the way to the monastery. A flicker of movement caught his eye, and he turned his head to see what it was, rotating slightly to keep the load he carried balanced.

As he turned, a loud crack sounded in the dark and a bullet slammed into one of his wings, ripping through feathers and cartilage. Searing pain bolted through his body and he plummeted through the air, Amaya's scream in his ear. Flapping his working wing wildly, they spun as he tried to slow their descent.

The ground rushed up to meet them. Deacon rotated so that he was beneath Amaya, breaking her fall as well as he could. He slammed into the ground, his head colliding with hard, packed dirt and the impact hard enough to rattle his bones. Blackness flooded his vision, and he sank into the cool darkness of unconsciousness.

Amaya landed on Deacon, her impact lessened by his body. She leapt to her feet, shedding the packs and clenching her fist, trading her jeans, t-shirt, and kevlar vest for skin-tight leather pants, knee-high boots, and a red and black leather bustier. Her hair hung down her back in black ringlets, and she held a whip in one hand and a sword in the other.

Cambion swarmed, surrounding her. Carefully, she placed one foot on either side of Deacon's unconscious body, shielding him with her own. When a Cambion charged her, she lashed at it with her whip, wrapping the cord around his neck and dragging it close enough to run it through with her sword.

She whirled when a second Cambion fired the shotgun he held, leaping to the side to avoid the slug. Dropping her whip, she grabbed Deacon and flashed fifty yards away, placing him behind a boulder before returning to the battle. Knowing using her powers was a risk, but unwilling to endanger him, she lobbed fireballs into the crowd of demons, killing three.

"No one gets to Saint Catherine's."

Amaya cocked her head at the Cambion who spoke to her, lifting her sword. "You're not doing a very good job at stopping me. I'm guessing you're the sentries Lucifer planted here."

"And you're Amaya Winslow." The man circled her, an axe in his hand. "It'll be quite a coup to kill you."

"If you think you can kill me, you know nothing about what I can do."

"I know you were nearly eaten by a hound in Purgatory. I know you watched as Lilith ripped Gabriel's Grace from his chest. I know you've hidden like a little bitch instead of fighting alongside your brethren. You're a coward, and you'll die like one!"

Battle was always a cost-benefit analysis. Amaya considered her situation as she surveyed the Cambion facing her. There were eight left. Logically, she knew there weren't likely to be more in the area. Her Nephil senses told her there weren't. If even one survived, Lucifer would be alerted to her presence in Sinai within minutes. Using her powers could allow him to track her location anyway, if he was actively looking for her at the moment she used them.

Choosing caution, she stooped to pick up her whip and charged the demons, the blade on her sword flashing in the light from the rising sun. Metal clashed with metal as she fought her way through them, using blade and whip in turn to hack through the demons.

Blood splashed on the ground, thick and black. None of the Cambion facing her were strong enough that their powers were useful on her. Amaya grunted as she drove her sword through the ribcage of a woman and shrieked when the sword of another adversary slashed deep into her thigh, hitting bone. Her flesh flayed and separated, red meat giving way to stark white bone.

Falling to her knees, she used her whip to slash at the two final Cambion, wrapping it around one by the neck and pulling tight, strangling life from him as she fumbled for her sword, lifting it to beat back the onslaught from the final Cambion. Using her powers to light the blade with flames, she swung wildly, making contact with the man's face and driving the tip of the sword into his skull.

Panting and out of breath, Amaya dropped her sword and looked around the desert, her eyes and powers scanning for any sign of other threats. Finding none, she flashed herself to Deacon and their packs, her attention turning to the gaping gash on her leg.

On the top of the mountain in the distance, just outside her range, Azazel stood watching. Smiling, he glanced to the Cambion next to him.

"Report back to Abalam. Tell him that Amaya and Deacon are nearly to Saint Catherine's. Do not get close enough to alert them of your presence. We watch until they emerge from Eden with the Rod. Gather more sentries to replace the dead ones."

"Why did you attack them?"

Azazel grinned, the wind whipping through his hair. "Now they'll think they've killed everyone we had stationed here. It might make them more reckless and may give us a better shot at defeating them once they come out of the Garden. Strategy, son, strategy." He glanced at the boy next to him. "Go, now. Make sure Abalam knows they're here and that things are being handled. The Rod will be ours. Tell him he can focus on collecting the witch."

The boy nodded. "As you wish."

CHAPTER NINE

DEACON WOKE slowly with the sun shining in his face. Panic rose in his chest, and he sat up, staunchly ignoring the dizziness that flooded him from moving too quickly. As his vision cleared, he saw Amaya sitting five feet from him, her back against a boulder, wearing nothing but underwear and a tank, one leg bent at the knee and the other straight out in front of her. Her skin was gray, and there was a puddle of congealing blood beneath her. One hand was pressed weakly to a bundle of blood-stained cloth held against her leg.

Any relief he felt at seeing her was replaced with abject panic at her condition. He scrambled to his knees and grabbed her face, shaking her until her eyes opened, the glassy green orbs unable to focus on his.

He grabbed one of the packs and dumped it on the ground, opening one of the bottles of water and dumping it on her head to wake her up, pouring water into her mouth until she coughed and gagged.

"Deacon?"

Relief washed over him and he crushed Amaya to his chest in a hug. "Yes, thank God, baby. What happened?"

She shook her head slowly, trying to clear it. "You got shot down and knocked out. I fought off the Cambion. Had to use my powers. One stabbed me. It's bad. I tried to stitch it, but I forgot the fucking first-aid kit."

Deacon pulled the bloody shirt away from her leg and paled when he saw the width of the cut. Grabbing his extra pants, he cut one leg into strips and wrapped the clean fabric around the wound, tying it tightly. When he pressed on the injury, tears flooded her eyes and a scream tore its way from her chest, her head falling back and digging into the rock behind her.

"You're gonna be okay. How long was I unconscious?"

"Couple hours. It's about eight, I think."

"Any sign of other Cambion or demons?"

She shook her head. "I killed them all."

Deacon kissed her head. "Good girl." He flexed his wings and winced at the pain from the bullet wound. "I'm going to get you to the monastery. Surely they'll have a doctor there."

Amaya offered a half-hearted smile. "I don't think I can walk, and you can't carry me."

"I'm going to fly you."

She shook her head. "It's too dangerous. It's daylight."

"Then I'll flash us."

"We can't use our powers."

He glared at her. "You just said you used yours hours ago, and no one has showed up yet to kill us. One flash isn't going to be noticed. If you killed all the sentries, it's a good bet no one is watching this area." Standing, he stared down at her. "Your choice, Maya. Flash or fly, but we're going one way or the other, and we're going now."

"Flash. A split second of exposure is better than an hour."

Deacon gathered their packs and lifted Amaya in his arms, cradling her against his chest. Taking care to make sure he was touching both packs, he flashed toward Saint Catherine's monastery.

The walls rose up out of the dirt, surrounding several white and tan buildings. On top of the walls were several people with rifles. Before Deacon could even take a step forward, the unmistakable sound of slides snapping into place permeated the air. Stretching his wings fully behind him, he extended them above his head, leaving no question of his heritage.

"It's an Angel!"

Within seconds, the gates opened and several men ran out,

rushing toward him. They were still armed, but the weapons were lowered. One of the men, a rangy blonde that looked to be in his forties, held up his hand to the others.

"Identify yourself, Angel."

Deacon cleared his throat. "I am Deacon, son of Michael, the Angel of War. I am Nephil, not Angel. This is Amaya Winslow. She's hurt badly and in need of medical attention."

The man's head snapped up. "Braxton's and Alaria's kid?"

Amaya turned her head, her eyes glassy and her lips cracked and dry. "Do you know my parents?"

"I fought with them in Colombia when Brad Dooley was there. God, I was just a kid when they were there." He nodded to the Warriors behind them. "Run and get the doctor." He gestured to the packs. "See that their stuff is brought in. Have a team sweep to make sure those fucking Cambion didn't follow them in." He lifted an eyebrow. "How did you get past the guards?"

"She killed them all. I was flying us in overnight and got shot down. Knocked me out, and she took them on. That's how she got hurt." Deacon followed the man into the monastery, taking in the small houses, the larger buildings and the church. "This is more like a city than a monastery."

"It's a bit of both. Saint Catherine City fell with everything else. Lucifer sieged on it hard, and it's nothing more than some rubble. We retreated behind the monastery walls and discovered pretty quickly that they couldn't get in here. All that biblical shit is apparently true. This place is protected. The fighting has died down since the beginning, but there are still little skirmishes every once in a while, especially at the Oasis. They don't like to let us farm, and we need the food to survive." The man looked at Amaya worriedly. "How long ago was she hurt?"

"A few hours. She's lost a lot of blood."

"Humans can't give Nephilim transfusions. It has to be from another Nephilim, and we don't have any others here, so it's going to have to come from you." He offered a terse smile. "I'm Harry, by the way. I don't think I ever introduced myself."

"I'd shake your hand, but they're both occupied at the moment."

Amaya managed a laugh. "I'd say he's not always so sarcastic, but it'd be a lie." She closed her eyes. "How many people are here?"

"Couple hundred. About thirty priests, eighty Warriors and a hundred civilians." Harry led them up a staircase and into one of the buildings. "What are you even doing in this part of the world?"

Deacon sighed ruefully. "We're looking for the Garden of Eden."

Harry drew to a stop, his eyebrows coming together as he stared at them. "What for?"

Amaya laughed deliriously. "We're after the sword in the stone! It's a grand adventure!"

Harry pressed his hand to her forehead. "She's getting a fever. Why you're here can wait. Let's get her taken care of."

The doctor was a young woman with quick hands and a hard face. She barked orders in two languages, directing four nuns and Deacon in rapid order. Before Deacon could wrap his head around what was happening, Amaya was lifted out of his arms and placed on a bed, and he was being shoved into a chair.

Gritting his teeth when a needle slid into his arm, he watched as blood ran out of his arm, through a slim tube and into a needle sticking out of Amaya's arm. The doctor glanced up at him from where she was preparing a tray of instruments.

"We don't have a way to monitor how much blood is coming out of you with a person to person transfusion, so you have to let me know when you start to feel dizzy. She only needs a unit or two, so being a hero and putting yourself in a bed next to her will do her no good."

Deacon bit his cheek to stop the grin. "Duly noted."

She looked at him sharply. "I mean it. She's not on death's door. She doesn't need half your blood volume or more. Giving it to her will only hurt you and not help her. Got it?"

He inclined his head. "Got it." He watched her fluid, efficient movements. "Do you have a name?"

"Cleo." She pulled on gloves and lifted Amaya's leg to tuck a towel under her thigh where the gash was. "How did your friend get hurt?"

"Fighting Cambion." Deacon winced on Amaya's behalf when the doctor started poking at the wound. "I believe it was done with a sword, but I suppose it could have been an axe."

"Definitely a sword." Cleo dragged a chair to the bed and plopped in it, lowering the tray so she could reach it and picking up a bottle of betadine. "I'm going to clean out the wound and disinfect the area. There's a lot of damage to the muscle, but it doesn't appear that any infection has set in, so she should heal well. It'll be a couple weeks before she's able to bear much weight on the leg, and I'd say four to five before you're ready to leave to go wherever you need to go. I'm not an orthopedic surgeon, and even if I were, I don't have the equipment to be able to really fix the muscles the way they should be done."

Deacon watched as she poured betadine into Amaya's leg. "Will she be able to walk?"

"Yes. She should have full range of movement, be able to train and do everything she does now. Unfortunately, there will be a significant scar, and she'll likely always have some pain in the area intermittently." Cleo rinsed the betadine away with water. "I can give her some morphine while she's here and some antibiotics, but our stores are pretty slim."

"You have morphine?"

"We grow poppies in the oasis not too far from here. I refine it into morphine. It's rudimentary but effective. I can only use it in small doses for a small amount of time because of the addictive nature, but it's better than nothing." Cleo began suturing the muscles together, her lip between her teeth as she worked. "You're damned lucky to even have found a doctor. Most people with a wound like this would die of infection if not from blood loss."

Deacon studied the doctor, taking in her pitch black hair, dusky skin, dark eyes and the accented lilt to her voice. "Where did you train?"

"Right here." She glanced up. "Do I seriously look old enough to have been around when there were still medical schools?" She scoffed. "I was on holiday here from Turkey when Lucifer escaped. My uncle was a physician in Saint Catherine City. I was visiting him during the summer. I was likely only four or five when it happened. My parents were here, too. They died in the fighting, and my uncle raised me. He taught me all I know about medicine until he died last year. I took over then." She rose and rounded the bed to check his IV, removing the needle from his arm with a practiced movement. "Everything is in short supply. We disinfect and reuse all we can, down to gloves and needles."

"Don't you send out people to look for supplies?"

"We do, but there aren't many places to look here. We have to cross the mountains or one of the gulfs to get somewhere else, which limits how far we can go. We're able to grow enough food to get by, and we can hunt and fish some, but supplies are hard to come by. There's always a squad out somewhere. Right now they're east of here in Israel looking for supplies. They've been gone nearly two weeks." She cut the sutures and brought together another layer of tissue. "We don't have Nephilim with long range flashing abilities here, so we're very limited with transport."

"Do the Cambion attack this place very often?"

Cleo pursed her lips and rocked her shoulders back and forth. "Meh, not really. They make noises a lot, but they don't do too much. A few little spats every year. It's not too bad. They hit us really hard at first, but they can't get through. I don't know why, but I'm damn glad they can't." She glanced up from her work. "Why are you here, anyway? People don't exactly stumble onto us, especially not very powerful Nephilim. You had to be aiming for this place."

"Rumor has it that the monks here can help us get to the Garden of Eden. We need to get something that's in there. If we're right, it's going to help us get our world back."

She bent her head back to her task and continued stitching. "This is our world, Deacon. It's all we've ever known. The world you want to get back is the world of our parents, not ours. None of us are going to know how to survive there." Her hands stilled for a moment. "Think about it. We don't have money, we don't live in houses or have jobs or go shopping. We don't do anything that they did. It's a hand-to-mouth existence. We wouldn't survive in their world."

Deacon leaned forward, bracing his elbows on his knees. "Do you not want to see Lucifer killed?"

Cleo's head snapped up, her eyes flashing. "I want that more than anything else in the whole world." She tied a stitch carefully, studying the thread for a long moment. "It just also happens to be the most terrifying prospect I've ever heard."

"It's going to take time for things to go back to the way they were. Decades maybe. Certainly not overnight. It's just not possible for it to happen that fast." He looked down at Amaya, relief sweeping through him when he saw that her skin was warm and pink instead of pale and gray. "Do you think it's possible to talk to the monks?"

"I don't see why not. I'm sure Harry will be coming back for you sooner or later anyway. He can take care of arranging all that. There are a few of us who speak English here, so you'll do fine with communication. All the Warriors do, I believe, but most of the nuns and monks speak Israeli or Egyptian. A few know a little English, but for the most part they've been pretty resistant to learning it." She shook her head in disgust. "I don't know what they intend to do in the next few years. Even the youngest of them is in their seventies. If they want their knowledge to continue, they're going to have to break down and teach stuff to one of us eventually."

"What's the bare minimum time she's going to need to recover?"

"Unless you have a Healer you can get to come and zap her good as new, I'd say a minimum of three to four weeks. I won't take the stitches out for ten to fourteen days, and after that she'll have to build back up to normal activity." Cleo reached for a roll of gauze and wrapped Amaya's leg. "If she heals faster it might go quicker, but don't hold your breath. Most Nephilim don't heal faster than humans." She peeled off her gloves and put them on the tray. "How do you feel?"

"Me?" Deacon lifted his eyebrows. At her nod, he shrugged. "Fine. Why?"

"If you want to, you can pick her up, and I'll show you to one of the empty rooms. You can get a shower, take a nap and keep an eye on her until she wakes up."

"Are you sure you don't need to watch her?"

"I'm sure. There's no reason to think she won't wake up as soon as the morphine I gave her wears off. She was conscious and talking when you brought her in. Once she's up and had some food, I'll give her some antibiotics to make sure there's no infection, and she'll be good to go." She smiled. "Follow me."

Deacon stooped and lifted Amaya into his arms, cradling her against his chest and following Cleo out into the hallway. She led them up a flight of stairs, down another hall and around a corner to a large room sparsely furnished with two beds, a chest of drawers and one chair.

"It's not much, but it's clean and comfortable." She stood by the door until Deacon had placed Amaya on one of the beds. "I'll see if we can find some clothes to fit you both and have your packs sent up. The bathroom is through the door. There's a shower, toilet and sink. Nothing fancy." She rocked back on her heels. "I don't normally do this, but I'm going to anyway. I got the feeling you and the unconscious one are an item, and if that's the case, awesome. If not," She offered a nervous smile. "I'm three doors down on the right."

Before Deacon could answer, Cleo pulled the door shut and disappeared down the hall.

Sighing, he glanced back at Amaya to make sure she was still sleeping and dropped onto the other bed, staring up at the ceiling while pressing his hands to his temples to fend off the threatening headache.

CHAPTER TEN

DECEMBER 23RD, 2060

SAINT CATHERINE'S MONASTERY

AMAYA OPENED her eyes and sat up with a jolt. The sun was slipping over the horizon, lavender, orange and red fingers of light crawling over the sand toward the mountains. She squinted and blinked in the dim light, shaking her head to clear it.

Her leg pounded rhythmically from the long line of black stitches marring her tanned skin, and she winced when she tried to swing her legs to the edge of the bed. Gritting her teeth, she grasped the nightstand and heaved herself to her feet, the need to both brush her teeth and empty her bladder overcoming her reluctance to feel the inevitable pain from placing any weight on her leg.

Biting her lower lip to keep from crying out, she limped into the small adjoining bathroom and twisted the knob to turn on the tap, sticking her mouth underneath to rinse off her teeth and tongue. Spying a toothbrush on the back of the sink and a tube of paste in a small basket, she shivered in delight and brushed her teeth enthusiastically.

Half an hour later, her hair hanging down her back in wet curls, her leg puffy and tender from the heat of the shower, and her bladder delightfully empty, Amaya hobbled back into the bedroom naked. There was one chair in the room, and she rifled through a stack of clothes someone had placed there, pulling on a pair of snug denim shorts and a black tank. Her boots were sitting by the door, and there were a pair of flip flops next to them. Checking the size, she slipped her feet into the sandals and opened the door, determined to find Deacon.

On the other side of the door, her hand poised to knock, was a pretty woman with black hair, dark eyes, and a small backpack in one hand. She stepped back when Amaya opened the door and fisted her free hand on her hip.

"Good, you're up. I see you found the clothes I left. I thought we'd be a close fit. I'm a bit smaller than you, so I knew they'd be snug, but I figured you could wiggle into my shorts just fine." The woman slipped past Amaya into the room, pulling the door shut behind her. "Lucky for you that our feet are the same size. There aren't very many women here, and even fewer are willing to part with clothes and shoes."

Amaya turned and stared after the woman. "Who are you?"

"You don't remember?"

"No."

The woman smiled and put the bag down on the second, still-made bed. "I'm Cleo, the one who sewed you shut yesterday. I came to check your leg out and give you another dose of antibiotics. Some pain meds, too, if you think you need them."

Amaya perched on the bed and lifted her leg up, laying it on the mattress to let the doctor check it. "I'm sore, but I feel mostly okay. It hurts to walk, but I can get where I need to go, even if it's pretty slow."

"Slow is the way you need to walk for the next bit." Cleo dabbed rubbing alcohol on the stitches. "You must have a very high pain tolerance. Most people would be lying in bed for days screaming for morphine."

"Lying in bed for days is no good for me or you. It'll heal faster if I'm on it and moving. There's less muscular atrophy that way, too."

Cleo glanced up. "Have you studied medicine?"

"I've just been hurt a lot." Amaya chuckled. "It's a rough world out there. We don't always have the luxury of Healers or doctors. Most of the time we patch ourselves up and hope for the best." She grimaced when the other woman liberally applied iodine. "Damn, that burns."

"At least I know you're not immune to pain." Cleo laughed and taped a gauze pad to Amaya's thigh. "I'm going to give you a shot of penicillin. You're not allergic, are you?"

"I have no idea. I've never had it."

Cleo unscrewed the lid on a bottle and drew some liquid into a syringe. "Penicillin is an antibiotic I can make here. There's a tiny medical ward with some basic equipment, and I was able to figure out how to make a few medications. I can manage antibiotics, some morphine, ether, a few other things."

"Nineteenth century medicine."

"Basically." She jabbed the needle into Amaya's arm and depressed the plunger. "All done. Hungry?"

"Starving."

"Good. You can follow me down to breakfast. I think that's where Deacon is. I lost track of him at some point last night."

Amaya cocked her head. "Hmm?"

Cleo stood and helped Amaya to her feet. "That man is gorgeous, isn't he?"

"He certainly is." She forced herself not to jump to conclusions. "I guess I just assumed he was staying in here with me."

"He was going to."

"But he didn't."

"I don't think so, no."

"Where did he stay?"

Cleo lifted one shoulder in an elegant shrug. "A girl never tells."

Amaya slammed her tray down next to Deacon so hard that her oatmeal sloshed out of her bowl and her coffee splashed. He jumped and looked up, his face splitting into a grin when he saw her. Rising to his feet, he slipped his arm around her waist and brought her close, bending to brush his lips over hers.

Surprised when she turned her head to the side and offered her cheek instead, he gestured to the chair. "Sit down and get your weight off that leg. I was just going over what we need with Harry. He's the Warrior leader here. He knew your parents from before."

Amaya offered a tight smile. "Nice to meet you." She turned back to Deacon. "I need to know one thing, and I need to know it now."

Deacon sipped his coffee. "Sure. What's going on?"

"Did you screw the doctor last night?"

Harry choked on a bite of eggs. "On that note, I'll excuse myself." He shook his head and stood, casting a sympathetic look toward Deacon. "Bad move, son."

Deacon held up a hand. "I most certainly did no such thing. Where in the world did you even get an idea like that?" He glanced at Harry. "You can stay. This isn't some big fight. I didn't do anything, and I'm not sure why she thinks that."

Amaya ignored the Warrior. "Then why weren't you in your bed when I woke up?"

"Because I left before dawn to tour the monastery and get a sense for how things work. I pitched in last night doing an inventory of the hospital and stumbled in after midnight. You were asleep when I got in and still asleep when I left. Cleo checked on you twice and said you just needed to sleep it off. Nothing happened with me and her. She invited me to her room, but I tracked her down in the hospital and explained to her that I am not available."

Amaya blistered. "She doesn't seem to understand the meaning of the word unavailable, since she was in my room this morning gushing about how you're gorgeous and that you spent the night elsewhere and how, and I quote, 'a girl never tells.'"

Harry huffed. "I'm sorry for this bit of drama. I'll speak to Cleo about it."

Deacon shook his head. "No need for that. Just a misunderstanding." He held out a hand to Amaya. "I promise nothing happened."

Amaya placed her hand in his. "Okay. So, what's the plan?"

"It'll take a while for you to be ready to move into the Garden, so we have to allow time for that. Harry's been telling me about the monks and their rituals. It seems they plan to begin a week of praying and rituals they won't cut short. It starts on Christmas and goes until New Years. Since you won't have your stitches out until then anyway, I see no reason to force the issue. We'll let them do their thing, and once they're done, the monks will give us the information we need about how to get into the Garden, and we'll move there as soon as you're healed enough to manage the trip."

Harry gestured with his fork. "These monks are super excited about you being here. They see it as a sign the war is going to be over. They knew there would be someone eventually, and here you are, so they're going into a tizzy with the prayers and the research.

Personally, I'm not sure they know how to get you where you need to go, but they swear they do."

"Michael said they would, and he's rarely wrong about these things." Amaya speared a bite of egg and brought it to her mouth. "How long do you think before they'll take us? I know the week for the Christmas stuff and to let me heal, but I mean after. Do they have to do research? Is that part done? Are they just going to guess?"

Harry shook his head. "Not a fucking clue. You two might as well get comfortable. You could be here for the long haul. They'll take you when they think it's right and not a second before. They operate on their own schedule and don't seem to care too much what the rest of us think about it."

Deacon scraped the bottom of his bowl of oatmeal for the last bite. "We don't want to stay here any longer than necessary. The longer we're here, the more danger you're in. I know they haven't been able to get in yet, but if Lucifer finds out Amaya's here, or worse, if my mother finds out I'm here, they'll have even more incentive to figure out a way in. It wouldn't be pretty."

"We can hold our own. Have been for thousands of years. We'll be fine, kids." Harry stood. "I need to head out to check the walls and finish up our ammo inventory. I'll catch up with you later." He slapped Deacon on the back. "Try to stay away from the pretty doctor if you can. You've apparently caught her interest, and I don't need romantic drama shit going on around here."

Amaya dropped her spoon into her bowl, waiting until Harry disappeared before she spoke. "We need to be moving as soon as possible. I don't give a flying fuck about their rituals. They need to tell us where the damn door is now."

Deacon nodded slowly. "I thought we'd be leaving as soon as we got here, too. Do you have a plan?" He lifted his eyebrows. "And was the reasonable Amaya you just showed Harry all for show? All the talk about letting the monks do their prayers and rituals and letting yourself heal?"

"I'm fine. I can walk. We can leave today if they'll spill the beans."

Looking at her out of the corner of his eye, he lifted one brow. "Really? You feel up to it even with that leg?"

She nodded, trying to appear more sure than she felt and hoping she was convincing him. "Definitely. Absolutely. Without a doubt."

Deacon sighed. "I was hoping you wouldn't make me do this. I never want to hurt you, Maya, but you're being both stubborn and unreasonable." He reached out and poked his index finger into the meat of her leg two inches below her incision, taking care not to touch the wound, but choosing a place close enough to make his point.

Tears sprang into Amaya's eyes and she bit down onto her tongue, trying desperately not to scream. She pressed her palm to her thigh and rocked back and forth, mumbling under her breath. For a moment, her power surged out of control and a blast rocketed out from her, shattering all the light-bulbs in the cafeteria.

"What the fuck, Deacon?" She glared at him, her eyes flashing with fury.

He looked at her calmly and picked up her bowl of oatmeal, moving it onto his own tray. "I was proving a point. You're not ready. You won't be ready for a while. We need to take the time for you to heal before we do whatever it is we need to do. There's no harm in it. It's not like we're on a deadline."

She waved her arm. "What do you expect us to *do* here for a week? Or more! Nap? Tan? We'd be better off calling for your dad, having him zap me up to Zeke so she can fix my leg, and then insisting that the fucking monks spill their guts about what's going on." She snatched the bowl back and plunked it on her tray. "That's mine."

"We both knew once we came down here, that was it. No flashing back and forth unless it was an emergency, and being forced to lay low for a few days isn't an emergency. We'll be fine." Deacon reached out to tuck a lock of her hair behind her ear. "Just take a few days to heal up. You need it." He chuckled when she grimaced at the taste of the cold oatmeal she didn't like. "You really gonna eat that?"

Knowing it was petty but not caring, and still angry about her leg, she stared at him stonily, deliberately taking another bite. "Every last bit."

CHAPTER ELEVEN

DECEMBER 31ST, 2060, 11:38 PM

SAINT CATHERINE'S MONASTERY

THE DESERT was beautiful at night. Amaya studied the way the moonlight danced over the sand and cacti as she peered over the balcony off her bedroom. She had a quilt from the bed wrapped around her shoulders to combat the chilly air~even in Egypt, it got cold at night in December~and leaned against the metal bars, bouncing on the balls of her feet to keep her blood flowing.

Glancing down at her watch, she toyed with the idea of going to bed, knowing it was late and she needed to. Discarding the notion, she slid down the wall and leaned against the side of the building, tucking the blanket under her feet to keep them off the cold cement.

She turned her head when the door leading back into the bedroom slid open and Deacon stepped out onto the narrow ledge, offering a smile up at him.

"Hey."

He looked down. "Hey. Everything okay?"

"Yeah, why?"

"Everything isn't normally okay when people hide outside late at night in the cold, by themselves."

Holding open an edge of the quilt, she patted the concrete next to her. "There's room for two under here."

Deacon shook his head in mild amusement and dropped to the ground, scooting close and tucking her against his side. "How's your leg?"

"Almost healed. The doctor says another few days and the stitches will come out. I'm not sure why they can't come out now, but I suppose that's why I'm not a doctor." She glared at him. "It's still sore, so no poking me again."

"It hasn't even been a week. I'm guessing they can't come out because no one wants to see your leg split wide open again." He stared up at the sky, admiring the black velvety sky and the stars that dotted it. "It is beautiful here, isn't it?"

"Mmhmm." She leaned her head against his shoulder. "New Years' Eve is always such a weird time. It's a holiday, and humans still celebrate it, but it's also the anniversary of the Choosing. Thirty-one years ago tonight is when our parents were fighting that battle. I can't help but wonder what they were doing right now."

"I know what you mean. Is now when Gage was running with Griffin from Azazel or is now when she was stabbing Beelzebub with the Jesus blade? Had Azazel already tried to chain your father to his rock or was that an hour ago?"

"It still bothers Dad—Braxton—that he was unconscious at the end. Azazel knocked him out in the chapel, and he still feels guilty about it."

Deacon shrugged. "That's life. We don't always get to say goodbye. We're not always there when we want to be. Shit happens." He laughed ruefully. "Hell, it's not like he can't just call her down from Heaven and talk to her now. As if our lives weren't weird enough."

"Tell me about it. I wonder how Zeke feels having her great-grandmother around."

"I doubt Zeke is thinking about it much. She's got the baby to occupy herself with, and it's not like she ever knew any of her family other than Damon and Greer." He turned her wrist to look at her watch. "Five till. They were definitely in the chapel by now. Alaria facing off against Azazel, Braxton unconscious in a corner, almost everyone else dead."

Amaya stared up at the sky. "Do you think in thirty years there will be someone, somewhere doing this about something we did?

Sitting somewhere on the night we fought and wondering what we were doing at that time?"

"Yes." He looked at her solemnly. "No one knew about Griffin. Most people still don't, because the world was different then, Maya. People had lives to be distracted by. They didn't know about what went on in the shadows. That's what life is now. Everyone knows about you, they know what we're supposed to do, and they'll know when we've done it. You're going to be a hero."

Amaya stared at him sadly. "I don't want to be a hero or some martyr. I don't want to be famous. I just want to know that if we die doing this, someone will remember us, too."

"They will." He looked at the face of her watch again. "Midnight." He lifted his hand to cup the side of her face. "Isn't there some old ritual about kissing at midnight at the start of a new year?"

Her brows furrowed. "I think you're thinking of mistletoe. Whatever that is."

Deacon laughed, the sound rumbling in his chest. "Whatever." He shifted to wrap the other arm around her. "I'm going to do it anyway. Unless you have any objections."

Amaya's eyes drifted closed on a sigh, her heart pounding from anticipation and desire. "None."

His lips were soft and smooth, and he tasted her mouth expertly, flicking his tongue against her lips and sinking between them slowly, flooding her senses with his taste. Amaya's fingers gripped his biceps, digging into the solid muscles she found there and holding tightly.

She responded eagerly to the kiss, her tongue brushing against his and her mouth hungry. What had started soft and slow escalated quickly. Their breath came in gasps, and the easy kiss turned deep and searching.

Deacon gripped her hips and lifted, dragging her into his lap so that one knee was on either side of his thighs and their chests were pressed together. The blanket slipped from her shoulder, pooling at her waist and leaving her bare arms exposed to the brisk breeze. The wind whipped through her thin tank, puckering her nipples and making her shiver in meager defense.

Amaya's head fell back and her chest jutted forward as Deacon's mouth trailed over her neck and around to her throat. Inch by painstaking inch, he worked her tank up until he could lift the scrap of fabric over her head and drop it next to them, her dusky skin exposed to his hungry gaze for the first time.

Her skin flushed with both desire and slight apprehension, Amaya stilled as he studied her, taking in the fullness of her breasts, the rose colored nipples at the tips, and the sweeping expanse of skin leading to the waistband on the sweatpants she wore. Slowly, almost hesitantly, he reached out and dragged one finger from her collarbone down to the peak of her breast, circling the tightly beaded tip with the pad of one finger.

A guttural groan tore from Amaya's throat and she rocked her hips against his, desperate for friction. Their eyes met and held and without breaking contact, Deacon dipped his head and lapped his tongue over her nipple, sucking it into his mouth and swirling his tongue around it. Lifting her other breast in his hand, he stroked his fingers over the soft skin, admiring the curves of her flesh before tugging gently on her other nipple, rolling it between two fingers as he sucked on the first.

Amaya couldn't look away. Her fingers tangled in his hair, holding tight to the pale strands. Her breath came in quick gasps as desire rocketed through her body until every nerve was simultaneously firing. Deacon sucked harder, rubbing his tongue against the sensitive flesh while his fingers worked sheer magic on her other breast.

With a wet pop, he released her and sat back, studying her face. Bringing the blanket back up to make sure she wasn't too cold, he pulled her closer until their chests were again pressed solidly together. When he spoke, his voice was deep and strangled.

"Do you want to go inside?" He pressed a kiss to the curve of her shoulder. "Will you let me take you to bed, Amaya?"

Amaya felt her heart swell at the question, and desire bolted through her, hot and strong. She closed her eyes and forced herself to breathe, leaning into his embrace. "There's something you need to know first."

Concerned, Deacon sat back slightly. "What's wrong? Is it your leg? Did I hurt you?"

Shaking her head, Amaya grabbed his hands and held them. "No, no. I'm fine. You didn't hurt me. My leg is fine. I just don't know what's going to happen in there, and I want you to be prepared for it. Michael was always afraid that sex would make my powers extremely difficult to control and that I could lose hold of them while in the...throes." She giggled nervously. "I was so scared at the thought of hurting someone and so perpetually tangled up with you that, uh, I never got around to finding out if he was right or not."

In the span of a heartbeat, Deacon's body tightened and hardened to the point he was concerned he would explode if she so much as looked at him, never mind what would happen if she laid one finger on him. Taking several deep breaths, he focused on calming himself down. After fifteen tense seconds, he felt able to speak, though his voice was still strangled.

"Never?"

Chewing on her lower lip, Amaya shook her head. "I didn't want to risk blowing anyone up. You remember what used to happen when I got mad or sad or had any really intense emotions."

A fleeting memory of being chased across the globe by Gabriel flitted through his mind, and he smiled. "I remember." He rubbed his hands up and down her arms. "Let's go inside and talk about this. It's too cold out here for you to sit half-naked."

Amaya dragged on her shirt and climbed out of his lap, limping into the bedroom. She waited until Deacon had closed the door before opening her mouth again. "I don't want you to make too big a deal about this. It's not some big thing. I don't need to be taught the ropes of sex. I know how everything works."

"I'm quite sure you do." Biting his cheek to keep from laughing, he perched on one of the beds. "I'm more concerned with the blowing up part. Did Dad ever say why he thought you should abstain?"

"He didn't. He sat me down right after the attack with Lilith and asked me if I was still a virgin. It's that way your dad has, even when he's asking prying questions. You just know he's asking for a good reason and it's important, so it didn't feel weird. I told him I was, and he asked me how far you and I had gone. When I told him we'd only ever kissed, he asked if there had been other boys, and I'm damn sure he knew there hadn't." She snorted. "I didn't exactly have time to date as a teenager. I think we were all late bloomers in that way. Not because we were sexually repressed but because of training and having to be adults before we were able to go out on our own. It made it really fucking hard to get laid."

Deacon chuckled. "We male types lamented the same sort of thing often during our teenage years. There was a lot of stuff going on in that house we'd like to think Dad didn't know about." He reached for her hand when she sat next to him. "Go on."

"Michael explained to me that since my powers are tied into my emotions, he was concerned that during sexual contact, they would be harder to control and I should take extra precautions to ensure I could be with..." She trailed off, looking amused, "...as he put it— either a male or female without incident."

"So you never did anything."

"Oh, I did stuff. I wanted to see if he was right. One night, Zeke and Lux got trapped in a sex shop in Boston and had to spend the night. This was a year or two before Michael sat me down for a talking to. Anyway, you know I was never allowed out by myself, especially after we ran from Gabriel that one time." She laughed at the memory. "I snuck out one night about a week after The Talk and found the store. I gathered myself a nice collection of vibrators and dildos and locked myself in my room. I determined an orgasm was not going to turn me into some uncontrollable beast, but Michael was right. It's still an emotion, and a powerful one at that. I experienced a power surge. I was able to control it, but it was there. It's always there, and it's hard for me to control what I have."

"You got scared."

Amaya nodded slowly. "Because it's scary. If I lose control, I could hurt whoever I was with, myself, or innocent people in other rooms or buildings. I wanted to be sure I could control things before I let myself be with anyone and took the risk. By the time I was sure I could, I didn't want it to be just anyone." She sighed deeply. "Don't get me wrong, I like sex. I have it with myself fairly regularly. I'm not some blushing virgin who has no idea how things work. I know exactly how it works and I'm relatively sure I'll enjoy actual sex. There just hasn't, as of yet, been the insertion of penis into vagina. That's all."

Deacon looked pain. "That's far from all there is to it, Maya." He rubbed her hand between his own. "That's the least of it."

Amaya squirmed uncomfortably. "I don't want you to make a bigger deal about this than it is. I just thought you should know what the situation is."

"I'm glad you told me." He studied her face intently. "Please don't take this the wrong way." He inched closer to her, sliding his hands up to grip her elbows. "We're not going to have sex tonight."

Emotions rose in her, confusion and fear battling anger and disappointment. She blinked several times, trying to carefully formulate what she was going to say. When she managed to speak, her voice was razor sharp and ice cold. "Why not?"

Deacon didn't release her. "Because if you're worried about

losing control of your powers, you aren't going to let go with me, and I'm not taking you to bed until I know you're going to be able to enjoy it. We'll wait until we're somewhere you can't hurt anyone even if you do let loose a little."

Softening, she smiled slightly. "You would be there. I could hurt you. That isn't going to change."

"You aren't going to hurt me. I have powers of my own, and I can handle you when you lose control. We've established that before. There's no danger in being with me. That comes in other people around, like here. So it won't be here." He drew her close, taking care to adjust her leg so that it was extended carefully. "Not because I don't want to. I want to. But because I want it to be the best for you that it can be, and that isn't going to happen here."

Amaya nodded slowly. "Okay." She offered a half-smile. "That doesn't feel like rejection."

Deacon brought her in for a kiss, sinking into her mouth and ravaging her until she was clinging to his arms for balance and panting. When he released her, she stared up at him with glassy, unfocused eyes.

"It's nothing remotely like rejection. I want you. Never think anything differently. We'll get there at the right time for us. Just because it's not tonight doesn't mean it isn't going to happen." He tucked her close. "And that doesn't mean we can't start with a sleepover." He nuzzled her neck with his nose. "I think we've been in separate beds for long enough, don't you?"

Amaya shivered and sighed as his arms snaked around her. "Uh huh."

CHAPTER TWELVE

JANUARY 8TH, 2061

SAINT CATHERINE'S

"WELL, I think your leg is good to go." Cleo pulled off her gloves and studied the scar on Amaya's leg. "How does it feel?"

Amaya stretched her leg back and forth. "Feels strong. I didn't lose as much muscle as I was afraid I would."

"Good. Do you know when you're leaving?"

"The monks are going to speak to us at sundown. I'll go directly there from here." She looked around the room. "Are we done?"

Cleo put her hands on her hips. "In a hurry?"

"Kinda, yeah."

"Sundown isn't for another forty minutes, Amaya. You've got plenty of time." Cleo rinsed her gloves in the sink and carefully laid them out to dry so they could be reused. "Is everything okay?"

Amaya struggled not to say anything. She forced herself to take several deep breaths and counted to ten three separate times. When neither tactic worked, she bit her tongue until she tasted blood.

Cleo turned to face the other woman. "Seriously, what's up?"

Amaya was certain that was more than even a saint could take. "You want to know what's up? Fine, I'll tell you." She hopped off the table and fisted her hands at her hips. "When I woke up from nearly bleeding to death, you took advantage of that to make me believe you and Deacon were sleeping together, knowing damn well that he and I are a couple. Instead of being a grown-ass woman about it and backing off when he told you he wasn't available, you schemed and plotted to get what you wanted, and now you're acting like nothing ever happened and pretending to be friendly with me."

Cleo lifted one eyebrow. "Are you really together, though? You've been here almost two weeks. I'm just down the hall. I never hear any moaning and groaning. Never see any kissing in the hallways, never any lusty looks or groping when you think no one's looking. You two are either the most private and quiet couple on God's green Earth or you aren't as together as you're letting yourself think you are." She smirked and turned back to her tray of instruments. "I like you, Amaya, and I'm not upset about your little outburst here. I wasn't trying to slide in where I'm not welcome, but Deacon doesn't put out 'spoken for' vibes, and quite frankly, neither do you. A man like that isn't going to sit around and wait for you forever. If you want him, go get him. Otherwise there are plenty of other women who would be glad to take your place. Me included." She finished replacing her instruments and strode to the door. "I'll walk you down to the monks."

Deacon and Harry were standing with a group of six elderly men wearing black robes and hoods when Amaya entered the room. The murmured conversations ceased as she entered the room and the men stared at her. Harry cleared his throat.

"They're a bit in awe of you, I'm afraid." He patted her shoulder as she stood next to them. "Are you ready to start?"

Amaya nodded. "I got the all-clear from the doctor, so let's get this show on the road."

Harry spoke to the monks in a language Amaya didn't know. There was a rapid exchange between the men, with much nodding and excitement. After several moments, Harry turned back to Deacon and Amaya.

"They say that there is prophecy about the one who will defeat Lucifer. They know of the entrance to the Garden and will take you there and show you how to enter it. Before they do that, however, they want to do a cleansing ritual and allow you to have a convening with God as Moses once did to purify your spirit and prepare your body and soul for the hardships you will face in the coming weeks.

Are you willing to allow them to do their rituals?"

Amaya and Deacon shared a skeptical look. She looked at Harry. "Do I get much of a choice?"

"I'm not sure if they'll take you if you say no. It's important to them. It's nothing that will hurt you, and it shouldn't delay the trip since we couldn't leave until morning anyway. They say it'll take a few hours."

She lifted a shoulder in a shrug. "Why the hell not?"

Deacon laid a hand on her shoulder. "What does it require her to do?"

"There was some mention of praying over her, communion, a foot-washing, then sending her out to Mount Sinai to see if God will give her a sign."

Amaya gaped up at him. "They want me to waltz out there and chat with a flaming shrub!"

Deacon covered his mouth to stop the snort of laughter. "Burning bush." He turned to Harry. "And what if the 'sign' doesn't come?"

"I don't know. They wouldn't say. They seem to be pretty sure that it will."

"God isn't too talkative with the Nephilim." Amaya rocked back on her heels. "I wouldn't expect a lot of theatrics. Besides, how are we going to know what's God and what I could do myself? I could probably work up some lightning or a burning bush."

Harry grinned. "I'm sure you could, but at least make an effort to placate them before you go faking it. At the very least, an appearance by an Angel wouldn't hurt. Splitting open the Heavens, coming down with a sword. Something like that. Not Michael, since that's Deacon's dad. Or Gabriel, since he's yours. Who's left that's good?"

Amaya's face darkened. "Gabriel is dead. He died killing Beelzebub."

Harry sobered. "I'm sorry. I didn't know." He awkwardly touched her shoulder. "I only met him once, but he was a decent sort."

Amaya nodded stiffly. "Thanks." She took an unsteady breath. "Let's get this going."

The monks led Amaya into the chapel where she was instructed to remove her boots and socks. One man lit incense while two others sang in a language she didn't know. Nervous, she looked at Deacon.

"If one of them pulls out a knife, I won't be held responsible for the damage I do to this place."

"Duly noted." He swatted her bottom. "Go on."

The rituals took over an hour. Amaya was told to kneel at the altar while the monks poured oil on her head while praying. She was fed bits of cracker and given weak wine to drink while being prayed over. Her forehead was smeared with ash and she was sprinkled with Holy water. Finally, she was placed in a chair, and each monk took a turn dipping her feet in a bowl of lukewarm water.

Uncomfortable but forcing herself not to object to the experience, Amaya gritted her teeth and let the monks do their ceremony. Finally, she was led out past the walls of the monastery and taken to the foot of Mount Sinai. The monks gestured to the mountain and retreated several yards. Harry cleared his throat and stepped up beside her.

"They say that they've prepared you to receive the word of God. You're to kneel and receive instruction from the Holy Spirit. Once you've received a sign, they'll take you to the entrance."

Amaya scowled. "What kind of a sign?"

Harry smiled tightly. "If nothing happens after a few minutes, just do what we talked about and get an Angel to come down here and impress them. It doesn't matter what is, Amaya. It matters what they believe. The power isn't in reality, it's in belief. They need to see a miracle, or what they perceive to be one, so give them one."

Amaya looked over her shoulder at the gathering of monks, then back up at the mountain. Muttering under her breath, she dropped to her knees and faced the pile of rocks.

"So, I'm supposed to talk to you and get you to send some sort of a sign so these old men over there will take me to the Garden of Eden." She looked from side to side, uncomfortable with the whole situation. "I don't really believe in praying. I think you're pretty much a jerk. I've read the Bible, ya know? Well, parts of it anyway." She cleared her throat and rubbed her hands over her thighs. "I read all these stories about how awesome you are and how much you love people and cared for them and now you've just left us all down here to die."

Amaya tipped her head back and stared at the velvety sky, taking in the twinkling stars. A breeze stirred the air and blew through her hair, gently moving it away from her face. Behind her, the monks stirred excitedly, apparently convinced that their miracle was imminent. Less certain, Amaya continued to speak, her voice soft.

"We're really trying. Any idiot could see that. We're dying for this. I almost died for this. Every time, we charge out into battle without a thought for ourselves, trying to save this damn world because it's the right thing to do." She scowled at the sky. "I don't know how much more you want from us. You ask us to fight, so we fight. You ask us to die, so we die. You require women to carry Nephilim, and they do. I know Lucifer keeps cheating, and I know there are some morons who follow him like lemmings, but there are plenty of us who move to block everything he does. This world is more good than bad, and it's not right of you to just sit up there and watch us all die for you and ignore the pain and suffering we're in just because you're pissed off. That's just not right. So pull your head out of your ass and give these silly old men some kind of miracle that will convince them this is what you want so that I can go get the Rod and the Spear and kill Lucifer once and for all. You're supposed to be a loving God, a merciful God, a caring God. One who cries and feels pain when we do. Prove it. Help me out here, dude. Give me something."

Frustrated, Amaya waited thirty seconds with no response. Climbing to her feet, she cast a look back to Deacon, about to call for Michael or Griffin when the sky split open and a streak of red lightning surged into the ground.

Dirt and sand flew up, erupting into flame and forming a column of fire. The monks jumped and held onto each other, watching with excitement and fear. The fire swooped down, spreading out until it came within a hairsbreadth of Amaya's feet.

Slowly, it rose off the ground, forming the outline of a human. One of the arms reached out until the hand was pressing against Amaya's forehead. Though she could see the fire burning, there was no pain when it touched her. After a moment of silence, a voice filled the air, seeming to come from nowhere and everywhere, all at once.

"Fear not, child, for I am with you. The Hand of the Lord is upon you, and your mission is Blessed. Blessed are those who help you, and cursed are those who oppose you. Heavy has been your load, Amaya, and heavier will it be still. Doubt not that your pain is known and that it is grieved. You have felt pain, and you will feel more yet. Fear has come and will be faced again. Cast it aside, for I am beside you." The figure brought the other hands up and pressed one to either side of her head. "You will walk through the Valley of the Shadow of Death and emerge victorious. You shall eat of Heaven's manna and drink from the Cup of Christ and be purified by the blood. You will be cleansed through fire and washed in baptism, and you will crucify Lucifer. I am your Heavenly Father. Go forth and do as I command. Feel my presence with you and know that you are loved and you are Blessed."

In less time than it took Amaya to blink, the fire was gone and the night was silent. She looked over her shoulder and saw the monks on their knees with their heads pressed to the ground and their arms stretched out in front of them, whispered prayers barely audible. She turned to Deacon and Harry, her eyes wide.

Deacon rushed to her, taking her elbow with one hand. "That was one hell of a trick. How did you do that?"

Amaya looked up at him as Harry came up on her other side. The Warrior clapped her on the shoulder, grinning widely. "Damn, girl. That was better than an Angel. They'll be talking about that for a thousand years!"

She shook her head, trying to reconcile what she was hearing with what she had experienced. "Deacon." Her voice was shaky.

Deacon looked down at her, concerned at her tone. "What is it? Did you drain yourself?"

"I didn't do that. I thought it was you."

Both men stopped walking. Deacon turned slowly until he was fully facing her. "I didn't do anything. Are you telling me that you didn't do what we all saw?"

Amaya shook her head, her ears ringing. "I didn't do that." She felt tears prickle her eyelids. "Deacon, my God! That was Him!"

Harry expelled a low whistle. "Holy shit. He does exist."

Deacon gaped at her, his heart pounding in her chest. "What does it mean?"

Tears were running freely down her cheeks as a wave of emotion swept through her. "It means we're going to be okay. He hasn't given up on us. He believes we can win." Laughing and crying at the same time, Amaya spun in a circle, her arms spread out to her sides. "It means we saw a miracle."

CHAPTER THIRTEEN

JANUARY 9TH, 2061

GULF OF AQABA

AMAYA DRESSED in the steely pre-dawn grayness. Sturdy hiking boots, khaki pants that zipped at the knee and thigh to become shorts, a black tank with a tan camp shirt overtop, and her hair plaited into a tight braid. As she checked over her bag to make sure it was stocked with supplies, she swore at her hands for shaking. Next to her, Deacon looked up from his identical task, concern in his eyes.

"You okay?"

She nodded. "Fine." Huffing, she sat back on her haunches and closed her bag. "I'm terrified and humbled and still reeling from last night. This all seems so much bigger now."

Deacon reached out and wrapped his fingers around hers. "I know exactly what you mean." He helped her to her feet and hugged her tightly. "Are you ready for this?"

Heart pounding in her chest, Amaya nodded. "I don't have a choice. I have to be ready for this." She snatched up her bag and shouldered it, strapping it across her chest. "I'm more nervous now than I was when we went into Purgatory."

"We knew what to expect down there. This is totally unknown. As far as we know, no one has been to the Garden since Adam and Eve. There's no way to tell whether we'll be the only living creatures there or whether we'll be hiding from dinosaurs and dragons."

She looked at him sharply over her shoulder as they descended the steps. "That's not even funny."

Deacon smiled wryly. "Who said I was joking?"

Harry was waiting for them at the bottom of the staircase. "Morning. Did either of you get any sleep?" When they both shook their heads, he grinned. "Neither did I." He gestured toward the door. "The monks are waiting on the bank. They've been out there since we arrived, preparing the water to transfer you into the Garden."

Amaya took a deep, trembling breath. "Then let's get this going."

Harry grabbed her arm. "Are you sure you're ready? This is really big, and I don't want you two to rush into something and get yourselves killed. I can spare a few Warriors to go with you. You don't have to do this alone."

"Yes, we do." Amaya squeezed his hand and pushed through the door. "You're doing your part in helping us get there. It's up to us to do the rest."

Deacon slapped the older man on the back as they walked. "We really appreciate everything you've done. Putting us up while she healed, feeding us, making sure we had supplies. It's above and beyond. I know you're short on everything as it is, but you made sure we had stuff to go do this. It's appreciated."

Harry pulled the door to the small house closed behind them. "My pleasure, guys." He stood back as the two Nephilim walked to the bank of the water, saying a quick prayer under his breath that they would make it back out alive before following.

Speaking to the monks in Turkish and Egyptian, he listened as they explained what was going to happen. Nodding and holding up a finger to keep them from continuing to talk, he turned to Deacon and Amaya to explain.

"They've said that the Gulf represents the entrance, but it's faith that will guarantee you safe passage through. They will take you into the water and baptize you in it. When they submerge you in the water, if your faith is strong enough, you will emerge in the Garden. If it is not, you'll be brought back above the surface and you aren't meant to cross over."

Deacon laughed. "Of course it's another test, just like everything else." He looked at Amaya, his eyes searching hers. "Good thing we both have some perspective on things after last night, huh?"

She smiled softly. "Mysterious ways and all that jazz." She stepped forward. "I'll go first."

Deacon took her arm. "Are you sure? I can go first. I don't mind."

Shaking her head, Amaya stepped into the water. "This is for me to do, Deacon." She gasped as the water turned from deep blue to blood red as she entered it. Looking over her shoulder to Harry, she lifted her eyebrows. "Did they do something to the water?"

Harry spoke to the monks rapidly before answering. "They say it's a sign that you're going to pass through. Baptism is a symbol of being washed in the blood of Christ. They consider this the embodiment of the promise God made to you that you would be washed through baptism. They don't think there's anything to worry about. This is all very exciting to them."

Amaya let the monks grip her by the arms and take her deeper into the water. They scooped up the red liquid and poured it over her head, murmuring prayers in a language she thought she recognized as Aramaic. She felt a gentle pressure against her knees and relaxed, allowing herself to float as the monks chanted and prayed.

In one smooth motion, one of the men clamped a hand over her nose and mouth, and she was plunged beneath the water, red engulfing her. Coughing and sputtering, she found the bottom of the river with her feet and stood, her head breaking the surface as she spit out water.

"What the hell, guys? You couldn't warn me?"

The rest of her outburst slid back down her throat as she realized she was alone. Instead of standing in a skinny strip of water in the desert, she was in a lush lagoon surrounded by thick greenery and brightly colored flowers. Above her, the branches moved with birds and monkeys, and in front of her was a thick carpet of dark green moss dotted with tiny white and pink flowers.

"Holy hell, I did it." Amaya hiked her pack higher on her shoulders and trekked out of the water, turning in a slow circle to take in her surroundings.

She had barely reached the bank before there was a large splash and Deacon was breaking the surface, scraping his hair out of his eyes and blinking rapidly as he tried to get his bearings. Relaxing when he saw Amaya, he walked from the water and dropped to the moss next to her, untying his wet boots to remove them.

"Seeing you disappear was fucking creepy." He looked around the jungle. "Any sign of things that can eat us?"

Amaya laughed and laid her socks next to herself to dry. "Not that I've seen yet, but I've only been here thirty seconds longer than you." She wiggled out of her wet camp shirt and laid it down. "We need to lay out all the wet stuff and let it dry, or we risk mold on everything in our bags and developing blisters on our feet from walking in wet boots."

Deacon nodded and began unpacking his bag. "Then it looks like here is home for the day. By the time everything dries, it'll be nearly dark if time is the same here as it is there."

"No reason to think it isn't." She stood to peel off her pants. "It'll only take an hour or two for our clothes to dry. The shoes will take a lot longer than that. We could venture a little ways barefoot, maybe find some fruit or something to eat."

Deacon glared at her. "We're in the fucking Garden of Eden. You're not eating any fruit off any tree, Amaya Winslow. There's no telling what bad things could happen if you picked the wrong one."

Laughter bubbled up from Amaya, and she laid back on the fragrant bed of moss. "I hadn't thought of it like that. Now that you mention it, our rations will be just fine." She propped herself up on her elbows. "Remind me what your dad said about how to find the Rod?"

"He said the Rod is at the entrance, but the only way to get it is to go through. That makes me think not everything in here is going to be as peaceful and quiet as it is right now or it wouldn't be much of a struggle to get it. The way Dad made it sound is that there's only one way through, so all we can do is keep moving forward." He wiggled his toes in the moss. "It's certainly pretty in here."

Amaya looked up at the sky and smiled. "Yes, it is." She rolled onto her side. "I feel like we're living in a fairytale right now. A magical land, a quest for a sword. This is something that should have been a movie fifty years ago."

"Maybe it will be someday." He jumped when a monkey swung from a low branch in one of the trees up to a higher one. "So much for us being alone in here."

"No one ever said we would be alone. We kind of assumed." She studied the water and the greenery. "I like how quiet it is in here."

Deacon frowned. "Don't get too attached. We're going straight through, and we're leaving right back out the way we came in."

Amaya laughed softly. "You have to admit it's nice not to be dodging bullets and demons for once in our lives. We're safe in here."

"As far as we know. That's no excuse to let our guard down." He cast a glance around the quiet jungle and the sparkling water. "I'm not convinced this place isn't just as deadly as Earth is."

"What's even supposed to be in here?" Amaya wiped sweat from her forehead as she followed Deacon up the slope of what had to be the tenth hill of the day. "So far I see trees, vines, monkeys, and some fish."

Deacon glanced over his shoulder. "Well, if you follow the Genesis version of events, Adam and Eve lived here until Lucifer convinced Eve to eat from the Tree of Knowledge. After, God cast them out and placed an Angel to guard the Tree of Life. I suppose it could stand to reason the Angel is still here. Maybe."

"If there's only one way through, we'll find out soon enough." She stopped to take a drink from the bottle of water on her belt. "It's fucking hot in here."

"It's the jungle. What did you expect?"

"Touché." She rubbed at the scar on her thigh and pushed herself to keep moving, the weight on her back starting to wear on her. "How is there a sun and moon in here? I thought we'd established this wasn't on Earth?"

"The same way there's day and night in Purgatory, I would think. It's adjacent to Earth and controlled by God, so we have day and night." Deacon drew to a stop at the top of the field and surveyed the slope downward that led into another patch of forest. "I swear everything looks the same. We could be going in circles for all I know."

"We're keeping the sun positioned so we're heading due North at all times. We aren't going in a circle unless the sun is also going in circles." Amaya dropped her pack onto the ground and held up her hand to shield her eyes from the bright light as she looked around. "I haven't seen any sign of human life in here, or Angels or demons. I don't think they're here."

"I'm beginning to agree with you, though we have to assume there's the one Angel guarding the tree until we're proven otherwise."

"Angels aren't a threat. They're on our side."

"Not all of them." He stooped to pull out an energy bar for each of them. Handing her one, he ripped into his own with gusto. "We know there are still some on Lucifer's side. I doubt the one that's been in the Garden of Eden for millions of years is among them, but you never know."

Amaya lowered herself to the ground and stretched her legs out in front of her. "If I didn't know better, I'd say it looks like rain."

Deacon looked up and studied the line of dark clouds against the horizon. "That's because it does. I imagine it can rain in here. There's vegetation and rivers and stuff. Those things need water to live."

"I kind of assumed they just always stay the same." She sighed as she chewed the chalky peanut butter bar. "This is disgusting."

"Yup." Cheerfully, he dropped next to her. "How's your leg holding up?"

"Sore, but I'm hanging in there." She flexed her thigh and winced when a bolt of pain streaked through the muscle. "It's only a couple more hours before we'll need to stop for the night. Less than that if we're going to get a storm."

"I'd like to get down into the forest before we stop. The cover will give us some extra protection from the weather aside from the tent."

"Agreed." She finished the energy bar and climbed to her feet, strapping her pack across her back and leading the way down the hill.

By the time they reached the bottom of the rocky slope, thunder rumbled in the distance and the clouds had rolled in, thick and black. Wind raced across the field to blow by them, and the leaves of the trees turned up, anxious for the promised rain. By silent consensus, both Amaya and Deacon quickened their pace, rushing for the tree line, trying to beat the quickly approaching storm.

They burst through the vines and entered the jungle together. Deacon used his machete to clear away the undergrowth from a spot between two large trees while Amaya unpacked the tent and supplies they would need. While she secured the nylon dwelling, he surveyed the area, venturing two hundred yards in every direction to check for threats before returning to the fully erected tent.

"There's no sense in putting out herbs or salt tonight. It'll wash away. We'll line the inside and put up wards, but that'll be the best that we can do."

"Did you sense anything?"

Deacon shook his head. "Not a thing. There's a small stream about a hundred and fifty feet west of here, but even if it floods its banks, I don't think it could do much damage. I didn't sense anything near us and nothing threatening at all. All the animals are all tucked away in their homes for the night."

Cold drops of rain broke through the canopy and splashed on them before they could get into the tent. Tossing their packs inside, Deacon ushered Amaya inside and zipped up the tent behind himself. She turned on a flashlight and unzipped the windows on the tent to allow some airflow and light in while he lined the edges with both salt and gunpowder before laying bundles of herbs on top.

"Are we good?" Amaya lifted her eyebrows questioningly.

"I think so." He sat back and shoved their packs into one corner, digging through his to pull out the thin solar blankets they had to use and the sleeping bags they shared. "Is the rain coming in through the windows?"

"Not right now. The canopy is giving us enough break from the wind that it's not blowing sideways at us. If it starts coming in, I'll zip them back up, but it gets really stuffy really fast with the tent completely closed."

"Even if it comes in sideways, rain can't come from four sides at once." Deacon unlaced his boots and tugged them off, placing them with their packs. "Might as well get comfortable. We're here for the night."

Amaya peeled off her boots and socks. "I'm going to lather our socks up with some soap and set them outside to get washed out. Both of my pairs are grimy and smelly." She rose to her knees to dig through the pack. "This is a good opportunity to do some laundry. Do you have anything that needs washed?" She cocked her head. "Is that stream big enough to wash clothes in?"

He chuckled. " It's six inches across, maybe. So, that's a no. As far as the clothes, we've been here two days, babe. We're both on our second set of clothes and those stink from sweat." Peering out one of the windows at the rain, he nodded. "Okay, we can spread things out in here enough to dry if we're careful with it. How's our soap situation?"

"We have two bars of soap and a small bottle of shampoo. We're okay." She crouched in the tent to shuck off her pants and then knelt to peel off her shirt, leaving her clad in simple cotton boyshorts and a sports bra. "I'll soap everything up and get it washed. You find me some good flat rocks to lay things on so they can get rinsed. If I put them on the ground, we'll have to deal with mud and dirt."

Deacon handed her a rifle and slung his own over his shoulder. "Keep an eye out. We don't want to let our guard down just because we think we're alone here."

Amaya scowled at him but took the weapon. "Neither of us have sensed a single being other than some animals since we got here. I think we're safe enough to do some laundry without getting murdered."

"Better safe than sorry." He held the door open for her. "Let's go get wet."

CHAPTER FOURTEEN

AMAYA CROUCHED in the rain, her hair soaked and plastered against her skin as she scrubbed Deacon's pants with the bar of soap. Deacon squatted next to her, a pair of socks laid across the rocks, bar of soap in his hand, working up suds in the fabric. Wrinkling her nose at the brown tinted foam, she grinned up at him.

"One of us had really smelly feet."

"I think we both did." He looked at the three pairs he'd already washed. "These were all equally bad."

"At least they'll be clean for tomorrow." She finished the pants and stretched them out on the rocks to be rinsed by the rain, standing to unfasten her bra and wiggle out of her underwear, her intention to wash both items. Not noticing Deacon staring at her, she began rubbing the soap into the sports bra. "If you take off your boxers, I'll wash them, too. I think the first batch of stuff should be about rinsed out. You could wring them out and lay them in the tent to dry if you want."

Deacon shook his head to clear it and stood up, stripping off his boxers and handing them to Amaya before gathering up the rinsed clothes and carrying them back to the tent. He twisted the pieces of fabric to expel the water gathered in them and ducked inside the tent to lay them out, taking care not to disturb the salt lines around the edges.

After determining that there was not enough space to dry their clothes on the floor of the tent, he dug through the packs until unearthing a length of rope. Fastening the ends to either side of the tent, he rigged a makeshift clothesline and hung the clothes up, going back outside twice to wring them out better when several pieces began dripping. After several minutes of work, he was satisfied that the job was done and returned to check on Amaya, who was finishing the underwear.

"Here, go lay these out. I'm going to wash off and scrub my hair while I've got a chance." She glanced over her shoulder as he took the garments from her. "The sun's going down and it's starting to get cool, so I'd recommend you do the same if you want to be clean."

Deacon headed for the tent, waving his arm when she yelled after him about finding her razor. He hung up the clothes, found her razor in the pack and spent a full sixty seconds debating how to go give it to Amaya without letting her see what the sight of her completely naked body had done to his penis.

After seriously contemplating the merits of wearing wet khakis out into the rain and considering whether or not he could venture out with one of the solar blankets around his waist, Deacon chided himself and left the tent, cursing his anatomy for being uncooperative the entire trek back to the edge of the wood-line.

Amaya was standing five feet from the rocks they had laid out, her arms raised above her head as she massaged shampoo through her hair with her face tilted up into the rain to keep the suds from getting into her eyes. Any progress he had made toward being flaccid was gone the moment the long lines of her bare body came into sight and he was able to feast upon the sight of her tanned skin, gentle curves, and sleek muscles.

Deacon raked his eyes over her, studying the column of her throat before allowing his gaze to dip down over her breasts. He took in every inch of skin, admiring the curve of the globes, their dusky peaks and the way her nipples jutted out in defiance against the cool raindrops. Beads of water ran down her skin, over her stomach, skating off what he knew were rock solid muscles covered with silky soft skin.

Amaya finished rinsing her hair and bent, picking up one of the bars of soap and rubbing it between her hands, working up a lather that she spread over herself, her hands skimming across her own shoulders, down over her breasts and down her body to her thighs and legs. Deacon nearly choked when one of her hands slipped between her own thighs to wash.

At his strangled gasp, she looked over her shoulder. "Something wrong?"

Deacon shook his head and jutted the razor in her direction. "I need to leave before my dick explodes." He laughed raggedly when she took the razor. "Seriously, you should not be allowed to do what you're doing right now."

Confused, she blinked up at him, the rain slowly washing the suds off her. The sight of white soap working its way down her slippery skin nearly made his eyes cross from desire. Amaya dropped the bar of soap onto the rocks and put her hands on her hips.

"I'm washing up, same as you should be. What's so bad about it?"

"I wish you could see yourself through my eyes, Maya. It's not as innocent as all that." He picked up the soap and retreated several feet. "I'll see you back at the tent. Be careful out here."

Bewildered, Amaya sat down on the rocks and ran soap across her legs to begin the process of shaving. By the time she finished the process, the sun was dipping beneath the horizon and the wind had turned from cool to cold. Chill bumps rose on her skin, and she gathered the soap and shampoo hurriedly, slinging her rifle over her shoulder and running back to the tent.

As she ducked her head and entered the tent, Amaya froze, a blush rising on her cheeks and heat pooling deep within her.

Deacon was laying on their sleeping bags, his eyes closed and one of his fists vigorously pumping up and down on his bulging erection. Noting with curiosity that he had not only brought condoms with them into the Garden of Eden but was wearing one, she cleared her throat to announce her presence.

Deacon jumped and jerked, hitting his head on the ropes holding their clothes and letting go of himself so quickly that he ripped the latex off himself and flung it in her direction. Amused, Amaya gingerly picked up the condom and laid it outside the tent before zipping the door and wrapping the soap she held in the plastic wrap it had been in.

"Amaya." Deacon's voice was strangled and his face blood red. "It wasn't what it looked like." He trailed off meekly.

Amaya laughed and looked over at him, her wet hair hanging

down her back in ropes. "I suppose we should have some sort of a sign, like hanging a sock on the outside of the tent if we want privacy or something." She giggled at the thought. "I didn't mean to interrupt your—uh—festivities." She knelt next to him and refastened the rope to the edge of the tent, her breasts swaying as she moved. "Do you want me to go back outside?"

Deacon shoved one of the solar blankets at her. "I want you to stop being naked."

Hurt flooded her eyes and she wrapped the material around herself. "Sorry. I didn't think it bothered you."

"You walk in on me jacking off and you don't think it bothers me?" He snorted. "For Christ sake, I've got a hard-on so stiff I could drill for oil. I need you covered if I want any hope of it going away."

Amaya blinked rapidly as the reason for demanding her coverage with the blanket sank in. Smiling, she dropped the blanket to the floor and reached out, placing her hands on Deacon's hips.

"Or, alternatively, you could, just maybe, possibly, put it to use." With each word, she eased closer until their bodies were aligned, his erection pressing into her belly, the velvety softness of the head of his penis brushing against the silk of her skin. "There's no one here for me to blow up."

Deacon closed his eyes and laid his hands over hers, squeezing her fingers gently. "I don't want you to do anything unless you're sure about it. It'll go away on its own. It won't be the first time my penis misbehaves, and I doubt it's going to be the last."

Amaya laughed at that. "I want to. I wanted to at Saint Catherine's, but there was a good reason not to. That reason doesn't exist here. We're alone, in a tent in the jungle with no other human being in this dimension—on this plane—whatever you want to call it. It doesn't get more remote. As long as you're sure you're not scared of me."

He shook his head. "I've never been scared of you. Your power doesn't worry me." He ran his hands up her arms to grip her shoulders gently. "I didn't want the first time to be on the hard ground in the middle of a storm after we've just done laundry caveman style and you walked in on me masturbating. I figured I'd take you somewhere remote and beautiful, and it would be slow and sweet and gentle."

A grin split her face, and she leaned up to brush her lips across his collarbone. "Welcome to our life. We don't always get what we want, and we have to make do with what we have." She gently pulled his hips into hers. "I want you, Deacon, and as long as I can have that, I don't need the rest." She lifted her eyes to meet his, rich green locking on icy blue. "Are you going to make me ask again?"

Deacon shook his head. "No." He dipped his head and laid his mouth against her throat, flicking his tongue against her skin. "I'm not a fool, and only a fool would make a woman like you ask twice."

Amaya lifted her hands to his shoulders and ran her palms over his skin, sliding them around to his back. He was paler than her, and his white hair was a stark contrast against her pitch black. Physically, they were complete opposites. Her dark to his light. Dusky tan to creamy pale. Pale blond to rich black. Sharp blue against emerald green.

Deacon nudged her back onto the sleeping bags, pressing her onto her back and laying on his side next to her. He braced himself on one arm, the other hand cupping the side of her face as he leaned down, capturing her mouth with his own. Gently, he parted her lips with his tongue and delved, her taste blooming on his tongue and flooding him with her essence.

Slowly, he slipped his hand from her cheek to her shoulder, massaging the flesh beneath his fingers. They trailed down slowly, brushing over her collarbone and the side of her breast before sliding up and finding her nipple. Amaya gasped at the touch, her body arching into his ministrations and her eyes drifting closed as a bolt of pleasure rocketed through her body.

He peppered kisses over her neck and throat, working his way down her body until he fastened his mouth on the other breast, drawing her nipping in with his tongue and teeth. He rubbed his tongue over the tightly beaded tip, tasting the remnants of rain on her skin as he sucked gently.

Amaya's hands fisted in the sleeping bags and she struggled to hold on to control. She felt a tidal wave of emotion as he feasted on her body with both his mouth and hands. Each stab of his tongue or scrape of his teeth sent a spear straight through her, making her ache for more and fear what it would bring.

Deacon released the breast he'd been stimulating with his fingers and continued his journey downward, dancing his fingertips over her stomach and hip before sliding them between her thighs and stroking gently over the juncture. When he nudged her legs apart, she opened them, allowing him to take possession of her with his hand, his fingers spreading the lips to her body and one digit sliding inside while the heel of his hand pressed against her clit, rubbing gently back and forth to give her stimulation.

Amaya sucked in a ragged breath at the foreign penetration and let herself float away on waves of desire. Her body tightened and loosened with his ministrations. The slight stubble on his jaw rubbed the skin on her breast as he released her nipple and nuzzled her gently before slipping downward.

Deacon stroked her with his hand, learning which movements made her gasp and groan until he had her panting and on edge. Only when he knew she was close to the cusp of orgasm did he withdraw his hand and lift himself to his knees, positioning himself between her legs.

Amaya forced herself to sit up, her eyes clouded with need, and stared up at him. "What's wrong?"

Deacon leaned over her, placing one hand on either side of her and gently pushing her back down. "Not a thing." He kissed her deeply, letting his tongue wander through her mouth until they were both out of breath. Sitting back up, he laid his hands on her knees. "Tonight is about you. All about you. I want to make this as special as I can, given the circumstances." He gazed at her, those icy blue eyes burning into hers. "I want to make sure you're ready for this, Maya. I don't want it to hurt."

She shook her head. "It won't. I told you. I've used vibrators and things."

"I know what you said. I just want to make sure." He very deliberately placed her feet on the sleeping bags. "I want to taste you. Will you let me get you off that way before we do this? Just to make sure you enjoy everything."

Touched by his slightly awkward request, she nodded. "If you're sure you want to."

"Oh, I want to." He adjusted his position between her legs, his hands gripping her ass. "Just enjoy, baby. I want you to enjoy this."

The first touch of his mouth to her thigh made her jump at the unfamiliar sensation. Amaya closed her eyes and tried to get used to the feeling of having someone's head between her legs. All thoughts of it being awkward slipped away when he touched his tongue to her, using his fingers to give himself access to her clit.

His mouth was warm and his tongue wet. He slid against her flesh, expertly working her up the crest of orgasm. Amaya lifted her hips, pressing herself against him, silently begging him to keep going. Deacon licked and sucked, using both tongue and mouth to bring her as much pleasure as he could. Slowly, he slipped one finger inside her body, thrusting gently as he laved attention on her, feeling a deep sense of satisfaction when he felt her contract and pulse around him, her body growing hot and wet as he brought her closer to climax.

Over and over he brought her to the edge then let her slide back down only to drive her up again without letting her fall over. Only when her whole body was covered in a thin sheen of sweat and her breaths were coming in shallow pants did he have mercy on her and push her over, watching as her body tightened and jerked as orgasm coursed through her.

Her eyes rolled back in her head and her muscles tensed and released. Outside, the rain pounded against the tent, and thunder sounded in the distance. The sky split with a bolt of lightning, illuminating her face in an ethereal light.

Before she had completely come back down, Deacon reached into his pack and drew out the box of condoms, tearing into one and rolling it over his erection. Lifting her hips in his hands, he positioned himself against her body and slipped inside slowly, easing into her inch by inch, taking care to make sure that his penetration was slick and easy.

Amaya gasped and grabbed his arms, her nails gripping his skin. Worried, Deacon stilled and stared down at her, his eyes belying his concern.

"Are you okay?"

Nodding, she wiggled her hips. "It feels good."

"Did I hurt you?"

"No." She forced herself to loosen her grip on his arms and stroked her palms up and down. "You didn't hurt me."

Deacon lowered himself until one hand was braced next to her head and the other was holding her hip to keep her lower body positioned where he wanted it. Locking his eyes onto hers, he began to move slowly, thrusting himself in and out gently, his body driving into hers at an infuriatingly slow pace.

Amaya hitched her legs up to wrap about his hips, anchoring their bodies closer together. She was wet around him, her body pulsing with each stroke. Her eyes drifted shut and her head fell to the side, exposing her neck. Outside, the storm raged around them, thunder and lightning ripping through the sky as rain pelted the tent.

She felt her power surging to the surface, and the ground shook as she struggled to control it. Losing focus on Deacon and their lovemaking, she clamped down on her power, concentrating on keeping it in check even as emotion and pleasure whipped up within her. Sensing the change, Deacon stroked his hand over her face.

"What's wrong?"

Struggling to control herself, Amaya blinked rapidly. "We need to stop. I can't stop it."

Deacon stared down into her eyes. "Yes you can." He held her hips still and stopped moving within her. "Look at me, Maya. Trust me. Be with me. You can do this." He dipped his head to press his mouth to hers gently.

"I don't want to hurt you!"

"You won't." He laid his head against her neck, every muscle in his body rock hard as he tried not to move. "Just relax. Trust me to handle it, honey. I've got you. I'm not going to let anything bad happen. I've got this."

Slowly, Deacon began moving again, thrusting methodically. Amaya's thighs fell open and her head tipped back. Lightning lit up the sky, thunder rolled, and the wind howled. A groan tore its way from her throat, and her body pulsed as she worked her way toward orgasm. Carefully, he allowed his own powers to ramp up, laying them on top of hers, forming the two together until he matched hers exactly, pressing himself against her in every way to ensure that she was controlled. If she wanted to, she could break through it easily. They both knew she was more powerful than he was, but he had the better control. Deacon's hope was that in the throes of passion, his power would be enough to manage the surge that escaped hers.

As his climax build, he pressed his face into her neck and drove his hips faster, pumping himself in and out. Amaya's hands stroked up and down his back as her body hugged him tightly. She exploded around him, clamping down on him as orgasm erupted within her. With a ragged yell, he followed her off the cliff, her orgasm triggering his own, and collapsed on top of her, his heart pounding and his breath coming in great heaving gasps.

After several moments, Amaya's voice sounded in the dark tent. "Well, I didn't blow anything up."

Laughter bubbled out of Deacon's chest and he rolled onto his side, withdrawing from her and removing the condom, tucking it back into the ripped package before setting it in the corner of the tent.

"No, you didn't blow anything up. I told you it would be fine." He drew her close and tucked her against his side, pressing a kiss to the side of her head. "Do you feel okay?"

Nodding, she rolled to wrap an arm around his waist. "I feel heavy and lazy and sleepy, but no different." She drew her finger across his chest idly. "Do you think people are going to be surprised that we're doing whatever we're doing?"

Deacon chuckled. "Do you need a label?"

She shook her head emphatically. "Not at all. I also don't want to call it something it's not and stick my foot deep inside my mouth." Smiling up at him, she stretched up for a lingering kiss. "Michael won't be. Neither will Dev, obviously, since he saw us. Zeke and Lux know."

"I think everyone knows, Maya." He ran his fingers through her hair. "If they don't, they're blind. We've been circling each other for years."

"I know." She stared at the wall of the tent, her eyelids getting heavy. "Thank you for making sure I didn't kill us both."

Grinning, Deacon yanked one of the sleeping bags up to cover their naked bodies. "I'm always going to take care of you. Don't worry about that." He kissed her forehead. "I love you too much to let anything happen to you."

Sleepy, she burrowed in closer. "Do you think we'll find the Angel tomorrow?"

"I hope so. The sooner we find the Angel, the sooner we get back to Earth. As nice as it is not to worry about getting slaughtered while we sleep, I also hate being unable to be in contact with our families. It makes me nervous." He adjusted his free arm beneath his head. "Get some sleep. Everything will keep until tomorrow."

CHAPTER FIFTEEN

THEY FOUND the Tree of Life and the Angel late the next day. After eight hours of hacking through the seemingly impenetrable jungle, Amaya and Deacon broke through into a field that stretched as far as they could see with nothing in it except for one tree.

The tree was so large that they could make it out from nearly a mile away. By the time they drew within a hundred yards, it was easy to tell that the tree stretched several hundred feet into the air. Its trunk was so thick Amaya thought it would have taken ten people holding hands to surround it. The limbs were thick, heavily leaved, and hung low with a strange red, purple, and orange fruit that looked to them like the embodiment of a sunset. Standing at the base of the tree, his hand on the hilt of a flaming sword, was an Angel.

The Angel wore nothing but a loincloth. Even his feet were bare. His hair was silver and flowed down his back, nearly hitting his waist in a straight sweep. His wings were charcoal gray, indicating that he was an Archangel. As Amaya and Deacon approached, the Angel lifted the sword and spoke, his voice booming to fill the field.

"Identify yourselves. I am Jophiel, Archangel of the Lord God. You have trespassed in His Garden and will be punished by His sword."

Deacon pushed Amaya behind him, muttering under his breath. "At least he speaks English."

"Angels speak whatever you speak, you know that." She shoved her way back out and stepped forward. "I am Amaya, daughter of Archangel Gabriel. This is Deacon, son of Michael the Archangel. We are here to retrieve Aaron's rod."

The Angel glared at them. "Step forward, daughter of Gabriel. I will look into your soul and see your truth."

Fearlessly, Amaya stepped forward and allowed the Angel to place his hand on her head. After several seconds, he stepped back, inclining his head at her.

"Yours is a pure mission, daughter of Gabriel. How is your father? It has been many millennia since I have laid eyes on my old friend. And you, son of Michael? How fares your father?"

Deacon answered. "Michael is doing fine. He's leading the Nephilim in war against Cambion. Lucifer is free on Earth. We're trying to stop him. That's why we need the rod."

Jophiel's brow creased. "How can that be? The Choosing would certainly have eliminated the need for the Apocalypse. Did the Chosen refuse to make the Choice?"

Amaya shook her head. "She Chose. Lucifer found a loophole. He managed to get the Hellgate open and got loose. It's war up there. The Angels are behind the Gates and aside from a few who have defied God's orders to help us, we've been on our own until recently. God has sent us to retrieve the Rod and use it against Lucifer. I'm supposed to be able to kill him."

"The only being that could truly kill the King of Hell is one who blends together human, Devil, and Angel. Tell me child, who is your mother?"

"My mother is Alaria, a Devil made human. She betrayed Lucifer during the Choosing in return for the Chosen to request her life from God as reward." Amaya smiled sadly. "I am all three."

"Does your father know you are here?" Jophiel leaned his sword on the tree. "I find it hard to believe Gabriel allowed his progeny to come to the Garden alone."

Her eyes directed downward, Amaya spoke softly. "My father died trying to kill Lilith. He's been gone a few months."

Jophiel closed his eyes for a long moment before speaking. "I am sorry for the loss of your father. Your grief is palpable. Please accept my condolences." He laid his hand on her shoulder. "Your father was a good friend and a fierce warrior. He would be honored to know his daughter is carrying on a legacy of honorable service to our Lord." He stepped back. "I am equally sure that your father is proud of you, Deacon. Michael is one I am lucky to call my brother."

Amaya cleared her throat, uncomfortable with the exchange. "Can you help us get the Rod?"

"I can, and I shall. First, however, I shall assist you with the rest of your task. You have been visited by the Eternal Spirit of God, have you not?"

Amaya thought of the scene at the foot of the mountain. "We saw something. I think it was God."

"To arrive in the Garden, you must be baptized and cleansed in blood, yes?"

Deacon nodded. "Yes, in the Gulf of Aqaba. It turned to blood when the monks took us there."

"You must also be purified through fire. In order to remove the Rod from the ground and pass through the exit back to Earth, you must be purified through my sword. I will touch you with it, and if you have sufficient faith to complete your task, you will be purified and declared worthy. If not, you will be turned to ash."

Fear bolted through Amaya's chest. "No one mentioned that we might get killed by an Angel in the Garden when we were asked to come here."

Jophiel cocked his head to the side. "You had the faith necessary to enter into the Garden. Do you doubt you have the faith to pass this test?"

Deacon laid his pack on the ground. "The worst thing that could happen if we failed that one is that we stayed in Egypt. If we fail at this one, we die. Besides, what if the standards are different?"

"If you possess the amount of faith as is in a mustard seed, you can move mountains, son of Michael. You who are the son of the Angel of War, do you doubt your Heavenly Father or your mission? Do you doubt that you are submitting to a Heavenly quest?"

"No."

"Then you have nothing to fear." The Angel grasped his sword and lifted it. "Which of you will go first?"

They spoke in unison. "I will."

Jophiel smiled. "Daughter of Gabriel, step forward. This is your mission more than it is your companion's. You will go first, and if you fail, he will take up your task in your stead." He waited until she had dropped her pack on the ground and taken three steps forward. "By the fire of my sword, I cleanse you in the name of God the Father, God the Son, and God the Holy Spirit."

Amaya gasped as the flames touched one of her shoulders and then the other. They surrounded her, leeching into her body and warming her until every inch of her tingled. She watched as the flames retreated from her body and back down the blade of the sword. A satisfied smile on his face, Jophiel lifted it and looked her in the eye.

"You have the required amount of faith, child. You have been purified by flame and declared worthy of the mission you are on." He turned to Deacon. "Step forward, son of Michael, and face your test."

Amaya watched with a knot of fear in her stomach as Deacon went through the same thing. When the flame moved from his body back onto the blade and he was left unburned, she expelled the breath she hadn't realized she'd been holding and rushed forward to grab his hand in hers.

"We did your test. Will you take us to the Rod now?"

Jophiel laughed. "There is no need to rush, child. You are not finished here." He reached up and plucked a piece of fruit from the tree, extending it to her. "Eat."

Amaya stared at the sunset like fruit and shook her head. "Oh, no. Bad things happen when you eat off trees in the Garden of Eden. I'm not falling for that trick. I'm smarter than Eve." She clasped her hands behind her back. "No way, no how."

Jophiel lifted his eyebrows. "I find your language most amusing." He sighed deeply and thrust the fruit at her again. "There are only unfortunate consequences when humans eat from trees they have been told not to eat from. Eve ate from the Tree of the Knowledge of Good and Evil. This is the Tree of Life. Eat from this tree, and you will partake of God's grace. This is close to—" He struggled to find the words that would make them understand what he was trying to understand. "—eating Heaven." he finished lamely. "That is not what I want to say, but I am unfamiliar with your vernacular."

"What will it do to me?"

"Were you told at the beginning of your quest that you had to be made ready to take in the Heavenly Spirit in order to defeat Lucifer?"

Amaya jerked her shoulder. "Something to that effect. I figured it was just talk. Most of the crap we deal with is."

"Eating from the Tree of Life allows one to literally take in God's grace. It's something no mortal other than Adam and Eve have ever done. It will allow you to take in the power of Heaven and wield it through the Rod in order to smite Lucifer and strike him down."

Deacon barked a laugh. "Eating Heaven was pretty close. Remember when Gabe told us that we had to become pure vessels and harness God's power?"

She nodded. "Vaguely. Why?"

"I think this is what Jophiel is saying, just in a more Biblical way. Basically, we've proven ourselves pure, now we have to eat Heaven~the fruit~and when the time comes, we'll be able to use the power we need to kill Lucifer and Lilith." He turned to the Angel. "Will this make us immortal?"

Jophiel shook his head. "No. You would only remain immortal as long as you continued to eat of the Tree of Life. If you wished to live in the Garden and dine on the flesh of the Tree daily, then you could live forever, but just eating of it once will do nothing to your natural life expectancy."

Amaya looked at Deacon. "No one said we'd have to do this, but no one told us we'd meet an Archangel with a flaming sword, either." She looked back to the Angel. "I hate to sound like I don't trust you, but how do I know this isn't a trick? We both know the story about Lucifer appearing to Eve and convincing her to eat fruit she wasn't supposed to eat. I don't want to do anything to jeopardize this."

Jophiel smiled softly. "Child, I am an Angel of the Lord. I would not lead you wrong. I was stationed here by God to shield the Garden from those who wish to use the flesh of the tree for their own designs. Your companion knows the story. Your fathers are my brothers. I understand your reluctance to do anything you view as a threat to your mission, but I can assure you that I mean you no harm, and nothing I would have you do will be unfavorable to my father."

Deacon ran his hand over his jaw. "Adam and Eve had also been specifically told not to eat off the trees. No one told us not to."

"Actually, son of Michael, they were encouraged to eat from the Tree of Life daily. It was the Tree of the Knowledge of Good and Evil that was forbidden to them. As descendants of Adam and Even through your human parent, you have already eaten of that tree. You know right from wrong, good from evil. You are able to choose your own path. When Eve ate of the fruit and convinced Adam to do the same, they were banished from the garden because to continue to eat of the Tree of Life after the Tree of Knowledge was forbidden as that person would then be able to harness the power of Heaven and use it. In your particular case, harnessing the power of Heaven is why you are here."

Amaya and Deacon exchanged a long look. After several seconds, Amaya shrugged and sighed deeply. "If something were wrong with what he was telling us, I have to believe that we'd be getting a sign of some sort. If they sent us in here unprepared for what we would find and we made a mistake because we ran into an Archangel who led us wrong, well then, that's something they're just going to have to deal with." She turned to Jophiel. "Do both of us need to eat or just me?"

"You are on this quest together, so both will partake of the flesh of the Tree." He plucked a second fruit for Deacon.

"But Deacon isn't human. Will that affect him differently?"

Jophiel lifted one eyebrow. "What do you mean by that statement? Is he not Nephil? Being Nephil necessitates being the child of an Angel and a human."

Deacon shook his head. "Michael is my father and Lilith is my mother."

"Lilith the second in command in Lucifer's army?" Jophiel closed his eyes and a look of pain washed over his face. "Oh brother, how far have you fallen to have carnal relations with a Devil?" He turned to Deacon. "Does your father still serve God?"

"My father is leading the Nephilim army against the Cambion and Devils. He is one of few Angels fighting on Earth. Lilith betrayed him. He has parted ways with Heaven, but not because of my existence. He disagreed with the decision to have the Host retreat behind the Gates and let the Nephilim fight on their own, and he disagreed with the decision to allow Angels to impress their essence upon human women to create Nephilim without their consent."

Jophiel looked pained. "I fear there is much I have missed during my time here." He handed them each a piece of fruit. "Eat quickly and I will take you to the Rod. After that, I will accompany you from the Garden and meet with my brother to determine how I might be of help in this war. My time here is of no use if Earth falls to Lucifer while I stand guard in a place that has long since been forgotten by those who wish to use it for evil."

Amaya bit into the fruit, her teeth piercing the skin and flavor erupting on her tongue. It tasted like a hybrid of peach and watermelon. She chewed slowly, apprehensively waiting to see what was going to happen to her. Beside her, Deacon did much the same, taking a bite, chewing slowly, waiting, then taking another.

After finishing the piece of fruit, she wiped the remaining juice on her pants and turned to the Angel. "I don't feel any different."

"You're not supposed to. You'll know what to do when the time comes." Jophiel slid his sword into a scabbard at his waist and began walking, his wings tucked tightly to his back. "Follow me. The Rod isn't far." He glanced over his shoulder. "Tell me, what garb will I need to appear as my brethren do in your time? It is our custom to appear in a manner humans are comfortable with."

Amaya fell into step on one side of him, with Deacon flanking her other side. "Most Angels I've ever seen wear suits. Michael's the most casual I've ever seen and he wears a buttondown and slacks with no jacket."

"This suit you speak of is some form of garment similar to that which the two of you wear?"

Deacon chuckled. "It's a dressier version. You'll see when we get to Dad's."

Jophiel led them through the field and back into the jungle. After two hours of hiking, the vegetation thinned and they emerged in the same clearing that they had come into when they had crossed into Eden from the Sinai Peninsula. In the middle of the river was an island with a sword sticking out of it.

Amaya cocked her head to the side. "Somehow I thought it would look more majestic than that."

Jophiel smiled indulgently. "The blade is made of sapphire, daughter of Gabriel. The handle was forged in the bowels of Hell. There is no weapon in existence more magnificent than the one you are about to grasp." He nudged her forward. "Go forth and withdraw it from the earth. Seize your destiny, Nephil."

Amaya took her boots off and rolled her pant legs up before splashing out into the shallow water. She climbed up onto the island and approached the sword's handle, noting the intricate carving on the handle. The metal shimmered and glittered in the sunlight. Beneath her bare feet, the ground trembled and shook gently, and the air around her hummed with energy. The blade was buried in the ground so deeply that she couldn't see anything other than the handle.

Grasping the sword in her left hand, she jumped when a bolt of electricity traveled up her arm to her shoulder, staying there until the entire appendage thrummed with energy. Closing her eyes and sending up a quick prayer that it worked, she gritted her teeth and yanked, falling backward into the water as the blade easily left the dirt and emerged into her hands.

The Rod's blade was deep blue, almost opaque and glimmered in the light, catching the rays of sun and reflecting them out into the clearing. Intricate carvings ran down either side of the sword, showing the story of Moses and Aaron in pictographs. As she watched, the images all shifted upward, compressing and miniaturizing. A new image formed near the tip of a woman drawing the blade from the earth and Amaya recognized herself in it.

Amazed, she looked back at Deacon and Jophiel. "I got it!"

Jophiel laughed warmly. "Did you doubt, Nephil?"

She climbed to her feet and slogged back to the bank. "I always doubt until I have something in my hand." She clenched her free fist to form a scabbard and secured the sword at her hip. "Now how do we get out of here?"

Deacon frowned. "At least take a minute to put on dry clothes and your shoes."

"I agree with the son of Michael."

Amaya put her hands on her hips and turned to the Angel. "If we're going to be together for a while, could you please call us Amaya and Deacon?"

Jophiel inclined his head. "I will make an effort to address you by your given names." He turned to walk away. "I will bring up the door back to Earth while you change."

Amaya changed quickly and was lacing her boots when Jophiel returned, a worried look on his face. Picking up on it, too, Deacon laid his hand on his rifle. "What's wrong? Please don't tell me we're stuck here."

"We are not stuck. I was able to bring up the door to the other side. However, I sense a powerful presence on the other side. I believe we will be exiting the Garden and going directly into an ambush. Prepare yourselves for battle. Azazel and Abalam have come for the Rod."

CHAPTER SIXTEEN

AMAYA'S FIST clenched at her side, and she was transformed into her battle garb of black leather tights, knee-high stiletto boots and a red leather bustier. In one hand she held a whip and in the other a gleaming sword. Deacon removed his pack and stripped off his shirt, allowing the tattoos that ran down his sides to erupt into wings--pitch black with red tips--that he folded against his sides. In one hand he held a sword and in the other a battle axe. Each had a rifle on their backs. Amaya kept the Rod strapped to her hips.

Jophiel made an approving noise in his throat. "I see you have both been in battle before. That is good." He led them to the door, which had appeared in the side of a stone cliff. "I want for you both to stick close to me when we get on the other side. I don't know quite how many demons and Cambion there are on the other side, but there are two Devils. Our goal is to get through the soldiers they have brought without them getting the Rod. Once we are free, we must go directly to Michael."

Deacon nodded. "We know how this is done. It's you who hasn't had to do anything with that sword in a few million years."

"I assure you that my skills are unrivaled with my weapon." Jophiel looked at Deacon drolly. "I fought with both your fathers when Lucifer led the siege against Heaven. I've not forgotten how to wield my sword. Are you both prepared to die today?"

Amaya grasped the handle of the door. "Let's hope it doesn't come to that."

He smiled. "You look so much like your mother. Let us all hope you are as effective on the field of battle as was she."

Amaya smirked as she yanked open the door. "I don't think you'll be disappointed."

The three emerged into the desert shoulder to shoulder, weapons raised. They were met with an onslaught of bullets. With a wave of his hand, Jophiel sent them flying into the sand. Abalam held up his hand to stop the Cambion from firing.

"Jophiel. What are you doing outside the Garden? Is God's golden boy leaving his post?" The Devil grinned and tapped his cowboy boot in the dust. "Did you get horny while you were in there? Need some nookie?"

Jophiel looked at Abalam with a scowl. "You've not changed, Abalam, and your presence is still distasteful to me." He lowered his blade slightly. "It has come to my attention that my presence is needed more on Earth than it is in the Garden. The greeting my companions and I are receiving reinforces that belief." He lifted his voice to speak to the group of Cambion and demons. "Flee now, sons of Devils and demons, and your lives will be spared. Stay and fight and you will know the bite of my blade."

Azazel laughed as he sauntered forward. "Do you really think you stand a chance against all of us? Twenty Cambion, a dozen demons, and two Devils, and there are two Nephilim and one rusty Angel who hasn't done anything other than stand under a tree for a couple million years. Yeah, we'll all just run and hide."

Not understanding sarcasm, Jophiel nodded. "That would be wise. We'll allow you to flee." He frowned when his statement was met with laughter. "This is not humorous. If you do not go now, your lives will undoubtedly be lost." He turned back to Azazel and Abalam. "Do you not remember how strong I am? I was Michael's second in command during the Fall."

Deacon filed that bit of information away for later use. He twitched his wings and tensed in anticipation of the inevitable battle. Amaya was on his other side, her stance relaxed and her grip steady on her weapons. He'd never seen anyone more comfortable charging into battle than she was.

Abalam chewed on his lip thoughtfully. "I remember how you could fight. You slayed hundreds of my brothers and sisters during the fall. You're part of the reason why there's only a few dozen Devils left and only three of the Archangel Devils left living. Well, four if you count the bitch's mother, but since Alaria's human now, I don't count her at all." He smiled. "Regardless, you didn't manage to kill either one of us, and there are two of us and one of you. I'm willing to take my chances that the army I brought can take out two Nephilim."

Jophiel looked at Amaya and Deacon. "They do not appear to see reason. I fear we must kill them all." He patted Deacon on the shoulder. "Take care not to die in the upcoming battle. I will take care of Azazel and Abalam. The two of you must destroy the others. Is that acceptable?"

Before Deacon could answer, Azazel sighed. "Enough with the chatting. Get the sword!"

Amaya barely had time to brace herself before she was surrounded with Cambion. Knowing she was stronger than most of them, she threw out her whip and used it to slash through the air, ripping through flesh wherever it touched. Deacon had dropped both his weapons and anchored his rifle to his shoulder, picking off Cambion as they rushed her, his finger steady on the trigger and his aim second to no one she had ever met.

Blood splattered Amaya's face as Deacon shot one of the Cambion that had managed to get too close to her. Bullets whizzed by her as they tried to shoot her. Jophiel kept sending the projectiles spinning uselessly into the sand.

The Angel had his flaming sword in one hand and a regular blade in the other. His silver hair blew in the breeze, streaming out behind him as he twirled both swords expertly and parried both Azazel and Abalam at the same time, fighting both Devils off.

The desert greedily lapped up the blood from the bodies that dropped to the ground. Some had bullet holes, others were bleeding from wide, gaping sword wounds. Amaya kicked one demon in the knee that managed to get too close before running it through with her sword and pivoting to face another, thrusting the sword again without having the time to withdraw it from the ribcage of the first demon.

When the weapon didn't come free with one jerk, she let it fall to the ground with the two bodies and planted her feet in the dirt, lashing her whip at the Cambion charging her. She wrapped the weapon around the throat of one and dragged it to her, drawing a slim dagger from her hip holster that she used to slit its throat before casting aside yet another body.

Deacon had run out of ammo and tossed his gun aside, stooping to pick up the axe he preferred. His first swing buried the edge in the skull of a Cambion. One jerk freed the blade and he swung it at the next, severing a hand from its connecting wrist before ending another life with a swipe of metal and wood.

He threw his elbow back, crashing it into the nose of a demon before bending and jerking his opponent over his shoulder and throwing it to the ground, stepping on its windpipe and swinging downward with the axe, spitting blood when it splashed into his mouth. Three Cambion charged him in unison and he held up a hand, throwing out a wave of power and tossing them back, reaching into them and clamping down on their windpipes, slowly crushing their throats until all three collapsed to the ground dead.

Several demons had already fled as they saw their numbers dwindling. Jophiel was viciously battling Azazel and Abalam, though when he saw that Amaya and Deacon were nearly done with the Cambion and demons, he backed up, allowing the two Devils to charge him. As they got close to him, Jophiel dropped to his knees and slashed up with his sword, running both Devils through with the blades.

"Quickly, Nephilim, I need your blood to send their essence to Hell. It will buy us some time before they can escape and report to Lucifer about what has happened here."

Amaya used her dagger to slash at her arms and dashed over, forcing one arm to each of the Devils, her blood choking them as their human bodies died. Their eyes flashed black and red, signaling that the spirit was descending to Hell before the host body collapsed onto the ground in a heap. Jophiel straightened and brushed dust and blood from his chest. He cast a glance around and nodded approvingly at the bodies and the now empty desert.

"You both fight remarkably well." He picked up his flaming sword and holstered it. "Are either of you injured?"

Deacon shook his head. "I'm good, I think."

Amaya nodded. "Just bumps and bruises. Nothing serious to report." She kicked Azazel's body with her boot. "I wish we could really kill them instead of just getting rid of them for a few hours."

Jophiel narrowed his eyes. "Do you not have the Spear of Destiny in your possession? It can be used to kill multiple Devils aside from Lucifer."

Deacon shook his head. "It's in Atlantis. That's the next thing we're going to go get." He slapped the Angel on the shoulder. "Let's get you to Dad. I want to be out of here before they come back."

"I concur. It is likely they would have many more soldiers the next time. They did not realize I would be accompanying you out of the Garden. Without my presence, I do not know if you would have survived this battle."

Amaya laughed. "We'd have done our best, but ambushes are no fun." She looked at Deacon. "I guess one of them must have gotten away when we fought the sentries on our way in to Saint Catherine's."

Deacon scowled. "Or they knew we would need the sword and have been hanging back just out of range and waiting for us to make a move for it. They're smart, Maya. We can't underestimate Lucifer."

Jophiel nodded in solidarity. "To do so would be deadly." He looked around. "Which way to your father's home?"

Deacon reached out and touched the Angel's forehead. "Let's go."

Michael came down the stairs when he sensed Deacon flashing into the house. Torn between concern and happiness, he loped down the steps and came to a stop on the landing, his face splitting into a grin.

"Jophiel. What are you doing here?" He rushed forward to embrace the other Angel.

Jophiel returned the embrace enthusiastically. "Brother, it is so good to see you. I've fought in battle with your son. You have much reason to be proud of him. He has honored you as his father. His skills during war are sharp and his aim true."

Michael embraced Deacon next, then Amaya. "I'm glad you're back safe. Did you get the Rod?"

Amaya patted the scabbard on her hip. "We had a welcoming committee when we came back through. Azazel and Abalam knew we were in the Garden and were waiting for us."

Michael sighed deeply and dropped into one of the chairs in the living room, gesturing for the others to sit. "I wish that were totally unexpected. Lucifer is very intelligent. It's not surprising that he figured out what weapon could kill him. We're fortunate they weren't able to find a way into the garden before we got to the Rod."

Jophiel perched awkwardly on the couch, unsure what he was sitting on or how to do so in his loincloth. "They would have never gotten past me, Michael. Surely you know I would have battled to the death."

"Depending on who they sent, it would have just as likely been your death as theirs, brother." Michael folded his hands on his knee. "Why did you leave the Garden? Does Father know you've abandoned your post?"

Jophiel shook his head. "Your son and his companion told me of Gabriel's death and the war that is upon the Earth. They told me of Lucifer's freedom and that the host cowers behind the Gates like children instead of fighting as warriors. I accompanied them from the Garden to offer myself to you again. It was an honor to serve in your ranks during the Fall, and I would be honored to serve with you again during this war. Together we can lead the children of Angels to victory against the children of Devils and demons, of that I have no doubt."

Michael considered that for a long moment, contemplating all angles before speaking. "It would honor me as well. First, though, we have to get you some appropriate clothing and get you up to date on what has happened between when you were assigned to the Garden and the time we're in now. Things have changed, and you need to know how to function in this world. You should also be aware that you may be punished by Father for betraying his orders. You've left your post and you're joining with me. I've stood apart from Heaven for nearly thirty human years."

Amaya squirmed. "Michael, there's something I need to tell you."

Jophiel held up his hand. "It can wait, daughter of—" he paused. "—forgive me. Amaya." He smiled at Michael. "I understand the repercussions and I accept them. My place is fighting with you and the Nephilim. I will take my comeuppance with no hesitation."

Michael turned his attention to Amaya. "What do you need to tell me?"

"I talked to God in Sinai." She waved her hands wildly to emphasize what she was saying. "The monks said they needed a sign, so they marched me out to where Moses talked to the fiery weeds and had me ask God for a sign. I was just getting ready to use my own powers to work something up when red lightning hit the ground and this man of fire came out of nowhere and told me that it was God and my mission is blessed and those who help me are blessed and those who oppose me are cursed and to go and do his bidding knowing that I am on a Godly mission." She gulped a breath. "It was incredible."

Michael smiled softly. "It certainly was." He reached out and took Amaya's hand, squeezing her fingers. "Thank you for telling me. It brings me comfort to know that Father is still keeping an eye on us, even if He and I disagree on things sometimes."

Jophiel narrowed his eyes. "Have you not had an audience with Father?"

"Not in many years."

"Nor have I. Not since I entered the Garden. I am willing to request one with Him if you feel it would be helpful."

Michael shook his head. "We have an emissary to Heaven through another Angel. Gabriel transferred his Grace to a spirit when he was dying. Griffin took his place and keeps us apprised of what is going on up there." He stood and looked at Jophiel. "If you're up to it, I would like to take you to Earth and bring you up to speed on everything that's been going on. We'll get you some clothes, I'll teach you more about the language and customs, and by the time we get back, you'll be ready to step in."

Jophiel stood. "I am ready whenever you wish to go."

"Just let me finish a couple things in my office and we'll go."

Deacon trailed after his father, following the Angel into the office and shutting the door, sinking into one of the chairs next to the desk. Michael bent over the desk, making a notation in his notebook.

"Something you want to talk to me about?"

Deacon crossed his arms. "Can we trust Jophiel?"

Michael looked up. "Undoubtedly. He was my first general during the Fall. I have fought with him many times. Jophiel is one I unhesitatingly trust my life to." He met Deacon's gaze steadily. "Is that all?"

Deacon sighed. "What are you going to do after this is all done? Do you want to go back to Heaven? Stay here? What is there for an Angel to do once the war is over?"

Michael smiled. "Just the fact that you've started worrying about that brings me great joy, Deacon." He sat down and looked at his son across the desk. "There's no place in Heaven for me. I know that. Jophiel will be able to go back. He's a soldier. He wants to serve me because it is what he has done before, but when this is over, he will return to his post in the Garden without hesitation. I'm unwilling to take a post in Eden or Purgatory or Heaven because I am unwilling to leave the Nephilim I have here." He smiled sadly. "You're the only one I made the human way, but Zeke and Lux have my essence in them. Carys and Elisa have been here for a decade. Dev and Zane for even longer. You're all my children in all the ways that matter, and I'm not going to leave you. No, after this is over, I will throw myself upon God's mercy and ask him to strip me of my wings. I finally understand why Alaria wished for humanity so badly because I, too, wish for it."

CHAPTER SEVENTEEN

JANUARY 15TH, 2061

FRANCE

LUX POKED her head into the kitchen of the house she was staying at and cleared her throat, getting Braxton and Alaria's attention. The two looked up, their discussion over patrol placement tapering off as they turned their attention to her. Braxton waved her in, smiling as he moved to the coffee pot to pour her a cup.

"Hey, Lux. What's up?"

"I just heard from Michael. Amaya and Deacon are back from the Garden of Eden. They got the Rod."

Alaria closed her eyes and sent up a quick prayer of thanks, relief coursing through her until her whole body hummed with the emotion. "Thank God they're safe." She rose to embrace the witch. "Thanks for coming to tell us."

"No problem." She tapped her toe at the doorjamb. "I've been asked for one of you or Dad to go back to Michael's and give them a rundown on Atlantis. Apparently that's where the Ark of the Covenant is, so they're going to have to time travel back to get it and Michael doesn't want to risk them running into any of you and messing with the timeline."

Braxton handed Lux the coffee and sat back down at the table, gesturing to her to join them. "That's a tough one because we weren't all together while we were there. During the battle, I was with Aradia, but we were outside the walls going after Garrick, so there's no risk of them running into her or me. Alaria, you were with Gage for most of it, right?"

She nodded. "Yeah. We went after Javal, but we got back a long time before you and Aradia. We fell back to the temple to guard the portal back to our time and stayed there for over twenty-four hours waiting for the two of you to get back. During the fight, the only two who were in the city were Damon and Greer. Unless Michael wants to pull them out of Heaven to talk to them, I don't think we're going to be able to tell Amaya and Deacon what was going on inside the city during the fight."

Braxton took a drink of his lukewarm coffee. "Why are they sending them back to the battle anyway?"

"In order to keep from messing with the timeline, they have to pull the box out right before the city sinks. So they're going to be on a tight schedule. They have to get it and basically be right behind us going through the portal or else they'll be killed in the flood."

Alaria leaned back in her chair and crossed her legs. "Couldn't you go with them to buy them some time?"

Lux shook her head. "No. I suggested that, too. Michael is afraid that since I got Mom's magic when she died that Mom would sense my presence when I went through. We don't want to risk that." She laid her head in her hands. "I'd love to go through, to see her again, but I know we can't take the risk. It's the same reason Zeke couldn't go, even if she hadn't just had the baby a few weeks ago. There's too much risk involved."

All three froze when the air shimmered and a pop announced the arrival of an Angel. Griffin stood in the kitchen, her hair perfectly coiffed in a French braid and her white suit pristine. She folded her wings tight to her body and offered them all a smile.

"Good evening." She looked at Lux. "How is your father?"

Lux frowned. "He's doing somewhat better. Not drinking as much. He's struggling to deal with Mom being gone." She bit her lip when tears gathered in her eyes. "So am I, but I have to focus on him right now."

Alaria stood and laid her hands on Lux's shoulders, rubbing gently. "Gage will be fine. This just brings back memories of all he lost before. He's hurting, but he'll pull out of it. I have no doubt of that." She turned to Griffin. "What brings you to Earth?"

"I came to take Lux back to Michael's. She'll need to prepare to take Amaya and Deacon to Atlantis."

Lux shook her head. "No. I'll work on the spell from here. I'm not leaving my dad until I have to." She scowled. "I still don't understand why Michael can't just send them back to where they need to go."

"There is less likelihood that Lucifer will detect a spell than an Angel altering the folds of time. In order for Michael to send them, he would open a crease in the fabric of time. A spell, if drawn correctly, can sidestep that and merely transport them through, leaving the fabric intact. It's a safety measure to keep anything from following them through."

Alaria drained her coffee and stood to put the cup in the sink. "I'm in favor of anything that keeps them safer."

Griffin flicked her wings. "Alaria, may I speak with you privately?"

Confused, Alaria jerked one shoulder in a careless shrug. "Sure, I guess." She looked around, thinking. "Umm, I guess we can walk down and check on the lines. They need to be brought in and re-baited before bed anyway." She grabbed her coat and stepped into boots, slinging a rifle over her shoulder and strapping a utility belt with a knife, stakes and Holy Water around her hips before opening the door and leading the Angel out. Together, the two women walked out of the compound and down the path to the water. "What do you need to talk to me about?"

Griffin stared stonily ahead. "I'm having memories. I think they're Gabe's. I feel like I'm losing me and finding him. It's getting hard for me to figure out where I begin and Gabriel ends. I don't know how to make sense of it. My memories of my time as a human seem to be fading and I keep remembering more and more about his past."

Alaria opened the gates and led Griffin to the edge of the lake. Silently, she began pulling in one of the lines to check for a fish. "I warned you that would probably happen."

"I know. I don't know how to deal with it,. I don't know what I feel and what he feels. I'm losing myself! This isn't what I signed on for." Griffin dropped onto a boulder and brought her knees to her chest. "I didn't want to be an Angel. I just wanted to be left alone and be dead. Now not only am I what I never wanted to be, I have to face the people I loved when I was alive, deal with Lucifer and this war all over again, figure out how to even *be* an Angel, and now on top of all the rest of it, I have Gabriel's memories erasing mine. Am I going to turn into Gabriel?"

Alaria laughed as she baited the hook and tossed it back into the water before moving on to the next pole. "No, you're not turning into Gabe. You're just going to have to figure out how to live with him inside you. You're sharing your body with his memories. Your time as a human isn't fading because of his memories, it's fading because you're not human anymore. You're not meant to have human emotions or memories or experiences. You'll know what you did, but you won't be able to remember how it felt. You won't wish for it." She expelled a breath into the frosty air, her fingers cold as she unhooked a fish and tossed it into one of the buckets. "It's complicated, I know."

"Every time I come here I'm afraid that seeing you with Brax is going to make me angry or sad." Griffin stared at the black water, her chin resting in her hand.

"Does it?"

"No. Or I didn't until tonight, but when I came in and saw the two of you sitting there together, I was filled with this intense jealously that I didn't know what to do with. I'd never felt anything like it."

Alaria tossed a second fish into the bucket and calmly baited the hook. "Did you bring me out here to tell me that you're going after Brax?" She tossed the line back into the water. "I mean, I appreciate the heads-up, but I'm an old woman now, Griffin. You're eternally thirty. I don't have anything on you in that arena, so if you go after him, there's not much I can do to stop you."

Griffin yanked on her hair. "I'm not going after Braxton." She looked up at the sky, tears gathering in her eyes. "I remember having sex with you on the desk at the Choosing Place. I remember screwing you brainless in the basement at Gage's, or in the hotel room at Damon and Greer's wedding, or in the shower. I remember it all. I know quite logically that it wasn't me and that these are Gabriel's memories, but they're in my head and they're messing with my emotions. I came in there tonight, and I suddenly understood exactly why he tried to stab Brax because I wanted to, too."

Very deliberately, Alaria wiped her hands on her jeans and sat next to Griffin on the rock, her mind racing as she tried to think of an appropriate response. After several moments, she sighed and opened her mouth. "You're attracted to me."

Griffin shook her head. "Am I? No. But Gabriel was, and his memories and essence is inside me and I'm struggling to control it. With him swimming around in my head, my body responds to memories of you the same way it responds to my memories of Braxton."

Alaria tapped her fingers together as she mulled the situation over. "Is it safe to say you never felt these things before you died?"

Miserable, Griffin nodded. "That's a fair assumption, yes. But what does that have to do with anything?"

"Just making sure it's all Gabe." Alaria chuckled. "I've been with a woman or two in my years, so it wouldn't shock me if you had, too." She patted Griffin's knee reassuringly. "You need to find one of the other Angels who has shared Grace and talk to them about this. I never did it, so I can't help you with this particular problem. I'm sure there's a way to keep Gabe's emotions from twisting you up."

Griffin ran her hands over her braid. "I never imagined what it was like to have a penis. Now that I know, I'm not entirely sure which I prefer."

Alaria's eyebrows nearly met her hairline. "An Angel with a gender identity crisis? God might pass out."

Giggling, Griffin wiped her eyes. "I didn't mean it that way."

"What other way could you have possibly meant it?"

With a sigh, she deflated. "I know it sounded bad. I just meant that now that I've kind of experienced sex from both sides, I'm not sure which is better."

"I don't think either is supposed to be better. Just different." Alaria shoved her hands into the pockets of her coat. "Look at us, all evolved. The dead wife and the current one sitting here talking about sex." She laughed warmly. "It's very progressive. But in all seriousness, I understand how hard it must be to have Gabe's feelings inside you. It must feel like a total crisis of identity. I strongly suggest working with one of the other Angels to figure out how to limit Gabriel's influence."

Before Alaria could say anything else, Griffin shifted positions, sliding her arms around her and kissed her. The Angel's lips were warm and soft, and her grip was tight around Alaria's waist. Shocked, Alaria didn't move for several seconds as her brain struggled to process what had happened. Gently, she grasped Griffin by the shoulders and eased the other woman back.

"Griffin, you really need to find one of those other Angels." Alaria rubbed Griffin's arms gently. "That wasn't you."

Embarrassed, humiliated, and hurt, Griffin disappeared. Flabbergasted by the entire exchange, Alaria finished checking the poles, collected the bucket of fish and made her way back to her house, dropping the fish off at the cafeteria before slipping in through the kitchen door. Lux had already left the room. Braxton was sitting at the table, his head bent over blueprints. He glanced up when the door opened.

"Good catch?"

"A dozen." She took off her coat and rubbed her hands together to get blood flowing to her frozen fingertips.

"What did Griffin want?"

"To talk about how she's getting Gabe's memories." She hopped on one foot to pull off her boot. "It's part of having his Grace. I told her she needed to find one of the other Angels who have shared Grace in the past to talk to them. I don't know how to help her. She told me that she remembers everything about his time as an Angel, including the time he spent fucking my brains out."

Braxton choked on coffee. Coughing, he slapped the table. "Say what now?"

Alaria laughed. "You heard me, old man. She's got his memories. That includes the time Gabe and I were together. So in some creepy, weird, roundabout way, we've both had sex with Griffin." She padded across the room in her socked feet and eased herself down into Braxton's lap, looping her arms around his neck. "Then, she kissed me."

Braxton gaped at Alaria. "Griffin kissed you."

"Yup."

"What did you do?"

"Told her she really needed to find one of those Angels because her door doesn't swing that way. She got embarrassed and disappeared."

"Damn."

"Yeah, pretty much." She studied his face for a long moment. "I don't know how to help her, Brax. This is out of my comfort zone. I know a few Angels have done it, but I never did, and I don't know how to manage the side effects. This is the first time I know of that an Angel did a complete transfer. Griffin is losing herself. She's becoming more like Gabriel. She's losing her human memories and emotions. I know there's a way to stop his from taking over, but I don't know if there's a way to stop her from becoming completely Angelic."

Braxton leaned his head on Alaria's shoulder, a wave of grief rolling through him. "Unfortunately, she's going to be an Angel for the rest of eternity. She has to learn to exist in that world. That's going to require not being human. I don't even think we should try to stop it, babe. It's not for us to do. This is her reality now. We have our own to deal with."

"I feel bad for her, though. I wish there was something I could do to make it all go away."

"So do I, but there isn't." He rubbed his nose against her neck. "She seriously kissed you?"

Laughing, Alaria nodded. "Right on the mouth. Tongue and all."

Braxton stretched up to brush his lips over hers. "Completely unacceptable." He stood, lifting her in his arms. "Eden and Lux and Zane are all in bed."

Alaria grinned at her husband. "It is pretty late."

"We should go to bed, too."

She was laughing as he carried her into their room off the kitchen. "Great minds think alike."

CHAPTER EIGHTEEN

LUCIFER GRIPPED the armrests of his throne tightly and stared at Azazel and Abalam, his eyes flashing with anger. Beside him, Lilith stroked her bulging stomach lovingly, enraptured by her pregnancy and seemingly paying little to no attention to what was going on.

"What do you mean, they got away with the Rod? How could that be? You took more than twenty of our soldiers to take on two Nephilim. Surely they aren't that powerful."

Abalam inclined his head. "Forgive me, but we did not anticipate that Jophiel would leave the garden. His years inside have not weakened him, nor have they dulled his skills. He was able to distract Azazel and me and allow the Nephilim to take on the Cambion and demons."

Lucifer straightened. "Jophiel came through? He left his post in the garden?"

"Yes. He came out with Amaya and Deacon. He was joined with Michael and is, to the best of our knowledge, staying on Earth for the time being. We don't know much else at the moment. It was quite unexpected to see him come through the gate. If it had just been the two Nephilim, it wouldn't have been a problem, but I'm sure you remember fighting Jophiel the first time." Abalam kept his eyes trained on the floor, trying valiantly not to anger Lucifer more than he already had.

Lucifer stroked his fingers over his chin thoughtfully. "That's certainly an interesting turn of events. It makes more sense why you failed so miserably with him there. I tried to turn him during the Fall, but the Angel was annoyingly loyal to both Michael and God. That was an unexpected complication." He sighed deeply. "What do you think, my love?"

Lilith glanced up, her hands stilling on her stomach. "I think we need to continue with our plan to capture the witch. If they have the Rod, they'll be going after the Spear soon. Once they have those two things, none of us are safe. If I know Michael, and I assure you that I do, he knows we could slip through with them were he to open up a wrinkle in time to send them through to Atlantis to get the Spear. That means he'll be having the witch do a spell to send them through without opening the fabric to allow for intruders. Our opening will be to find them and snatch the witch once the spell is completed, which is when she'll be her weakest. If we can't follow them through and get to the Spear in Atlantis, we can at least have the witch in our control."

Azazel cleared his throat. "If I may, I think Lilith has a sound idea. Magic like that would drain the witch, and if we could arrange some sort of distraction that would appear to be unrelated so as to keep the others away while Lux is sending them through time, it should be simple for us to collect her. Ideally, I would suggest not having a shootout with Michael and his Nephilim over the witch because then we wouldn't have any time to work on her before they would be after us. If we can find her alone, we could have her well-hidden before they even realize she's gone."

Lucifer tapped his fingers on his chin as he mulled over the situation. "I was ready to skin both of you alive today, I hope you know that. When I heard you failed to get the Rod, I couldn't contemplate a situation in which failure wasn't a complete affront to me. The presence of Jophiel has earned you a modicum of mercy. I want you to collect the witch for me. If you fail, I promise both of you that you'll be praying for the Nephilim to come and kill you with the Spear." He stared at them both steadily. "You may be the one who tortures souls, Abalam, but I know a few tricks of my own, and I will not hesitate to string you up on your own rack. Find her, bring her to me, and turn her to our side. If you don't, there is no more mercy to be had."

Abalam inclined his head slightly. "I will not fail. Your will be done."

Lilith smiled softly. "We'll succeed, darling. We've been ahead of them since the Choosing. There's no reason to think they're going to defeat us now. They have their little victories, but when it counts, they fall flat and we succeed. They learned that lesson when you escaped Hell, and they'll learn it again when they come to kill you."

Lucifer took Lilith's hand and brought it to his lips, pressing a kiss to her knuckles. "I hope you're right, darling. This will be the biggest test any of us have faced. They aren't just coming for me, but for all of us. They come for my children, for my mate, for both of you. They wish to eradicate us from Earth and kill those who follow us. We must stop them. There is no other option or our very lives are at risk. This isn't just war for Earth anymore. It's a battle for our lives."

Abalam placed his hands on his hips and stared up at the ceiling. "I would be remiss if I didn't caution you both about what we're doing. Kidnapping the witch will bring their wrath upon us. Michael gave his essence for the creation of that particular Nephilim, she is the mate of the son of the Angel of Death, and her father is the vampire turned human. They would not rest until they found her, and it would be their sole goal to destroy all of us. If they have the Spear, the likelihood of them being able to do so increases exponentially." He paced back and forth in front of the thrones. "Please don't think I'm refusing to do as you wish. I'm not. I'll go get her, and do it as ordered. I just want you both to understand the brevity of the situation."

Lucifer stood, descending from his throne until he stood toe to toe with Abalam. Slowly, he reached out and laid his hands on Abalam's head, bending his own until their foreheads were pressed together.

"You've always been such a loyal servant, Abalam. No one has ever looked out for my family the way you have." He pressed a kiss to Abalam's cheek. "I want you to know that your loyalty is appreciated. I understand the risks, and this is what I want you to do. Succeed, and your reward is great. Fail me again, and there is no hole small enough or remote enough in which you can hide. I will tear your skin from your bones and ensure that feel pain for the rest of eternity. Know that beyond doubt."

Abalam didn't let his fear show. He met Lucifer's gaze steadily.

"I won't fail. We'll have our victory. I'll bring you the witch and I'll turn her to our side."

Lucifer released the Devil and stepped back. "I have full confidence in your talents. I'll arrange to have a Healer at your disposal to ensure she doesn't die while you're working on her. Lilith, darling, do you feel up to working with the witches to ward one of our safe-houses to make sure the witch will be unable to blast her way out? We'll need to find a way to control her magic and her Nephil powers and to keep her from flashing."

Lilith tapped her fingers on her stomach. "I think I can muster up the energy, my love. Where would you like her to be stored?"

Lucifer turned to Abalam, answering Lilith's question as he spoke to the other Devil. "As much as it pains me, I fear we'll need to draw on the power of Hell to contain the witch so we will have to find a place close to a gate or another place of supernatural power. I can't be present there, obviously, and it's too dangerous for Lilith and Serafina to be where Lux is, so you won't have our powers to help contain her. Once we have the witch, our focus is on turning her and using her as a weapon against Amaya and Deacon. We'll lure them in and kill them." Lucifer returned to his throne and draped himself across it casually. "Go now, I tire of discussing this. You know your tasks."

Amaya lay next to Deacon in the dark, her head on his chest and one of her arms around his waist. His hand was on her shoulder and his fingers rubbed back and forth gently, stroking her skin as they lay quietly. After several moments, Amaya sat up, tired of the silence.

"What's wrong?"

Deacon stared up at her, his features barely visible in the dark. "Why do you think something's wrong?"

"Because I know you, and I know when something's bothering you. Talk to me. Tell me what it is."

Sighing, he sat up and shoved his pillows behind his back so he could lean against the headboard. "My dad is going to ask to give up his wings."

Amaya sucked in a breath and pressed her hand to her throat as the weight of his statement sank in. "What? Why?"

"He said he doesn't want to go back to Heaven and be a soldier and that he's unwilling to go to some post like Jophiel has been at. The only alternative he sees is to give up his wings and Fall."

"Can he even do that? God wouldn't let my mom Fall millions of years ago."

"Dad's been standing apart from Heaven for a long time. I don't think God would let him back in even if Dad wanted to go. He's stuck in limbo. He's an Angel, he's immortal, and he's here, but he's not a part of the decisions. It's like he's been neutered."

"But why does he want to be human? He could just keep doing what he's been doing. It'll take years more to clear out all the Cambion and demons, if we ever get them all. Add in the vampires, werewolves, hounds, and witches, and this fight isn't going to be over just because we defeat Lucifer. It could still take generations."

Deacon took Amaya's hand in his and held it. "Babe, Dad doesn't want to watch us grow old while he stays as he is. He looks at us all as his kids. He loves us and wants to live with us. He doesn't want to be an Angel anymore. He's done. He wants the life your mom has had. He wants to experience humanity."

"But he'll die if he does that."

"I think that's the point. He doesn't want to watch us grow old the same way Gage didn't want to watch Aradia and Lux grow old and die. He willingly gave up eternity for a human life with the people he loved, and that's what Dad wants. Physically my dad is my age. He could meet someone, settle down and have half a dozen kids. He could have a life. If that's what he wants, it's what I want for him."

Amaya leaned her head against the wall, mixed feelings raging within her. "I don't know what I think. Michael has always been the constant. The one I always knew would be the same, who would always be there. My parents are getting old, Deacon. They won't be around forever. Zeke's are gone. Lux's mom is gone. The six are down to three, and we've still got the biggest bit of this whole fight ahead of us. I don't know if we could reasonably expect that we'll all survive. But your dad? I never questioned having him. He's always been there, and I always knew he would be. I'm not sure how I feel about him being human."

Deacon chuckled. "I've had those feelings about it, too. But I have equally confusing feelings about being an old man while my dad looks thirty forever."

Laughing, she turned her head to look at him. "There is that." She bumped him with her shoulder. "Look at us talking about the future like we're actually going to get one."

"I think we are." Sobering, he drew her close to his side. "Since

Sinai, I really think we're gonna do this, Maya." He hugged her tightly. "I think I'm finally starting to get some of that faith we've always heard so much about."

Amaya kissed his cheek and laid her head on his shoulder. "I hope you're right. Though how will you explain to people that your father looks young enough to be your twin brother?"

"That's probably exactly what we'll say. If he doesn't lose his wings, eventually, he probably won't be able to go out in public much. People will go back to the way it was pretty quickly. They'll start setting up governments and cities and doing the same things they've always been doing. Angels won't be welcome."

"And what happens if he does become human, find some woman, settle down, and start having babies? Are you going to be a part of that family?"

Slightly insulted, Deacon removed his arm from around her shoulders. "What the hell does that mean?"

"Just that it's complicated and there are a lot of things that need to be considered before he does this. If it's just going to be the two of you, it's no big deal, but if he wants a life like the rest of the people on this planet get, then he's going to have to tell the person he's with, or you're going to have to lie to her for several decades. It's a lot to think about."

"I think we need to get through one thing at a time. There's no guarantee that God'll even go for making him human. Dad's the Angel of War. It's a longshot to think He's going to let him go. All we can do is wait and see and hope." He ran his hands over his face. "I hate thinking about what's going to happen after this. It'd be easier if I could just keep my focus on the next step, which is going to Atlantis and getting this damn Spear."

"Michael got in touch with Lux, who was going to ask one of my parents or her dad to come here and give us a rundown of what Atlantis looks like, where people are and where we need to go. There's going to be an attack going on while we're there, so it's going to be tricky. We have to stay out of sight, not mess with things, and stay alive, all at the same time."

Deacon whacked his head against the wall twice to relieve his frustration. "Okay. That's good. Do you know who it's going to be?"

"Not a clue. Maybe all of them. From what I know they were in different places doing different things. Could be beneficial to have a couple of them tell us what was going on." Amaya stifled a yawn and squinted to read the dial on her watch. "It's really late. We should try to get some sleep." She grimaced when she heard the baby start crying down the hall. "Poor Zeke and Dev. I swear Caleb cries every two hours."

"He's only a month old. That's what they're supposed to do at that age, isn't it?"

She nodded. "Oh, yeah. He'll do that for a while." Scooting down into the bed, she tucked the pillow under her head. "I'm going to get some sleep. I'm exhausted. Do you feel like you can sleep?"

Deacon lay on his side, cramming his pillow between his arm and his head. "I'll at least give it a shot. Tomorrow night we might be sleeping in a barn in a city about to sink to the bottom of the ocean."

Amaya giggled. "That's one way to look at things." She leaned forward and pressed a gentle kiss to his mouth. "Goodnight."

Deacon tucked a lock of her hair behind her ears. "Night, baby."

CHAPTER NINETEEN

JANUARY 17TH, 2061

THE MANOR

MICHAEL WAS sitting at his desk when Griffin appeared in the room, Alaria and Braxton on one side, Gage and Lux on the other. He rose to greet them, hugging each warmly before looking critically at Gage. The man's face was lined with worry, his eyes were sunken and ringed with dark circles, and he appeared to be more than a few pounds lighter than the last time they had been together.

"How are you, Gage?"

Gage offered a tight smile. "I'm pulling myself together. It's been a few dark months, but I'm getting there. There's not another choice. I have other things to live for. Aradia wouldn't want me to live like this."

"No, she wouldn't. I can't imagine the pain you both feel." Michael looked at Lux, including her in the statement Dent. "I miss her very much. I miss them all." He turned when a knock sounded at the door. "It seems your presence has been noticed." He smiled and moved to open the door, letting Zeke~her son cradled in her arms~ in.

Lux darted for her friend, scooping up the baby and cradling him against her chest, cooing at the infant and bouncing on the balls of her feet when he whined. "Oh, he's grown so much! Zeke, he's gorgeous!" She wrapped one arm around Zeke. "How are you? How's Dev?"

"We're tired." Zeke laughed and moved to hug Alaria before wrapping her arms around Gage. "He's up every couple hours. It's exhausting. Amaya was nice enough to take him for a few hours last night and let me sleep some, so I feel pretty good right now. I got four hours in a row before my boobs woke me up."

Alaria chuckled. "Even when the baby sleeps there's no respite from nursing." She looked around the office. "I think we'd do better in the living room with some more space. Is Amaya still sleeping? And where's Deacon?"

"I think they're still upstairs." Zeke led the way into the living room. "I can go up to their room and get them."

Braxton lifted his eyebrows and exchanged a look with his wife over Zeke's statement, but didn't address it. "They'll be down when they're awake. It's only seven-thirty, and if she was up late with the baby, I want her rested. We're not in a hurry, are we?"

Griffin shook her head, speaking for the first time. "No. You're quite secure here." She cleared her throat. "If you'll excuse me, I think I'm going to take a walk around the grounds until you're ready for me."

Michael watched the other Angel leave with concern. "Is something wrong with Griffin?"

Alaria cringed. "She's currently having some issues with her memories. As in, she's getting all of Gabriel's and is having a hard time figuring out where she ends and he begins. It's making things rather complicated for her. One of the other Angels who shared Grace is helping her manage it. Hopefully she's getting better, but it looked like it was getting pretty out of hand."

Braxton laughed. "Look at you, Miss Diplomatic." He sighed deeply. "She's struggling with maintain separation between her own memories and Griffin's memories. It's affecting everything about her."

Michael frowned. "That is concerning. I'll have a talk with her after this is done." He glanced back toward the kitchen. "If you'll excuse me for a moment, I'll put on some coffee and fix something for breakfast. I have a house full of Nephilim who will be waking soon, and they're going to want to be fed before they head out."

Amaya stepped out of the shower and reached for a towel, rubbing water droplets off her body and padding across the tile to the mirror. She bent, wrapping the towel around her hair and standing to wipe her hand across the mirror, clearing steam from the glass.

As she dressed and dried her hair, her mind wandered to the path still ahead. Mentally, she went over what she needed to pack for Atlantis. When her parents had gone, they hadn't been able to take weapons back because of the risk of tampering with the timeline. Unsure if accessing the doomed city via magic would have a different result than a split in time, Amaya pondered whether it was worth the risk to pack guns and ammo.

Deciding it was always worth the chance at having a rifle, she left the bathroom in jeans and a sweater and made her way out of the bedroom, dropping her wet towel in a heap on the floor, smiling when she thought briefly how annoyed Deacon would be by it before stooping to pick up the offending object. Slinging it over the back of the chair, she jerked open the door and headed down to the living room where voices were trickling up.

Her smile widening as she recognized her parents' voices, Amaya quickened her pace and loped down the stairs, skating around the banister and swinging into the living room, squealing with delight at seeing Lux and Gage as well. She rushed forward, managing to envelop both of her parents and Lux in a hug all at the same time, accomplishing the feat by plopping in her father's lap and stretching across her mother to reach Lux.

"I'd hoped you'd all come, but I didn't really think you would!" She kissed Alaria soundly on the cheek. "I've missed you!"

"We've missed you, too." Alaria scooted to make room for Amaya to sit down. "We want you to be as prepared as possible for what's you're doing. We were so spread out during our time in Atlantis that I thought it made a lot of sense for us all to come."

Michael crossed one of his legs over the other and cleared his throat. "Let's get on with it then. Lux, how close to the battle will you be able to put them?"

Lux chewed on her lip thoughtfully. "I'm working on a spell that will allow me to detect large waves of magic. My theory is that Garrick and Mom were putting off huge signatures when they were fighting and that if I can find it, I can send them back in the middle of things."

Gage leaned forward, bracing his elbows on his knees. "Garrick started things two days before Aradia ended them. If you're off and you send them back at the beginning, they're going to have to hide for a while. She was using quite a bit of magic on the trek up the mountain, wasn't she, Brax?"

Braxton nodded. "Yeah. Alaria and Gage were off chasing Javal, Damon and Greer were inside the city managing the battle, and I went with Aradia up the mountain after Garrick. When we came back down, they were all in the tunnels waiting for us to get back so we could get out through the portal. If you can't take the Spear until the very end, and have to follow us out, you'd better be right on our tails." He shook his head in disbelief. "Honestly, I don't know how you're going to get through without us seeing you. The water was right behind us. It's a matter of seconds at best."

Lux threw up her hands. "That's why you should let me go with them! I could stop the water, buy us a few seconds to get through the portal and make sure they don't die. As it is they're going to have to activate it with new coordinates or they'll follow you right back out into Gage's living room circa thirty years ago."

Deacon took a gulp of coffee as he thought about the situation. "What if we went through just ahead of them? Were you guys hiding in the room with the portal or somewhere else?"

Gage answered. "We were in the castle by the tunnel leading to the portal. Damon was at the door standing guard. When Damon saw Brax and Aradia coming, we all ran outside. That would be your chance to come in and slip ahead of us. It took Greer a minute to heal Aradia before we headed into the tunnels, but you're going to need to know exactly where you're going. If they got in when we came out to get Aradia, they'd have a solid ninety seconds before we went in after them. That's enough time to get to the portal, activate it, go through and we'd have never noticed." He patted Amaya's knee. "I can draw you some schematics of the castle, the tunnels and the portal room so you'll know exactly where to go."

"Okay, so now that we know how to get out, the question becomes how do we hide for what could be a couple days while we're there? If Lux drops up in at the beginning of the fight, we have to go through nearly forty-eight hours without being seen and without interacting with anyone." Amaya raked her hands through her hair. "Why does this have to be so complicated?"

Michael laughed. "It's not. You can interact with people who are in Atlantis. Vampires, Atlanteans, anyone who's going to die when the city sinks. You cannot alter the timeline. That means stopping the sinking or changing anything key. It's safest if you manage to slip in, hide somewhere until you go through the portal and then leave with no one ever seeing you, but it's not the end of the world if you do. Atlantis sank a long time ago. No one makes it out alive. As long as you don't change that, you're not affecting the timeline, I promise."

"So where do we hide? Anywhere? Do we stay inside the city? Do we wait outside? Where is going to be the best place to not get seen by anyone?" Amaya looked at her mother. "How long were Damon and Greer inside the city alone before you came back in?"

Alaria closed her eyes briefly. "Honey, Gage and I were after Javal for a few hours. It was a long hike to get to him, then a hell of a fight and a trek back. Even when we got there, we weren't together the whole time. I can't tell you where I was every minute of those two days let alone where they were. I can't tell you if they ever left the city either. After we came back from killing Javal, I know I didn't leave the walls again. Gage, did you?"

Gage shook his head. "No. I stayed with Aradia's father's body most of the time. King Liam was the vampire that turned me, and I needed to make sure that he ended up rising so that I would be turned to preserve the timeline. I wasn't with Damon and Greer much at all. They checked in with me every few hours, but they were in full-on soldier mode." He turned to Zeke. "Did your parents give you any other details about where they may have been during the battle?"

Zeke stared down at her baby's face. "I know they were together and that they were managing the fighting. Past that, they didn't ever tell me much. It was war, it was a fight. They didn't give me a play by play on where they were and when they went there."

Deacon rubbed his palms on his thighs. "Okay, so we know that Braxton and Aradia weren't in the city from the time the battle started until after Garrick was dead. Alaria and Gage were outside the city for a few hours, then came back inside and stayed there until Braxton and Aradia came back and you all went through the portal. At what point were you all hiding in the castle? How long were you there before Aradia and Brax got there?"

Gage looked at Alaria, wracking his memory. "A couple hours, maybe. Not long. Garrick had brought the night with him to ensure that his vampires could invade the city, and when Aradia killed him, the darkness went away and the vampires were forced to leave. Aradia brought the darkness back pretty quickly, but a lot of the vamps had run away because they didn't want to die." He leaned back against the couch. "You have to remember, this was a two day fight. We had a lot to do and a lot to manage. Not everything about it was memorable. We'd had no sleep, there was smoke in the air, blood everywhere, no one had eaten, water was scarce. We're lucky we can remember whether or not we won."

Michael frowned, considering. "Preserving the timeline is very important. We have to ensure that Amaya and Deacon don't run into any of the original six. Even the briefest of interactions could have long-reaching effects. We also must ensure that they don't stop you from interacting with someone you interact with. It's not the people of Atlantis I'm concerned about, but what ramifications this could have on the six of you. One misstep by either of them and the whole present shifts. We need to know where Damon and Greer were at all times. If they left the city, we need to know where they went. It is imperative that the two of you remain out of sight of anyone who interacts with the six."

Annoyed, Deacon glared at his father. "Well, unless you can somehow bring them down here and ask them that, we're not going to get those answers! It's a best guess situation!"

Griffin cleared her throat from the door leading into the kitchen. Everyone in the room turned to look at her, not having realized she'd come back from her walk. "I'm sorry to interrupt, but I can assist in this particular issue." She stared at Zeke, her eyes betraying her sympathy. "When I inherited Gabriel's Grace, I also got his abilities. I believe it is within my purview to call your parents from Heaven in the same way Gabriel called me forth. We could ask them."

Zeke's eyes filled with tears. "You can bring them back?"

Michael moved to sit next to Zeke, taking her hand in his and wrapping his other arm around her shoulders. "No, child. Griffin can bring their spirits out of Heaven for a very short period of time. It would be the same as when Gabriel sent her to relay a message to you. It's not permanent. It's a temporary thing that is not done often. You would only have a few minutes, perhaps half an hour, with them before they would fade and return to Heaven."

Griffin shifted uncomfortably. "I don't want to do anything to cause more pain than I already have. I don't know if I could bring them both back or if I could only bring one, but I'm willing to try to bring them both if it's something you think would prove helpful."

Michael inclined his head. "I don't see as we have another

choice. Ezekiel, do you want to be here when this is done? There's no shame if it would be too painful."

Zeke sniffed back tears and looked at Lux. "It doesn't seem fair that I'm going to get to see my parents and you won't get to see your mom."

Lux offered a tight smile. "My mom isn't in Heaven. She's just gone. She got killed in Purgatory. There's no Heaven or Hell from down there. Griffin couldn't bring her here for me to talk to even if we needed her." She exchanged a pained look with her father. "Don't think about us, Zeke. It's an opportunity you might never have again. You should take it."

Zeke nodded. "Okay. I promise I'll ask them about what you need, but do you think I could be alone with them when we do this? At least for a few minutes. I know everyone else will want to say goodbye, but I'd like a few minutes for them to meet Caleb and for us to be alone."

Michael looked at Griffin. "You'll hold them here as long as you can?"

She nodded. "I will. You have my word."

Deacon stood. "I'll leave you guys alone for this. There's no need for me to be here for it."

Lux joined him. "As much as I'd like to see them, this is for you guys. I'll be upstairs."

Amaya nodded. "Me, three." She leaned over to hug Zeke before heading for the stairs. "Do you want me to send Dev down?"

Zeke nodded. "If you don't mind."

"Not at all."

Griffin took a deep breath and reached inside herself, calling on the power she was still learning to control. It took several tries, but within two minutes, Damon and then Greer appeared in the living room. Without a word, and struggling to hold onto them, she slipped into the kitchen where she could be alone.

Michael stood and embraced Damon and Greer. "I know this is confusing."

Damon looked around, an expression of concern on his face. "Where am I?" He focused on Greer. "How are you here? I heard you die!" He grabbed his wife in a hug, crushing her to his chest.

Greer held Damon tightly. "We are dead." She looked at Michael, tears shining in her eyes. "We're dead, aren't we?"

Michael nodded sadly. "Yes. You've been brought out of Heaven temporarily because we need some information only you can give us. I'll make it quick so you can have as much time as possible with Zeke before you have to go. When you were in Atlantis, did you ever venture outside the city after the battle had begun?"

Greer nodded. "I went to the stables a few times and down to the beach at least once."

Damon thought back. "I don't think so. I stayed near the walls to run the defense."

Gage spoke from the couch, his voice choked with emotion. "Did either of you go to the grotto?"

Greer looked confused. "I don't even know what that is. Damon?"

He shook his head. "Not a clue, so I guess not."

Gage smiled. "Then I know where you can hide." He stood and went to Damon and Greer, embracing them both. "I'm so sorry about what happened to you. I could kill you for not calling and letting me help you." He kissed Greer's cheek. "You have no idea how badly I want to yell and scream right now."

Alaria elbowed him out of the way and wrapped her arms around them both, tears streaming down her cheeks. "Oh, I've missed you both." She hugged them tightly. "The kids are doing great. Lux and Zane did their part. Beelzebub is dead. Zeke and Dev succeeded with getting the sword. Amaya and Deacon are halfway to killing Lucifer. They're going to win."

Damon closed his eyes. "Then all of this is worth it." He shook Braxton's hand as the Warrior moved to stand in front of him. "Thank you all for helping take care of our baby." He looked around. "Where's Aradia? And Gabriel?"

Gage's eyes darkened. "They didn't make it. They were killed in Purgatory." He took a shaky breath. "Gabriel gave his Grace to Griffin and made her an Angel when he died, so she's the one working with Michael and the kids now."

Greer's hand flew to her mouth. "But in Purgatory..." She trailed off, looking at Gage apologetically. "I am so sorry."

He hugged her again. "Me, too." Looking around, he gestured to the other room. "Let's give them some time with Zeke."

Zeke stood as the others filed from the room, taking several steps forward. "I had a baby." She shrugged. "With Dev. It's a boy. We named him Caleb Gabriel Damon Deveraux. It's a big name, but I think he'll live up to it." She took a deep breath, trying to hold back the sobs. "I'm so sorry I shot you, Daddy!"

Greer rushed forward, enveloping her daughter and grandson

in a hug, rocking back and forth, both women crying openly. Damon wrapped his arms around them both, holding his wife and child tightly, his eyes angled up at the ceiling and filled with emotion.

After several moments, Greer wiped her cheeks and stepped back, making a visible effort to control her emotions. She rubbed Zeke's arms briskly. "Let me see that baby."

Zeke shifted the infant from her arms to those of her mother, dropping to the couch. Damon sat next to her, holding her hand in one of his and wrapping his other arm around her shoulders.

"I don't know how much time we have here, so you need to listen to me, Zeke." Damon pulled her in close and wrapped his arms around her. "You have nothing to be sorry for. I told you then and I'll tell you now that you did nothing wrong. You did what I asked you to do, nothing more. I'm proud of you for having the strength to do what was asked of you, and even prouder still for being strong enough to finish everything that's come since then."

Dev came into the room and uncomfortably cleared his throat. "Amaya said I should come down, but I can come back."

Greer shook her head and extended a hand. "No, come sit. You're a part of this, too." She smiled when he perched on the coffee table. "Your son is beautiful." She brushed her finger over the baby's soft cheek. "I so wish I could know him. Do you have any family living, Dev?"

"No. Well, Michael raised me, so I have him."

Damon laughed softly. "We all have Michael, don't we?"

Greer smiled down into Caleb's face. "Everyone should be so lucky to have someone like him." She looked over at Zeke and back at Dev. "We're together in Heaven, and we're not in pain. When we're up there, we don't remember what happened down on Earth. Neither of us blame you, and we're not angry." She gently handed the baby to Damon. "Here, meet your grandson. I think he has your eyes."

Zeke closed her eyes and fought back tears. She felt Dev's hands on hers and squeezed them tightly, pain rocketing through her. Her mother's hands were cool on her face as Greer tugged her close.

"It's okay, darling. Be sad. Be whatever you need to be. There's no shame in grieving. You never expected to be without us so young. You're going to raise your son without your parents to guide you, and that's sad." Greer pressed a kiss to Zeke's cheek. "Honey, you're strong. You have a wonderful man by your side and you're surrounded by people who love you. Alaria and Braxton and Gage and Michael are all here for you the same way we would have been. They'll love you in the same way."

Choked with tears, Zeke couldn't speak. She buried her face in Greer's shoulder and sobbed, crawling into her mother's lap. Greer hugged her child tightly, tears running down her own face.

"I'm sorry we had to leave, baby girl. I'm sorry you got dragged into this."

Damon handed Caleb to Dev and turned to his daughter. "Zeke, you need to pull yourself together. Everything's okay."

Zeke wiped her hands over her cheeks and looked at her father through red eyes. "It's not okay. You're dead!" She gagged. "I put a gun to your head and pulled the trigger. How can you even look at me right now?"

Damon grabbed her face and pressed his forehead to hers, forcing her to meet his eyes. "You listen to me, Ezekiel Mackenzie. You did what you had to do in order to survive. You owe no apologies and you shouldn't feel bad about that. Ever. You did what you had to do. Nothing more, nothing less. I am proud of you for having the strength to do what I couldn't. I wanted you to live. Your mother and I knew what was going to happen to us, and we made a choice for you to live. We bet on you. I'd do it again a thousand times. It's time to stop torturing yourself over something you couldn't help. Suck it up and get over it."

Griffin poked her head into the room and cleared her throat, getting their attention. "I'm sorry to interrupt. Really, really sorry, but I don't think I can hold it very much longer. You may want to say your goodbyes."

Damon nodded. "Thanks." He hugged Zeke tightly. "We're always looking out for you, Zeke. Just because we're not here with you doesn't mean we're gone. We're still in Heaven, and we still love you. Nothing will ever change that."

Greer hugged Zeke again. "I want you to be happy. Finish this with Lucifer, have a life. Raise your family, protect them. Grow old and play with your grandchildren the way I'm never going to play with mine. Do whatever makes you happy, my love." She kissed Zeke's forehead. "My greatest accomplishment in life was being your mother. You've become a wonderful woman. I know you'll be a marvelous mother to that beautiful boy." She smiled sadly. "You've made us so proud, Zeke. I love you."

Zeke hugged both her parents at the same time, one arm

around each. "I love you both. I don't want you to leave!"

As they faded and Zeke was left alone with Dev and Caleb, she gave herself over to another wave of tears and grief.

CHAPTER TWENTY

"HOW'S ZEKE?" Deacon walked into the library, carrying a bottle of beer in one hand. Amaya looked up from where she was sitting on the floor in front of the couch staring into the fireplace.

"She's doing okay. Dev took her upstairs to bed. My mom is taking care of Caleb for the night. She and Dad are heading back to France in the morning. Gage and Lux already went back. Lux said she'll be ready by the weekend to do the spell."

"So three more days before we head to Atlantis."

Amaya laughed as Deacon slid down the couch and dropped next to her. "Eden, Atlantis, next thing we know we'll be jetting off to Mars for something." She brought the glass she held in one hand to her lips and sipped the dark amber liquid. "What does it say about me that I'm jealous of Zeke?"

"That you're human." He reached out and toyed with a lock of her hair. "Are you drunk, Amaya?"

She shook her head. "No, I've only had two drinks." Looking up at him, she offered a watery smile. "I hated Gabriel when he was alive, and now that he's dead I wish he was still here so I could keep hating him. How fucked up is that?"

"I don't think it's fucked up at all. I think it's normal. Zeke got a chance to say goodbye to her parents and have that closure that you and Lux won't ever get. I'm sure she's feeling the same thing you are."

"Lux seemed happy for her. She's sad and missing her mom, but she's so worried about Gage right now he's all she sees."

"He seems to be doing okay." Deacon took a pull from his beer bottle and let it dangle between his fingers. "We're almost done. One more thing."

"It's really like five things. Spear, Lucifer, Lilith, Serafina, baby Devil. Not in that particular order."

"We're going to do it." He set the bottle aside and watched with thinly veiled concern as Amaya drained her glass. "If you don't stop with the drinking, you're going to wind up an alcoholic."

Amaya glared at him, her eyes flashing with heat. "Don't you dare start with that. It's not like I'm drinking myself unconscious day in and day out. I've been on the road with you for weeks and had zero alcohol. I didn't have a thing since we got back until tonight, and I'm still stone cold sober. I've had two drinks in the last hour."

"I hate seeing you drink to bury it. Cry, yell, scream, grieve, do something, but don't just sit here and do this."

She stared into the empty glass. "I'm good at this. If I let my emotions get away from me, I put the people I love in danger. This is safer for everyone. I pout and sulk, drink until I go numb, sleep, puke, wish I was dead and then move on. It's a cycle that works for me." She sighed and placed the glass on the floor. "Will it make you feel better if I stop at the two?"

"Much."

"Then I'll stop at two."

He turned his head to look at her. "Have you talked to your mom and dad about how you're feeling about this?"

"No. I don't want them to be worried about me." She shook her head emphatically. "They have enough to worry about. Eden and Donovan are fighting, Finley has the baby, they're getting older, it's too much to ask them to worry about me, too. And I'm fine. This is a lot that we have to do, and I have some mixed up feeling about Gabriel. It's nothing I can't handle. I was handling it very well, in fact, until today when Griffin yanked Damon and Greer out of Heaven and I got reminded that Gabe and Aradia are nothing. They aren't in Heaven. They just disappeared. They don't exist anywhere anymore. They're just gone." She wiped at the tears on her cheeks. "I hate that so damn bad!"

Deacon tugged her into his lap, cradling her against his body. "I know, and I hate it, too. I want to make it better for you, but I can't." He brought her mouth to his, brushing a kiss over hers gently. "I love you, Maya."

Smiling, Amaya bumped her nose against his. "I know. I love you, too."

Serious, he shook his head and cupped her cheek in one of his hands. "No, I mean I'm in love with you." He placed his other hand on her hip, kneading her skin gently. "I love you so much I can barely see straight. You're the first thing I think about when I wake up and the last thing before I fall asleep. I'll spend the rest of my life loving you if you'll let me."

Stunned, Amaya sat back, staring into Deacon's eyes. "I've been head over heels in love with you since I was seventeen years old. I never thought you felt the same way. We've always been such good friends that eventually the feelings ebbed into this warm friendly sort of love." She leaned forward to brace her forehead on his. "The moment I kissed you in the kitchen they all came roaring back, and I've been sitting on them trying not to slap you with them until you figured it out for yourself."

Deacon crushed Amaya to him, claiming her mouth with his own. His tongue swept past her lips, inundating her with his taste. Amaya twined her arms around him, pressing herself against him feverishly. As his mouth trailed down her neck, she threw out one hand and flicked her wrist, turning the locks on the door to the library. She tore at his shirt, ripping it over his head and casting it to the side.

Deacon fumbled with the buttons on her shirt before getting frustrated and ripping it open, sending buttons flying. His hands took possession of her breasts, kneading the mounds of soft, supple flesh through the thin barrier of lace and silk. Her nipples jutted through the bra and he rubbed them with his fingertips, enjoying the feel of her flesh in his hands.

Slowly, he slipped the front enclosure loose and eased the cups away, freeing her breasts to his gaze and touch. Dipping his head, he laved attention on her with his mouth and tongue. Amaya arched her back, pressing herself into his mouth, groans tearing from her as he sucked and licked her nipples.

Bolts of emotion raced through her and her powers threatened to surge out of control. Tamping down on it, Amaya forced herself to control the waves of power. Sensing what was happening, Deacon very carefully ramped up his own abilities, molding them to hers and using his to help her control her abilities.

Her hands tore at his belt, ripping the strip of leather from the belt loops. Lithely, she popped the button from the loop and eased the zipper down, the sound of the hiss artificially loud in the room.

"I don't want to go slow." Her voice was a pant in his ear as she struggled to pull off his pants. "I just want you."

Deacon stripped her pants down her legs, throwing them to the side and streaking his hands up her flesh, kneading them gently. He grappled for his own pants that she had yanked off, fumbling for the slim foil packet in the back pocket. Amaya lifted her eyebrows.

"Do I even want to know why you have that in your pocket?"

Deacon smirked as he rolled the condom onto his bulging erection. "I came down here with the intention to lure you somewhere quiet and take advantage of you. I didn't anticipate tearing each other's clothes off in the library with ten other people in the house."

Amaya straddled his lap, gripping the base of his penis in one hand and easing down onto him, sighing with pleasure as he slipped inside her.

"There's something to be said for being spontaneous." She smiled when his hands gripped her hips as she rocked back and forth. "Am I doing it right?"

Deacon met her gaze steadily. "As if you could ever do anything wrong." He brushed a kiss over her collarbone. "Do you feel in control?"

She nodded, her concentration on the feelings washing through her. "Whatever you're doing is helping." She rolled her hips against his, quickening her pace. "It feels like every time my power starts to spike, you're calming it down."

Deacon stroked his hands up her ribcage and around to her breasts, teasing the tips with his fingers gently. He kept his eyes on her face, watching the expressions that moved across it as she rode him. Her movements had started slow and hesitant, but as she grew more confident, they sped up until their hips were colliding rhythmically.

Keeping her gaze, Deacon reached between their bodies to where they were joined, parting the folds of her body and stroking the pad of his thumb over her clit. The stimulation from his hand combined with the sensations from the thrusts was enough to send her soaring over the cusp of climax and Amaya came, panting and moaning as her body tensed and released.

Without missing a beat, Deacon grabbed her hips and flipped her onto her back, never sliding out of her. He wrapped her legs around his waist and drove himself deep within her, bracing himself on one arm by her head and keeping the other hand on her hip.

Amaya's head thrashed on the floor and mumbled nonsense spilled from her lips as she lost herself in the waves of pleasure that crashed over and through her. Before she had even come down from her release, he was driving her back up. Her breath caught in her throat and she clawed at his arms, dragging him closer, her mouth seeking and finding his.

Deacon slowed his thrusts, moving almost completely out before sliding back in slowly, rocking himself against her, continuing to give her the friction and stimulation she needed to keep building her back up the crest of release. The hand on her hip slid around, finding her clit and stroking the bundle of nerves slowly, his finger sliding around, using the moisture from her body to glide over the nub, bringing her bolts of desire.

Over and over again he pushed into her, planting himself deeply and then rocking back and forth before pulling out until only the tip of his penis penetrated her, then sinking back in and starting the cycle again. Amaya was covered in sweat and her breath caught in her throat as she struggled to grab hold of the orgasm he held just out of reach. Her chest was flushed with color, her body pulsed around him, and her fingernails dug into his arms.

Taking mercy on them both, Deacon sped his pace, using his fingers to bring her quickly to orgasm, finding his release when her body clamped down around him during hers.

Panting and out of breath, he rolled to his side, gathering her close and holding her tightly against him. Amaya wrapped her arms around him, pressing herself firmly against his chest, her power spiking almost uncontrollably. Continuing to press his own power onto hers, Deacon managed to dampen it enough that she could bring it back under control.

"Will I ever be able to experience intense emotions and not have to worry about blowing things up?"

Deacon toyed with a lock of her hair and smiled down at her softly. "You don't have to worry about it because I won't let you while you can't control it, and eventually you'll learn how to, just like you have everywhere else. It's you and me, Maya. As long as we're together, I'm not going to let anything bad happen. You've got more power, but I've got more control. Together, there's nothing we can't handle. I believe this is how it was always supposed to be. You weren't ever meant to do things alone."

Amaya curled closer to him, yawning. "I hope you're right." She sighed deeply. "I feel like this thing with my powers is just that sex is so new to me. I remember when I couldn't control it if I got pissed off or upset. I'd start crying and lightbulbs would start exploding. I eventually got used to it and was able to control it in those contexts, but I had to learn how to keep it under control in each specific situation. I'm hoping that's what's going to happen here. We'll get enough practice and I'll figure out how to keep myself in control here the same way I had to learn everywhere else." She shrugged and tucked her head against his shoulder, closing her eyes and giving into the urge to sleep. "That's my hope, anyway."

Watching her as she slipped into sleep, Deacon cast his eyes to the ceiling. "Me, too."

Close to an hour later, Deacon carried Amaya from the library. Her hair hung over his arm as he cradled her head gently in the crook of his elbow. A blanket was draped around her shoulders and over her body, covering her top half to disguise the fact that her shirt had been destroyed in the course of their frenzied lovemaking.

Halfway up the stairs, a voice stopped Deacon cold.

"Once you're done there, come on back down to the kitchen. I think we oughta have a conversation, you and I."

Turning slowly, Deacon met Braxton's steely gaze. "I'd tell you this isn't what it looks like, but I don't know what else to say it is."

Braxton stared at him with a stern expression, though Deacon thought he saw his lips quirk in the threat of a smile. "Smart move. I'll be waiting."

"Yes, sir. I'll be right down."

Heart pounding in his chest, Deacon ascended the rest of the stairs and took Amaya into his room, tucking her into his bed before stopping to take what he was sure was one final look at the current arrangement of his facial features before returning to the kitchen.

Braxton was sitting at the table, a beer open at his elbow, and a second sitting across from him. When Deacon entered the room, the older man gestured to the unopened bottle. "Take a seat. I think we need to have a chat."

Deacon dropped into the chair and looked at the beer. "Did you poison it? Because I could really use a drink if you didn't."

His angry expression melting into an amused one, Braxton barked a laugh. "No, I didn't poison it. Get a drink before you pass out." He glared at the Nephil. "What did you expect? Did you really think no one in a house this crowded would see you sneaking her out?"

Deacon looked at his watch. "It is past midnight. I was hopeful."

Braxton leaned back and regarded the other man coolly. "You're not a kid anymore, Deacon." He shook his head. "My problem is that I keep seeing you all as kids. God, I remember when we found out about you. We had no clue what you were or if you'd be good or evil. The girls took turns taking care of you when Michael couldn't be here, and then when we lost against Lucifer he was thrown into the fire headfirst. No one left to help. He adjusted well to parenthood for anyone, let alone an Angel that's never supposed to experience it."

Deacon shifted in his seat, obviously uncomfortable. "I thought I was getting a lecture."

"You are. I'm just getting warmed up." Braxton offered a smile. "I do have a point. It's hard for us in this situation because I have almost as many memories of you over the last fifteen years as I do my own children. I changed your damn diapers, boy, and that makes this fucking awkward for me."

"I share your pain there, sir." Deacon had started feeling slightly nauseous. "But I won't apologize for loving her."

"And I'd like you a hell of a lot less if you did." Braxton finished the beer and rose to retrieve a bottle of bourbon. "We need something stronger, I suspect." He snagged two glasses and returned to the table. "I feel like I'm morally obligated to do this, but I don't want to because I feel as protective of you as I do of Amaya." He took a deep breath. "Is it just physical or are you serious about each other?" He held up a hand. "Before you answer, let me tell you I don't care which it is, and it's between the two of you. You're adults who make your own decisions. I'm just being nosy I guess."

"It's serious." Deacon straightened in his chair and accepted the drink. "I'm in love with her."

"Does she feel the same way?"

"Yes, sir, she does. I think we've been circling this for years. It started when we were teenagers, but Dad sat us down and told us that we couldn't be together because of my mother, and we never even tried to go behind his back. We were just friends up until a few months ago. Before we went to Purgatory, things had started to start."

"Started to start?" Braxton laughed. "I don't want the gory details. Michael told us years ago that any sort of physical relations Amaya has could be dangerous because of how much power she has and how hard it is for her to control it. It's nice to know he was wrong."

"He wasn't. She struggles with it." Looking uncomfortable, Deacon drained his cup in one gulp. "If we're going to talk about sex, I need another drink."

Obligingly, Braxton poured one. "I don't want to talk about sex. It's not right to discuss something about Amaya when she's not here and it's awkward for both of us. My daughter is an adult, she's capable of making her own decisions and she's a wonderful, smart, beautiful, strong woman. I'm not going to ask uncomfortable questions and ask you to give me painful answers. Alaria and Amaya would both knock me loopy if they knew I was talking to you at all." He looked pained. "It's not that I think they're any less capable than I am. I don't. But sometimes, a dad just wants to poke his nose where it doesn't belong, flex his muscles and make the young man involved with his daughter uncomfortable. Is that so wrong?"

Recognizing that there was only one answer to that question, Deacon shook his head. "Not at all. I'd do it myself if I had a daughter." Thinking about it, he was rather positive he would. Feeling better about the situation, he sipped from the second drink and relaxed slightly. "I can lay my powers over hers and keep them from spiking out of control."

Curious, Braxton looked at him over the rim of his glass. "Could you do that in other places, too? She's always had problems controlling her abilities because she has so much power."

"I think so, but we've never tried. She's really very good at controlling herself now. She very rarely loses control of her emotions more than it takes to blow out some lights. There hasn't ever been a need to try."

"If I've learned anything in the last sixty some odd years, it's that these things don't just happen for no reason. If you can overlay her powers with yours to give her more control, it's an ability that's going to be needed at some point." Braxton looked at the bottle, then back at Deacon appraisingly. "I do believe it is my God-given responsibility to get completely shit faced after the level of discomfort I have put us both through tonight. Care to join me?"

Deacon sighed deeply. "And I suppose it's my God-given responsibility to bond with my future father-in-law in drunken camaraderie." He lifted his glass. "Are we going to tell Amaya and Alaria about this?"

"Fuck no! Do you have a death wish, boy?" Braxton looked incensed as he drank. "This is between us." He glared at Deacon. "I like you. More than that, I love you like one of my own, so don't fuck up, okay? And make sure she doesn't fuck up, either. I don't want to see either of you hurt."

"I don't plan on it."

CHAPTER TWENTY-ONE

JANUARY 20TH, 2061

THE MANOR

AMAYA STOOD back and surveyed the packs, checking off the last items on her list. "I think we've got everything. I've checked it twice off your list, Zeke." She glanced to her friend and smiled when she saw the other woman was distracted by her son. "Zeke!"

Zeke's head snapped up. "What?"

"I said I finished packing the bags. We're ready to go."

Zeke looked sad for a moment. "I hate to let you go. I really wish I could go with you, but I know you have to do this alone the same way I had to do my part in it." She stood and crossed the room. "I'll go get Lux and let her know you're ready."

Before either could move, Griffin appeared in the room, her hair askew and her jacket torn. "Michael! Michael, come quickly!"

Michael came out of his office, concern evident on his face. "Griffin, what's wrong?"

"Lucifer is sieging on Heaven. Azazel is leading troops against the Gates! Angels are being slaughtered!"

Michael held up his hand as everyone in the house gathered. "Calm down. How many are there?"

"Thousands. He's brought Devils, demons, and Cambion. The Gates will not hold! We need the Nephilim! You must come now!" Griffin wrung her hands together, her eyes darting around the room.

"Okay, stay calm. We're going to handle it. I want you to go back to Heaven and get a squad of Angels to guard the souls. If Azazel gets through the gates, you're to gather the souls together into a vessel and run with them to Earth. Do you understand?"

Griffin nodded, the panic in her eyes starting to ebb. "What are you going to do?"

"I'm going to handle it." He looked around the room. "Zeke, take Caleb to Alaria and Braxton, then suit up. You're going to have to go. Carys, you'll take her to Earth to drop off the baby and then come back here immediately.

With a hoop of excitement, Zeke nodded. "I'm ready."

"I know you are. Go now." He didn't wait to see if they'd gone. "Lux, you are still going to send Deacon and Amaya through to Atlantis. We can't take the risk that this is a distraction. The timing is very suspicious to me, so we can't allow this to affect our plan. Once you're done with them, come straight to Heaven to help." Moving on, he turned to the others. "All the rest of you, you have your assigned Nephilim base to go to in the case of an emergency. I want you to go to them immediately and gather all available Nephilim. Send them out to the other bases and have them come here as quickly as possible. I want as many Nephilim as we can get here within ten minutes. Go!" He looked at Deacon and Amaya. "I know you'll do well. I have to go collect Jophiel and the few Angels on Earth." He laid a hand on each of their shoulders. "I'm sorry we don't have time for proper goodbyes, but I don't doubt you can accomplish this. Stay safe and know my thoughts are with you both. I love you."

Amaya grabbed Michael's arm before he could flash. "You should let us come help. We have the sword. If Lucifer is there, I can kill him."

Michael shook his head. "Not without killing Serafina and the unborn child first. No, you need to stick to the plan and go to Atlantis. I suspect this is a trick to allow Abbadon and Lilith to get access to Atlantis. They may be trying to get there ahead of us and get the Spear. You need to get there and execute the plan as we discussed."

"Can they even get through time?"

Deacon crossed his arms. "If we have a witch that can do it, we have to assume they can find one, too. I know Lux is the most powerful, but we don't know if this is something only she can do or not."

Lux looked between them. "I can certainly tell you I haven't sensed the power signature necessary to get a time portal opened up. If that's the plan, they haven't done it yet, but I agree with Michael. This smells like a trick to stop us from getting the Spear. Let them handle it, and I'll send you two through. I think it's for the best." She turned to Michael. "I'm using the Choosing Place for it. The residual magic there from the spells my mom cast and the Choosing itself will help bolster the spell. I do believe that's the one place on Earth this can be done from. There's nowhere else with as much power, and to get the boost to go that far through time you need a hell of one."

"Then I will assign protection to the Choosing Place once this is done." Michael cast one last look at them. "I must go."

Amaya grabbed her bag as the Angel disappeared. "Let's get this going then. I want to get there ahead of them if they're trying to trick us into anything."

Amaya could feel power humming in the air as they walked through the heavy wooden doors and into the Choosing Place. Leaves and snow had blown into the entry way and dirt coated the floors. The piles of rubble had shifted over more than three decades, with stones falling from the ceiling and walls as the structure became less stable.

"If someone doesn't do something soon, this place is going to fall in on itself." Deacon carefully stepped over a beam and held out a hand to help each of the women over it.

Lux led the way down the hall to the sanctuary. "No it won't. The magic is holding it up. This place is too important. The Lucifer gate is here, the Choosing Place is here, this is where our parents failed. There's a lot of blood and power here." She pushed open the door to the sanctuary and stood for a moment. "I can feel it."

Candles still stood in a circle, covered in a thick sheen of dust. Protections were painted on the walls, the floor, and the ceiling. Chains were anchored that had been used to hold each of the Devils as their wing roots were carved from their backs. A brown stain on the floor showed where Griffin had died.

Amaya took a deep breath and cast her eyes around the room,

feeling as if she should whisper. "I feel like we should turn this place into a museum after all this is over. So much happened here." She walked to one of the pews and sat down. "My mom took her first breath as a human here. My parents got together here. Dad married Griffin in this room. Lux, your dad was here for the battle at the Choosing, too."

Lux glanced up from unpacking her bag of supplies. "I know. He speaks fondly of Griffin. This place feels Holier than any church I've ever been in. I look around and I can picture them all standing, holding hands, trying to re-chain Lucifer." She flicked her wrist and lit the candles that had been left. "I'm going to use what Mom did. Layers of power."

Amaya wandered to the corner where Braxton had once lain unconscious while Griffin and Alaria fought to get to midnight. "Should we try to bring Lucifer here to kill him? Finish it where it started. There's something about that that feels right to me."

Lux lifted one shoulder. "If it was me that had to do it, I absolutely would, but that's because I have to draw on magic to do things. I need those layers, that outside influence. You're supposed to have everything inside you, right where you need it. Getting him here could be difficult, but there's no downside of doing it here." She brushed off her hands and stood back. "Okay, I need you two to stand in the middle of the circle. Hold hands so that you're connected. I've never done this before, so I want to make sure you're going to the same place at least."

Deacon's head snapped up. "You mean there's a chance we don't end up in Atlantis?"

"There's always a chance. Nothing is ever guaranteed. I'm opening a rip in time, looking back and trying to find my mother's magic signature. Hypothetically, I could end up taking you to Atlantis or to Scotland thirty years ago, or to Purgatory six months ago." She handed each of them a piece of paper and a citrine. "This is a spell to call for me. It'll bring my astral projection to you. If you land in the wrong place, cast the spell and I'll figure out how to get you to where you need to go. Remember not to interact with anyone and not to be seen if you land somewhere else."

Amaya tucked the rock in her pocket. "Suddenly I wish Michael was doing this."

Lux smiled. "I'm mostly sure this will work. And no one's going to be able to hitch a ride, which is the point." She drew a blade across her palm and winced when it cut through flesh. "Now be quiet, both of you. This is some major magic and I need to concentrate on it."

Lux let her magic whip up within her, still unfamiliar with the amount of power she contained after Aradia's death. She focused the magic into one stream, braiding it together into a strong cord that she could use to weave the spell she was casting. Softly at first, then louder as the magic built, she began to chant the words to the incantation.

"Hear my words, hear my cry, bless my Quest, help me fly. The time is here, the enemy close. We beseech the Gods to fly from this world to another. Walls of time, tunnels of space, open the door, allow entrance to the wonders of Atlantis. I seek entrance to the fabric of time. Rip form, tear open. Two to fly, two to return. Magic seeking magic, time across time, blood to blood, child to mother. I call upon the blood of my blood. I call upon the source of my magic. I seek the time of Atlantic, and the vessel of Christ. Our hearts our pure, our mission true. Grant our Quest, free two to fly. As I will it, so must it be!"

Amaya gaped as a swirling blue and silver mass rose out of the floor and opened in front of them. Lux yelled triumphantly, then bent over to grab her knees, tired from the spell.

"That's the door! Go through! If you end up somewhere wrong, use the spell and I'll get you where you need to go." She looked at each of them, holding their gaze for a long moment. "I love you both. Come home safe."

"We will." Amaya offered her friend a smile. "Be careful going to fight. Be safe. I love you."

Lux watched as Amaya and Deacon disappeared through the portal, satisfied at the spell. She flicked her hand to extinguish the candles, deciding to leave them where they were in case they were able to lure Lucifer there to kill him. Each big spell cast layered more residual magic, giving them a bigger boost for the next. The less she moved, the better off they would be for the next time.

Gathering her supplies, she strode from the sanctuary, intending to leave the building before flashing back to Michael's. Her thoughts already on the battle raging in Heaven, she was distracted enough that she didn't sense the flash signature until after it happened.

Before Lux could do more than pivot, she was faced with a man in a red suit. His hair was white, slicked back from his face and shiny with gel. Icy blue eyes glowed in a face of sharp lines and harsh angles. She leaped back, only to crash into Lilith, who shoved her angrily forward, cradling her bulging stomach protectively.

"You bitch! You could have hurt my baby!"

The man cleared his throat. "I don't believe we've ever met in reality. You're Lux Windsor. I'm Lucifer."

The tendrils of panic that had been curling through Lux's gut turned to ice. She tried to flash, only to find herself anchored to the stone floor. Ramping up her magic as high as it would go, she threw out a wave at both Devils, managing to blast them back several feet. Turning on her heel, she ran.

She burst through the door and charged across the lawn, trying over and over to flash. Before she made it to the driveway, Lucifer came out the door and stretched out one hand, closing his fist. Lux felt a crushing pain in her chest and her feet stopped moving. She jerked against the force, trying to use magic to blast her way free of it, but unable to do so.

Desperate, she flung open the doors to the black magic she hadn't accessed since the death of her mother. It flowed through her unchecked, rupturing her citrine and refracting through her body, pouring out wildly from her. She threw waves at Lilith, driving the she-Devil back over and over. Blood streamed from her ears, eyes, and nose, choking her as she tried to breath. Spells jumbled together in her mind as she tried to do everything from re-open the rip in time to escape to get to Heaven to call for Michael.

"She's going to blow herself up like her fucking mother did if we don't get her under control!" Lilith's voice was a screech that barely penetrated Lux's fog of black magic.

Lucifer looked around, his eyes alight. "She's got so much power, my darling. I cannot wait to harness her ability." He reached out with his own power and broke through her wave, slamming himself against her magic.

Lux screamed from pain as Lucifer's power collided with her own. Her whole body felt as if it was on fire. Pain erupted in every nerve, scorching her skin and muscle. Even her bones felt like they were on fire. When he crashed into her again, the pain overtook her and her magic extinguished, unconsciousness overtaking her. Her body crumpled to the floor into a heap, twitching as her nerves continued to fire from the pain coursing through them.

Brushing his hands on his pant-legs, Lucifer stooped and lifted Lux in his arms, cradling her as he would a small child. He glanced at Lilith. "Call off the siege on Heaven. We got what we wanted.

Have the witches standing by to sever the link with the other Nephilim immediately. We cannot have him finding out where she is. He may already know she's been injured so it's just a matter of time before they know she's missing."

Lilith inclined her head and disappeared. Lucifer looked down at the unconscious witch and began walking down the driveway, holding her gently.

"I wish you wouldn't have fought so hard. I hate seeing you in pain, my darling." He stroked one hand over her face, removing the blood and using his power to ease the pain in her nerves. "I dislike seeing you in pain." He bent his head to press his lips to her cheek. "The power coursing through you is so great. Amaya has to die. That's an unfortunate reality since she has even more power than you do." Conversationally, he continued to speak to Lux's unconscious form as he walked aimlessly toward the main road. "I like collecting powerful things. You're going to help me siege on Heaven. I'm going to help you realize your full potential. You're so much more powerful than Garrick ever was. There's so much magic you can use to help me take over. Together, my darling, you and I are going to take over Heaven." He trailed one finger down her chest and over her breasts. "Lilith will be my Queen, of course, but every King needs a mistress, and I think you'll do quite nicely."

CHAPTER TWENTY-TWO

ZANE CHARGED a Cambion, his sword raised, ready to run the creature through with it when the man disappeared. Skidding to a stop, he looked around to see demons and Cambion disappearing from everywhere. Before he could open his mouth to ask what was happening, a searing pain ripped through his head, driving him to his knees.

Broken images filled his mind. Lux running, fighting, flailing. Magic swirling, black pouring from her. Zane held his head and screamed, rocking back and forth as agony ricocheted through him. The pain ebbed slowly, allowing him to climb to his feet slowly. All around him, Nephilim he didn't know were staring at him in concern, some still afraid to touch him.

Not even sparing them a word, he flashed to Earth, heading directly to the Choosing Place.

The first thing he saw when he arrived was scorched grass and melted snow. Blood smeared the ground, and there was an indent where a body had landed. Seeing no sign of Lux, he raced for the door.

"Lux! Are you here?"

The first floor was empty, the candles from the spell she had cast to send Amaya and Deacon to Atlantis still warm. Panic rising in his chest, he took the stairs to the second floor two at a time and rounded the corner quickly, searching each room, knowing as he did it that Lux wasn't there.

Focusing on the flashes of memory he'd experienced, he tried to eke out more details about what had happened but got nothing more than a flash of a red suit, a lot of pain, and even more power. On his way back outside, another bolt of pain rocketed through his skull, knocking him off his feet again. By the time he could see through the black haze of debilitating pain, the only thing he felt was emptiness and all he heard was silence.

Lux was gone. Their link was severed.

Panic rose in his chest, hot and thick. Nausea rolled through his gut, churning until he thought he would puke. Desperate and scared, he flashed back to Michael's, searching every room. While he was tearing through them, the others arrived, their voices filled with excitement about having run the demons and Cambion off.

Zane raced down the stairs and ran straight for Michael, grabbing the Angel's arms.

"It was a trap! They've got Lux. The link is gone. I can't feel her in my head! They have her!"

All conversations ceased. Michael grabbed Zane by the arms, mirroring Zane's grip on his, and shook him roughly. "What did you see? Show me everything."

Zane carefully replayed the memory he had seen through the link while Michael looked into his mind. Withdrawing from the Nephil's mind, Michael kept hold of his arm. "Dev, Zeke, my office. Everyone else, go get cleaned up and back to your patrol schedule. I want two of you on the Choosing Place at all times. Go!" He looked toward Jophiel, who was standing to the side. "Would you join us, brother?"

Jophiel straightened. "It would be my pleasure. The Nephilim I have been training have returned to their base and are cleansing themselves from the dirt of battle." He followed Michael into the office and sat in one of the chairs. "What is it that you need assistance with?"

Zeke closed the door behind them. "What's happened to Lux? Where is she?"

Michael dropped into the chair behind his desk. "Lucifer has her." He held up a hand when the three Nephilim burst into conversation. "Hush for a minute. I don't think they took her to kill her. Lucifer made it clear that he wanted to harness her power and use her as a weapon against Heaven, so we have no reason to believe that he's doing anything else. I know that doesn't make things feel better and it doesn't lessen the need to get to her with all expediency, but we can safely assume that she's alive."

Zane ran his hands through his hair. "She could be getting tortured, raped, starved or worse! There's no telling what they're doing to her!"

"I know, and it will be our primary goal to get her back. I'm going to go to the Choosing place and see if I can get a sense for where they may have taken her. With any luck, I'll be able to read the trail they left and get a general location. Jophiel, please go to the Nephilim bases you're overseeing and arrange for searches of the various sectors. We need to find where they've taken her as soon as possible."

Jophiel lifted his eyebrows. "You would devote so many resources to one Nephil? That seems to be a waste of time and energy. I understand that you have an emotional attachment to this particular one, but I urge you to be logical about the disbursement of resources."

Michael grabbed Zane's arm as he launched himself from his chair. "Sit down before he slices you in half." When Zane reluctantly sat, Michael continued. "Lux isn't just a Nephil. She's also the singular most powerful witch to have ever lived. She has powers that Lucifer believes can help him defeat God. He wishes to control her and use her as a way to take over Heaven. His possession of her is a direct threat to everyone."

Jophiel nodded. "In that case, I concur with your assessment of the situation and will arrange the patrols immediately." He stood. "Is there anything else with which I can be of help?"

"No, thank you, though. I'll check in with you shortly on the state of the patrols." Michael was silent until Jophiel had left. He gripped Zane's hand tightly and looked at Zeke, who was holding Dev's arm with both hands, panic evident in her face. "We'll find her. I need to check with your father, Zane, to make sure that he can monitor her soul and alert us if her condition is degrading. He may also be able to help us find a location, so I'll try to convince him of that as well." He sighed deeply and looked pained. "Someone needs to tell Gage."

Zane paled. "Oh, God. Gage. Fuck. He's going to go off the deep end."

Zeke shook her head. "No, he won't. It's his daughter. He's

going to find her. He holds it together when it counts."

Michael stood. "I'm going to go. Zane, I think you should as well. Zeke, Dev, I want the two of you to make a list of the places that we know of on Earth they could have her. We are going to find her, no matter how long it takes."

Gage was eating dinner when Michael appeared with Zane at his side. He rose, looking at Alaria and Braxton with trepidation.

"Where's Lux?"

"She's alive." Michael's voice was clipped. "The attack on Heaven was a distraction. Unfortunately, we fell for it. Lucifer's target was Lux. He's kidnapped her. We believe he wishes to turn her and harness her power in order to use it against God and overthrow Heaven. The link between Lux and Zane has been severed, but I've checked with the Angel of Death, and he has assured me that she is still alive." He laid a hand on Gage's shoulder. "I have Jophiel organizing patrols with the Nephilim. Zeke and Dev are making a list of possible places she could be. We're going to find her, Gage. I promise you that."

Gage looked at Zane. "You're sure the link was severed?"

Zane nodded. "It was the worst pain I've ever felt, and I can't feel her anywhere." He shrugged ruefully. "On the upside, I'm still not killing people when I touch them. At least not yet."

Michael looked at everyone in the room in turn. "I'm going to the Choosing Place as soon as I leave here to see if I can trace the flash trail. Since it was Lucifer that took her, I don't hold out much hope that'll work, but I'm going to try nonetheless." He focused on Gage. "Is there anything I can do for you right now?"

Gage shook his head. "I need to go to your place. I have to work on figuring out where she is. I have contacts I can get in touch with. I need to arrange for weapons and ammo. I'll need to see maps of where the patrols are being done. If you have a working computer, that would be great and make things easier. We'll need to check Purgatory as well. I wouldn't put it past them to send her there. The same with Hell. That's Lucifer's realm, so if we can't find her on Earth, then we need to look elsewhere." He paced the kitchen stiffly. "It's Lucifer, so we don't know what protections they might have. A brief patrol isn't going to do it. It's going to have to be a room by room search of every place on this planet to find her. I want all the manpower we have devoted to this."

Michael nodded. "It's our first priority right now. Amaya and

Deacon got through into Atlantis safely, and if we haven't gotten her back when they come back through, we should be able to use Amaya to locate Lucifer at that time if he's the one who has her. We'll find her one way or another."

Gage stopped pacing and stared at Michael, his eyes steely. "Wherever she is, I'm going with you. I'm going into this fight. I've lost my wife. I'm not losing my child, too."

Michael looked pained. "Gage, as much as I cherish the memories of fighting alongside you, I don't think your place is going into battle against Lucifer. The odds of your survival as a human are slim to none. This isn't your war anymore."

Gage's eyes flashed with fury. "Then change me back." He threw up his hands in frustration. "You think I'm so old and feeble? Change me back! Do it!" He slammed his fist into the counter. "I wanted to be human to spend my life with Aradia! She's gone! My daughter is in the hands of Satan himself! My wife dead, my daughter kidnapped, and you tell me I'm too weak to fight for them? Then change me back!"

Alaria cleared her throat. "Gage, think about what you're asking. Lux isn't dead. Would you really want to watch her grow old and die while you continue to live as you used to be? Or watch all of us die off and leave you alone?"

"It's better than the alternative!" Gage whirled to face her. "I was happy, Alaria. I was fine as a vampire. I had friends and a good life doing what I wanted, and then all of you came along. I love you all. You're my family, and I wouldn't trade the years we've had together for anything, but it wasn't the two of you or Damon and Greer who made me want to be human. I'd have grieved you when you died and remembered you for the rest of my days with great fondness, but it was Aradia I wanted to spend a *life* with. That's been ripped away from me by this fucking thing, and I'll be damned if I let it take my child, too! I would rather watch Lux grow old and die then have her die now because her father is too old and weak to help find her. I'll make that same choice a thousand times straight if given the chance." He looked back to Michael. "Turn. Me. Back."

Michael looked pained. "Gage, I don't even know if I can. I can heal people, but death is not within my purview. In order to revert you back to your vampiric form, I would have to kill you. That isn't something I can do. If you were to die, we have no reason to believe you would be anything other than just dead."

"Then find someone who can! Drag a fucking vampire in here!

Make me a goddamn Angel! Give me some of your Grace! Kill me, send me to Heaven and give me some of it! I'll be like Griffin. I'll take Angelic powers over this. Do something! God damn you, that is my child out there! My baby! How would you feel if it was Deacon and someone was telling you that you couldn't go save him?" He looked at Braxton and Alaria. "Or if it was Amaya or Finley or Eden or Donovan and you couldn't get to them? Damon and Greer died for their child. Aradia blew herself up to save all our asses! I'll take the sacrifice. I'll give up my soul. Find me some Devil to make a deal with."

Michael blanched. "I would never tolerate you giving up your eternal soul so rashly." He leaned against the counter and stared at Zane. "You're being very quiet. What are your thoughts?"

Zane looked at Gage as he spoke. "I love Lux. I also think I know her better than just about anyone. I want to marry her and have a family with her and grow old with her. I want forever with her." He smiled sadly. "Sir, I know your daughter, and I know that the most important thing to her is her family. It's more important than this mission, it's more important than herself, it's more important than anything else. She'd never forgive herself if you gave up your humanity for her. But I also know how I feel about her, and were I standing in your shoes, I'd never forgive myself if I didn't, knowing that I had a chance to save her if I did." He shrugged helplessly. "Logically, I know we'll probably find her and could go get her without you. Even as a vampire, you going in against Lucifer is damn near suicide. This isn't about logic. It's about you and Lux and you needing to know that you're doing all you can to save her and being able to live with yourself if we can't. I don't think either of us could if we didn't try. I wish you'd reconsider because I know what this is going to do to her, but I completely understand why you're doing it, and I would make the same call." He looked at Alaria and Braxton. "You would, too, if it were your child and not his."

Gage glared at Michael. "Find a way to turn me back or I'll go do it myself. There are plenty of vampires around here that I'm sure would jump at the chance to help me."

There was a shimmer and an Angel appeared in the room. He was dressed in all black, had pitch black hair, eyes so dark they were nearly black and his wings were inky black save for silver tips. Zane knew immediately he was looking at his father.

Michael stepped forward. "Death. Have you news on Lux?"

The Angel shook his head. "I do not. Her soul is still anchored to its physical body, and there is no change in her condition. She is still alive and well. I have not been able to locate her on Earth. It appears her captors are blocking Angelic interference." He looked around the room. "It is another matter on which I am here." He took a step toward Gage. "Do you know who I am, human?"

Gage squared his shoulders. "You're the Angel of Death."

"My brother may not be able to control life and death, but I can." Death lifted one hand and looked at his fingers. "With one touch, I can bring death, or I can give life. Though I have never done it before, I believe that I may be able to deaden your body and revert it to when you were a vampire. In this manner, you would be as you were then, with the same abilities, strengths, weaknesses, and powers. You would live on blood, be cold to the touch, have your resistance to sunlight, and continue on as an immortal. However, since you would not truly die and then rise to begin anew as a vampire, your soul would remain within your body and upon your eventual death, you would be judged as every other human soul." He looked at Gage solemnly. "Since I have never before done this, the possible consequence is that you would die and your soul would be judged now. Do you wish for me to attempt this?"

Braxton spoke for the first time. "Gage, if I were in your shoes, I'd be crawling out of my skin wanting to do something. I get why you want to do this, but you need to be sure that you're willing to take a chance on being really completely and totally dead before you say yes. This isn't something reversible. No more prophecies, no spells, nothing. You wouldn't be human anymore."

Gage glanced toward his friends. "I spent fourteen centuries as a vampire and a combined six decades as a human. I know what I'm getting into."

Alaria's voice was gentle. "You've never had to watch your child grow old and die. Or your grandchildren. How many generations will you watch live and die?"

"No, I didn't watch my children grow old and die. I ate them." Gage's eyes were filled with pain. "I've lost children before, Alaria. I'm not going to let the worry of future pain control the chance to save the one child I have left." He looked at the Angel. "Do it. Turn me back. I'm sure. I'll do anything to save Lux. With Aradia gone, she's all I have left, and I'll be damned before I sit back and let other people be responsible for getting her back. I'm ready."

Death reached out and laid his hands on Gage's head. There was no flash and bang, no fireworks or explosions. Gage paled, his chest stopped rising and falling and he fell to the floor, limp and gray.

CHAPTER TWENTY-THREE

AMAYA AND Deacon emerged through the portal onto a beach. Looking around, Amaya lifted her hand to shield her eyes from the sun.

"Well, fuck. Obviously the battle isn't already going on or the sky would be black." She looked around, making sure that there was no one around to see them. "We need to get to the grotto Gage told us about and hunker down until we figure out how long we have to wait."

Deacon grimaced. "If the battle hasn't started, we can't go to the grotto. Gage and Aradia will be there. They were on their way back from it when Javal killed Liam, remember? If we walk into that clearing, we're likely going to walk in on them going at it, scaring ourselves and them eternally and doing only God knows what to the time line."

"They'll only be there if this is literally right before it starts. Lux was trying to pick up on major magic signatures. Maybe it was when Aradia and Graciela were practicing with the citrines or something. Or maybe Aradia has just defeated Garrick and the sky will be darkening any second now." She turned in a slow circle. "Regardless, we need to figure out how long we've got and find a safe place to hide until we can go get the Spear."

"Agreed. We'll head in the direction of the grotto, but we're going to have to go slow, be quiet and keep our distance. Gage is still a vampire in this time. He'll be able to sense us from quite a distance if they're there."

Amaya stooped long enough to pull out the map Gage and Alaria had drawn them and positioned it so she could orient herself to the city. Determining which direction they needed to go, she pointed toward the trees and struck out.

"I think it's about five miles this way, depending on how accurate Gage and Mom's memories are after thirty years."

Deacon grinned and withdrew his machete from his belt. "I'd say they're both still pretty damn sharp, actually." He glanced over his shoulders at her as they walked. "It's hard to believe it's been thirty years since they did this."

"My mom was pregnant with me while she was here. If you want to make your brain bleed even more, Aradia's mom is pregnant with her here, too. So my best friend's mom is both an adult and a fetus right now, just like me."

He sighed. "I'm not going to think about it too hard."

They trekked through the woods toward the creek and pool. Less than two miles from the beach, the wind picked up and clouds moved across the sky, darkening it to nearly black, blotting out the sun until not a single ray penetrated the thick wall. A grim smile on his face, Deacon drew to a stop.

"I think it's safe to say the battle's started. We know from right now that we have two days before Aradia and Braxton come back down the mountain." He reached into his pocket and withdrew a stopwatch, pressing the button to start the timer. "All we have to do is not interact with anyone until then."

Amaya set her own timer as a backup. "I'm really glad the spell got around the rule of not bringing anything back that didn't exist in the receiving time." She patted her pistol. "Not that I want to have to fire a gun in Atlantis, but I feel better having it anyway."

"The one advantage we have is that we know everyone here except Graciela and the six are going to die. We can't possibly do too much damage."

"I wouldn't hold your breath on that. Michael wouldn't have pressed us so hard on being quiet and staying out of sight if we didn't need to be careful."

"I'm just thinking about all the changes your parents made when they were here. Training, running the battle, killing Garrick.

Aradia was the one who sank the city. It was completely different than the first time. The only thing that matters is that the city sinks and the people who survive don't know we're here so we don't affect their futures. Pasts. Present. Whatever it is." He shook his head. "God this makes my head hurt."

Amaya chuckled and began walking in the direction indicated by the map. "Let's just get to the grotto and get hunkered down. We can deal with everything else later. We need to get this done and get home."

Forty minutes later, they emerged into a clearing. Amaya pointed to a pile of broken branches and foliage.

"There's where Aradia and Gage tied the horses. He said from here that the only way to get to the clearing is to get wet."

Deacon scowled. "So we get to spend the rest of the day waiting for our stuff to dry again. Great." He dropped onto a branch of the tree to tug off his boots. "Why do we always have to get into the water? First in Eden and now here."

Amaya opened her bag and withdrew two large plastic bags. "I thought ahead this time. We can stow our packs in here so they won't get wet. If we strip down naked, we won't even get our clothes wet."

"Do we really want to be naked in a place we've never been that's crawling with evil warlocks, super powerful demons on a mission, and a vampire army?"

"All of which are occupied with the city. We have no reason to believe we'll be anything other than completely safe out here." She shrugged. "And I never said we wouldn't be armed. I don't intend to let my gun out of my sight. I can wear a holster and my utility belt on bare skin." She ramped up her powers, reaching out and feeling for the presence of any beings. Finding none, she glanced back at Deacon. "We're alone. There's nothing here. I'm positive of it."

Amaya methodically removed her clothes, folding them and placing them in the bag, tucking her pack in it and pressing the edges together to form a seal. She strapped her utility belt and shoulder holster on over bare skin and waited on the bank while Deacon followed suit, rolling her eyes when he left his boxers on. Shrugging, he followed her into the water.

"Sorry. If someone comes after me, I want my dick to have at least some level of protection."

She snorted. "You think one layer of cotton is protection?"

"I fully understand that it's psychological, but that makes it no less important."

The water deepened quickly, rising to their waists before they were forty feet downstream. Within thirty yards, Amaya was able to kick off the bottom and begin swimming, keeping one hand on her bag as she paddled with her other arm and her legs.

The brook opened up into a grotto. The creek emptied into a deep, clear pool. At one end, it flowed out over a cliff that led down to an inlet and then, further out, the ocean. To the opposite end was a rock ledge behind a waterfall being fed by a small river. The bank on the side closest to where they had swum in was thick with vegetation, but on the opposite side, there was a thick carpet of moss. Amaya gestured to it.

"I think that's where we put up the tent." She climbed from the water and opened the bag, pulling on a shirt and underwear. "Let's get protections put up. Lux sent crystals to block Garrick from knowing we're here and some herbs. There's a spell to cast. If we use our regular stuff on top of it, we're going to be pretty damn safe." She handed him a chain with several twinkling pieces of stone. "Lux said to wear that while we're here. It'll shield us from being detected by other witches or warlocks and help limit the effect we have on the environment here."

Deacon looped the chain over his head and picked up a can of spray paint. He began spraying the moss and nearby trees with protection symbols to establish a boundary, keeping demons and Devils from flashing in to where they were. Within twenty minutes, the protections were in place and Amaya was putting up their tent, her movements quick and methodical.

"I think we oughta not light a fire if we can keep from it."

Amaya glanced up from driving a stake into the ground. "It's warm. We'll be fine without one." She glanced at her watch. "This being dark all the time thing is going to mess with my sense of time." She looked up at the thick cloud cover. "At least it's not so dark that you can't see."

"No, it's just like it's going to storm all the damn time." He tossed their packs into the tent. "It's too hot to stay in there until it's actually night. We can't really go anywhere. If you want to take a swim, I'll stand guard."

She lifted her eyebrows. "What happened to it being too dangerous?"

"That's why I said I'd stand guard and make sure you're safe. I don't sense anything, you don't sense anything. From what we know, the battle is concentrated in the city, which is miles from here. Other than Javal killing Liam on the way back to the castle, we have no reason to believe anything ever happened out here. There's nothing telling us that there are any other demons or Devils here aside from Javal. Besides, I feel much better now that we've got all our protections laid down. That gives us some extra security." He grinned at her. "I think we're safe, at least for the moment. When else are you going to have an opportunity to skinny dip in Atlantis?"

Amaya's eyes lit up as she grinned. "Technically, I already did that." She stood and unstrapped her holsters. "You sure you won't come in with me?"

"I'm sure. One of us needs to be on guard."

"You could come in and we'll fool around in the water." She wiggled her eyebrows as she shucked her underwear down her legs. "Not many people can say they had sex in Atlantis, either."

Deacon sat down on a boulder and stared at her stonily. "Stop trying to convince me."

"I packed a few condoms just in case." She waded into the water and tossed her shirt back at him. "They're in the front zipper pocket of my pack. Just in case you change your mind."

Amaya sliced through the water easily, enjoying the feel of it on her skin. She turned over, floating in the pool and staring up at the thick canopy of greenery as she mulled over the stories Gabriel had told her as a child.

"I always wanted to come here. Gabriel told me all about the tasks my parents had to do." She righted herself and bent her knees to stay submerged up to her chin. "I remember thinking that this was one of the places I so wished I could have experienced for myself. Now that I'm here, it feels weird to be where they are when they're here. I know from the stories that Gage and Aradia were having sex on that rock shelf right before we got here. He bit her, marking her as his, and now she's dead. Atlantis is where Mom told my dad she was pregnant with me. They weren't even together yet, not really. Aradia's father is dead now, when an hour ago he was riding out to warn Gage and Aradia about the battle."

Deacon leaned forward and balanced his elbows on his knees. "Don't get too caught up in the past, Maya. In thirty years your children will be talking about the stories of your glory days in that same tone. It's the nature of what we do. If you kill Lucifer, people are going to be talking about you like you talk about them for the rest of human history."

"I like to remember where we came from. It makes me feel better to know that we're not the only ones who have had to do this. Knowing they went through this before we did is comforting to me." She kicked her legs beneath the surface. "It's nice to know they all managed to do normal things in spite of it. It makes me feel less guilty about trying to talk you in here to seduce you while we're here to get the Spear. We had sex in the Garden of Eden, Deacon." She laughed softly. "I feel bad about things like that until I remember that we're allowed to still have lives, too. If we're not in danger, not actively fighting someone and it's not causing us to jeopardize our mission, there's no sin in having some fun wherever we can find it."

"That's one thing I think everyone has been very clear on. We all have jobs to do, but we have lives to live, too. There's nothing wrong with living them."

Amaya swam toward the shallow end of the pond, standing up so that the water was at her waist. "Still won't join me?" She trailed her hand across her shoulder and over her chest, grazing her own nipple with her fingertips. "I don't sense anyone within my range of detection."

Deacon swallowed and closed his eyes, squirming on the rock to try and loosen his suddenly too tight fatigues. "I don't want to take the chance, Maya."

"Do you really think there's a danger, or are you just being stubborn because you started off saying no and you don't want to backtrack?"

"Both." He offered a disarming grin. "We've only been here a couple hours. Feels kinda wrong to be stripping down and going at it so soon after arriving."

"Why?" She walked several steps out of the water, her skin glistening with moisture in the low light. "We're here, we're safe, we have nothing better to do and there's no one around for me to hurt if you can't help me stay in control." She smoothed her hands down her abdomen and slipped her fingers over her thighs. "Of course, if you're not interested, you can watch while I take care of things for myself."

Deacon stood and disappeared into the tent, re-emerging holding one of the sleeping bags. He unzipped it, spread it out on the moss and then went back into the tent, returning with a condom in his hand.

"I'm not coming into the water. If we're going to be reckless, let's at least do it up here with weapons within easy reach."

Amaya climbed from the water and went into his arms. "You're so responsible when you're reckless."

They were both laughing as he lowered her to the sleeping bag.

CHAPTER TWENTY-FOUR

JANUARY 21, 2061

JERUSALEM

LUX REGAINED consciousness slowly, becoming aware of her surroundings bit by bit. The temperature of the air hit her first, causing her whole body to shiver as cold ripped through her. She jerked, her eyes snapping open when she realized she was tied down. Blinking rapidly to clear her vision, she took stock of her surroundings, taking in the stone room, the pallet on the floor, the trays of instruments lying next to the chair to which she was confined.

"Welcome back." Abalam strode into her field of vision. "You took quite the nap. How are you feeling?" He held her head up and pressed a cup of water to her lips, watching with something akin to pity as she drank greedily.

"Where am I?"

"The Garden of Gethsemane. Jerusalem. We set it up as a sort of base of operations to work out of." He unfastened one of her hands and picked up a sandwich. "Eat. You need to keep your strength up. Are you cold?"

Lux goggled at him. "Who are you and what have you done with

Abalam?"

Abalam pulled up a stool and perched on it, crossing one leg over the other. "People have a very twisted view of me. I'm not at all unreasonable. As long as you cooperate. It's when you refuse to cooperate that we have problems." He nudged the water closer to her as she ate. "You need nutrition and liquid to survive, so I provide it. You need a bed on which to sleep, so it's available for you. There are facilities for you to relieve yourself, you'll be provided with clothing, bathing opportunities, and a Healer is here to make sure that you aren't too badly hurt for us to continue if that becomes necessary." He patted her knee gently. "I hope it's not."

"What do you want with me?"

"You know what we want. We want you to join with us and help overtake Heaven. If you are willing to swear loyalty to Lucifer, then give us information in order to ensure that we can find and kill those seeking to kill him, you will be released from here immediately and be hailed as a Knight of Hell. As much as it irks me, you would be my equal." He lifted one eyebrow appraisingly. "I'd be willing to bet God hasn't made you any sort of offers of preferential treatment after this is done. Don't you think all you've accomplished should be rewarded?"

Lux closed her eyes and concentrated on calming her racing heart. Her magic was being dampened by the protections they had in place. She was unable to access any of her powers. The link to Zane was severed. For the moment, she was as helpless as any human would have been.

"How did you turn off my powers?"

"We have a coven of witches working with us that placed protections here. In addition, while you were unconscious, Lucifer took advantage of your weakened state and placed walls inside your mind to keep you from accessing your abilities. It's a multi-pronged approach. I wouldn't try to mess with it. Only he can take them out."

Fear knotted in Lux's stomach as she considered the ramifications of that. She finished her sandwich and stared at Abalam steadily. "So let me get this straight. I can walk out of here right now if I swear an oath to Lucifer and turn over everyone I love so they can be butchered?"

Abalam nodded decisively. "Precisely. What do you say?"

"What do you expect me to say?"

His eyes twinkled. "I remember when your father and Michael

and Damon were in Purgatory and killed Abaddon. They took him from me after hundreds of millions of years together." He curled his lip in a snarl. "I'd love nothing more than to make them feel some of the same pain I've felt in the years since then. I'm hoping you say no so I can kill you, Lux Windsor. I'm hoping you keep saying no until Lucifer realizes what I've always known. The only use you have is dead."

Lux closed her eyes and took a deep breath. "They're going to find me eventually, and when they do, they're going to make you wish you'd never been created."

"Oh, Alaria got ahold of me once." He shuddered at the memory. "She's talented with a scalpel, that one. I'm man enough to admit that I wept like a child from some of the things she did to me. I never thought she had it in her. It was an impressive amount of balls for her to do it. God, I still remember the feeling of that screwdriver plunging into my thigh." He grinned maniacally. "It almost made me come on the spot. Such pain and vitriol while the body of Braxton's sister lay cooling on the floor where I could still see it, where I could still smell the blood."

Lux felt tears prickle the back of her eyelids. She looked around the room, desperate to figure out a way to escape. There were symbols drawn on every inch of the walls and ceiling. She was contained in a circle of crystals and herbs that she recognized as a witch trap. Inside it was the same symbol she knew was the Nephilim trap Lilith has used on her before. She could feel the edges of the walls Lucifer had put in her head to block her access to her powers and knew that as long as they were intact, she was stuck. Her only hope, save being rescued, was to fight her way past the walls, and manage to get out of the trap. If she could accomplish those two things, she stood a chance.

Abalam gripped her chin in his hand and forced her to look at him. "There's no need to be scared, darling. All you have to do to make it stop is say you'll join us." He smiled brightly and released her chin. "While you're considering your options, why don't I go over with you how my part of things works, hmm?" When she didn't answer, he continued. "As long as you're saying no, you're a threat. That means that you're a prisoner and you'll be treated as one. You have information I need, and I'm going to get it. I ask questions, you answer questions. As long as you answer the question asked with an honest, correct answer, there's no pain for you. If you refuse to answer, smart off to me, or lie, then I use one of these tools~" he gestured to the trays surrounding the chair Lux was strapped to, "to encourage you to talk."

"How will you know I'm not lying to you if I say yes?"

"Because you're going to forge a mental link with me. I'll be in your head, and I'll know if you're planning to betray us. There would also be a contract gifting your soul to Hell if you were ever to go back on your word." He cocked his head to the side. "Surely you're not already considering that? It would take all my fun away."

"Why did you pick Jerusalem?"

"Avoiding the question isn't nice." He glared at her. "I'll forgive it this once since you don't know all the rules yet." Sighing, Abalam toyed with a scalpel. "Gethsemane is where Lucifer went to Jesus on the eve of his crucifixion and offered to take the Cup of Wrath from him as his Father would not. Peter denied Jesus three times in this place and led to the killing of Christ. It's a very important place to God. It makes me exceedingly happy to torture Nephilim here. A little "fuck you" to the big guy. Beyond that, since this has been the place of important supernatural events in the past, the barrier between Hell and Earth is thinner here and we've been able to access the power of Hell, which allows us to keep your power drained more effectively while charging me up. Win-win for everyone. Well, except you, of course."

"This isn't one of the Hell Gates."

"Nope, it isn't. We don't enter and exit here. Think of it as an exhaust vent." Abalam leaned back in his chair and considered the situation at hand. "It's up to you what happens next, but I do need your decision."

Knowing she was out of time, Lux took a deep breath and offered a bright smile. "I'm going to have to decline."

Abalam stood. "Good. I was hoping you'd say that." He cracked his knuckles and rolled his shoulders. "I'm pretty anxious to get started, so I think we'll jump right in." He snapped his fingers to gather her hair back into a ponytail, keeping it off her face. "This is going to be extremely unpleasant for you." He picked up a pair of shears and cut her shirt off her body and slashed her jeans off at the knee before removing her shoes and socks. "Remember, I ask questions and you answer them. You must tell me the truth, and you must answer the question asked. If you fail to do so, you'll be punished. The longer you go without giving me the information I desire, the more unpleasant this becomes. Do you understand?"

"Yes."

"See? You know how it works! Have you done this before?" Abalam looked at his trays of tools admiringly. "Have you ever been tortured before, Lux? I won't continue to ask twice. When I ask a question, I expect an answer."

"No."

Pouting, he lovingly ran his fingers over the instruments. "What spell did you use to unlock time and send Amaya and Deacon through to Atlantis?" When she looked surprised, he smiled. "Oh, yes, we know about that. Unfortunately, Lucifer and Lilith arrived after you had cast it and were unable to document the spell you used. We'd like you to tell it to us so our witches can cast it and we can go after your friends."

"I don't remember."

Abalam's smile got wider. "I was so hoping you'd give me a reason to do something nasty to you." He flicked his hand and hummed as classical music began playing in the room. "I like music while I work." He perused the selection of tools before picking up a clamp in one hand and a scalpel in the other.

He stood and walked to the side of the chair, leaning over until his face was mere inches from her neck. Lux felt warm breath on her cheek and trembled, her whole body shaking in the cold air. Abalam's tongue darted out and brushed over her earlobe, tasting her skin and sucking the flesh into his mouth.

"There are many erogenous zones on the human body. Earlobes are one of the most overlooked. A scrape of teeth or a flick of a tongue can bring sexual arousal." He brought the clamp up and pressed the cold metal to her skin. "The opposite side of that coin is pain. The more nerves that are in an area, the greater the amount of pain I can bring you with very little effort." He clamped the tool down on her ear and pulled the flesh taut. "Feel how much that hurts with just a little pinch?"

Lux bit her lip to keep from crying out at the pain. Her hands dug into the armrests on the chair, and she broke one fingernail from gripping it so tightly. Abalam lifted the scalpel and pressed the blade against her cheek, drawing the edge through her skin, barely slicing through the first layer.

"This is going to hurt, darling girl. Take care you don't bite off your tongue."

With one slash, he ripped through the chunk of skin holding her earlobe to her ear, severing it from her body. Holding up the clamp with a jubilant cry, Abalam studied the bloody chunk of flesh in the cold light from the lamp.

Lux surged against the straps holding her down, struggling to get free. A strangled cry ripped its way from her throat, tearing from her against her will. Her teeth sank through her lip, the taste of blood blooming on her tongue as she rode the waves of pain. Little by little, it faded to a throb and she was able to concentrate on what was going on around her.

Blood ran down the side of her neck and arm, dripping off the side of the chair to form a small puddle on the floor. It stuck to the few pieces of hair that had escaped her ponytail as she struggled, turning the coppery red strands bloody and sticky. As the pain ebbed to a level that allowed her to think, Lux focused on what she had learned from that first slash of the scalpel.

Much as she had physically thrown herself against the leather straps holding her to the chair, she had flung herself against the mental walls Lucifer had implanted into her psyche that were holding her magic out of her grasp. As she brought herself back under control, she felt for the edges and detected a bit of wiggle in them.

She tried to wrap her mind around the walls and tear through them, but found them too strong. They were slightly weaker from the assault she had been able to put on them while in pain, but they still held.

The only unknown was whether or not the Healer Abalam had brought would be able to heal the damage she had done to the walls alongside the damage he had done to her body.

Knowing that accessing her magic was the only way in which she would be able to get out of the room alive, Lux gritted her teeth and straightened her shoulders before addressing the Devil.

"Is that all you got? Cutting my earlobe off? I thought you were supposed to be some savant of torture. Instead you do something a ten year old could have figured out. Pathetic, really. I thought you were better than that."

His eyes alight, Abalam looked at his tray. "Oh, my darling. I'm going to have so much fun with you. I think you need to learn some respect." He picked up a drill and pulled the trigger, the sound of the bit turning filling the room. "Let's get to work, shall we?"

CHAPTER TWENTY-FIVE

"IS HE alive? Did it work?" Alaria jumped from her chair, the legs scraping the floor as the furniture wobbled on its hind legs before falling to the floor with a loud clatter.

Zane crouched next to Gage's prone form, pressing his fingers to the man's throat. "He's dead."

Death looked affronted. "Of course he is. A vampire is not a living being like humans or Nephilim."

Alaria covered her mouth with her hands, tears welling in her eyes. "He's not getting younger. It's not working!"

"It takes time for the process to reverse, sister. Give it a few moments. The reversal begins on a cellular level and emerges from there. It could take a matter of seconds or several minutes for physical signs to begin to manifest. His soul is not loosening from his body, so I have no reason to believe that he is truly dead." Death fluttered his wings and looked at Michael, who was standing silently. "You're being quiet."

Michael sighed deeply. "I'm not in favor of this decision. I don't think Gage is thinking clearly, and I dread what Lux is going to feel when she finds out what her father has done. I understand why he's made the choice, and in his position, I would have been hard pressed not to do the same, but I still don't believe it to be in the best interest of either Gage, Lux, or this mission. A vampire against Lucifer is little better than an old man."

"That presupposes it is Lucifer himself who is in possession of Lux. Isn't it more likely that he will have assigned the torture and rewiring of the witch to Abalam?" Death cocked his head to the side. "That is, after all, his specialty."

Zane crouched next to Gage. "This isn't about whether or not he can actually help. He's been lost since Aradia died, nearly drowning himself in the bottle, and Lux hasn't been able to snap him out of it. With her gone, too, he wouldn't be able to survive not doing anything. He'll never forgive himself for not being there when Aradia died. If he'd still been a vampire, he could have been. This is his way to make amends for what he views as his sin." He shrugged. "I don't agree with him, but I can certainly understand it."

Alaria waved her hand. "Look!" She pointed to Gage's hair, which was changing in color from gray to black, the lighter color receding from the roots and working its way off the shaft before dripping off the ends.

Death smirked. "It would seem the process is working." He cast a glance around the room. "With that, I will take my leave. I would suggest you arrange for some blood. He is likely to be ravenous when he awakens."

Braxton sighed deeply. "I bet he didn't think about that. We're going to have to take turns feeding him. There aren't blood banks like there used to be."

Michael's wings jerked in displeasure. "He'll feed from the Nephilim. It will give him additional strength, and they replenish the blood at a much faster pace than humans do."

Zane didn't look up from staring at Gage. "He can feed from me. I don't mind." He rocked back on his heels. "I keep waiting for him to breathe or something."

Michael's mouth quirked in a smile he didn't want to let take hold. "It shouldn't be long. He looks almost as he was."

Alaria put her hand over her mouth. "He's thirty again." She chuckled. "This is going to be so weird."

Braxton tucked her to his shoulder. "Don't get any ideas about us becoming immortal along with him. One life is enough for me."

She leaned her head on him and slipped one arm around his waist. "You only say that because you've never been immortal."

Michael shook his head. "There comes a time when all beings want to rest. Life is not meant to stretch out forever with no end in sight. It loses its meaning when that happens. Life is frenzied and desperate and beautiful because it is so painfully short." He looked sad. "For me, these years will be nothing more than the equivalent of one of your commercials. A very memorable one, mind you, but that short. When time extends without end in either direction it becomes difficult to find enjoyment in it."

Alaria eased away from Braxton and studied Michael. "You sound a lot like I used to."

"Having a family has changed my opinion on immortality. I don't wish to stay as I am, an outcast from Heaven, and apart from Earth, a member of neither place for the rest of eternity. I have no desire to see my children grow old and die, to watch their children after them. I'm tired. I understand you now in a way I never before did, Alaria. To see Deacon and Dev and Zane, the girls, and know that soon they will appear older than I do, to see all of you grow older while I stay the same. I don't enjoy this process."

Braxton crossed his arms. "Do you have any options, though? It's not like there's another Choosing."

"My only option is to be cast to Earth." Michael gestured to Gage. "I believe he is waking up."

Gage groaned and rolled onto his side, coughing and choking as his body couldn't make use of the air he had sucked in. Gagging, he rolled to his knees and grabbed the bucket that served as a trash can, vomiting into it.

Alaria grimaced. "A vampire can't make use of human food, so his body has to expel it. They can still manage liquid since blood is a liquid, so he'll be able to drink things, but no solid food anymore."

"One less mouth to feed." Braxton's voice was heavy with sarcasm.

Gage sat back and wiped his mouth, his eyes glowing red and his fangs fully extended. "You all need to get out of here. I've got to go hunting. I forgot how hungry you are when you wake up." He grabbed his head. "Go!"

Zane crouched and held out his wrist. "We talked about this while you were asleep. Michael thinks it would be best if you fed from Nephilim. You can take more, we replenish it faster, and you'll take on some residual strength from the Angel in my blood." He jutted out his wrist. "Go on, drink."

Gage looked crazed. "Don't let me take too much. I nearly killed Aradia once when I was in a state like this. Vampires~we can't control ourselves when we get like this."

Zane looked at him drolly. "No offense, but I'm not in love with you. Eat enough to take the edge off. If you take too much, I'll knock you the fuck out."

The vampire grabbed the proffered wrist. "I like you. You're good for Lux." He sank his teeth into Zane's skin and growled as blood flowed over his tongue.

The taste was sweeter than normal blood. Gage soon learned that Nephil blood made his whole mouth tingle as it flowed over his tongue and seeped down his throat. The thick blood coated his throat and stomach, easing the gnawing hunger until he felt able to control himself. Retracting his fangs, he lifted his head and wiped his mouth gently, looking at the others apologetically.

"Sorry about that."

Zane stared at him. "That's it? You drank for like twenty seconds. Maybe."

Michael's brows drew together. "You couldn't possibly be fed, Gage. I suspect you need to feed for at least two minutes to extract a quart of blood from the vein. You've only ingested approximately three-quarters of a cup."

"I feel okay." Gage shrugged. "Maybe it's the Nephil blood. Makes my mouth tingle and feel funky. I suppose it could fill me up faster, too."

Zane shrugged. "Whatever it is, just be sure you aren't going to go homicidal on us. I can part with some more." He cast a glance around the kitchen and helped Gage to his feet. "Now that that's done, let's get back to the problem at hand, which is that we have no clue where Lux is."

Michael cleared his throat. "As I was saying before the transformation, I have assigned all available Nephilim to the task of locating Lux."

Gage brushed himself off. "I need equipment, transportation, and to get to your house, Michael. If anyone can find her, it's going to be me. I need to feed twice a day, so we'll either need to develop some sort of storage system, which isn't a problem when I have a fridge, or there will need to be a Nephil available for me."

Zane glanced at his wrist, which was already half-healed. "I'll take care of it. You can munch on me for the time being." He cast a glance around the room. "I know I don't have much experience with Abalam, but if I find him, I'm going to rip him apart with my bare hands."

Braxton's expression was sober. "The last time one of ours was captured by Abalam, they didn't make it." He held up his hand when Gage started to speak. "I know Lux is different and that they intend to turn her, so I'm not comparing the situations. Sam was a human, Lux is a Nephil, there are differences. I'm just saying that we need to all prepare ourselves for not getting her back. We've lost people already and we knew there was a very real possibility we would lose more. Our priority, as much as it pains me to say this, is to kill Lucifer. While Amaya and Deacon are in Atlantis, we can divert all our resources to finding Lux. Once they're back and we're ready to make a run at ending this, that has to be the focus, even if it means not going after Lux as hard."

"We're not just leaving her." Gage's eyes flashed red. "You wouldn't be saying this if it was one of your children."

"Yes, I would." Braxton's jaw was set. "We've all sent our kids out to fight. We've all sent them out to maybe die. We all knew the risk when we took this on thirty years ago, we knew the risk when Aradia and Greer agreed to carry Nephilim, and they knew the risks when they started this. I love Lux as much as one of mine, just like I know you love mine the same as you do yours. It'll tear me to pieces if we don't get her back, and I'm not suggesting we ever stop looking or stop trying to get her back. I'm just saying that we still have to be smart about it and stick to the plan, which is to get Amaya and Deacon to the point that they can kill Lucifer. Everything else--my life, yours, Lux's, Zane's, Michael's, everyone's--is secondary to that."

Zane spoke up. "He's right." He laid a hand on Gage's shoulder. "I love Lux more than anything in this world. I'd give up anything for her. But Braxton's right. We need to stay focused. They know how important she is to us and how hard we'll be looking. We can't let them sneak in under our noses and catch us off guard. We'll find her, but we have to be smart about it, and we can't take unnecessary risks."

Gage inclined his head sharply. "Let's just get this started. The longer we stand around talking about it, the deeper they could be going into hiding and that does no one any good."

Michael stepped forward. "I'll transport you to my home and make sure you have everything you need." He glanced to Braxton and Alaria. "Call for me if you need anything or if you find out any information. I'll be in touch soon."

Michael reached out and touched Gage and Zane on the forehead before snapping his fingers and sending them careening through space.

CHAPTER TWENTY-SIX

JANUARY 22, 2061

ATLANTIS

AMAYA GLANCED up as the sky lightened from black to blue. "That's the signal. Aradia just killed Garrick. We need to pack up and get moving to the city."

Deacon was already shoving their stuff into the packs. "Once we get there, we'll find a safe place to watch the entrance to the castle and wait for the others to come out when Aradia and Braxton come back down from the mountain."

She strapped her utility belt across her hips and slung a rifle over her shoulder. "Well, let's get there and wait. No use wasting time."

"Hurry up and wait." Deacon shook his head and began picking his way through the thick vegetation to a narrowing in the pool where they could cross without getting their boots wet. "Just like a woman."

"Shut up." Amaya's grin was good natured as she slapped him on the back. "We won't have long to wait. This is a long walk from the city."

Together, they trekked through the forest until breaking

through the trees into a field, a task that took two hours on foot. Picking up their pace to a brisk walk, Deacon led the way toward the city—thick black smoke billowing into the air an obvious sign of where to go.

After nearly three hours, they hit the wall. Her hand on a stake, Amaya pressed her back to the stone and felt her way along it, squinting in the low light to find a weak spot or hole in the wall that they could fit through without being detected. After fifteen more minutes of searching, she found a crumbled space in the wall and climbed through, crouching on the other side while Deacon followed her over.

The city was on fire. Houses still smoldered and burned, bodies lay in the street with vampires feeding on them. Screams could be heard from a distance as the wave of creatures moved their way through the huts and houses, dragging out those who had hidden from the battle and either eating or slaughtering them.

Deacon lifted his rifle when he saw two vampires tackle a woman to the ground and rip her dress off, their intention of rape obvious. Amaya shook her head and laid her hand on the barrel, pushing it down.

"We aren't here to change it." She looked at the scene in disgust. "Let's get to the castle and wait until Dad and Aradia come through. It should be soon, so we don't have a lot of time."

"How long do we have?"

She glanced at her watch. "It's been five hours since the sky turned. Braxton said it took them nearly seven to get back, so we've got less than two hours before they'll be here."

"Two hours is a lot of time to sit somewhere and not be seen."

"We don't want to miss it. Come on." She wound her way through the city back toward the castle. "The Ark is in the temple, which is where the entrance to the tunnel is, so once we see them head out, we're going to have to do this fast."

The doors to the castle had been blasted in. The walls were smeared with blood, and bodies lay in the entrance. Carefully, they picked their way over the carnage and entered the structure. Amaya clicked on her penlight to see by and pulled the map Gage had drawn from her bag, opening it and studying the rendering of the main floor of the castle.

"It looks like the temple is adjacent to the castle at the end of a long hallway. It's that hall where Damon is standing guard, so we're going to have to be really careful not to let him see us, but we need to be ready to run through when they come out."

Quietly, they picked their way over the rubble, pausing several times when one heard a noise. By the time they got near the hall leading to the temple, another thirty minutes had elapsed. Amaya grabbed Deacon and dragged him up a set of stairs to the left of the hall, crouching behind a pile of stone that had dropped from the ceiling. Peeking out from behind it, she could just see the top of Damon's head.

They sat silently for over an hour, counting each breath and holding it to make sure they made as little noise as possible. Three times Gage came out into the rotunda to look anxiously around before retreating to the temple.

"I'm telling you, there is something alive in this castle. I can smell it." Gage's voice trickled back to Amaya, followed quickly by Alaria's.

"I'm sure there is. A maid hiding under a bed or a kitchen wench bleeding out in the pantry. I don't sense any demons or vampires, do you?"

Gage's tone was sullen. "No."

Amaya smiled tightly. "I wonder if we just created a new memory by being here."

Deacon chuckled softly. "Knowing what we do about time, if we were always meant to do this, then maybe we were here like this when they were and we'd have really altered the timeline by not being here like this at this particular moment."

Amaya squinted her eyes and shook her head. "I'm choosing not to think about that. It makes my brain bleed." She wiggled her toes to keep them from going numb after being in the same position for so long. "We're down to twenty minutes or less."

"Almost there."

They both jumped when they heard a noise at the front of the castle. Damon ran to the entrance to the rotunda, a sword in one hand. Blood was smeared across his face and his hair was streaked with dirt and sweat. Amaya felt tears prickle her eyes at seeing him so young and alive. The knot in her throat swelled when she heard Greer's voice call out from behind him.

"What is it?"

"I don't know. Stay back there. I don't see anything yet." Damon retreated back to the entrance, his voice lowering. "If they don't come soon, we're going to have to go looking for them. It's been damn near seven hours since the sky lightened. That should mean

Aradia killed Garrick. What if they're up there bleeding to death or dead or something?"

Gage's voice was sharp and angry. "I'd know if she was dead. We're bonded. She's not dead. We'll give them two more hours. If they aren't here by then, I'll go look for them."

Amaya tapped Deacon on the arm and pointed. Braxton walked around the corner, Aradia in his arms, her arms around her neck and her face drawn in pain. They saw Damon rush forward.

"It's them! Aradia's hurt!"

The other three ran from the temple, crowding around Braxton. Gage took Aradia from his arms, cradling her against his chest. Amaya leaped from the stairs, darting behind the group and racing for the temple, Deacon on her heels. They skidded into the temple, running full bore toward the tunnel.

"Where's the Ark?"

Amaya cast a quick glance around the room, looking for the chest. "There! Dammit, it's big."

Deacon grabbed a pair of pliers from his utility belt and wrenched the lock off the Ark, yanking open the lid. The Spear of Destiny was six feet long with leather cording holding a rudimentary head to the staff. The jar was small enough to stuff into one of their packs, which Amaya did while they raced down the hall.

"Do you remember the buttons to push?" Deacon peeked out the door. "Hurry. I can hear them."

Amaya studied the stone console and withdrew the paper with the symbols written on it her father had given her. Pressing them carefully, she stepped back with her hands up, waiting with her heart in her throat for something to happen.

The portal glowed and turned blue. Smiling triumphantly, Amaya snatched the spear from the ground and grabbed Deacon's arm.

"Let's go!"

Together, they dashed through the blue light, disappearing into time mere moments before Gage strode into the portal room and laid Aradia on the floor for Greer to heal.

They emerged into the Choosing Place. Amaya lurched forward, holding her stomach as nausea churned through her. Deacon grabbed the strap on her pack to keep her upright while stumbling himself.

Straightening, Amaya looked around curiously. "I figured Lux would be here waiting for us."

"They had no idea when we'd have been back through. Let's head outside and flash back to Dad's. We'll figure out how to divide this Spear into pieces and then go after Lilith before she has the baby."

Deacon led the way into the courtyard. As they crossed through the door, both stopped. The grass was scorched and the scent of power hung thick in the air. Amaya breathed in deeply, holding it tightly in her lungs as she tried to get a feel for what had happened since they had gone through the portal.

"It feels like Lux. I can feel her magic."

Deacon's mouth was set into a grim line. "I feel my mother, too. She was here. And someone else I've never encountered. It's a powerful signature. More powerful than anything I've ever come up against."

"Lucifer." Amaya's voice was a panicked whisper. "Lucifer came after Lux!" She gripped Deacon's arm. "We have to get to the Manor and let them know! We have to go after them!"

"Calm down. We don't know how long ago this was. Lux might have gotten away, she may be back home, or they may have gotten her back already. There's no reason to panic before we get to the Manor and find out what's going on for sure."

She took a deep breath, forcing herself to settle. "You're right. You're absolutely right." She reached out and grabbed his hand. "Let's go find out what's going on."

Deacon flashed them to the non-place, arriving with a slight pop in the middle of the living room. When no one came rushing to greet them, they exchanged a worried look. Amaya laid her hand on her scabbard, fingers resting lightly on the handle of a short sword.

"I'll check down here, you sweep upstairs."

Deacon looked down at her worriedly. "We have to consider that we've come back to the wrong time. They might not be here because this is in the future or the past."

"Only one way to find out."

Amaya moved quietly through the main floor, checking in each room until she got to Michael's office. Nudging open the door, she stopped in shock when she saw Gage at the desk. Staring at him, panic rose in her throat. Gone were the gray hair and deep lines on his face, replaced with the smooth skin and pitch black locks of youth.

Gage looked up when the door opened. "Good, you're back." He stood and came out from behind the desk. "We were starting to worry about you."

She blinked rapidly. "How do you know me?"

Gage looked confused for the first time. "Is everything okay, Amaya?" He took a step forward, concerned when she took an equal one backward.

"When is this? What's the date?"

"It's January twenty-second, why?"

Amaya's voice was tense and harsh. "What year?"

Realization dawned in Gage's eyes. "Oh, sweetheart, it's okay. It's twenty sixty-two. You're in the right place."

"Then what are you and where is Gage?" She drew the sword, the Spear clattering to the floor. "What have you done with everyone? Deacon! Get down here!"

Gage held up his hands. "Calm down. It's okay." He extended his fangs and let his eyes flicker to red. "Death turned me back. I know I look different, but it's me, I promise."

"Promises don't mean much these days." She glanced over when Deacon appeared next to her.

"Shit. We're thirty years in the past. He's not even human yet? How the fuck did this happen?" Deacon plowed his hands through his hair. "Goddammit this is going to fuck with the timeline so bad!"

Gage cleared his throat. "You haven't messed with the timeline at all. You're exactly where you intended to be." He sighed deeply. "I suppose we really should have considered the fact that I was a human when you left and a vampire when you were coming back, but with everything going on, it slipped our minds. Deacon, call for your father and let him explain all of this. Obviously neither of you are going to listen to me. You think you're three decades in the past, and she thinks I'm some sort of piss poor shape shifter or something."

Deacon put his hands on his hips. "Dad! Dad, we need you!"

Michael appeared with a crack, taking in the situation quickly. He placed a hand on Amaya's shoulder. "Lower your weapon, child. It's Gage."

Amaya sheathed her sword, but the look on her face remained skeptical. "Someone had better tell us what the hell is going on here. He was not thirty years old and immortal when we left. And what happened to Lux? We caught the scent of a hell of a fight at the Choosing Place when we came back through."

Michael gestured for them both to sit. "And all will be explained. First, though, did you complete your mission successfully?"

Deacon picked up the Spear and handed it to his father. "The manna is in her pack. We got through just ahead of the six. It was tight, but we weren't seen."

"Good." Michael perched on the edge of the desk. "After you went through the portal, Lucifer attacked and captured Lux. She's being held in an unknown location, we suspect by Abalam, and we're searching for her. Death turned Gage back into a vampire at his insistence so that he would be able to help with the rescue. He's working on finding a location."

Amaya gripped her head in her hands, the sound of her blood pumping through her veins the only thing she could hear. Her power surged and the lights flickered twice before the bulbs exploded from the surge. Struggling to control it, she breathed deeply and mentally coached herself into a calmer state.

It wasn't working. The curtains blew as a wind ripped through the main level, blowing papers from the desk and scattering them. In the fireplace, the glowing embers flashed into flames and leaped up, turning from orange to white as they spiked in temperature. Amaya's fingers bit into her skull as she tried to physically press her powers back inside.

"Calm yourself, Amaya. Control the power. Don't let it control you." Michael's voice was soothing. "You've done this before, and you can do it now. Bring it down slowly, like walking down a set of stairs. One step at a time. Breathe deeply and feel the air calming you." He glanced at Deacon. "If you can do something, now would be the time."

Deacon reached out with his own powers, fitting himself over her, unsure if he could help outside of the context of sexual contact. The spikes in her power were violent and dangerous. She was holding on by a tenuous thread as grief and anger coursed through her--both emotions more powerful than lust.

Where she surged, he laid himself on top, smoothing out the jagged edges and helping give her control back until she could bring herself back down. Slowly, she released her head, the tiny half-moon nail marks in her skin a stark reminder of how desperately she had been trying to stay in control.

Michael reached out and patted one of Amaya's hands. "There, you did it. Nicely done." He looked back at Gage. "We need that location quickly. With them back, we have to find out where Lilith and Serafina are as well. Killing Lucifer has to be the priority."

"No." Amaya's voice was ragged. "Lux first. She's family. We find her first, then the rest. This doesn't get in the way of family. It can't."

Deacon nodded. "I'm with Amaya on this one. We find Lux, then we go for the rest."

Michael smiled grimly. "Okay, then. Let's find Lux and bring her home."

CHAPTER TWENTY-SEVEN

JANUARY 24TH, 2062

JERUSALEM

LUX SPAT blood and jerked as the scalpel dug deeply into her flesh. Blood ran down her arm and dripped off her fingertips, the sound of the droplets on the concrete floor echoing through the room. She gritted her teeth and concentrated on not screaming as Abalam methodically severed her skin from her body.

"You're a tough little witch, I'll give you that." Abalam tossed the strip of skin onto a tray with a wet plop and leaned back, picking up a towel to wipe the blood from his hands. "We've been at this for a couple days now. I'm sure you're quite tired. I'm getting fatigued myself."

Lux took a deep breath, the air catching in her chest as she tried to expel. She coughed, gagged, nearly puked and heaved before managing to speak. "Poor baby. Do you need a nap?"

"I need a rest, as do you. Along with a shower, some food, and clean clothing." He crossed one ankle over the opposite knee. "We haven't taken our first break yet, darling, and I don't want to wear you out too much." He perused the trays of instruments, taking great satisfaction in the sticky, congealing blood still coating some of them. "Three days we've been at this and you with no sleep and no food. If I don't give you a break soon, you might die, and I can't have that."

Lux sagged against the leather straps holding her to the chair. Her hair was sticky with blood. A mixture of saliva, tears, blood, and dirt coated her face and chest. Her left leg hung uselessly off the footrest, her knee broken from Abalam's hammer. Both of her earlobes had been cut off, he'd driven nails under her fingernails until the discs of tissue had peeled off her fingers with a sucking noise, the strings of flesh holding them on snapping one by one and the nail sank deeper.

Her right arm had been carved open so that all the veins and nerves were exposed. One touch to the nerves sent white hot pain rocketing through her whole body. Abalam had plucked the strands of nerves over and over again until she had passed out from pain.

But each injury, each slice of his scalpel or strike of the hammer got her one step closer to wiggling her way past the barrier in her mind. Accessing her powers was the key. If she could reach them, then she was a match for the Devil.

Abalam studied her closely, clucking his tongue. "You're so defiant. Even now, after all this, I can see that look in your eye. If you could just get to me. If I'd just give you your powers back. If only it was a fair fight. Sorry, sweetheart, I'm a Devil. I don't fight fair." He leaned forward and released the straps holding her to the chair. "Let me be clear. This is just the first chapter. We've still got a whole book to write, and I can make you scream and writhe from pain in ways you've never even imagined. The next bout when I come back is going to be with the drill. You're going to find out precisely how easily those bones break when I apply pinpoint pressure with a drill bit."

Lux fought the urge to vomit. "What's stopping you? Go ahead. I'm here. I'm ready."

"If only I were allowed to kill you." He sighed deeply and patted her broken knee, relishing in her muffled scream as she sank her teeth into her lip. "I'm going to send in my Healer, who will make sure you're all ready to go for the next time. You'll have some food, some water, a shower, some warm pajamas and a good night's sleep on a clean bed. Then, in the morning, I'll be back for you and we'll start this all over again. I'm going to drill into your cheekbones. I'll break your ankles, shatter your fingers, and drill holes into your legs. Maybe I might pop off a toe or two. My Healer is pretty sure she can put them back, so I'll give her an opportunity to try. Maybe I'll reach into your brain and replay all the torture I've done to other people so you know what you have to look forward to. I'm going to chain you up and whip you until the flesh peels off your bones, then I'll rub salt in it and leave you sobbing in your chains until you're ready to tell me what I want to know." He stood abruptly. "Doesn't that sounds like a lot of fun?"

"Barrels." Lux's voice was raspy and thick, but there was still fire in her eyes. Abalam laughed.

"I'll see you in the morning. Goodnight."

Lux was still slumped in the chair when a slight woman with dirty blonde hair and muddy brown eyes entered the room. She walked to Lux and laid her hands on the witch, efficiently healing her. As the pain ebbed and her skin knitted back together, Lux felt for the wall in her brain, looking for the edges and desperately hoping they weren't being healed as well. When she still felt the distinct wiggle and cracking that she had managed to put there throughout the torture, she nearly sobbed from relief.

"Come with me. I'll take you to the shower and for some clothing." The woman gestured to the door through which she had come. "Your bed is in a room adjacent to this one. I'll bring you a tray once you're settled in your room."

"Why are you helping him? You're human, right? Not a Cambion because the hair and eyes don't match. I don't sense demon, so unless they managed to strip my senses, you're completely human." Lux stood and followed the woman, debating on whether or not killing her would do anything other than annoy Abalam.

"My loyalties are none of your business."

"Luciferian then. I see." She stripped off the tattered remains of her pants and stepped into the shower, waiting until the cold water hit her in the face. "I don't know why I was expecting warm."

"Warm water was never promised." The woman handed her a bar of soap. "Wash quickly. You have three minutes."

Lux gamely rubbed the soap between her hands and continued making conversation with the reluctant Healer. "Have you always worshipped Lucifer, or did you come to it later in life? I suspect being a Healer upped your value, so that's why you're not possessed by a demon yet. Would your abilities still work if you were possessed?"

The woman scowled. "Stop talking."

"No one said I couldn't chat while I bathed." She rubbed the soap into her hair and rinsed it quickly in the chilled water. "Do you have a name?"

"It's none of your business."

"Well, no, it's not, but that doesn't stop me from asking." She cocked her head to the side as she took the towel being held out and wrapped it around herself. "You know, if you were to come with me, I could guarantee that you'd be safe and protected. All you have to do is help me get out of here."

"I don't need your help. I'm fine here." The woman jerked open a door and led Lux into a small room with a narrow cot. "There are clothes on the bed. Get dressed and I'll bring you your food. Then I suggest you eat and sleep. Abalam will be back for you in the morning."

Deacon looked at the Spear and considered how he was going to separate it. The rod was warm and heavy in his hands, the wood smooth and worn from age. Turning it over and over, he tried to determine the best way to turn a chunk of wood with a spear tip into multiple weapons meant to kill Devils.

"Just cut into it already." Amaya's voice was irritated as she sat and watched him.

"It's not quite that easy. This is the one thing we know can truly kill a Devil. I don't just want to cut it in half and only get two uses out of it. Azazel and Abalam are still alive and lots of other Devils that weren't Archangels. There are a lot of uses for this thing and I don't want to waste any of it."

Amaya cocked her eyebrow. "Could we turn it into bullets? I bet you could get a hundred bullets from that thing."

"There's a lot of waste with bullets because of shaping it down, but that's not a bad idea. If we melted the spear head down, I bet I could get half a dozen arrow tips out of it." He looked at the hunk of metal on the end of the spear. "That's a good sized piece of metal there. At least two pounds worth."

"I'm not sure how anyone used that. It's heavy and unwieldy."

"It was meant to knock people off of horses, kind of like a rudimentary jousting stick."

"A jousting stick?" Amaya bit her tongue to keep from laughing. "What the hell is a jousting stick?"

Deacon glanced over at her. "You pay zero attention to history, huh? A joust was an event where two knights would try to knock each other off their horses in a competition back in the Middle

Ages. I'm sure there's some technical term for what they called the stick, but I'll be damned if I know what it is." He cut the leather cording tying the metal onto the rod. "I guess I could make some knives out of this. Those would be easier for us to wield than the arrows."

"I like knives. Go with that. Knives and bullets."

He looked at the staff woefully. "I feel bad destroying a piece of history like this. It feels wrong."

"No, what feels wrong is leaving it intact and getting ourselves killed because you don't want to ruin some future museum display." Amaya rolled her eyes and climbed to her feet. "Get it done, Deacon. The sooner we have this thing made into something we can use, the sooner we can turn our focus back to finding Lux."

"Dad is still looking for her." He stood, tucking the Spear under his arm. "I'll go get started on this. What are your plans for the day?"

"I'm going to help Gage try and find Lux and Lilith. Whoever we find first is where we go."

Amaya waited until Deacon had left the room before winding her way through the house and into Michael's office where Gage was sitting behind the desk, working on a computer he'd managed to get running. He glanced up when Amaya entered the room and gestured for her to sit in one of the two chairs facing the desk.

"Everything okay?"

Amaya nodded. "I figured you could use some help. Deacon is working on separating the Spear, and everyone else is down on Earth looking for Lux. I'm supposed to stay here so I don't get into trouble." She rolled her eyes as she dropped into the chair. "I'm dying to help find her. Or do anything other than sit on my ass and wait."

Gage leaned back in his chair. "You've done plenty. Getting the sword from Eden, taking on all those demons and Cambion yourself in Sinai, then time-traveling to Atlantis and managing to get the Spear and manna without altering the timeline. None of that is insignificant." He turned back to the computer screen. "The worst part is yet to come, I'm afraid. There are still three beings that must die before you can kill Lucifer. Killing Lilith won't be easy even under ideal conditions, and these are not that. We don't know what Serafina can do, and we know we're pressing against when she's going to deliver her second hellspawn." He rubbed one hand over his face. "This makes me long for the past when I could pick up a fucking phone and find out what I needed to know."

She chuckled. "This is all I've ever known so it's not even frustrating to me." Picking up one of the maps, she studied it. "Is this the map of places Lux isn't or where you think Lilith might be?"

"It's one of the seven maps I have to mark where Lux is not." He pointed to the red X's on the page. "Each city that's been thoroughly searched is marked off. The world is a small place. They won't be able to hide her for long."

"Unless they take her to a nonplace."

"I don't believe they'd risk that. Lux is too powerful. She could tap into the power of a nonplace and use it to blast her way out. It's not nearly so easy to neuter her in a nonplace as it is on Earth."

"What about Purgatory?"

"There's a team of Nephilim down there now searching. Zane was able to open it up for them to go down. We're working on it, Amaya. We'll find her."

Amaya brought her knees up to her chest and studied Gage. "Can I ask you something?"

Nodding, he continued to work on the computer. "What's up?"

"What's Lucifer like?"

Gage's head came up and he studied her. "What do you mean?"

"I've never met him. I don't know what to expect, only that I'm supposed to kill him. You've at least been in the same room as him. What's he like?"

"He's cocky. Powerful." He folded his hands on the desk. "Are you scared?"

"Terrified." She exhaled nervously. "I'm absolutely terrified. It's not the fact that I might die. I accepted that a long time ago. It's knowing I might not be able to do what I'm supposed to on my way out. If I have to die, I want to leave the world a better place, I want to know I did my job. I don't know how to fight this unknown enemy."

"None of us know much more than that you're supposed to harness the power of God and use it to kill him. I would have to assume that you'll know more precisely what to do once you've eaten the manna. That's supposed to be some direct link straight to the will of God, so I'd hope you'll be able to figure out what to do at that point." Gage scowled when his stomach rumbled. "I miss the days of just being able to nuke some blood in the microwave."

Amaya stood and rounded the desk, offering her wrist. "Help yourself." She chuckled. "Blood on tap."

Gage looked at her pointedly. "I'm glad you think this is funny."

"I don't think it's funny. There's nothing the slightest bit humorous about any of this." She winced when his fangs sank into her wrist. "I'm fucking nursing a vampire that just so happens to be the father of my best friend, who has been kidnapped by Supreme Hellacious Grand Torture Master in order to turn her into some weapon for their side. Instead of being out looking for her, I'm up here worrying about whether or not I'm going to be able to kill Satan himself." She shook her head as Gage drank. "If this wasn't my life, I'd call anyone telling me about it a liar."

Gage withdrew his fangs and soothed the bite with his tongue to help it heal faster. "I think we've all said that exact same thing a time or two." He wiped his mouth and released her wrist. "Everything will be fine, I promise."

"You can't promise me that, and we both know it. I'm not eight anymore. I don't believe the lies."

Gage's eyes were sad as he looked at her. "If only you knew how much I wish you all still did. It seems just yesterday I was scaring the monster under the bed away for Lux and earlier this afternoon that I started training you and Zeke. Now, I'm watching those I love like my own children head out into a battle I failed to prevent from happening, knowing that some or all of you might not come home." He shook his head. "There's nothing good about any of this."

They both looked up when Michael appeared in the room. Without waiting for either to greet him, the Angel spoke. "We've sensed a great surge of power on Earth. It would seem we have either located Lilith or Lux. I've dispatched a team with instructions to find out which so we can prepare."

CHAPTER TWENTY-EIGHT

"MY TEAM has indicated that the surge of power we all felt was from Moscow, which is in what used to be Russia." Michael pointed to a spot on a map that had been circled in red ink. "However, it is not Lux that has caused the surge. There is a high level of demon activity around the area which limited how close we could get without being detected. It appears that Lilith has gone into labor, which would explain the surges. That means we need to act soon in order to kill her and the child at the same time to avoid having three individual beings to kill."

Amaya crossed her arms and studied the map. "Is Serafina there?"

"A small child was seen, so it seems that she is. There was no sign of Lucifer being present."

Gage cleared his throat. "I've done some looking and there is tunnel access to the building where they are. The issue is going to be getting you in undetected. There are a lot of demons and Cambion wandering the compound, so they'll sense any Nephilim a couple miles out."

Deacon grinned sharply. "Then let's set up a diversion. They did it to us and it worked. There's no reason to think it wouldn't work on them, especially with Lilith in labor and Lucifer nowhere to be found. Amaya and I will go in after Lilith and Serafina. The rest of you will flash into Moscow somewhere close. Engage them in a fight when they come to inspect. With any luck, they'd leave only a few guards for Lilith and we could take them out easily. If we flashed in at the same time, we might be able to confuse their senses enough that they wouldn't be able to pick us up as long as we shut down our powers and run cold as soon as we get there. We take out the demons and then we go after the kid and Lilith."

Zeke pursed her lips. "I could go with the two of you and shield you with my powers. That way there would be less risk of you being sensed."

Amaya shook her head. "No. I don't want you in anymore danger than necessary. You'd be safer with the others."

"And you'd be safer with me there." Zeke looked at Michael imploringly. "Back me up here."

"Ezekiel is right, Amaya." Michael crossed his arms and stared at her evenly. "She could shield your arrival and assist with the demons while you find Lilith and Serafina. I would insist, however, that you leave as soon as the demons are taken care of, Zeke." He turned to her and continued. "I don't want for Lucifer to focus on you as another target when we're so close, so the less seen of you, the better it will be."

Deacon sighed deeply. "I don't like taking anyone else into danger. This is for me and Amaya to do. I'm afraid anyone else would end up being collateral damage."

Zeke smirked. "I'm hardly collateral damage. Besides, Michael agrees with me which makes it as good as settled."

Gage leaned over the map again, studying it. "I think three is more appropriate than two, especially because Zeke can shield you from detection." He gestured to an area on the map. "I think around here is a good place for the battle. There are plenty of buildings to extend the area in, many places to hide if that becomes necessary, and it's close enough that we could draw out the demons. The best way to go in is to make it look like we're searching for Lux. That's something we've been doing all over the world anyway. They'll know we sensed the power surge, but it's quite reasonable it could have been Lux that produced it. That should keep them from just flashing out with Lilith and going into hiding somewhere else."

Reluctantly, Amaya nodded. "Okay. When do we move out?"

Michael tapped his fingers on the desk. "It'll take me a couple hours to gather enough Nephilim for a search party to give it the appearance of the rest. Gather weapons and supplies and be ready to leave at dark."

Amaya twisted her arms behind her back to finish braiding her hair, securing it with a black ponytail holder. Her pack sat at her feet, loaded with supplies. Clenching her fist, she smiled slightly as her jeans and t-shirt were replaced with red and black leather and knee high boots.

Stooping, she snagged her utility belt and strapped it around her hips, checking each pocket to make sure she had everything she would need. She looked up when the door opened and offered a tight smile to Deacon as he entered.

"You ready to go?"

He held out a knife. "I finished with the Spear. There's a knife for all three of us, and I loaded a clip of the wooden bullets for each. There's still half the staff left here that I didn't get to, so we can make more bullets if we need to."

Amaya took the knife and tested the weight in her hand. The handle was heavier than the blade, giving it an odd balance. "It's good enough to get the job done."

"I didn't have enough metal to properly balance the blades. Or time." He smiled ruefully. "Things moved pretty quickly."

She tucked the knife into one of the loops on her belt and secured it before taking the clip Deacon offered and zipping it into one of the pockets on her bag. "Everything will be okay. We're going to be just fine and we'll kill all three of them."

"I'm not worried about that part." He reached out and tucked a loose strand of hair behind her ear. "I'm worried about what doing this is going to do to you. We have to go in there and kill two kids. That was weighing pretty heavily on you before."

Amaya frowned. "It still does. I don't believe in being doomed by birth. I think we all make our own decisions and even with bad parents, I think a kid can choose a different path. Your mother is Lilith, too. Yet here you are, fighting for God. My mother was a Devil. She chose a different path, and I'm here fighting right next to you. Mom and you are both shining examples of people not being pigeonholed by what they are. We're taking away Serafina's chance to choose another path. We aren't even letting this baby have a shot at it. That eats at me, but I know I can go in there and do what needs to be done because this is the only way I kill Lucifer. If there was another way, I have to believe Michael or Gage would have found it." She picked up her pack and slipped her arms through the holes. "But that doesn't mean I like what we're doing. It's wrong. This is a bad thing, and I'm going to pay for this every day for the rest of my life."

Deacon gripped her arm in his hand to stop her from leaving the room. "You shouldn't feel like that. We're only doing what's necessary. It's not about one or two lives. It's about hundreds of millions of lives. Every human being on Earth will die if we don't do this. I know it sucks, and it feels wrong, but there isn't a choice. It's not wrong to sacrifice two to save a billion."

Amaya offered a tight smile. "That doesn't make it feel any better." She glanced toward the door. "We need to get down there and get going. The longer we wait, the more likely I'm going to have to slaughter an infant."

Together, they descended the stairs where Michael had gathered everyone else. Zeke moved to stand next to them, handing Caleb to Alaria. Alaria bounced the baby expertly and settled him in the crook of one arm.

Michael cast a glance around the room. "We'll go in first to begin the search. The three of you should flash in near the area where we detected the surge, but not so close as to be seen. Find a good vantage point and wait until you see the demons and Cambion leave. The rest of us will put on a search for Lux until the enemy arrives. At that point, it will be an intense battle as we will be significantly outnumbered. Use the city to your advantage. Don't exhaust yourselves with needless flashing. We'll reconvene here after the fight is done or whenever one of the three going in after Lilith and Serafina notify us that they're leaving. Questions?"

Gage handed Amaya a map. "I've drawn you a schematic of the sewer systems running underneath. I think that will be the easiest place to gain access to the building where Lilith is. Once you're in, you'll have to rely on your own senses to find her. I haven't been able to get any better intel on that, and we don't have the equipment we used to." He scowled. "The last time I needed to find this bitch, I used infrared scanning to determine precisely how many people were in the house and where she was. Unfortunately, that stuff isn't as easy to get anymore."

Deacon grinned. "The difference is that we're used to doing stuff without the bells and whistles. We'll be fine."

Michael laid his hand on his son's arm. "Don't do anything stupid." He turned to Amaya. "Keep each other safe."

Zeke rolled her eyes. "Let's just get going. I don't want anyone to get sappy here." She glanced to Alaria. "If I don't make it back..." Her voice trailed off as Alaria nodded.

"Don't worry about a thing. I'll keep him safe until this is done." Alaria turned to Amaya. "Be careful. I love you."

Amaya didn't have a chance to respond before they were all flashing.

She stumbled forward half a step as they landed and brought her rifle to her shoulder, casting a glance around to make sure they'd landed somewhere abandoned. Zeke turned, pressing her back to Amaya's, and Deacon pivoted to face away from them, each sweeping a portion of their surroundings.

"It's safe." Zeke adeptly twisted a silencer onto her gun and anchored it to her shoulder. "We need to find a point to watch them. I need somewhere high that I can be effective with my sniper rifle."

Amaya pulled out the map and studied it. "The building where they are is about three blocks north of here. If we go about halfway there and find a roof, that should be good for watching them and keeping enough distance that they won't see us."

Deacon slung his rifle over his shoulder and drew a pistol to carry. "Is your shield up, Zeke?"

"Hmm?" Zeke glance over her shoulder. "Yeah. It's up." She gestured to a building in the distance. "I want that one. It'll have a good sight line and it's high enough. If we get inside the top floor, that'll give you two cover while I watch them."

Together, they began the trek over the rubble-filled streets to the building Zeke had chosen. The block and a half trek took twenty minutes with them pausing every few yards to make sure they weren't being followed. Once they arrived at the building, Deacon shouldered his way in through a side entrance.

"We need to be careful. We don't know how sturdy this thing is." Amaya pulled out a penlight and shined the slim beam of light around the room. "It looks pretty bad in here."

Zeke glanced up at the crumbling walls and the rebar poking out of them. "I think it's okay." She opened the door to the stairwell and shined her own light inside. "The stairs are mostly intact."

"Mostly?" Deacon's voice was incredulous. "That gives me a ton of faith that we aren't going to fall to our deaths."

"Says the man with wings." Amaya shouldered her way past him and started up the stairs. "They're holding me just fine. Come on."

Amaya's thighs were screaming from exertion by the time they got to the top floor. They exited the stairwell together and split up, covering the whole floor to make sure there were no other occupants before gathering back at the stairwell door. Deacon closed the door and jammed a piece of rebar he'd found on the floor through the handle to keep it from being opened from the inside.

"Pick your spot, sniper girl."

Zeke stuck out her tongue at Deacon and chuckled. "I know where I'm going. You two hang out back from the window. No reason for all three of us to risk being seen."

Zeke knelt in front of one of the windows and carefully removed the last pieces of glass before balancing the barrel of her weapon on the sill and pressing her eye to the sight, moving it back and forth until she had it focused on the entrance to the building where Lilith was.

"Looks like they're staying in some sort of palace."

Deacon settled himself against the wall by the stairs. "It's the Kremlin palace. Lilith isn't going to stay in anyplace not fancy, so it must be in pretty good shape inside."

"Thing is fucking huge. It's three times the size of the Choosing Place. It could take us an hour or more to find them once we're in, and that's if we don't run into trouble."

Amaya fingered the blade made from the Spear that was buckled into her belt. "We'll find them." She glanced up. "What do you see?"

"The demons are gathering out front and they're armed, so either the ploy is working or they've sensed us despite my shield and are on their way to kill us."

"Reassuring." Deacon idly tossed a chunk of concrete and caught it in his hand. "What are the odds of the second one?"

"About as good as this whole building collapsing in the next ten seconds. My shield is effective. Unless they have Lucifer in there with them, we should be safe."

"We'll either live or we won't. No use dwelling on it." Amaya fought down licks of panic at the thought of what she was about to do. "Are they still there?"

Zeke made a noise in the back of her throat. "The one in charge is talking to them. A few are stepping back toward the palace." She angled her scope slightly. "They're flashing out. Looks like about forty went and around ten left to hold down the fort." She glanced over her shoulder. "I could snipe a few of them from here."

Amaya shook her head. "Too risky. We don't want them to know we're coming." She stood. "Let's get moving. We need to get into the sewer system and work our way up into that monstrosity."

Deacon stood and unblocked the door leading to the stairs. "Let's go kill us a Devil bitch."

Amaya snorted. "That Devil bitch is your mother."

His expression was grim as he led the two women down the steps. "All the more reason to eliminate her."

CHAPTER TWENTY-NINE

THE SEWERS were long empty, devoid of water or waste. Several rats scurried as Amaya dropped through the manhole and into the tunnel, and she turned from side to side quickly, scanning for any threats. Finding none, she motioned to Zeke and Deacon to join her, waiting until Deacon had pulled the cover back over the hole in the sidewalk to speak.

"If Gage's map is right, we're about half a mile from the entrance to the building Lilith is in. We'll come up into a cellar or basement. Once we're there, we'll need to split up to avoid being seen and to cover the house quicker. As far as we know, there aren't any cameras or security systems, but we need to be prepared if there are."

Zeke nodded. "I'll take the first floor and the outside to eliminate all the demons out there. I should be able to keep my shield up to cover the whole house, so as long as you don't leave the building, you'll be shielded."

Carefully, they trekked through the tunnels until they found the entrance marked on the map. Deacon climbed the ladder and eased it aside, sticking his head through, a pistol in one hand. Careful to be quiet, he heaved himself out of the tunnels and crouched in the dark, eyes darting around, checking for any threats.

Finding none, he waved to Amaya and Zeke, standing to shield them as they climbed up. Amaya slid the cover back into place and stood, brushing her hands against her pants.

"Okay, well, that was easy enough."

Zeke scoffed. "This was the first step. We've still got the whole marathon ahead of us." She fished radios out of her bag and handed one to both Amaya and Deacon. "Keep these close. That way we can talk without any power usage. I'll sweep the main floor and the grounds. Call for me if you get into trouble."

Amaya tucked the radio into her belt. "Stay safe."

Together, the three climbed the stairs out of the basement and emerged onto the main floor. The only light was from oil lamps and candles, and the house was silent. Using hand signals, Zeke directed them toward the stairs before slipping to the right and disappearing around a corner.

Deacon laid his hand on Amaya's shoulder. "You take this wing, I'll cross the main level here and go up the west stairs."

"Yell for me if you need me."

"You, too."

She slipped up the stairs, pressing close to the wall. Her rifle was strapped to her shoulder, and she had a pistol on either hip, but she'd chosen a bowie knife to carry in her hand, preferring the silence of a blade to the distance of a bullet.

Amaya methodically cleared each room on the second floor, checking in closets and under beds before marking the door with a black marker and moving on. She knew there were ten demons left but had no idea where any of them were.

On the third floor, she froze when she heard singing. The voice was child-like and young. Amaya's gut clenched as she realized who it was most likely coming from.

Moving stealthily toward the voice, she pushed open the door and looked down at a small child. The girl blinked and looked up at her, the singing stopping.

"Who are you?"

Amaya flexed her fingers on the knife. "My name is Amaya. What's yours?"

"Serafina." The child looked around the room. "Did my mother send you?"

Amaya made a noncommittal noise in her throat and closed the door behind her. "What are you playing with?"

The girl's face split into a wide grin. "Daddy sent me a present.

Do you want to see it?"

The absurdity of hearing Lucifer referred to as 'Daddy' had Amaya biting her cheek to keep from laughing. Instead, she offered what she hoped was a comforting smile and nodded. "I'd love to."

Serafina went to her closet and opened the door, revealing a Nephil tied to a chair. The woman's head lolled to the side, her eyes alarmingly blank. Blood was pooled beneath the chair, sticky and black. Amaya swallowed a wave of nausea and tucked the bowie knife into her belt.

"Why did your Daddy bring you this as a present?"

"I asked for a body to play with. He brought me a real-live Nephil." The child bounced on her feet excitedly. "I've gotten to torture her! It's been so much fun." Pouting, Serafina turned to stare up at Amaya. "But I don't think she'll live very much longer. I'm going to need a new toy to practice on. When I get big and strong like Mommy and Daddy, then I'll be able to go kill all the nasty Nephilim I want." She batted her eyes. "Have you killed many?"

"A whole bunch." Amaya's fingers shifted toward the blade made from the Spear. "Does Daddy bring you toys often?"

"No." The pout became more prominent. "He says I'm too little to have much fun with them." Her eyes flashed red. "I try to tell him I'm strong, but he won't listen. I'm not a little girl!" Serafina stomped her foot, making the room shake from the bolt of power. "I'm a Devil!"

The power of the evil rolling off Serafina was enough to make Amaya dizzy. Torn between wanting to finish part of her mission and the grief she felt from killing a child, she slowly unsnapped the blade, allowing her to draw it from the sheath.

"I can tell how powerful you are." Amaya kept her voice low and soothing. "What will you do to the Nephil?"

Serafina bared her teeth in a parody of a smile. "Kill her, of course. What else would you do with Nephilim?"

"Have you killed before?"

"A couple times, when Daddy brought me presents. I killed my Nanny the last time they had one. She was a witch, but not a very powerful one. She wouldn't let me play outside in the snow, so I ripped out her throat with my teeth."

Amaya pressed one hand to her stomach in a futile attempt to quell the nausea. There was no good in the child. Nothing but pure evil.

"Are you my new Nanny? I liked having one, but Mommy and

Daddy said I couldn't have another one because of what I did. Daddy liked the witch I killed, but I didn't. She wouldn't let me play in the snow."

"I'm not your new Nanny. I just came up to check on you while your Mommy's having the new baby."

Serafina's eyes lit up. "I don't want Mommy to have a new baby." She lowered her voice to a conspiratorial whisper. "I think I'll kill it, too. I like killing. It's fun to have their blood on my hands. Mommy doesn't like it when I ruin my dresses, but she always gets me more." She twirled, making her skirt fan out. "I think once Mommy is sleeping after the baby, I'll sneak in and snap its neck. That way Mommy won't be mad about my dress."

When Serafina turned to look at the Nephil in the closet, Amaya made her move, drawing the blade and grabbing the girl by the hair, dragging her head back to expose her throat. Before the child could struggle, she slashed with the blade, burying it deep and gagging as blood sprayed the wall.

Black and red flashed in Serafina's eyes as she died, the body crumpling to the ground in a tiny pile. Amaya stepped over it and rushed to the Nephil in the closet, tearing her radio from her belt as she did so.

"Zeke, come in."

Zeke's voice was soft over the radio. "What's up?"

"What's your location?"

"I'm just finishing up the guards out front. Is something wrong?"

"I'm on the third floor, East wing. There's a Nephil here that's been held captive. She's very badly hurt. I need you to come heal her."

"I'll be there in five minutes or less. Is my path clear?"

"Should be. Serafina is dead."

Deacon's voice sounded. "Good job. I ran into some company on the second floor and just got searching for Lilith. I took out three demons. Zeke, what's your count?"

"Five. That leaves two."

Amaya pressed the button to talk. "They're probably in with Lilith. I'll continue searching my wing once Zeke arrives here."

She crept to the door and peered out, waiting until she saw Zeke's head coming up the stairs. Waving the other Nephil into the room, she carefully closed the door. Zeke went straight to the woman tied in the closet, laying her hands on bare skin to heal her.

"Thank you." The Nephil rubbed her wrist with the opposite

hand when Zeke released the ropes holding her. "Thank you so much!"

Amaya pressed a finger to her lips. "Keep your voice down. There are still two demons in here that we don't know a location of." She glanced at Zeke. "Is she strong enough to flash?"

"I can't flash." The woman spoke softly. "I never developed the ability. I don't have much in the way of powers. That's how they got me so easily."

Zeke lifted her eyebrows. "Fuck. We have to get her out of here."

Amaya paced the length of the room twice while she mulled over the options. Finally, she turned to Zeke. "You have to take her out of here. Get her back out of range and flash her out."

"If I'm flashing anywhere other than Michael's, it'll drain me. You know my range isn't very far."

"Then take her to Michael's and back down to Earth from there. Or leave her at Michael's. Or find her a car. Just do something and then get somewhere safe. As soon as you leave, the shield will drop because we'll be too far away. Once you're out, there's no coming back."

Zeke shook her head. "No, I'm here to help you and keep you shielded. I'll just sit here with her until it's over."

Amaya started to argue but saw from the look on Zeke's face that it was useless. "Promise me that if you get into trouble, you'll take her and get out of here. I don't want anything to keep you from getting home to Caleb."

Zeke nodded and unfastened her blade, handing it to Amaya. "I promise." She nodded to the knife. "Take that so you can kill one of them if you get the chance. We'll be right here."

Amaya left the room and slipped into the hall, continuing her search of the east wing. She moved swiftly through the rest of the rooms on the third floor before moving onto the fourth. When neither the fourth or fifth floors revealed any activity, she loped back down the stairs and entered the main floor, heading to the other stair case, determined to help Deacon find his mother and kill her.

Lilith relaxed into the pillows, relishing in the pain coursing through her as her son tried to force his way out of her. She gripped the mound of her stomach in both hands, screaming as another contraction tore through her. Panting, she lifted her nightgown to stare at the bulge, smiling as her skin moved and stretched from the baby tearing at it.

"Soon, my love. Soon you'll be in my arms." She cooed to her belly as she stroked it. "We'll rule this planet together."

The demon at the door cleared his throat. "My Queen, do you require assistance delivering the child? Lucifer left strict instructions that I care for you. My host body was an obstetrician before I possessed him, so I have some medical knowledge that may be helpful to you."

"No. I don't need any help. The child will do everything he's supposed to. Devils don't have children as human women do. This baby is going to tear his way from me."

Lilith reached out toward the table next to her, folding her fingers around a dagger and lifting it. Carefully, she drew the edge across her swollen abdomen. Blood pooled in the slice and dribbled down the sides of her stomach, staining the sheets beneath her.

Pain speared through her as her son tore at her from inside, straining to emerge. Lilith tossed her head back and cried out, the power from her child coursing over her.

"Yes, my child. Come meet your Mommy."

Her skin split wider and a face appeared~the small round features of an infant visible through the amniotic sack. Lilith used the dagger to puncture it, shivering when the fluid gushed from the incision and soaked into the bed. Lovingly, she reached into her stomach and pulled the squirming infant from herself, using the dagger to slice through the umbilical cord before cradling the baby against her chest.

The demon at the door watched in a mixture of curiosity and abject terror, his mouth slightly open and eyes wide. Lilith stared into the face of her son and stroked one hand down his cheek, savoring the feel of soft skin. Lusty cries filled the room as the baby took his first breaths.

"I'll be moving to the room next door while you clean up the mess. Make sure his bassinette is next to my bed and once you're done, fetch Serafina. She'll want to meet her brother."

"Yes, Highness. Do you require any medical attention?"

Lilith laughed melodically. "No, silly boy. I heal on my own." She pulled her nightgown up, exposing her intact stomach. "Devils heal almost instantly."

Rising, Lilith allowed the fabric to slip from her shoulders and pool at her feet, walking into the adjoining room naked, her son cradled against her chest. She turned when she heard a thump and lifted one eyebrow when she saw the demon dead on the floor and Deacon standing over him.

"Hello, son."

"Mother." Deacon lifted one eyebrow at the blood. "Please tell me you didn't deliver me that way."

Lilith laughed. "Goodness, no. You're half Angel. You emerged in a very human way. I labored with you for hours, then pushed you out as humans do. It's only a Devil child that tears its way free." She continued into the bedroom, placing the baby in a bassinette and drawing a clean gown over her head. "You've come to kill me, yes?"

"Yes."

She looked at him over her shoulder. "Then let's get on with it, shall we?"

CHAPTER THIRTY

DEACON STARTED to draw his knife, then thought better of it and held up his hands, palms up. "I was hoping to get to you before you had the baby. But since that obviously isn't going to happen, I'll make you a deal."

Lilith lifted her eyebrows. "What kind of deal?"

"If you tell me where Abalam is holding Lux, I'll let you live. You can just go, right now. No questions asked. I only need to kill the baby."

The Devil's eyes flashed to red. "No one is laying a hand on my child."

Deacon laughed. "Oh, don't pick now to get righteous and maternal. We both know there isn't one nurturing bone in your body. You're nothing but a selfish bitch. I'm sure Amaya's already taken care of Serafina. Just let me do what I came to do and we can both get out of here in one piece."

Lilith whirled, putting herself between the baby and Deacon. "I'm a good mother, you ungrateful whelp. I'll not let you take him from me! As for Amaya, well, Serafina is quite the little handful."

"And she's strong enough to kill Lucifer. I think she can handle one first-grader." Deacon shifted his hand to the pistol loaded with the wooden bullets, considering the angles. "I've dreamed of this moment most of my life. The moment when I'd finally be alone in a room with you and strong enough to take you out. No one has ever hated their mother as much as I hate you."

"Without me, you would not exist. How can you hurt the being that gave you life?"

"You birthed me and handed me over to a nanny. You never wanted me for anything other than a weapon against Michael."

Lilith shrugged. "Well, there is that, I suppose."

"You tried to kill my friends."

"I'll give you that one, too." She smiled beguilingly. "I'm a Devil, darling. Why do you constantly expect me to behave as something different?" She tapped her nails against her leg. "Your father always expected that, too. He remembered our time as Angels together and expected me to be the same. He was always surprised when I did something really, really bad."

"Nothing you do could surprise me." Deacon thumbed the safety off on the gun and waited for a perfect time to fire it. "Amaya may be meant to kill Lucifer, but you've always been meant for me."

"You, with your Cambion hair and eyes. It's so pitiful to see you trying so hard to fit in with the Nephilim. They'll never trust you fully. They'll always look at you and see me. Especially the humans. You're cursed to be Cambion. Accept your fate and come with me. You could rule next to me."

"Stop with the desperate begging. We both know even if I did that you'd just stab me to death in my sleep."

Lilith cocked her head and stared at her son with wide eyes. "You are so much like your father." She cast a glance at the infant in the bassinet. "I have such high hopes for your brother. My biggest wish is that he doesn't disappoint me like my first two sons did. Beelzebub's whelp was weak and pathetic from the start. You could have been great." She took a step toward him, lifting one hand. "You truly could have been great, my darling. Even now I can sense evil lurking in you. You hide it well and you work hard to fit in with the Nephilim, but deep down you know that it's my blood running through your veins. It's my voice you hear urging you to slaughter them all. It's my genes making you what you are. There will come a day when you can no longer hide your true nature, even from yourself. When that day comes, you'll regret what you're here doing on this day."

Deacon's upper lip curled. "Don't fool yourself. The only thing I'll regret about today is that it's taken me so long to do it. I've dreamed about the day I got to kill you since I was a child."

"And what does that say about you as a Nephil that you dream of bloodshed instead of peace?" Lilith jutted her chin up defiantly. "Deny it all you want, son, but you're more like me than you'd like to believe."

Deacon's finger twitched on the trigger, his hand itching to draw the gun and aim at Lilith. "Killing you ensures peace. That's all." He held up the gun. "I made the Spear into bullets. Efficient, right?" He smiled sharply. "Easier to shoot you than to stab you with a giant spear."

"Clever boy." Lilith looked nervous for the first time. "I wonder how you'll explain to that God you love so much that you killed your postpartum mother in cold blood and then slaughtered an innocent baby that hasn't even been on this Earth an hour yet."

"I think He'll understand, given the circumstances." Deacon looked down at the weapon and then back at his mother. "Do you even have enough energy to fight me?"

"I have more than enough." Lilith's eyes flashed red. "But you're not here for a fight. You're here for an execution." She concentrated on trying to whip up enough power to blast her son back, but found she barely had enough to stir the air. "You knew how weakened I would be after birthing your brother and you took advantage of it."

As Deacon drew the slide back, Lilith charged, throwing herself at him, slashing with claws and clamping her teeth down on the side of his neck. The gun hit the floor with a dull thump as mother and son battled for the upper hand.

He dropped to his knees from the weight of Lilith on his back, scrambling to flip her over. Claws dug into his arms, ripping through skin and digging into his muscle. He threw his elbow back, colliding with her nose and grunting in brutal satisfaction when blood spurted and dribbled down her face and onto his neck.

Lilith locked her legs around Deacon, using every bit of strength she had to try and flash. All thoughts of her child forgotten, she focused on escaping with her life. She felt the familiar burn in her chest as she tried to pull herself apart and released her son, springing back from him. Casting one glance at the bassinette, she made a mental calculation and decided she couldn't get to the infant.

With a loud crack, Lilith disappeared, leaving Deacon alone with his infant brother.

Amaya burst into the room, her gun drawn. She scanned the

room and went to Deacon, helping him to his feet.

"What happened? Where's Lilith? Is she dead?"

Deacon rubbed his hand over the bite on his neck, scowling when his fingers came away coated in blood. "Fucking bitch. She was weak from the delivery, and I got too damned cocky. She worked up a flash and got away." He winced as he applied pressure to the wound. "What about Serafina?"

"Dead." She looked toward the small bassinette. "Is the baby in there?"

He nodded. "Yeah, she didn't even try to go for him." He bent to retrieve the gun and turned it over in his hand. "Do you want to wait outside while I finish this?"

Amaya closed her eyes for a brief moment. "I wish there was another way. When I found Serafina, I spent a little time with her, hoping against hope that I found something redeemable. She was pure, unadulterated evil. No bones about it evil. She wanted as much blood on her hands as possible, and she was only six years old. I can't imagine what she would have been like as an adult." She shivered. "She made Lucifer look like a fluffy bunny, and they think this child is going to be worse. If they're right, there's no choice."

"There's no choice even if they're wrong." He snapped a round into the chamber. "Wait outside. You don't need to see this."

Shaking her head, Amaya grabbed Deacon's hand. "No, there's no need for you to do it alone. This is ours to do together. If we're going to Hell over it, we'll go together."

Deacon took a step forward, leveled the barrel of the gun, and pulled the trigger.

Zeke lowered the barrel of her gun when she saw Deacon and Amaya come through the door. Holstering the weapon, she stepped forward and laid her hand on Deacon's neck, healing the wound before speaking.

"Is it done?"

"The baby's dead. Lilith got away. She left him to save her own ass." Deacon closed the door. "We need to get out of here before she gets back with Lucifer and a ton of demons and Devils."

Zeke nodded and turned to the Nephil standing behind her. "Come stand over here so Amaya can transport us out. She needs to touch you in order to do it."

Amaya reached out and touched each of the others, focusing on Michael's nonplace. She snapped her fingers and reveled in the jerk behind her sternum as they were all propelled through space.

Michael's house was quiet and still. Amaya glanced to Deacon. "I'll take her back to wherever she wants to go, you let your dad know that we're done with what we needed to do. We should reconvene here to figure out what we do next. "

Deacon nodded and flashed out again. The Nephil looked around nervously.

"What is this place?"

Amaya offered a smile. "This is a nonplace. Angels and Devils can create them adjacent to Earth. Haven't you ever been to one?"

She shook her head. "No. I fell in with a group of other Nephilim when I was about eighteen. My mom died when I was a kid, and I lived on the streets for a while, just scraping by. When I figured out what I was, I joined up with the first group I found. They all got killed in the fight when I got captured. I don't really have anywhere to go."

"What's your name?" Zeke leaned against the counter in the kitchen, her legs crossed at the ankle. "I never thought to ask you."

"Katie."

"Well, Katie," Amaya laid her hand on the younger woman's shoulder. "I can take you to one of our Nephilim camps. They'd give you a safe bed at night, food to eat, and the training you need to survive. It's dangerous, but not as much as trying to live on your own as a not-very-powerful Nephilim."

The girl nodded. "Anything's better than what I had. That was no sort of life."

Amaya glanced at Zeke. "I'll take her down to my sister. Eden will get her set up and started on things. You go let Mom and Gage know about everything. Gage is probably in the office."

Zeke nodded. "I'll take care of it. Be careful."

Amaya grinned as she grabbed the other girl's arm. "I always am."

Zeke shook her head as the two women disappeared. "Cocky. She's so damn cocky I can't stand it." Smiling, she grabbed a bottle of water from the fridge and made her way into the office where Gage was sitting at the desk, his head bent over maps.

He looked up when she opened the door, his brows drawing together. "Is everything okay? Are you the only one back? Where's everyone else?"

Zeke held up one hand. "Whoa. One question at a time. Serafina and the baby are taken care of. Lilith got away. She sacrificed the infant to save her own butt." She scowled at the thought. "Deacon is letting Michael know so they can pull back. Amaya is dropping off a Nephil prisoner we rescued to her sister for training. As far as I know, everything is fine."

Gage closed his eyes and leaned back in the chair. "Oh, thank God." He stood and crossed in front of the desk to hug her. "Alaria is upstairs with Caleb. She was putting him down for a nap."

"I'll head up there then. I'm going to change out of my battle gear and wait for the others to get back. Hopefully it won't be too long." She cocked her head. "Speak of the Devil. I detect some flash signatures."

Gage grinned when Michael entered the room. "Is everyone okay?"

Michael nodded, flicking his wings. "We're all fine. There are some minor injuries. Zeke, if you don't mind, would you tend to the wounded? I don't believe anything is life threatening, but there are some things that could benefit from your attention."

"Sure." Zeke brushed her hand over his sleeve as she left the room.

Michael turned to Gage. "We need to increase our security here. I fear there will be significant backlash from what we've done. We also need to get Lux back with all possible expediency. Her expertise in preparing for battle is necessary to ensure victory." He glanced back toward the door. "You understand that there's a high probability Lilith takes out her anger on your daughter, don't you?"

Gage's eyes flashed. "The thought's crossed my mind. We need to find her."

Michael nodded. "We needed to find her yesterday. My patrols won't sleep until it's done."

The vampire inclined his head slightly. "Then neither will I."

CHAPTER THIRTY-ONE

FEBRUARY 4TH, 2061

JERUSALEM

LILITH PACED in front of Lux, her blonde hair swept out of her face with pins and her heels clicking on the floor as she walked, gliding over the pool of blood spreading out from the witch. Lux spat, blood slapping the stone with a wet plop.

Lilith looked at Abalam, who held a pair of pliers in his hand. "Again."

Abalam lifted one eyebrow. "If we do too much more, she'll die."

"Then heal her and start over!" Lilith's voice rose to fill the room, the high-pitched shriek painful to Lux's ears.

Abalam crossed one leg over the other and stared at Lilith. "You aren't in charge of me in here. I'm the one Lucifer gave the witch to, and it's up to my discretion what we do with her. When I say she's had enough, that means she's had enough." He waved his hand in Lux's direction. "I've ripped off all her toes twice now on your command, and now we're moving on to her fingers, which is great fun, don't get me wrong, but it does very little to accomplish our goal, which is to bring her over to our side."

"I don't want her on our side. I want her to pay for the deaths of my children!"

Lux perked up slightly. Warm relief swept through her. If the children were dead, that meant Amaya was one step closer to killing Lucifer. She coughed to clear her throat and tried to swallow before speaking.

"I didn't know until now they were dead." She peered at Lilith through the one eye she could open. "How do you think this is my fault?"

"It's your fault because I say it's your fault!" The Devil pivoted and stomped to Lux, bracing one hand on each of the armrests. "Your friends butchered my babies in cold blood! They infiltrated my home, where I was laboring, trying to bring new life into this world, and they set up a diversion to lure out my protection. Then, my own flesh and blood and his whoring piece of ass sneaked into my home and slaughtered my children! I barely escaped with my life. They will pay for that. I'll send them little pieces of your body until there's enough to put you together. But first," her eyes lit up. "I'm going to make him torture you until you beg for death."

Lux ran her tongue around the jagged edges of her teeth, feeling where they had been broken and ripped out. Her gums were swollen and painful, and the edges of the teeth she had left pricked her tongue—the taste of blood blooming in her mouth.

"They'll be coming for me, and when they do, they'll slaughter you the same way they did your abominations."

Lux sank her teeth into her tongue when Lilith's fist collided with her jaw. The impact of the punch reverberated through her skull. Her vision went cloudy and it was all she could do to throw herself against the wall in her mind again. It had been getting constantly weaker. She could sense her power just out of reach, writhing and struggling at the blockade.

The second strike took her breath, and she focused on clawing through the barrier. Lux could feel her power, the warm comfort of it, just beyond her reach. When Lilith leaned in, her breath hot and putrid on Lux's face, the witch bit the proverbial bullet and slammed her head forward, head-butting the Devil as hard as she could.

Lilith sprang back, grabbing her nose and screeching as blood spurted between her fingers. She whirled to face Abalam, who was barely restraining his amusement.

"Kill her! Rip her limbs from her body and bleed her out on the floor! Do it now!"

Lux saw Abalam pick up a handsaw and charged the blockade with every bit of strength she had left. Magic rushed into her body as the wall crumbled and she sent out a blast of power, knocking both Devils back several feet. Power flowed through her and out of her hands, uncontrollable in its intensity.

Black flooded her, roaring in as she tried to slam the door. Unable to stop it, Lux embraced the power, melding it with hers and wielding it furiously. When Lilith sent out a wave of power, Lux batted it away and sent the Devil flying into the wall. Abalam was stronger and held his ground against her, his power colliding with hers so strongly that the skies split open and poured rain down, the sky rippling with thunder and cracking with lightning as nature voiced her displeasure at the show of magic.

Lux's eyes shifted to white, then black, finally settling on blood red. Her canines lengthened into fangs and magic whipped up inside her. She used a thread to unfasten the binds holding her to the chair and stood, cursing at her weak legs. Finding that walking was nearly impossible with no toes, she remained in one spot, thrashing out with power until the whole building shook and rattled as it strained to contain her magic.

"She's going to explode if she takes more!" Abalam's voice was high-pitched and panicked. He looked at Lilith, laying on the ground disoriented from her assault by Lux's magic. "You need to get out of here now!"

Lilith disappeared in a flash of lightning, leaving Abalam to deal with the out-of-control witch on his own. He brought up all the power he had and sent it hurtling at Lux, trying desperately to contain her. The traps on the floor and walls dissolved as her magic ripped through them. Cracks in the wall began to form and the fissures spread, slowly and then faster and faster.

Chunks of rock fell from the ceiling, striking the floor and bouncing, dust filling the air. Lux punched out with power, driving Abalam back and slamming him against the floor. Wind roared outside the building and the roof shook as the storm raging tried to rip it off. Abalam sent one look around and disappeared, following Lilith out of the building with a crack and blast of light.

The house couldn't take any more. It crumbled, pelting Lux with debris as it collapsed around her. She used magic to blast it back, sending the falling chunks of stone and flying into the storm. Rain struck her head and hands, the wind streaked over her naked skin, chilling her as she was soaked by the water falling from the wickedly swirling clouds.

The threat eliminated, Lux struggled to bring her magic under control. Blood ran out of her eyes, nose, and ears, washed away quickly by the pelting rain. She wrenched the door shut to the black magic and collapsed to the ground as the flow of power was cut off.

Lux lay on the ground, naked and cold, staring up at the storm raging over her head. Pain from her injuries coursed through her, stealing her breath as it all rushed back. She closed her eyes, reveling in the cool relief of the rain pelting her face. Knowing she would die quickly if she didn't heal, she concentrated on Michael's nonplace, letting the familiar process of flashing fill her. With a sharp crack and flash of light, she hurtled herself through space.

Amaya opened the door to the fridge and rifled through the contents. She rubbed her gritty eyes with one hand as she fished for a bowl of leftover soup with the other. A glance at the clock told her it was nearly four in the morning. Sighing, she poured soup from the larger bowl into a small one and sat it in the microwave, hitting buttons to warm it before putting the rest back in the fridge.

Perusing the beverage selections, she shrugged and snagged a bottle of wine from the counter, pouring half a glass. She rose onto her tiptoes to stretch her tight calf muscles and rolled her neck from side to side, trying to alleviate the pain from sitting in the same position for multiple hours.

Since killing Lucifer's children, there had been very little rest and even less sleep. Amaya scowled as she fought the urge to yawn and took a deep drink of the wine, swishing the ruby red liquid around her mouth.

The beeping microwave startled her out of her thoughts and she used a potholder to hold the hot bowl as she moved to the island to eat. She grabbed a spoon from the drawer next to the sink and perched on a stool, dipping the utensil into the steaming broth.

With the first bite almost to her mouth, Amaya glanced up when she heard the crack of a flash. All thoughts of eating fled when she saw Lux lying on the floor in a wet, naked heap, with blood seeping from what looked like every orifice.

"Zeke!" The scream was shrill and panicked as Amaya launched herself from the stool. "Zeke, I need you now! Oh, God, now, Zeke!"

Zeke raced into the room, her shirt half unbuttoned and her hair mussed from sleep. She opened her mouth to speak, then snapped it shut when she saw Lux. Kneeling, she laid her hands on her friend, delving deep within her to heal the wounds.

Soft yellow light emanated from Zeke's hands as she worked. She forced herself into Lux, sealing cuts, knitting bone, forming the strands of muscles and flakes of skin. The black taint of death was heavy within the witch, and Zeke knew she had only moments to save her.

Working quickly, she raced to Lux's heart, checking the organ for damage. Healing what was there, she hovered for a moment to make sure the heartbeat was strong and steady before sliding through the vessels and riding the wave of pumping blood to Lux's brain.

Synapses were still firing, but they were sluggish. Zeke touched each of them, sending a jolt of power through each of them. She watched as they fired stronger, the light from the brain waves bright and brilliant. That job done, she stopped briefly to check the heart again and then moved down to Lux's hands and feet, bracing herself for the exertion of reforming fingers and toes no longer there.

Healing something broken was easy. Reforming a body part severed was much more difficult. Zeke focused on one digit at a time, building bone and muscle, forming the nerves and tendons and weaving skin to cover the newly formed extremity. Each one took longer than the previous as Zeke's energy waned. By the time she reached the last finger, she was struggling through each step, barely able to finish the healing before being tossed out of Lux and back into her own body.

Zeke collapsed to the floor, her chest heaving as she tried to catch her breath. Her arms and legs were as heavy as lead and she struggled to sit up, her only concern that of Lux and her wellbeing.

"Easy, babe. I've got you." Dev's voice was soft as he helped Zeke sit up, supporting her until she waved at him, signaling that she was fine.

Amaya yanked off her sweater and laid it over Lux's body, leaving her clad in a camisole. She glanced at Dev. "Go get Gage and a blanket. Send someone to get Michael and Zane. Then go get Deacon from wherever he is. We need to get her into bed and find out what's happening and how she's here."

Dev nodded and disappeared, loping up the stairs toward Gage's bedroom. Amaya looked at Zeke and wrapped her arm around her friend.

"Is she okay?"

Zeke nodded. "She very nearly wasn't. I don't often get brain-drained by healing, but that almost did me in." She glanced up when she heard footfalls pounding down the steps. "Here comes Gage."

Gage flew into the kitchen and dropped to his knees, picking up Lux's shoulders and holding them in his lap, tears streaking down his cheeks as he held his daughter and rocked back and forth.

Amaya reached out and laid her hand on Gage's arm. "We need to get her dressed and into bed. Will you let Zeke and me take care of her? It'll only take a couple minutes. We'll wash her off and get her all tucked in and then you can see her."

Gage nodded, unable to talk through the knot of emotion in his throat. He stood and took a step back, allowing Amaya to lift her friend, cradling her against her chest. Zeke climbed to her feet and hurried after the other woman, darting around her on the stairs to hold open the door to Lux's bedroom.

Together, they used warm water and towels to wash the blood from Lux's skin and out of her hair. Once she was dried off, they carefully tucked clean pajamas on her before bundling her into the bed. Amaya dragged her forearm across her head to mop up sweat before speaking.

"How long is she going to be out?"

Zeke shrugged. "She's healed, so she just has to wake up. It could take a minute or an hour. She was unconscious when she hit the floor, so it might take a little while. There's nothing wrong with her, though. At least not that I can tell."

"If anyone could tell, it would be you." Amaya went to the door and held it open for Gage to come in. "She's cleaned up and sleeping. We'll let you sit with her for a while."

Gage grabbed Amaya and Zeke in a hug, crushing them each to him. "Thank you for taking care of her."

Zeke rose onto her tiptoes and pressed a kiss to the vampire's cool cheek. "She's our sister. Of course we took care of her. That's what family does."

Zane appeared in the room, his eyes alight with panic and hope. He whirled, looking for Lux, his eyes finding the bed and her prone form. He spun back to face the other three.

"What happened? Where did you find her? Is she okay? Why isn't she awake?"

Zeke held up her hand to stop the flood of questions. "We don't know what happened. She flashed into the kitchen but was unconscious when she got here. She'll be fine, she just needs to rest. She'll wake up when she's ready." She leaned against the door. "I'm going to go finish nursing Caleb, since that's what I was doing when Amaya started screaming for me. Yell if she needs anything."

Amaya squeezed Zeke's hand as the other woman passed by her on her way out of the room. She smiled softly at Zane and Gage. "I'll leave you two to be with her. I'll go fill Michael in on what's going on and then I'm going to get some sleep. Come get me when she wakes up."

Gage nodded. "Of course. Thank you, Amaya."

She shook her head. "No thanks necessary. I just screamed for Zeke. She did all the hard work."

Closing the door, she trailed back down the stairs to where Michael was studying the spot Lux had appeared in. He glanced up when she entered the room.

"I don't feel any other flash signatures. I believe we can surmise that Lux got here under her own volition."

"Do you have any idea how she got out?"

"There was a large power signature from the Garden of Gethsemane in Jerusalem. I was there investigating it when Dev came for me. I believe that's where they were holding her. Somehow she was able to get loose enough to use her powers. She destroyed the building they were keeping her in and caused a severe disturbance with the weather. Without her citrines to cleanse and focus the amount of black magic she would have needed in order to do what was done, I believe that she would have been deep inside a power drain by the time she arrived here." He looked at Amaya. "Was she badly injured?"

Amaya inclined her head slightly. "All of her toes had been cut off. About half of her fingers. Her teeth were broken off, some were missing. It looked like Abalam had been at her for a while. Zeke was able to put her back together though."

"Good. Is Gage with her? And Zane?"

"Yeah, they're up there." She sat down on the stool and reached for the spoon in her now-cold bowl of soup. Idly bringing a spoonful to her mouth, she swallowed. "Where's Deacon? I sent Dev for him."

"They should be getting back shortly. I asked them to inform your parents of Lux's location and to let Jophiel know he can call off the search. Now that Lux is back, we can focus on luring out and killing Lucifer."

Amaya swallowed another bite of the soup and gulped the remainder of the wine left in her glass. "She'll need a few days to rest up before she's ready to help with something like that."

"Then we take the time. We only have one chance to get this right. Lilith surviving is an unexpected complication, so we'll need to address that as well. I need some time to formulate a plan. Gage will be assisting with that, and input from the rest of you is necessary, of course." Michael sat next to her on the stool. "Both you and Deacon will need to eat the manna."

"I don't relish the idea of eating several thousand year old moldy bread. It's likely to give me some horrid disease."

The Angel's mouth twitched as he tried not to smile. "Don't worry about that. It won't be moldy. It's a heavenly substance meant to connect you to God. That's part of the requirement. You are going to wield the literal power of God through that sword you have.""

"I know all that. It doesn't make me like the idea any more." She finished the soup and rinsed her bowl in the sink. "I'm going to go lie down for a while. I was up all night studying the maps looking for Lux, so I haven't even been to bed yet."

Michael lifted one eyebrow. "I was wondering why you were having wine at five a.m."

"Because I don't think it counts as morning until one has actually been to bed." She grinned as she rinsed her glass. "Besides, a glass helps me sleep." She patted Michael's arm as she passed by. "Wake me if you need me."

CHAPTER THIRTY-TWO

FEBRUARY 5TH, 2061

THE MANOR

LUX STIRRED in the bed, her eyes moving behind closed lids as she fought her way through to consciousness. She blinked against the light streaming in through the window and sighed deeply as her vision cleared.

As her eyes focused on the man sitting in the chair at the edge of the bed, panic rose in her throat. A harsh scream tore from her throat, and she threw her hands out, sending a wave of power at the sleeping Gage.

The vampire flew across the room, smacking the closet door and cracking it as he struck it. Leaping to his feet, he whirled, fangs extended and eyes flashing red as he tried to find the threat. Only when a second bolt of power struck him did he realize it was Lux.

The door flew open and Zane raced in, Amaya right on his heels. Both Nephilim ran straight for Lux, Amaya wrapping her arms around the redhead and Zane perching on the edge of the mattress, concern evident in his face.

"What's wrong? Why were you screaming?" Amaya smoothed Lux's hair away from her face. "Are you in pain?"

Lux blinked rapidly and stared at Amaya. "How are you here? I'm in the wrong time. Did I drag you through, too? Does Michael know? Is my mom here? Where's Gabe? How are we going to get home?"

Realization dawned in Amaya's eyes, and she tightened her grip on Lux. "We're not in the wrong time. You're at Michael's manor. We're all here." She glanced at Gage. "She thinks she time-traveled because she didn't know to expect you looking like that."

Lux grabbed Amaya's arms and shook her friend. "What are you talking about? Is this a dream? I can't be in the right time, or he's traveled forward, because my father is not still a vampire!"

Gage took a step toward the foot of the bed and stopped when Lux crawled back, a mewling cry escaping her. He looked to Amaya and Zane, the plea in his eyes clear. Amaya inclined her chin slightly and turned back to her friend.

"When you got taken, some things happened. Zane and Michael went to tell your dad about Abalam getting you, and he was desperate to come find you. Because he was human and getting older, Michael wouldn't let him be involved in the rescue. Gage demanded that Michael turn him back, but Michael doesn't have that power."

Zane took over the story then, holding Lux's hand in one of his. "Baby, my father came down from Heaven and offered to turn Gage back into what he was before the prophecy was completed. The Angel of Death transformed him back into a vampire and made him the way he was before he became human. We're all in the right time, it's just that your dad's different than he was."

Lux's eyes filled with tears as she stared at her father. "Daddy, no." She raked her hands through her hair. "You'll have to watch me die. Your friends. All of us. Why would you do this to yourself?"

Amaya left the bed to make room for Gage, watching as he rushed to his child, enveloping her in his arms. When he spoke, his voice was choked with emotion.

"Because I'd rather watch you grow old and die than have you ripped from me young and vibrant. I'd already lost your mother. I wasn't going to sit around and lose you, too. I needed to be there for you in a way I couldn't be there for Aradia. If I'd never changed, maybe she'd still be alive. I couldn't run the risk that my humanity would endanger your life. It's not worth that. Nothing is worth watching you die. I lost my children once because of what I am. I wasn't about to go through that again."

Lux clung to her father, burying her head in his neck and crying piteously. Gage rocked her back and forth, murmuring words of comfort softly as he held her. When the tears finally ran dry, she sat back, wiping her moist cheeks and looking at the other two people in the room.

"Lilith was there the last few days. She was pissed as hell about her kids being killed and she wasn't pregnant anymore. Did you kill them?"

Amaya nodded hesitantly. "Yes. Lilith got away, but the baby and Serafina are dead."

"So we need to make a move on Lucifer." Lux threw back the blankets. "I can't lay here dwelling on things. I need to get to work. What do you need me to do?"

"We need to get Lucifer where I can kill him. And we need to figure out a way to hold him while I stab him."

"I can use the same spell Mom tried to use to hold him. Well, a modified version of it since some of the participants of that circle are now dead." Lux heaved herself to her feet, wobbled, but managed to stay standing. "I need to eat, and then I need my books. It'll take some time to work the spell and figure out what we're doing, but I can get on it. Dad, I could use your help with it."

Gage nodded. "Anything." He looked at Zane, a pained expression in his eyes. "But I think you should take some time to rest and build up your strength. You had quite the ordeal and I want you strong for this."

Lux glared at them over her shoulder. "I know my limits. I'm the one who got ripped to pieces for damn near two weeks. I think I can handle some spell writing." She jerked her head toward Amaya. "Let's go make some food."

Deacon found Amaya on Earth, her shoulder hunched against the cold, with snow halfway up her leather boots and her hands shoved deep into her pockets. Bare trees jutted into the sky, breaking up the monotony of the gray. Surrounding her were headstones, marking graves of people long dead.

"What are you doing here?"

Amaya turned and glanced over her shoulder, offering a small smile when she saw Deacon. Her cheeks were red from wind, and the sting of it made her eyes bright with moisture.

"Thinking."

He moved to stand next to her, his white blond hair and icy

blue eyes a stark contrast to her inky black and vibrant green. "What're you thinking about?"

She gestured to the chunk of granite in front of her. "This is where Griffin's body is. Or used to be. I'm not sure there'd be anything left after thirty years." She waved her hand. "It doesn't matter whether there is or there isn't. What matters is that I can come here and remind myself that I'm not the only person who's ever had to go through this and that there is someone who has had it worse than me. It keeps me sane." Her breath was a frosty puff. "At least I don't have to kill myself for us to win."

"I always wondered why she had to die. I understand being willing to sacrifice yourself to make the choice, but I still don't understand why she had to actually die. God brings people back to life all the time. Lazarus, Jesus, so on and so forth. Why not her?"

"I'm glad He didn't." When Deacon's eyebrows shot up, Amaya laughed. "What? If she hadn't died, Eden and Donovan wouldn't exist. My mother wouldn't be human. I probably wouldn't exist because Mom would still be a Devil. Don't get me wrong, I think it sucks what happened to her, but looking at it from thirty years into the future, I can't say I wish it would've turned out differently. I like having a brother and sister, and I like my parents being together."

"Griffin really got the short end of the stick, didn't she? Never knowing her son, never knowing her granddaughter, dying so young, then getting ripped out of Heaven and implanted with Gabriel's Grace." He glanced around the graveyard. "Do we know how she's doing with the memory thing?"

"No one's said anything since she kissed Mom. I know one of the other Angels was working with her up in Heaven, but I don't know if they're making any progress. I'd like to think they are. It would really suck if she goes the rest of eternity with Gabe's memories. I wouldn't wish those on my worst enemy."

Deacon bumped her shoulder with his own. "It might not be such a bad thing, her having his memories. At least not if she can learn to differentiate between hers and his. One good thing would be if she could give you some of the answers about him that you want. The why of it all."

"I don't need the why." Amaya scowled at the grave. "I don't need someone else to tell me what my father thought and felt. He should have told me himself, and I don't need to feel guilty about our lack of a relationship after he's dead." She rubbed her hands together to warm her fingers and then stuffed her fists back into her pockets. "I just like reminding myself of what's come before. It's good for me to keep perspective."

"Perspective is good as long as it doesn't get in your way of hope." He laid his hands on her shoulders and pulled her back against his chest, resting his chin on top of her head. "We'll get through this."

"Not all of us."

"No, not all of us, but we all knew that going in. The original six all knew that going in." He rubbed his cheek on her hair. "No matter what happens, I'll still love you at the end of this."

"Same goes for me." She tipped her head back and peered up at him. "Is that supposed to be news?"

Deacon chuckled and kissed her forehead. "No, but I feel better saying it. We've had to do some horrible things, and I know there's more ugliness left to come. I want to make sure you know it doesn't change how I feel about you."

"I appreciate it. I've struggled with everything, but I think we have to accept that Michael won't lead us wrong." She bit her tongue to keep from giggling. "Besides, your sister was a crazy, psycho, evil bitch."

"She took after my mother."

The deadpan delivery had Amaya dissolving into a fit of giggles. Deacon cocked one eyebrow and stared at her in mild amusement.

"What's so funny?"

Amaya bent over and rested her hands between her knees, taking several gulps of cold air. "It's just the way you said that. So matter-of-fact." She straightened and turned to face him. "I'm sorry."

"I'm used to you, Winslow." He grinned at her. "You're just lucky I love you so damn much."

Amaya closed her eyes as a wave of warmth floated over her. The words skated over her skin, barely brushing her before burrowing deep into her chest and settling into her heart. She studied the feeling, mulling it over and letting it fill her before opening her eyes and staring up at Deacon.

"I'm not one for declarations." She laid her hands on his cheeks. "You know that, so you didn't do a big thing to tell me. Just matter-of-fact because that's us. No apologies, no explanations needed. We are who we are and we feel what we feel and that's okay because we know each other so well." She tipped her head back and stared up at the darkening sky and the snowflakes falling from it. "I love you, Deacon. More than as a friend or a boyfriend. Even before we were together, when I let myself think about the future, you were always in it. Now that we get to find out who we are together, I know more than I ever have that you and I were made for each other. I feel like I was made to love you." She paused. "And kill Satan, obviously. But to love you, too."

Deacon chuckled and tucked her head underneath his chin. "Always practical, aren't you? Can't just be romantic for even one solid minute."

"If you wanted romance, you should have stuck with the doctor at the monastery. I'm a commonsense kind of girl." She rubbed her nose on his neck, warming it. "But that doesn't change how I feel about you."

He tipped her chin up. "I want forever with you, Amaya. When this is over, I want it all. We'll build a house somewhere. Anywhere you want. We'll get married if that's what you want, but I don't care as long as we're together, and then we'll have babies. I'm thinking at least two since you have siblings and are used to a big family, but we can have as many as you want since you're the one doing the heavy lifting on that particular issue."

Amaya grinned up at him, her eyes alight with good humor. "Been thinking about this, have we?"

"Only since I was a teenager." He stooped and pressed a kiss to her cold lips. "I don't hear you arguing."

"I'll want to be close to my family. And to Lux and Zeke."

"Fine with me. Anything else?"

She shook her head and wrapped her arms around his waist, pillowing her head on his chest. "As long as I have you, I'm good." She smiled at the sound of his heart beating under her ear. "I love you, Deacon. I'll love you until I take my last breath."

"Let's make sure that's not for about seventy more years." He glanced around. "We need to get out of here. It's getting dark quick, and it's risky for us to be on Earth anyway." He held her tighter. "Shall I flash us back?"

She nodded. "Vacation's over. It's time to get back to work."

CHAPTER THIRTY-THREE

FEBRUARY 8TH, 2061

THE MANOR

LUX SAT back in her chair and regarded the group of people surrounding her. "I've been thinking about how best to do this. In order for Amaya to kill Lucifer, she has to get into the same place with him. Luring him out is going to be damn near impossible since he knows his kids are dead, and I've had no luck in finding him. He's more powerful than me, so he can shield himself from my detection spells."

Amaya rubbed her hands on her jeans. "You wouldn't have called for a group powwow unless you had something more than 'I don't know,' so spit it out already."

"I've been trying to tweak the spell my mom used to bring him out of Hell and hold him in the Choosing Place while they cut his wings out. Obviously we aren't pulling him out of Hell, so I have to change some things, and we don't need to get something from him, we just need to stab him." Lux jerked her shoulder. "So I basically ended up trashing the whole thing and starting over."

Gage chuckled. "She's not joking about that. I have about a hundred pieces of paper with different versions of that spell on it in my office."

Lux glared at her father. "Anyway. To get back to what I was saying, I've been trying to figure out the best way to go about this and then it hit me. When this started back when Zeke and Dev went to LA, Gabriel said that in order for Deacon and Amaya to get to where they are, their closest companions would have to be determined to be worthy as well. That's why Zeke and I and Dev and Zane had to go through what we did. To prove that we have the same faith they do and that we can stand up for Heaven. If we had to go through that, then there had to be a way to use it to win."

Michael crossed one leg over the other. "I'd be inclined to agree with you. Father rarely issues edicts without there being some deeper meaning. The fact that Gabriel specifically divided the six of you into pairs makes me think there's something to it. Have you developed a spell to take advantage of that?"

Lux shifted nervously. "I think what it means is that they were never meant to do it alone. It was always supposed to be six into two and two into one. Amaya is the one meant to kill Lucifer, but Deacon has an important part in this as well. He has the ability to suppress her powers with his own and help her stay in control of them. That's huge for her since she's had so many problems in the past with controlling the power she has. What I've developed is a spell that will give our powers to Deacon and Amaya temporarily. Literally six into two. From there, Deacon will use his powers to help Amaya control hers, giving her the self-restraint needed to wield the power of Heaven. Two into one. It's about us being a circle, literally and figuratively, and standing together against this one final threat."

Gage patted his daughter's thigh. "It's a brilliant spell. It takes all the elements of Aradia's original spell and just improves on every one of them. Lucifer isn't going to know what hit him. It's no wonder he wanted to keep Lux in chains and lure her to his side."

Amaya smiled tightly. "So what do we need to do? When can we do this?"

Lux shifted uncomfortably. "That's where we run into a bit of a problem. Samhain isn't until the end of October, and that's the most powerful Wicca holy day. Oestra is in March—the Spring equinox—but that's still six weeks from now, and Oestra is a minor holy day to begin with, so I wouldn't get much boost from it. I'd say we could look to New Years Eve, at midnight to mirror when Griffin died and tap into the power of the Choosing, but that's even further than Samhain. I feel like we should take advantage of everything we can for this, so I want to pick the right day to do it and the right place."

"The Choosing Place. Obviously." Amaya sat up straighter. "We'd have the power of the Choosing and of the original spell Aradia tried, plus the residual energy from the Devils getting their wings carved off."

"I can't argue with anything you said." Lux tapped her fingers on her legs. "But I will say I think they'll sense that coming a mile away. It's certainly one of the most powerful places on Earth, and there are some huge benefits to doing it there, but we'd be taking a huge risk even going there to prepare. I'm sure Lucifer has demons watching it to make sure we don't. Do we want to go for power or for the element of surprise?"

Deacon leaned forward in his chair. "Do you have another place in mind? If you don't want to do it at the Choosing Place, you must have a secondary sight in mind."

Lux smiled. "I've been giving it some thought. Atlantis would be a good second bet, but that's out for obvious reasons. Beyond that, I'm still doing some research on a good balance between safety and power. It needs to be somewhere we can get to inconspicuously, that Lucifer won't see coming, and that could still help increase the power of the magic we're going to be using. If it's far away from humans, that's even better because we don't want a high amount of collateral damage."

Amaya looked at Deacon, staring at him for a long moment. "What about Griffin's grave? Wouldn't that give us the same boost as the Choosing Place would?"

Lux bit her lip thoughtfully. "It's a good idea. I'd need to go there and get a feel for the spot before we decide for sure, but it's definitely possible." She looked to Michael. "Do you have any suggestions?"

The Angel ran one hand through his hair. "I'm thinking of places like the Vatican or Saint Catherine's. Either of those would have a power boost. The Garden of Gethsemane is another place you'd find a boost, as is Mount Sinai. I lean toward Sinai because that is where Amaya has already had one encounter with God. The power there is fresher than anywhere else, and it would be relatively subdued from human interference. Everyone there is Warrior or Nephil, and as such would be willing participants in our war."

Lux tugged on the ends of her hair as she mulled over what

Michael had said. "I need to go to the places and get a feel for the power there. Those places are all going to be full of magic and energy, but it needs to be the right kind of power and energy. I can't decide on a place until I get there and can feel what it's going to do to me for this spell and what is going to be passed into Amaya and Deacon through the spell."

"I'll take you to each of them." Michael glanced to Gage. "I assume you can arrange for all the supplies she'll need for the spell?"

Gage leaned back in the chair and tapped his fingers together. "I do still have my ways, even in this world. I'll get everything we need. It could take close to a week to gather it all."

Lux shrugged. "It'll take me nearly as long to select the right place and finish gaining my strength. I need to visit each place at different times of the day. Midnight, sunrise, and sunset. Those are the most powerful times throughout a day and I need to see when each has the most power in each particular spot. I'm also going to need the remaining candles and magic implements from the Choosing Place." She held up her hand when Amaya started to speak. "I know it's risky, but there's a lot of power there in those candles and in the blade they used. I want to have those things to bolster our spell."

Michael nodded. "I'll take care of it." He stood. "If there's nothing more, we should get started on this. I'll retrieve the items from the Choosing Place now, and then we'll leave for the first of the places you want to see in the morning before sunrise."

Deacon cleared his throat. "I think it's naïve of us to think we're only going to have to go up against Lucifer. Lilith is out for blood, and we still have Azazel and Abalam to deal with. There could be a whole fucking army of demons and lower level Devils there, not to mention the Cambion. We could be outnumbered a hundred to one easily. We need to be prepared for that."

"I'll have Jophiel bring all of our prepared Nephilim to the place we choose. If they bring an army, we'll have one waiting for them." Michael's expression was stony and set. "I agree with you that we'll likely have more than Lucifer to deal with, but he is our focus. If we kill him, the rest is just cleanup."

Amaya cleared her throat. "I could talk to my parents about brining Warriors in for it. I know they're human, but it would bolster our numbers, and they're well trained. It could make a difference."

"I agree that we need to discuss this with them and have the

Warriors brought in for it, but I don't think you should be the one to go. From this point until we make our move, I think we need to keep both you and Deacon here. Lucifer and Lilith will be looking for both of you and there's no reason for the two of you to be in more danger than necessary." Michael looked at both of them sternly. "That means no more jaunts to Earth."

Amaya blushed. "I didn't think you knew about that."

He sniffed indignantly. "I know about all things that go on under this roof. It's my job to keep you all safe and that's one I take very seriously." Brushing his hands over his arms, Michael glanced around the room. "I'll speak to Jophiel and then to Alaria and Braxton. Lux, be ready to go thirty minutes before dawn."

"Do we just eat it? Or is there some sort of ritual we need to do first?" Amaya glanced at the small urn she and Deacon had taken from Atlantis. "Is it moldy?"

Deacon opened the container and peered in. "It looks like balled up bread." He upturned it and dumped the manna onto the table. "Are you sure you want to do this now?"

"We have to eat it. Might as well do it when we're here and can have some time to adjust to the effects of the manna if there are any."

"Somehow I don't think it's like eating poison, Amaya." Deacon looked at her drolly. "Let's just get it over with."

Together, they each picked up a chunk of the white substance and ate it. Amaya grimaced at the slightly sticky, grainy texture. The manna stuck to her tongue and mouth, coating it with something akin to gritty honey. She swirled her tongue around, trying to rid her mouth of the feeling. Reaching for a bottle of water, she gulped half the liquid before handing it to Deacon, who drained it gratefully.

"Well, that was disgusting." Deacon scowled at the empty urn. "He could at least have the decency to make it taste like something yummy." He glanced sideways at Amaya. "And can I just say that way too much of this whole thing has involved me eating stuff I don't want to eat."

Amaya chuckled. "Well, I think that was the last one, so we should be in the clear now." She put the lid back on the urn and sat it in a cabinet. "I don't feel any different, do you?"

He shook his head. "Not one damn bit. Maybe it takes a little while, or maybe it's not going to be activated until we need it."

"We'll figure it out either way." She reached for a bottle of wine and the corkscrew. "I need something other than water to wash the taste out of my mouth." Deftly uncorking the bottle, she snagged a glass from the counter and poured it half-full. "Want a glass?"

Deacon took her glass and sipped. "I think I'm going to go burn off some energy in the basement. We can't train enough right now."

Amaya jerked her shoulder. "Speak for yourself. I'm gonna drink my wine, take a long, hot shower and go to bed. Naked." She smiled saucily. "Maybe you'll come join me."

Deacon grinned. "Maybe I will."

CHAPTER THIRTY-FOUR

FEBRUARY 14TH, 2061

THE MANOR

AMAYA STEPPED into the frothy water, sinking down slowly into the tub, immersing herself in heat and bubbles. A sigh of pleasure slipped out from between her lips and she closed her eyes, enjoying the warmth of the bath. Her muscles ached from training and several bruises purpled over her body, evidence of the grueling work she had been doing.

Lifting one hand out of the water, she studied her torn knuckles with disinterest and reached for the glass of wine she'd placed on the edge of the tub, bringing the cup to her lips and sipping, the cool wine sliding down her throat. After replacing the glass, she sank deeper, wetting her hair in the water and taking all but her head beneath the surface.

Ignoring the tightness in her chest as she realized there were only a few hours before they left for Sinai, Amaya reached for the shampoo and squirted gel into the palm of her hand, rubbing it into her hair until lather dripped down her shoulders and into the bubbles floating on top of the water.

The door to the bedroom opened and Deacon stepped in, his

face shining with sweat and an icepack on one of his hands. He crossed the room and leaned against the entrance to the bathroom, watching her with mild interest.

"What happened to your hand?"

Deacon laughed and dropped the bag of ice onto the sink as he started stripping off his t-shirt, nodding pointedly toward her swollen and discolored knuckles. "Same thing as yours, I imagine. I crammed it into Zane's face several times. That boy is wily and strong."

"It was Dev for me. Zeke was taking care of the baby and Lux is already at Saint Catherine's so he was the only one left to spar with." She ducked beneath the water to rinse her hair, then straightened and looked at him, water running down her face. "You heading to the shower or getting in here?"

"I'm not much for baths." He grimaced. "There's something yucky about sitting in grime mixed with water. Besides, I can smell the perfumey shit from here. No way do I want to smell like a bouquet of flowers."

Amaya laughed and playfully flicked water at him. "Fine, take your shower, then. I didn't want you to get in with me anyway."

"Liar."

She lifted one eyebrow, enjoying the light banter. "Oh, yeah? Maybe next time I'll make sure it's your face I break my knuckles on."

He shook one fist at her, the grin and light in his eyes belying the gesture. "Bring it on, baby." Shucking his pants, Deacon padded to the shower and turned on the water, facing her as he waited for it to heat up. "Is your pack ready to go?"

"Everything is set. I went through and checked it before I got in here and I'll run over things again in the morning. I'm ready. Well, as ready as one can possibly be when going into battle against Satan himself."

"We're going to be fine. In thirty or so hours we'll be back here getting shit-faced drunk in celebration of killing Lucifer and actually managing to save the whole fucking world." He stuck his hand under the spray from the shower to check the temperature, then stepped in. "It'll be okay."

"I hope you're right. I need you to be." Amaya picked up her razor and idly spread shaving cream on one of her legs. "But this is going to be the hardest thing we ever have to do. Logically I know we're ready. We've trained like crazy, we all know Lux's plan backward, forward, and sideways, but that doesn't make it any less worrisome right now. I don't think I'm going to be able to sleep a wink and I don't want to get drunk because the last thing I need is to charge off into the battle of my life with a fucking hangover."

Deacon laughed from inside the shower, poking his head out from behind the curtain. "Being so exhausted you can hardly keep your eyes open isn't going to help you any more than a hangover would." He disappeared back into the shower stall, continuing to speak. "Who's taking care of Caleb while we're all off saving the world tomorrow?"

"My parents. Mom and Dad are going to be here. Dad's at Saint Catherine's now arranging all his Warriors and getting things set up with Harry. They're evacuating all the civilians to the compound in France that Mom and Dad have been staying at. Donovan is holding things down there and Eden is leading the Warriors tomorrow." Amaya took a deep breath. "My baby sister is going into battle with us."

"Eden is more than capable of handling herself. She may not be Nephil but she's far from helpless. She'll be just fine. We all will be."

"It's crazy to think we aren't going to have at least some casualties. Odds are that some of them are our friends and family." She closed her eyes for a brief moment, then forced herself to continue shaving her legs. "I wish I could just stuff all of you in some basement somewhere and go do this alone so that no one else I love has to die. If I could keep you all safe, I would."

"You know we're all going into this with you." Deacon turned off the water and stepped out of the shower, reaching for a towel. "We're a family, Maya. This is what family does."

He used the towel to mop the water off his body, running the cotton over his shoulders and down his chest. Amaya watched as he dried himself, her eyes trailing over his creamy skin and hard muscles. She bit her bottom lip, chewing on the supple flesh as she stared. Deacon lifted his eyebrows and grinned at her, the expression cocky and self-assured.

"You're staring."

"I know."

He hung the towel up on the hook and strode into the bedroom naked, Amaya watching every step. Her gaze raked over the solid planes of his back and down to the curve of his backside. Snagging a pair of sweatpants, Deacon jerked them up over his legs and returned to the bathroom, leaning against the door.

"How long do you plan on sitting there in a bucket of your own sweat and crud?"

Amaya rolled her eyes and pulled the plug out of the bottom. "I had planned to sit in here until it got cold in hopes the heat would relax me enough to go to sleep, but now I have other plans." She stood and reached for a towel to wipe off the bubbles clinging to her slick skin.

"Other plans, hmm?" He crossed his arms over his chest and stared at her, his pale blue eyes warming. "What plans would those be?"

Stepping out of the tub, she bent to dry her legs before straightening and rubbing the towel over her hair, leaving her body bare and exposed to his gaze. Once her hair was no longer dripping, she draped the towel over the rack on the wall and left the bathroom, sauntering toward the bed she and Deacon shared.

"This might be our last night on Earth. I think we probably oughta enjoy it."

A grin spread slowly across Deacon's face. "I think I like where this is going. Tell me more."

Amaya perched on the edge of the bed and crossed one leg over the other. "I just meant that maybe we should take advantage of each other's company while we still can."

Deacon pushed off the doorjamb and strode across the room until he was standing directly in front of Amaya. "Why Miss Winslow, unless I'm sadly mistaken, it sounds like you're propositioning me."

She grinned up at him, tipping her head back to see him fully, her damp hair trailing down her back. "Does it? I was wondering if maybe that wasn't coming through clearly enough."

"I got the message. Loud and clear." Deacon bent, bringing their faces to the same level. "Sex might help you sleep anyway. It's the least I can do for the good of the world. You need to be rested for tomorrow and if an earth-shattering orgasm is what it takes to make sure you're rested, well, I think it's my God-given duty to provide it to you."

Amaya shivered. "Earth-shattering, huh? That's quite the promise. What happens if you don't manage it?"

He lowered her to the bed, stretching out next to her, his hand cupping her hip. "Then I'll just have to keep trying. Over and over and over again until I get you there."

Amaya's breath caught in her chest and her body tightened

from anticipation. "Think you have the energy for that many tries?"

Deacon was laughing when he kissed her. He tasted rich and dark, his flavor flooding her senses. The hand on her hip shifted up, skimming over her ribs and finding one of her nipples, the pad of his thumb rubbing over the protruding nub gently. Breaking the kiss slowly, he stared down at her, his gaze heated and filled with desire.

"I have the energy for as many tries as it takes."

Deacon brushed a kiss over the line of her jaw before sliding down her body, his hand trailing from her breast over the softness of her belly to the juncture of her thighs. Amaya inhaled on a gasp and spread her legs, her hips arching toward his hand. Gently, he parted the folds to her body and stroked her with one finger, rubbing softly while continuing to scatter kisses over her neck and down onto her chest.

He took one nipple into his mouth and sucked strongly, sending waves of desire through her as he did so. Amaya's hands fisted in the sheets and she lifted her upper body slightly, encouraging him to keep going. Swirling his tongue around the slightly rougher texture of her nipple, he used one finger to slide into her body, flicking her clit with his thumb as he did so.

Amaya's legs fell open, exposing her completely to his ministrations. Her eyes drifted closed and she let the waves of need and desire wash over her, relaxing into Deacon's skilled movements.

He released her nipple with a slight popping sound, his breath warm on her skin as he nuzzled her. Shifting slightly, he gave her other breast the same attention, tasting her skin and rubbing the tip with his tongue. His fingers increased their pace between her legs, sliding in and out, slickened by the evidence of her desire.

Deacon stood, grabbing her calves in his hands and scooting her down to the edge of the bed, arranging her feet where he wanted them. Kneeling at the foot of the mattress, he pressed a kiss to the inside of one of her thighs, making her whole body tense in anticipation of what was coming next.

When he licked her, Amaya nearly came off the bed. Before her power could spike, she felt the calm, warm waves of his surrounding her, bringing the spikes back within her control. Trusting him to handle it, she relaxed into the soothing sway of his power, letting it envelop her into warmth and safety. Slowly, he parted her, stabbing his tongue into her clit and using mouth, tongue and teeth to bring her pleasure.

Amaya's body tightened with need as she felt the beginnings of an orgasm form deep in her gut. She reached up with one of her hands and slid her fingers over her own nipples, tugging on the nubs and rubbing them between her fingertips. Deacon gripped her thighs in his hands, pulling her harder into his mouth, the intense stimulation sending her rocketing up the crest of release.

She gasped, one hand sliding down to tangle in his hair, the silky strands sliding through her grip. Her hips bucked and jerked and a loud groan tore from her throat. The light flickered as their combined power spiked, one bolt of fear jolting through her before the calming wave of Deacon's power settled hers.

He sent her careening into climax, the pleasure sweeping through her, hot and hard. Before she had finishing shaking, Deacon was sliding up the bed to lay next to her, his skin smooth and warm against hers. She turned into him, wrapping her arms around his chest and hugging him tight to her, the craving for close contact overwhelming. He hugged her to him, one arm banded around her waist. When he spoke, his mouth was next to her ear and his voice was a raspy whisper.

"How'd I do? Did I achieve Earth-shattering?"

Amaya laughed despite herself. "You were pretty damn close."

"I'll get there yet." He left the bed long enough to shuck off his pants and retrieve a condom from the nightstand drawer, rolling the latex barrier over his bulging erection before returning to the bed.

Amaya reached down and stroked his condom clad penis gently. "I figured you'd let me give as much as you did."

Deacon cupped her face in one of his hands, his eyes boring into her. "Tonight is about you, Maya. I just want to be with you."

She rose onto her knees, her body shimmering with sweat. He took in every inch of her luscious, dusky skin, burning the image of her into his mind. When she pivoted so her back was toward him and glanced over her shoulder, her eyebrow cocked invitingly, Deacon grinned.

"Oh yeah?"

She wiggled her eyebrows. "You did say Earth-shattering. I figure the best way to get there is hot, hard, and fast." She lowered herself to her hand and knees. "You want to be with me? Well then take me."

Deacon gripped her hips in his hands, yanking her back against himself and stroking into her with one solid thrust. Amaya gasped at the penetration and bit down onto her lip, her already sensitive body positively humming from the sensation of being filled.

Slowly, he rocked his hips back and forth, sliding in and out gently, his strokes methodical. Her body clenched around him and warmth surrounded his penis as she dampened. Her fingers grasped the sheet, pulling on it.

Deacon held her hips reverently in his hands, his body stroking in and out of hers more quickly, then quicker still until they were colliding with every thrust, the sound of flesh meeting flesh filling the room. Amaya moaned loudly, her body tightening around him as she worked her way toward orgasm, every thrust of his hips driving her closer, and closer still, to the edge of climax.

Amaya looked back over her shoulder, her eyes finding and holding Deacon's. She pushed herself back against him, seating him deeply within her. He withdrew, pulling all the way out before thrusting back in fully. A strangled cry of want tore its way from her throat and he repeated the motion before continuing his methodical, deliberate strokes.

As Deacon's orgasm began to threaten, he moved one hand from her hip to the entrance of her body, sliding his fingers over the wetness there and up slightly to her clitoris, stroking the bundle of nerves gently, pressing on it and rubbing back and forth. With a strangled cry, Amaya toppled into her second orgasm, her body clenching around him. Driving into her several more times, his own climax swept over him, his hips jerking into hers as he came.

Together, they collapsed onto the bed in a tangle of arms and legs, laughing as they shifted around one another until they laid face to face. Amaya rolled onto her stomach, propping her chin on one hand and stared at Deacon, reaching out with the other to brush a lock of hair away from his face.

"I think you officially achieved earth-shattering."

Deacon rolled to the side to dispose of the used condom before speaking. "If not we got pretty damn close." He grinned at her. "Feel like you can get some sleep now?"

She jerked one shoulder in a shrug. "I don't think there's anything out there that could make me sleep tonight." Sighing, she flopped onto her back and stared up at the ceiling. "On one hand I wish tomorrow would hurry up and get here and on the other, I wish it would stay tonight forever so I didn't have to actually do this."

"No one would blame you if you needed more time. Or if you refused to do it at all."

"Yes they would." Amaya laughed half-heartedly. "Everyone would blame me and they'd have every right to. This is my birthright. It's why I exist. I can't deny that. I have to go through with tomorrow and I will. Fortunately, having to do something doesn't mean I have to like it while I do it." She turned her head to stare at Deacon. "I need you to promise me something."

He raised up on an elbow to look down at her. "Don't ask me to do anything that's going to lessen your chances of survival. I'd hate to have to lie to you."

"If things go south tomorrow, I want you to get our friends out safely. Lucifer isn't going to stop with just me if he wins. So if I die—if he gets the better of me and I'm dead—I want you to promise me that you will make sure everyone else gets to safety. I've accepted that I might die. We've know that's the reality since the beginning, but I refuse to accept they'll die. And Eden. Make sure Eden gets out, too. I know she's not one of our friends, but she's my baby sister and I can't stand the thought of anything happening to her." She cupped Deacon's cheek in one of her hands. "Can you promise me that?"

Blue eyes bored into green, Deacon's gaze steady and intense. "I promise I'll do everything within my power to make sure all of our friends and family make it out of tomorrow safely."

CHAPTER THIRTY-FIVE

FEBRUARY 15TH, 2061, 10:47 PM

SAINT CATHERINE'S MONASTERY

HARRY PACED back and forth in the entry to the monastery, his hands on his hips and the scabbard for his sword hitting his thigh with every step. Deacon leaned against the newel post, his arms crossed over his chest, watching the Warrior pace.

"If this goes right, you'll be in all the history books."

Harry's head snapped up and he drew to a stop. "I don't want to be in the history books. I don't want to be here at all."

Deacon's brows drew together. "If you don't want to fight, I can take you to the compound with the rest of the civilians."

"I'm not afraid to fight, boy." Harry jutted his chin up defiantly. "I'm not afraid to fight or die for this. I'd do so happily and without any promise of people knowing my name. That's not important to me. What's important is keeping as many of these people alive as I can and we all know that's a pretty fucking tall order given that we're about—" he checked his watch, "—

seventy-two minutes from hailing Lucifer here to try and kill him."

"I never promised you easy." Deacon straightened and adjusted his utility belt. "The Warriors should stay in here until the battle gets going. We're going to have the element of surprise with as many as there are and I don't want to waste it too soon. Michael has the remnants of the Spear, so he's going to be the one fighting the Devils."

"Don't you worry one of them will get the better of him? He's your father."

"I know he is. I love my dad, but we both know that one or both of us might not come out of this still breathing. He's the best shot we have at killing the Devils so he's the one who'll go against them. It's just the way it has to be."

A shimmer near the door alerted both men to an Angel appearing and they turned, Harry smiling and Deacon frowning when they saw Griffin. She flicked her wings and tucked her hair behind her ears.

"Michael will hardly be alone. I'll be fighting alongside him." She looked at Deacon somberly. "I started this sixty-two years ago. I want to be here when it ends."

Deacon inclined his head in a ghost of a nod. "Any help is appreciated. We could use it. Dad's at the base of the mountain helping Lux get things ready."

"Where is Amaya?"

"She's upstairs getting herself ready."

"I'll poke my head in on her and then help your father." Griffin began to ascend the steps. "There isn't much more time to prepare so I'll make this quick."

She continued up the stairs and down the hall to the room where Amaya was going through her pack, checking things off on her list and rearranging the contents to make them fit better. Griffin leaned against the doorway and smiled, clearing her throat to alert the Nephil to her presence.

"When it was my day, I remember trying to peek out the window through a little hole in the wood covering it. All I had was that one knife. During the battle, when things started to go crazy, I ended up with a pack. I don't even remember who gave it to me now. It was one of your parents. Alaria was with me the whole time, fighting until the end."

"Mom's good at fighting. It's all she's ever known." Amaya turned to face the Angel, her face drawn and tight. "I kinda wish she was here today."

"I imagine she's worrying about you. Your dad, too."

"If all goes well I'll see them in the morning."

"It will. The way I see it, God owes us one. They failed the first time because He'd given up on them." Griffin smiled sadly. "Do you need anything, Amaya? I know I'm not your mom and you're probably not even happy to see me, but I'll do anything in my power to help you through this. I know more than anyone what you're feeling right now."

Amaya's hands trembled as she fastened her scabbard around her hips. Aaron's rod gleamed in the light from the lanterns in the room, the sapphire blade reflecting the light. She glanced down at the pack sitting on the bed, then up at Griffin.

"I don't need that, do I? All I'll be able to use is this sword. Nothing else is going to help me."

Griffin crossed the room and laid her hands on Amaya's shoulders. "Your friends are going to help you. Michael and I are going to help you." She placed one hand on Amaya's chest. "All you need, you carry in your heart."

Amaya blinked back tears and looked up at the ceiling, trying to hold them off. "I'm scared."

"You'd be a fool not to be."

"Were you scared?"

Griffin looked at Amaya, into the green eyes her children might have had if she'd lived long enough to have them. She thought back to the sense of calm she'd felt on the day of the Choosing, remembering the way her body had prepared her for death. The all-encompassing knowledge she'd woken to on the morning of the Choosing that she was fulfilling her destiny. She remembered that feeling—the relief, the calm—and looked into Amaya's eyes. And she lied.

"I was terrified." Griffin drew Amaya close, wrapping her arms around the woman and hugging her tightly. "You're going to be okay. You'll survive this."

"What if I don't?"

"Then you'll be at peace in Heaven."

Amaya laughed bitterly. "Cold comfort."

"Is still comfort." Griffin pulled back from the hug. "Now that I have my memory issue fixed, it's easy for me to tell what were mine and what are Gabe's. I can tell you beyond doubt that your father had no fear you wouldn't succeed at this. He believed it with every fiber of his being. I believe it, too. You're going to fight and live. All you need is some faith."

Amaya's smile was watery. "Now you're starting to sound like an Angel."

Griffin grinned. "I'm learning the lingo well enough." She wrapped her arm around Amaya's shoulders. "Let's get down there and help your friends prepare."

11:02 pm

"Fifty-eight minutes and counting!" Lux called out the time from where she was spray-painting the ground.

Michael glanced around. "I believe we're fine on time. Everything is nearly complete." He glanced up when Amaya and Griffin came into view. "Is everything okay?"

Amaya nodded. "Griffin's here to help."

Michael offered a wry smile. "I'm surprised Father is letting you come down to fight in the battle."

Griffin shrugged. "I'd say what He doesn't know won't hurt Him, but He obviously does know."

"You're here without leave from Heaven?"

Griffin shifted uncomfortably. "It's like I told Amaya. I was the one who started this more than six decades ago. I want to be here to see it finished."

"And so you should be." Michael handed her a dagger. "This is one of the two remaining knives made from the tip of the Spear. It will kill a Devil. I suggest you use it for one of the three who were once Archangels." He set his jaw. "I would also prefer that Lilith be left to me, but if you see an opportunity to kill her do not waste it."

Griffin tucked the knife into a pocket of her suit pants. "I don't intend to waste an opportunity to kill any ally of Lucifer." She smiled tightly. "I haven't yet forgotten what they put me through while I was still human. I doubt I ever will."

Lux looked up from spray painting. "Everything's done. If you have anything you want to do in the next thirty minutes, I suggest you go do it. I need everyone in their places at five minutes till midnight. The spell has to be in process when midnight hits. That'll give us the most power."

Michael cast a look at the gathered group, his eyes bright with emotion. "Make yourselves ready. If there are things needing said, say them. We all know there's a good chance some of us won't make it out and a chance none do. Don't charge to your deaths without making your peace with those you love. There is no room for anything other than hope and ferocity in your hearts tonight."

Amaya laid her hand on Michael's arm as the rest trickled off to walk aimlessly, talk, hug, or just stand waiting. He looked down at her, his expression softening.

"How are you?"

She shrugged, hunching her shoulders against the chilled air. "Scared out of my mind. Other than that, I'm good. Lux put up some blocking spells so once we call Lucifer out we might have a minute or two before the cavalry comes for him. They'll be able to get through quickly but we'll have a minute or two."

"For what it's worth, I think you have every right to be scared. I'm scared." He rubbed her shoulder gently. "I can't imagine how you feel tonight. The weight of the world is on you."

"And I feel every ounce of it." She tipped her head back and looked up at the sky. "This is the place where I saw God. In that moment, I believed with everything in me that we would do this. If Lucifer had appeared right then, I'd have absolutely believed I could take him on with my bare hand. I *saw* God with my own two eyes. Tonight I don't feel nearly so confident. Tonight I feel like I'm going to die."

"Then know we will all fall with you." Michael hugged her gently. "Thirty-two years I've fought this fight. Tonight it ends, one way or the other. I had faith in your parents, in all of the original six. I had faith in Zeke and Dev, in Lux and Zane. I have faith in you and in my son, but more than faith, you have given me hope, Amaya. Victory is within our grasp. All you have to do is reach out and take it."

"I'm flailing for it with both hands. I'll fight with every breath I have." She grasped his arm in both hands. "I need you to know that I'm going to try the best I can, that I'll fight with all I have and that I will die for this if I have to. I don't want to die, but I will lay down my life without hesitation to win this. I know what's at stake and I don't take it lightly." She blinked back tears. "I feel the weight of every person left on Earth. I won't fail."

Michael laid his hands on Amaya's face, bending to kiss her forehead. "I wasn't the one telling your stories as a child. I wasn't the one there when you took your first breath. It's not my essence that runs through your veins, but since the moment you came to me all those years ago, I have loved you as my daughter. I love all of you as my children. You have made me prouder than any parent has ever been of any child." He stared into her eyes, his own moist with emotion. "It has been my honor to train and guide you. In all my lifetimes, being here with you, going through this with the original six, those have been the single most important things I have ever done." He released her and stepped back. "You should say all you need to say to the others. I don't want you to go into this with anything left to be said."

Before Amaya could even move, Lux's voice sounded above the quiet rumblings of the other Nephilim.

"I need everyone to start getting ready. All Nephilim not directly needed for the spell should move back to the cover of the monastery. Everyone else, it's time to take your places. I need to be able to tell you what you're doing before we start." She glanced to Michael, then over at Griffin. "I want both of you to stay close. You're both needed for this, even though you don't have an active part in the spell."

Griffin lifted one eyebrow. "What do you need from me other than in the battle?"

Lux smiled tightly. "That's simple. I need your blood."

CHAPTER THIRTY-SIX

FEBRUARY 15TH, 2061, 11:52 PM

MOUNT SINAI

"THIRTY-ONE YEARS ago, six gathered in the Choosing Place and put all they were on the line for the sake of people who didn't even know they existed." Lux spoke loudly and clearly, lifting her voice so that everyone could hear her. "Tonight, we do the same. We will finish what was started before us, and we will stop future generations from having the same hardships that we've had."

Picking up the Choosing knife, she held it close to her chest and closed her eyes briefly. Next to her, Zeke had stuffed her hands in her pockets. Zane was on one side and Dev on the other, with Lux sandwiched between the two men and Amaya and Deacon in the center of the circle.

"As my mother told the six years ago, there is magic in everything. Energy and power in the ground we stand on, in the air we breathe, in the magic we make between people. Tapping into that and bending it to our will is how we use magic to make things happen." She took a deep breath. "We've used the candles in six groupings of thirteen, both because those numbers are important in the practice of witchcraft and because these same candles were used thirty-one years ago. There is power left in them from that spell, and we'll push more yet into them tonight.

"This isn't going to be easy. Blood has been spilled on this ground before, and more will be spilled between now and dawn. God has been on this dirt, sent his power into this mountain, and we will use it tonight to take on a Godly task. In order to succeed, we must all believe we can. God must believe we can." She met each gaze in turn. "In order for Amaya to kill Lucifer, we had to complete tasks to prove our worth as her allies. Tonight, we must stand strong against Hell and lend her all we are. It must be given without hesitation, without apprehension and with open hearts and minds. Does anyone here have doubt?"

When Lux was met with silence, she nodded sharply.

"Good." She bent and picked up a goblet from between her feet. "In order to strengthen the spell, I'm going to ask Michael and Griffin to put thirteen drops of blood into the cup." She handed Michael the blade and Griffin the cup. "Through blood runs power, life, and soul. We need all three to succeed." She watched while each Angel used the knife to cut their hands and carefully squeezed blood into the container.

Once both Angels had provided blood, Lux took it back and held it between her hands, staring into the deep red liquid.

"Blood of Angels, blood of friend, strengthen our plight to reach the end. Freely given, sacrifice made, give us rest, come to aid."

When the blood began to boil, Lux dipped the Choosing knife into it, swirling it around until the blade was coated red. Lifting it out of the cup, she poured the rest of the blood into the center of the circle, the dirt sizzling and boiling where it landed.

"Three to two, two to one, tonight we fight, our task is done. Power to power, blood to blood, brother, sister, lover, friend. The blood of the ones who have come before flows strong within us. Together we come together to fight." She glanced around. "I'm going to link Zeke and myself to Amaya, and Dev and Zane to Deacon. Once I've got that, I'll tie the two of them together and then we'll hail Lucifer. Any questions before we really get started?"

Zeke laughed nervously. "I thought we were starting."

"This is just the first act." Lux gestured to the center of the circle. "I want Deacon and Amaya to stand here, facing one another. Dev and Zane, stand on either side of him. Zeke, stand to her left, and I'll stand on her right, but don't go out of the edges of the circle."

Everyone shifted to their places, taking care not to cross the bounds of the salt lines. Lux handed Zeke the Choosing knife.

"Zeke, I want you to score your palm—a shallow cut is all that's needed—and repeat after me. Blood of the Healer, freely given. All I am, I give to she. Power to power, blood to blood. I give of myself willingly, openly, and fully."

Zeke repeated the words while slicing open her hand. "Now what?"

"Hand the knife to Amaya. She's going to slice her palm and then you're going to join hands so that your blood touches."

Lux watched with an eagle gaze as the two women followed instructions before turning to face the three men. "Dev, your turn. The exact same thing." She handed him the knife. "Blood of Nephil, blood of friend, I give all I am to Lucifer's end. All I am, I give to he. Power to power, blood to blood. I give of myself willingly, openly, and fully."

Dev repeated the chant, then opened his hand and passed the knife to Deacon, waiting while his friend followed suit. With a long glance at one another, they joined hands, a flash of light passing between them. Lux smiled tightly.

"Blood of the witch, freely given, I pass my power to please Heaven. By all I am, all I will be, I give to you, I give of me. Power to power, blood to blood. I give of myself willingly, openly, and fully."

When Amaya sliced open her other palm and then reached for both women, closing her hand around each of theirs, bright flashes of light tore through the sky. She gasped from the power flowing through the three of them, into each and then into the other. Lux looked at Zane.

"You know the drill by now. Son of Death, son of man, I hold life in my hand. I offer up all I am without hesitation. Brother to brother, friend to friend, we join together till this we end. Power to power, blood to blood, I give of myself willingly, openly, and fully."

Zane followed the steps, waiting until Deacon was ready. When their hands were clasped, he sucked in a deep breath as his power flowed out of his hand and into the other Nephilim. He got a blast of power he thought felt like Dev before it flowed back out and into Deacon.

Lux cleared her throat. "We've now joined six to two. I want Amaya and Deacon to release our hands on my count and grab each other's. Then Zeke and I are going to hold hands, so are Dev and

Zane. We're going to form a circle around them so we're all four holding one another. Three, two, one."

Amaya stepped forward, grasping Deacon's hands in hers as the others folded around them. He offered a tight smile as he looked down at her. Lux's voice broke through the silence, filling the air.

"Six to two and two to one, our tasks fulfilled, four victories won. Lucifer weakened, his sword destroyed. Links are severed, weapons gained, we gather together to fight again. Brother and sister, lover and friend, we give of ourselves toward Lucifer's end. Nephil, Healer, human, witch, to each other, we willingly hitch.

"Blood of the Choosing, we remember our past. Blood from the first circle, we will be the last. Blood of Heaven, blood of Hell, we forge our circle and slice through the veil. Three to one and one to two, magic and power in the witching hour. Power surge, magic rise, blood meld, links form. Together we fight, together we live or die. One falls, all fall. Together we win, together we fail. In fighting for Heaven, we split open Hell. Blood freely given, hearts open, minds clear, we seek to join together. By the power of our blood, I beseech the elements. By the power of our magic, I implore of God. Six and three, two and one, we stand together, are tasks are done. One last fight, for Heaven or Hell. We've fought and died and served you well. By the power given to we, as we command it, so must it be!"

Amaya jerked and shrieked as power rushed into her. Her head filled with it, the strength threatening to drown her. The skies rumbled with thunder, lightning ripping through the clouds. She looked around, panicking.

"I can't control it! You need to get out of here!"

Deacon squeezed her hands harder. "Look at me, Amaya!" He jerked on her hands. "Look at me, dammit! I can control it. That's what I'm here for. Trust me!"

Slowly, she felt Deacon's power—the power of all five of her friends—flow over her, helping calm her down until she felt she could wield the new abilities like a scalpel or sword.

Lux raised her voice to speak over Amaya. "You need to leave the circle now. I have to put up protections to keep us safe while you fight. You're going to be without us during this. We have to stay linked in order to keep our power flowing into you."

Amaya nodded and dropped Deacon's hands, stepping over the edge of the circle. "I understand." She drew the Rod from the sheath at her hip and held it in front of her. "I'm ready."

Lux squared her shoulders. "I've modified my mother's original spell for this. It adds another layer of power. If it works, Lucifer will be dragged here as soon as it's done. After that, Amaya, it's up to you. Are you ready for this?"

Amaya closed her eyes and offered up a quick prayer that she was. "As ready as I'll ever be. Let's do this."

"The time has come, the hour has struck. Tonight we fight, we test our luck. Power rise, magic flow. God on high, Lucifer below.

"Chains of God, doors of stone. Summon Lucifer from his hell-fire home. Circle round, power strong. Hold him here, do no wrong. Power of mine, power of they. Hear my plea, do as I say. I call upon the Witching Hour, heed my magic, fear my power!

"Open the gates, unlock the door. Where he is, he is no more. Conveyed to this circle, blood of my kin, Lucifer shall appear, covered in sin. Chains shall form, holding him tight. Mask his power, take his sight. Hail him to this holy place. Heed my words, by God's Grace.

"Power of magic, power of word. Obey me now, let me be heard! Crack open the gates, unlock the chain. This is the end of Lucifer's reign! Hear my words, obey my plea. As I command it, so shall it be!"

Her heart pounding in her chest, Amaya faced the circle in the dirt, watching as it started glowing and the ground shuddered beneath her feet. And she waited for Lucifer.

CHAPTER THIRTY-SEVEN

AMAYA PITCHED forward when an earthquake rolled beneath her feet. The mountain shook in resistance to the force of the power surging through it. Fire rained from the sky, striking the dirt and igniting it. The flames flickered and danced before sputtering out with a pop and hiss. Inside the circle Lux had drawn for Lucifer, the ground split, a gaping cavern opening up.

A blast of blue and white flame slashed up from the opening, extending high into the night sky. Flame and smoke obstructed Amaya's view of the circle and she lifted one hand to shield her eyes. The ground roared in objection as it was sealed back together, extinguishing the fire and causing the smoke to clear. As it cleared, she became aware of a lone figure standing in the center. Lucifer had arrived.

Satan was perfectly coiffed in a white suit, red boots, a red tie, and a scabbard with a sword sitting at his hips. He lifted one eyebrow at Amaya when he saw her and she thought she saw a quick flicker of fear cross his face as his gaze settled on Aaron's Rod.

"It takes guts to summon me here." He cocked his head to the side. "I wonder what yours look like."

Amaya shivered as his voice cut through her. She tamped down on the knot of fear in her gut and focused on keeping her grip on the sword steady.

"You'll never find out."

"We'll see." He looked past her to the others. "It's quite the gathering you've got here. Lux, how nice to see you again. Are you all healed up from your time with Abalam?"

Lux sneered. "Fuck you."

"Succinct. Pithy. I like it." Lucifer smiled cockily. "Michael. Griffin. Always a pleasure. My associates will be here to take care of you momentarily. I'm sure you're aware of that." He turned back to Amaya. "You understand that there is only one outcome of tonight. One of us dies."

Amaya nodded sharply. "All I have to do is make sure it isn't me."

He smiled and drew his own sword, turning it over to study the blade. "I do so wish your friends hadn't melted my sword. I'd had that blade since the Fall. Such a shame for it to be melted."

Amaya set her feet and held the sword in front of her. "Enough talk."

She didn't give him the opportunity to charge her, choosing instead to be the one lunging. Their blades met with an earth shattering clap of thunder and the sky turned red.

Amaya gritted her teeth and charged forward, swinging the sword and parrying every strike from Lucifer. Each clash of their swords sent a jolt of electricity up her arm, weakening her grip and making her hesitate to strike again.

She threw out one hand, sending out a wave of power and catching him off guard. He stumbled, nearly fell, then righted himself and blasted back, sending Amaya flying several feet backward. She hit the ground with bone breaking force and lay there for two counts, trying to get her bearings.

Her vision clouded from the force of the impact, her back aching, she barely managed to roll to the side in time to avoid being sliced by Lucifer's blade.

Rolling again to avoid a second strike, she leaped to her feet and threw out power over her shoulder, not looking back to see whether or not it hit him. Whirling when she thought she had some distance, she pivoted just in time to see the army of Cambion, Devils, and demons appear in front of the monastery.

Wildly slinging power to keep Lucifer at bay, she looked around for Michael, meeting his eyes across the battlefield.

"Lilith! Azazel! Monastery!"

Looking back toward the monastery, Michael turned and ran.

Gage stood inside the door, watching as the Cambion army flashed in. He turned to face the Nephilim and Warriors, drawing his sword as he did so.

"Here they come. Ready yourselves!"

Gage threw open the door and charged through them, entering the fray of Cambion with his sword flashing. Avoiding the bite of a blade, he ran his first adversary through, stepping over the body as he continued forward, slashing with his blade as the Cambion folded in around him, streaking past the lone vampire to engage the Nephilim.

The sound of the two forces meeting was that of a thunderstorm. The scream of metal meeting metal filled the air. Gunshots rained down from above as both the Nephilim snipers and the Cambion snipers took aim.

Gage caught sight of the three Devils who had once been Archangels hovering near the edges of battle. Lilith wore a blood red dress cut high on her legs and low at the bosom and spike heels that twined up her legs with strips of leather. Her hair—blonde and curly—flowed back over her shoulders and down her back. He focused on her—the one who had killed his wife—and shoved his way through the Cambion, his one intent to kill Lilith.

He caught a flash of movement and saw Michael entering the fight from the direction of Mount Sinai. Jophiel appeared in a flash of lightning and the two Angels charged the three Devils, Jophiel twirling a sword in each hand and facing the two men while Michael squared up face to face with Lilith.

Michael glanced over his shoulder and looked at Gage. "Go be with the children. Protect their circle from attack. I'll handle her. For both of us."

Gage jerked his head in a nod and sprinted toward the mountain where his daughter, and those he loved as his own, were engaged in a battle for their lives.

Michael looked at Lilith with deliberate detachment. "Lilith, how wonderful of you to make an appearance when I finally have a weapon to end you for good."

Lilith smiled and cocked her head to the side. "Do you have the gun our son had when last he and I met?" She touched one hand to her hair, adjusting the curls. "He couldn't bring himself to kill me, either. You aren't going to have the strength or the will. We both know you look at me and see the Angel you once loved, the mother of your son, the woman you bedded for millennia."

Michael held his sword in front of his body. "That's where you're wrong. I look at you and I see the Devil who betrayed me, the bitch that hid my son from me, and a woman who has never felt anything even remotely like love."

"I'm going to kill you, and then I'll go kill the son I made you and end that circle once and for all. Without him anchoring that bitch of Alaria and Gabriel's, she'll spiral out of control and blow up this whole country."

"Good luck with that."

Michael made the first move, swiping down with his sword and catching Lilith off guard enough that she stumbled and fell while leaping backward. She conjured a whip of fire and cracked it at him, the tail of the weapon catching him across one cheek and singing down to the bone. He winced against the pain and lopped the whip in half with his sword.

Lilith climbed to her feet and cocked one hand on her hip. "This is going to be fun." She threw out a bolt of power, striking Michael on the side and cutting through his suit to skin. He formed a ball of fire in one palm and threw it at her, striking her shoulder and breaking the bone. With a grimace, the Devil rolled her shoulder, popping the bones into place as they healed.

"You can't kill me, Michael. All you have is that fucking gun of Deacon's. You don't have it in you to shoot me."

"You have no idea what I'm capable of." Michael struck with the sword again, slicing down to the bone in her arm and glancing off it. "I'll cut you into a hundred pieces and be glad of it."

Lilith sneered and blasted him with fire, burning some of the feathers off one of his wings.

"Michael!" Jophiel's voice broke into the battle Michael fought with Lilith. "I need a blade or bullet."

Michael turned his head and saw Jophiel with Abalam anchored to the side of the monastery, a sword pinning him to the wall. Blood ran out of the Devil's mouth and dripped onto the dirt. Azazel was charging Jophiel, his head bent and blood streaking his bare chest.

Michael drew the blade he carried at his waist and tossed it to Jophiel, who caught it handily. He flipped his second sword around and struck Azazel with the handle, breaking the Devil's nose. Azazel dropped to his knees, looking up at Jophiel.

"Brother, show me mercy."

Jophiel dropped his sword and held the blade made from the Spear of Destiny. "There is no mercy for those who betrayed our father." He laid his hand on Azazel's head. "Your punishment this time is exceedingly worse than eternity chained to a comfortable rock in a nice, cool cave. This time, you burn."

Before Jophiel could strike with the knife, Azazel conjured his own dagger and surged up, driving it deep into the Angel's chest. The blessed blade hit the ground and Azazel followed the dagger with his fist, reaching deep into the chest cavity until he found the slippery strands of Grace. Jerking hard, he ripped the silvery threads from the Angel, watching jubilantly as Jophiel crumpled to the ground, his eyes glassy and lifeless.

Before Azazel could climb to his feet, Michael flashed to the spot with the knife, snatching it up and grabbing Azazel's hair, yanking his head back and using the blade to slit his throat.

The blade turned from silver to black, then to red, heating up and severing muscle and sinew as it sliced. Azazel's eyes filled with the purple and black fog of his Devil essence and bugged out until they burst, allowing the fog to lead out and dissipate over the ground.

Michael didn't wait for Azazel to finish dying before drawing the gun loaded with bullets made of the staff from the Spear. He thumbed off the safety, took aim at Abalam, and pulled the trigger twice, both bullets striking him in the chest.

Turning to face Lilith, who was watching in horror, he holstered the gun and stooped to pick up his gun. As he walked, both Devils exploded as their essence pried its way from the cavities of their bodies, the force of the explosion slinging Michael several yards. He landed on the ground with a sickening crunch, his head striking a rock and rendering him unconscious.

Lilith landed several feet past Michael, still conscious. She rolled to her knees and then climbed to her feet, brushing dirt off her dress as she sauntered to Michael's unconscious form. Standing over him, her hands on her hips and her feet shoulder-width apart, she stared down at the bruised, bloody face of the man who had fathered her son.

"It's no fun to kill you while you're unconscious." She tapped one red fingernail against her mouth, considering the situation. "I want you awake and aware when I rip your Grace from between your shoulders. I want you staring into my face while you die, knowing that you once loved me and I feel nothing for you." She crouched and sneered at him before flicking her wrist to bind him hand and foot. "Good luck getting out of these. I'm going to go slaughter all those children you love so much and then come back to you carrying our son's head in my hand with a belly full of his blood." She straightened and stared down at him. "See you soon, lover."

Lilith glanced toward the monastery where her two companions had been killed, feeling nothing but ambivalence at their deaths. She reveled in the trill of excitement at the ongoing battle—Nephilim and Warrior against a force of Cambion, demons, and Devils—and turned toward Mount Sinai, sauntering toward where Lucifer and Amaya fought, humming softly and swinging her hips as she went.

CHAPTER THIRTY-EIGHT

AMAYA HIT the ground again, her teeth smacking together from the jar of the impact. She gasped for breath and swiped one arm across her head, mopping up blood and sweat with her sleeve as she rolled away from Lucifer, forcing herself to climb to her feet.

Her lungs burned as she sucked in a breath, and she swung the sword wildly to block a slash by her opponent, falling to her knees from the force of the blow. Haphazardly, she tossed out her hand and blasted him with energy, driving him back enough to allow her to again climb to her feet. She blasted again, ripping his sword from his hand and slinging it several yards away.

"The one thing about this that almost makes me feel sorry for you is that I'm not human at all. I don't tire, I don't run out of energy. I can do this for much, much longer than you can." Lucifer shucked off his suit jacket and cast it aside before picking up his sword and turning to face Amaya. "You're all going to die. You've always been going to die. It's time for you to realize it. I'm Lucifer, the Light-Bringer. I sat at the right hand of God and nearly brought Heaven down around Him. I've ruled Hell for millions of years." He tipped his head up and stared at the sky. "All the damage I did and this is the best you can do? A little girl who doesn't even know how to use what she is?"

Amaya rolled her shoulders and adjusted her grip on the handle of the sword. "You will run out of energy, the same as we all do. You've had thirty years to find me and kill me and haven't managed to do that, so I don't want to hear about how much more powerful you are." She took a deep breath. "You will not win here. Not today."

Lucifer flicked one wrist and sent a writhing mass of snakes hurling at Amaya. She whipped her sword through the air, hacking several of them to pieces before they got to her. Others, though, landed on her, their skin cold and smooth as they slithered over her. Plucking at the reptiles, she threw them aside, using the sword to slice at them, wincing when two managed to sink fangs into her hand as she tossed them away.

"Symbolic." Amaya sneered at him and hurled her own blast of power, smacking him with a gust of wind and knocking him down. "Too bad I'm not scared of snakes."

"Snake bites are poisonous and your Healer is busy at the moment. How long do you think you have before you either die from the venom or they break their circle to help you?"

Fear gathered in Amaya's gut. The bites on her hands were red and bleeding sluggishly. Discarding the worry, she turned back to her opponent.

"I'm calling your bluff."

She dipped her shoulder and charged him again. As she did, she caught a flash of movement as Lilith appeared. Amaya's heart tumbled in her chest, fear icing her blood in her veins. Gage was the only one there able to fight and the vampire stood no chance against Lilith.

Gage saw the she-Devil appear as well and bared his fangs. "I was hoping you'd show up."

Lilith smiled as she sauntered toward him. "I'm going to need you to step aside and let me kill those five whelps."

"I'm afraid that isn't going to be possible."

Lux's voice was a whisper. "Daddy, no. Please, no."

Gage's head pivoted to look at her, his eyes shining with an expression of love. "Do not break the circle. I've got this." He looked at Zeke and Zane, who stood on either side of Lux. "Don't let her break it, no matter what happens. It's going to be okay."

Lilith clucked her tongue. "How sweet. Going to sacrifice yourself before I slaughter your children." She lifted her hands and watched with rapt attention as her nails lengthened into claws. "I'm going to enjoy this. Azazel should have killed you all those years ago during the Choosing when you put yourself between him and that bitch Griffin. I'm going to put my hand around your cold, dead heart and rip it from your chest. Your daughter will see you turn to ash. It will be the last thing she sees."

Gage didn't respond. He leaped and tackled Lilith, driving her to the ground and slamming her head against the dirt. Before she could react, he slammed his fist into her face, breaking her nose and splitting the skin on her cheek. The Devil coughed and gagged from the force of the impact before blasting out with her power and sending him flying through the air.

Using his vampiric strength, Gage pivoted and managed to land on his feet. He jumped to avoid a stream of flame and then rolled, landing in a crouch. As Lilith approached, her whip in her hand, he drew a hatchet from his utility belt and threw it at her, feeling great satisfaction as the blade buried itself in her chest.

Lilith stumbled three steps from the force of the throw. She looked down, studying the blade protruding from her sternum and looked up at Gage, a smile turning up the corners of her mouth.

"Nice shot."

She grasped the handle of the hatchet and pulled, yanking it from bone with a resounding crack. Tossing the hatchet to turn the handle toward her, she caught it handily and launched it at Gage, just grazing his arm as he dove out of the way.

Lilith approached slowly, raking her eyes over Gage as she walked. "I'd have liked for you to be on our side. I'd most definitely have taken you for a test drive. Vampires have such good stamina, and I love a man who'll take a good bite out of me in the sack."

Gage laughed as he rolled to his feet. "Come on over here, baby, I'll take a good bite out of you now."

She waved the suggestion away. "It's no fun unless there's sex involved." She cocked one eyebrow. "Of course, if you want to blow this place, join me, and then we'll go fuck like bunnies, well, we could discuss that option as soon as I kill the other five."

Gage backed up, very deliberately putting more distance between them and the circle. Moving toward the mountain, he stopped when he felt the bite of stone into his back. Slowly, he reached into his pocket and folded his fingers around the blade Michael had given him—the blade formed from the head of Aaron's Rod.

Grief filled his chest as he considered what he was about to do.

All the moments he would never see. All the time not spent with his daughter. Putting the sadness aside, he focused on the task in front of him.

"You killed my wife. I'd never bed you."

"I didn't kill your wife. She blew herself up trying to kill me. Not my fault she wasn't strong enough. She's in good company. Gabriel wasn't strong enough. He's dead. Michael wasn't strong enough. Will be dead soon enough. Aradia wasn't strong enough. She's dead. Deacon couldn't do it. Soon to be dead. Lux wasn't strong enough. Also soon to be dead. The ones that take me on die. You're not strong enough, and you're about to die." She gestured to Mount Sinai. "In case you didn't notice, there's nowhere else for you to run. Unless you think your vampire strength allows you to jump over mountains the way the cow jumped over the moon."

Gage cast a look back toward the circle, taking in the faces of all five of them. He shifted to see Amaya, battling fiercely with Lucifer, the look on her face stubbornly defiant. Looking back at Lux, he locked eyes with his daughter and read fear in them. Shifting to look at Zane, he smiled while the Nephil nodded. The decision made and communicated, he turned back to the Devil.

"I don't need to go anywhere. Here is just fine for this."

Lilith tipped her head to one side, looking at him inquisitively as she stepped toward him, bringing herself within arms' reach. "You're not going to try and run?" She clucked her tongue again. "You can't blow yourself up. You're not a warlock. I'm going to stick my hand in your chest, and you're just going to be dead."

Swiftly, Gage brought the blade up and stepped forward into Lilith's punch, driving the knife into her chest even as her hand penetrated his, her fingers wrapping around his heart.

Lux's scream echoed through the entire valley, bouncing off the mountain and sending a bolt of regret through Gage.

Lilith's eyes bugged out as her essence forced its way into them. "I'll take you with me."

Gage smiled, the sight steely. "All I needed to know was that I took you out. You killed my wife. I'll die happy, knowing I don't have to watch my child—children—die."

With one yank, Lilith ripped Gage's heart from his chest, the organ dissolving to dust. Gage had time to turn and take one last look at Lux before he exploded into ash. Lilith thrust her arm up triumphantly, smiling as her essence poured out of every orifice, her human form dissolving and floating away on the breeze as she died.

Lux shrieked, the sound filled with grief and anger. She lunged forward, trying to run to her father. Zeke and Zane tightened their grips, holding her within the circle. She yanked on her hands, desperately trying to free them. Reaching for her magic, realizing it was gone—given to Amaya to use against Lucifer—she hated her friend.

"Lux, listen to me." Zeke's voice was tender and soft. "There's nothing you can do. He's gone." She swallowed her own tears, memories of Gage holding her as she sobbed after her own parents' death filling her mind. "He's gone, sweetheart. It's over. We have to stay here and help Amaya finish this. We can't let Lucifer win."

Zane's voice, deep and strong, seeped through the fog filling Lux's head. "You need to focus on this. There's time for grief later, after this is over. Gage isn't suffering. He's gone. He's in Heaven. He knew what he was doing, he made the sacrifice willingly. It was an opportunity to kill Lilith, and he took it. He's a hero."

Lux closed her eyes and pushed the emotions aside, clearing her mind and forcing herself to focus. She stepped back into the circle, retaking her place and breathing deeply. Opening her eyes, she focused on Amaya, who had hit the ground yet again as she struggled to best Lucifer.

"She has to do this. All this death can't be for nothing. She has to win."

Deacon's gaze was steely. "She will. It isn't for nothing. She'll win." He smiled when Amaya again managed to get to her feet. "She's got this."

Amaya took gasping breaths, trying to suck in enough air to power her body. Lucifer laughed as she gulped.

"Running out of wind, are you? Should we take a break and reconvene when you're slightly less pathetic?"

"Shut up." She swung with the sword, smiling tightly when it glanced a blow off his forearm. The skin sizzled and hissed where the sapphire blade made contact, and Lucifer winced from the pain of the hit. "One good stick is all I need."

He looked pointedly at her swollen hand. "I don't know how much longer you can keep this up. That hand is looking pretty nasty. The venom from the snakes is working its way through your body. I see the black there on your knuckles that tells me the flesh is turning necrotic. Toxins coursing through your bloodstream, slowly and surely making their way to your heart. If I had to guess, I'd say you've got about fifteen to twenty minutes before you can't even walk from the strength of the poison."

"A snake isn't going to be the end of me." She swung again, grunting when the sword met his and bounced off the steel. "But a little, pathetic girl is going to be yours."

"It's a nice sentiment. Almost poetic. David and Goliath all over again. Except this time, the giant is going to crush the boy's skull like a coconut." Lucifer jabbed out with his sword, smiling when the tip sank two inches into her side. "That had to hurt."

Amaya pressed one hand to the wound, scowling at the blood pouring out. "Well, hell. You're letting all your poison out."

Her movements slowed both by the venom coursing through her body and by the wound in her side, Amaya barely avoided a jab from Lucifer's sword as he moved quickly. She blocked it with her own, clenching her jaw as pain reverberated through her. He follow up the jab with a slash and then a strike, managing to land two of the three blows, cutting deeply into one of her arms and then striking a glancing blow on her left hip. She whirled to avoid another strike and tripped on a rock, sprawling to the ground. A muffled shriek pushed its way from her lips as Lucifer's sword dug into the dirt next to her head. Glaring up at him defiantly, she began speaking.

"Though I walk through the Valley of the Shadow of Death, I fear no evil."

"Shut up." Lucifer's face began to turn red as he angered. "Don't quote to me from that hell-awful book. I won't tolerate the insolence! You show respect when you're in my presence."

"For you are with me. Your rod and staff, they comfort me."

"I said shut up!" Spit rained on Amaya's face as Lucifer screamed. "You will *not* talk to me like that!" He bent and lifted her by her collar, shaking her so hard her brain sloshed against her skull. "You *will* show me respect!"

Amaya managed to keep her grip on the sword. "I can do all things through Christ who strengthens me."

Lucifer threw Amaya back to the ground, picked up his sword and swiped down. She brought hers up, blocking the jab and slashing at him, cutting into one of his calves. She blasted out with power, driving him back two steps before he threw his own power back at her. The stream was hot and red, and she struggled to hold hers as his crashed against it. Feeling herself weakening, knowing she had very little strength left, she tipped her head back and stared up at the sky.

"I'm sorry. I tried."

Before Lucifer could react enough to run her through with his sword, the sky split open and rain pounded the dirt. Thunder rolled through the valley, lightning slashing through the night. Red flame poured from the sky, striking the ground and rising up into the form of a man. Lucifer dropped Amaya and stalked toward the figure.

"This is not your fight! Get out of here! It's her, and it's me! Daddy doesn't get to come in and rescue her at the last minute. No fucking flaming white horses here. Get out! You have no place here!" The Devil threw out both his hands and streamed power at the figure, who batted them away with a flick.

It turned to Amaya and extended one arm. "Take my hand and wield the power of Heaven. Ask and ye shall receive. Come to me and know your task is blessed." It turned to Lucifer and spoke again. "Your place was to battle against the full power of the Lord God. That is what you shall do."

Amaya climbed to her feet, picked up the sword and ran for the figure, thrusting her hand into the flame and closing her fist around what felt like thick air. Her whole body stiffened as power raced through her. In the span of what felt like a lifetime but might have only been a blink of an eye, she had the ability to do anything, to be anyone. She held life and death in her hand, could wield destruction with a look, bring peace with a thought.

Focusing that power on Lucifer, she whipped a cord of power around him, lifting him and slamming him into the base of the mountain. He threw a wave of power back at her, which she dispersed with a wave of one hand. Twirling the sword, she walked toward him, slowly and deliberately. When she spoke, her voice was not her own.

"Tonight I am the hand of God, and I will be your destroyer."

Amaya's blade clashed with Lucifer's. They fought violently, each battling for survival. Lucifer hurled snakes at her, watched as she ignited them into flaming serpents and sent them back. Slashing at them with his blade, he lobbed fireballs that dropped to the ground—frozen into balls of ice. Steady and strong, Amaya continued to progress toward him.

"This time, God hasn't given up on us. This time, He's given us his blessing and anointed our quest. This time, you burn."

She held out one hand, clenching her fingers into a fist and bringing Lucifer to his knees. The Devil grabbed his head and screamed from pain, tearing at his hair in a useless effort to stop the pressure inside his skull. Amaya approached him slowly, every step deliberate. She knelt next to him, her eyes boring into his.

"This time, you lose."

With a smooth motion, she stood, gripped the sword in both hands and swung, the heavy sapphire blade cutting through Lucifer's neck and separating his head from his body, his form turning to dust before it hit the ground. Turning, she stared at Michael, who had just run toward them from the monastery, his sword gleaming with blood, with alarmingly blank eyes and extended a hand toward him.

"My son. You have served me well, even when disobeying me. Your loyalty to the chosen humans has never faltered and your love for me has never been in doubt. Through this vessel, I grant you what you desire. You are free of the chains of your wings. Go forth and be happy."

Amaya wobbled as the power left her body. She blinked rapidly, trying to clear her vision. The spell giving her the power of the others snapped, sucking that from her as well. Left alone with only herself, her power spiked beyond her control, streaming out through her hands and wildly blasting. Deacon ran to her, laying himself on top of her power and forcing it back within her control. With not even a word, Amaya collapsed backward into his arms, falling into the inky blackness of oblivion.

EPILOGUE

JUNE 15TH, 2065

SCOTLAND

AMAYA STARED down into the face of her daughter, memorizing every curve and detail. She trailed one finger over silky soft skin and brushed her hand over the downy soft, pale gold hair. From the chair next to the bed, her father spoke.

"When you were born, your mother and I were in hiding. Aradia had come to deliver you, but she had to leave as soon as the delivery was done. We didn't know where we'd be the next night or how to keep you safe. We'd just gotten Finley back and had two babies to take care of." Braxton smiled softly at the memory. "The thought of trying to raise you was the most terrifying thing I've ever felt in all my years."

Amaya leaned back into the pillows. "I feel pretty terrified myself, and I'm not facing all that."

"Parenthood is scary no matter what's going on, I think." He stood and crossed the room, perching on the edge of the bed. "I looked down into your little face—no bigger than hers—and I'd have gladly given my life to keep you from doing what you had to do. I've thanked God every day since you finished it that no more children would grow up to fight that war."

"Things are getting better. Governments are getting up and running, commerce is going. Deacon and I actually went to a grocery store last week."

"I haven't been to one of those in thirty years except to scavenge what was left." Braxton chuckled. "God this is weird. I spent my first thirty-five years with all the modern amenities, then I spent the next thirty in the Middle Ages, and now things are going back to the way they were." He reached out and touched the baby's face. "She gets a whole new world." Staring into the child's deep blue eyes, he smiled softly. "Have you picked a name?"

Amaya laughed. "We talked about naming her after one of the ones who died during all this but decided she needed her own name. It took some back and forth, but we finally agreed on Ashlyn Faith Winslow."

Braxton's eyebrows went up. "Winslow? Your last name?"

Amaya shrugged. "Deacon doesn't really have a last name. He sometimes used Michaels if he needed to have one, but even Michael has taken to using Windsor as a last name just because it's easier than explaining that he used to be an Angel."

Both looked up when someone knocked on the door. Braxton rose to answer it, stepping aside to let Lux, Zeke, and Alaria enter the room. Amaya sat forward and glanced out into the hall.

"Where's Deacon?"

Alaria rolled her eyes and climbed into bed with her daughter. "He's downstairs fretting. Dev is calming him down." She held out her arms. "Hand over my granddaughter."

Before Amaya could shift the infant from her arms to her mother's, the room filled with a soft light and Griffin appeared.

"I wanted to come and share my congratulations on the birth of your daughter." Griffin took a half-step forward. "She is beautiful."

Amaya smiled. "Thanks." She handed the baby to Alaria and swung her legs to the edge of the bed, putting her feet on the floor. "How is everything?"

Griffin touched one hand to her hair. "Since Lucifer's defeat, God has allowed the Host back to Earth to begin guiding humans into colonies and to assist with the eradication of all demons, Cambion, and Devils left. There is significant progress being made in that fight. The assistance given by the Nephilim and Warriors has been very helpful. With any luck, things will be stabilized within the next five years. Most governments are in their infancy, but they are beginning to run. Angels are providing transportation and information relay for the people working on that particular task. Things will be back to the way they were. It appears the worst is over."

Braxton grinned ruefully. "I'd have a huge problem if something else reared its ugly head after getting through everything we have."

"I don't believe that will be the case." She ran her hands over her suit jacket. "How is Michael adjusting?"

Zeke snorted. "He's fine. It's been four and a half years since God made him human and he's doing fine." She giggled. "He actually had a date last week. I think all the years of living with us made him familiar with all things human. The transition was pretty seamless."

Amaya yawned and stretched. "I'm going to take a shower and try to get some sleep while I have all of you here. I just fed her, so she should be good for a couple hours." She rose. "Thank you for coming, Griffin. I appreciate it."

Griffin looked around uncomfortably. "I'll understand if you say no, but I would like to meet your child and place a veil of protection over her. There's nothing coming for her that we know of, and no reason to think anything is going to happen, but I would feel more secure knowing she is protected and shielded from the remainder of the demons on Earth."

Amaya smiled softly. "I think that's very thoughtful. Thank you."

Alaria slipped from the bed and handed Ashlyn to Griffin, the two women exchanging a long look during the exchange. "We'll give you a few minutes. Call if you need me."

Griffin waited until she was alone with the infant. Rocking from side to side, she dropped into the rocking chair next to the bed and crossed one leg over the other. Brushing her hand over the baby, a silvery fog drifted from her hand and hovered over the baby until she had breathed it all in.

"You'll be shielded from all those who would do you harm." She stared at the child, her own heart constricting with a mixture of grief and longing. "I'm going to watch over you, little Ashlyn. Your grandfather would want me to. He would have loved you very much. He was a good man, despite his flaws. One day, when you're old enough, I'm going to tell you about him. Perhaps I'll be Aunt

Griffin as he was you're mother's Uncle Gabe." She rocked back and forth slowly. "I think I'd like that."

Griffin sat for several minutes, rocking and humming under her breath as she looked down at the baby. After a while, she shifted slightly and spoke.

"Your grandfather used to tell your mommy stories. I have the memories of them. I think I should be the one to tell them to you, but I'm going to leave out all the risqué parts that Gabe didn't." She laughed out loud at the memory. "Here we go. Once upon a time, there was nothing but empty space. No planets, no people, no animals, nothing. And God was lonely by himself. So He created Heaven. And to keep Him company, He created Angels. Because the Angels needed something to care for, and because God craved more, He created Earth and humans. Angels were in charge of taking care of the people, and people were supposed to worship God. But eventually, one of the Angels, God's most precious Angel, decided he wanted to be in charge instead of God."

She paused and patted Ashlyn's back when the baby mewed, bringing her up and balancing her on her shoulder, tucking the tiny head into the curve of her shoulder. Quoting the story Gabriel had once told to Griffin, she continued to speak.

"Lucifer, the special Angel, tried to convince the other Angels to join with him and fight against God. And many of them did. They fought brutally. Many Angels died on both sides, and at the end, God was forced to create a special place for all of the Angels that betrayed him. So He created Hell. It was horrible, hot, ugly, and a place that no one was ever meant to go. Lucifer became the King of Hell—much the same way that God was the King of Heaven. They each had Angels, but God wouldn't let the others be called Angels. So they became Devils. They were evil and received pleasure from causing others pain. But this fight left one thing undecided.

"Both God and Lucifer wanted the people. When God made Earth, He never thought that they would go anywhere but Heaven. Lucifer wanted a chance to get some of them to Hell so that his Devils could hurt them forever. This hurt God's heart because He knew that the only way to avoid an ongoing war was to come up with a compromise. So He held a meeting. He met with Lucifer, one Angel, and one Devil to decide how the world would end. Eventually, after several hundred years, they decided on a system. One person would be born, and would have a choice to make. Heaven or Hell. For twenty-nine years, this person would be shielded by a Veil placed on her by the Devil and Angel in charge, not unlike the shield I just put on you. The Devil would get ten events to wipe out the natural inclination of humans to follow God. It would make her a blank slate. After twenty-nine years, both sides would be able to make their case. Then, on her thirtieth birthday, she would have to make her choice. This choice would have a great price. She would have to give up her life because this was not a choice that could be made lightly. By requiring her blood, both sides ensured that she would take it seriously and be sure about her decision."

Griffin paused again and closed her eyes, breathing in the scent of baby as memories washed over her. She smiled, the expression tinged with pain, and continued.

"If she decided not to pick, the Apocalypse would happen. Jesus, the Son of God, would come back and would take home everyone who had already given their soul to Him. Then, Lucifer would get seven years to convince humans to come to him. Anyone who refused to go with Lucifer after the seven years would be taken to Heaven and humans would cease to exist on Earth. A lot of people would die bloody, horrible deaths, and there would be a lot of suffering. This was to ensure that she would pick. Failing to would put the blood of millions on her hands. But both sides wanted her to Choose because it ensured that Earth would continue. If she Chose God, Devils would be stuck in Hell for a million years, and Angels would have free reign over Earth. After the million years were up, everything would go back to the way it was before, with both sides competing for souls. If she Chose Lucifer, it would be the opposite.

"If she died before her birthday it would be the Apocalypse. That was one of the rules. Neither side was allowed to kill her or the End of Days would start immediately. So no one wanted that. They both wanted her to pick. Not only would it delay the Apocalypse, but it would give one side a million years without interference from the other. In addition, if Heaven won, there would never be an End. People would go on forever. If Hell won, at some random point, after the million years ended, the Apocalypse would still happen, and the world would still end but only God would know when, and it would give Lucifer seven more years to make a play for souls.

"It was decided that the Chosen would be a birth out of death. No one would know what that meant until it happened, but everyone thought that it meant the Chosen would be born after her mother was already dead. She would be ripped from the womb, not born, and she would live a life of pain and suffering. All of those things: the events, the absence of God, the inability of the Angel to interfere until the twenty-ninth year, the pain and suffering—it gave an advantage to Lucifer. But God was confident that His creation would still pick Him."

Griffin continued to rock, the sleeping baby warm against her shoulder. She thought back over the events of her life and how she had died. The nights tangled up with Braxton, days running from Alaria—memories of Sam and Finn, both long dead. Of Allen and Miranda—the first people to show her kindness. Tears thick in her throat, she continued to speak.

"The Devil is your grandmother, and the Angel is your grandfather. See, Carys, nothing is ever black and white. Good will always triumph over evil, and love transcends everything—even Heaven and Hell." She paused and wiped tears from her face with one hand. "It all started sixty-seven years ago in a hospital in a place called New York City. There was a good doctor named Allen Winslow who was working on New Years' Eve. In that hospital was Gabriel—the Angel, and Alaria—the Devil. They were there to watch the birth of the Chosen, a tiny baby born from a dead mother. A baby named Griffin Javensen."

Amaya and Deacon's child in her arms, a child whose grandparents included Gabriel, Alaria, Michael, and Lilith, Griffin stared into the face of a child born into a world without Lucifer as she rocked. And as she rocked, she continued to tell the story.

ABOUT THE AUTHOR

Sirena N. Robinson is an author who lives and works in the foothills of the Appalachian Mountains. When she is not helping her characters defeat unspeakable evil, she spends her days working as a drug and alcohol counselor and as a court-appointed attorney in the local Juvenile Court. A firm believer in wearing many hats, she spends many weekend traveling the country with her husband, daughter and Bengal cats attending cat shows. On off weekends, she can be found with the rest of her family at a hunt-test or field trial helping shuttle dogs or holding down the fort at home, caring for the menagerie of dogs and cats living in her house.

Sirena writes in several genres, focusing primarily on novels with paranormal or supernatural elements. She has several other novels in various stages of planning, including a futuristic crime series. She writes both because she loves it and because she has no choice and is a self-proclaimed slave to her characters. She considers herself incredibly lucky to be the one chosen to tell their incredible stories.

Keep in touch with Sirena via her blog at sirenanrobinson.blogspot.com or through her publisher Supposed Crimes, at supposedcrimes.com.